Médicis Daughter

ALSO BY SOPHIE PERINOT

The Sister Queens

Médicis Daughter

A Novel of Marguerite de Valois

SOPHIE PERINOT

Thomas Dunne Books
St. Martin's Press ⚓ New York

THOMAS DUNNE BOOKS.
An imprint of St. Martin's Press.

MÉDICIS DAUGHTER. Copyright © 2015 by Sophie Perinot. All rights reserved. Printed in the United States of America. For information, address St. Martin's Press, 175 Fifth Avenue, New York, N.Y. 10010.

www.thomasdunnebooks.com
www.stmartins.com

The Library of Congress Cataloging-in-Publication Data

Perinot, Sophie.
    Médicis daughter : a novel of Marguerite de Valois / Sophie Perinot. — First edition.
        p. cm.
    ISBN 978-1-250-07209-2 (hardcover)
    ISBN 978-1-4668-8348-2 (e-book)
    1. Marguerite, Queen, consort of Henry IV, King of France, 1553–1615—Fiction.
2. Catherine de Médicis, Queen, consort of Henry II, King of France, 1519–1589—
Fiction.   3. Henry IV, King of France, 1553–1610—Fiction.   4. Guise, François de
Lorraine, duc de, 1519–1563—Fiction.   5. Saint Bartholomew's Day, Massacre of,
France, 1572—Fiction.   6. France—History—House of Valois, 1328–1589—Fiction.
7. France—History—16th century—Fiction.   8. France—Court and courtiers—
Fiction.   9. France—Kings and rulers—Fiction.   10. Nobility—France—Fiction.
I. Title.
    PS3616.E7446M43 2015
    813'.6—dc23

                                                                        2015034669

Our books may be purchased in bulk for promotional, educational, or business use. Please contact your local bookseller or the Macmillan Corporate and Premium Sales Department at (800) 221-7945, extension 5442, or by e-mail at MacmillanSpecialMarkets@macmillan.com.

First Edition: December 2015

10 9 8 7 6 5 4 3 2 1

To E, K, and C,
Never let any person's will
supplant your own,
nor anyone's advice override
the dictates of your
conscience.
Not even mine.

Médicis Daughter

PART ONE

Si jeunesse savait . . .

(If only youth knew . . .)

PROLOGUE

Summer 1562—Amboise, France

In my dreams the birds are always black.

This time when I wake, breathless and frightened, I am not alone. Hercule, perhaps disturbed by nightmares of his own, must have crawled into my bed while I was sleeping. I am glad to have his warm little body to curl around as I try to go back to sleep. No, he is no longer called Hercule, I remind myself sternly. Since his confirmation he is François, the second of my brothers to bear that name. The older, other François was not my friend or playfellow but rather the King of France. He has been dead nearly two years.

My nurse claims it is *because* King François II died young, and my father

King Henri II died tragically before him, that large black birds fill my nightmares. She insists images of weeping courtiers clothed in somber black etched themselves upon my youthful mind and were turned to birds by my overactive imagination.

I know she is mistaken, but I bite my tongue.

My brother Henri was equally mistaken. When we shared a nursery at Vincennes, he teased me that the birds were crows, noisome and noisy but, *à la fin,* harmless. They were not crows then, nor are they now. Crows with their grating clatter have never frightened me. Besides, my birds are silent. Silent and watchful. And always one is larger than the others. This one stares at me with beady eyes as if she would see into my very soul. I recognize my mother, Catherine de Médicis, Queen of France, even if none to whom I relate my dreams ever see her.

Putting an arm around my brother, I pull him close and smell the summer sun in his hair. I recall this night's vision—the birds arrived out of the northern sky, swooping over Amboise. The one in the lead was so large, she obscured the sun. Lower and lower they flew, until they came to rest on the spire of the Chapel of Saint-Hubert.

My mother is coming. Even as I close my eyes and my thoughts blur, I know it. I am as certain as if I had received a letter in her own hand declaring it.

The next morning, standing at the limestone parapet in the château garden, I feel rather smug. My *gouvernante* laughed when I said Her Majesty was coming, but crossed herself when the messenger arrived, proving me right. Madame kept giving me strange looks all the time she was fastening me into one of my best gowns—the one Monsieur Clouet painted me in last year, all heavy cream silk and pearls. Looking down to make certain my hem did not become dirty as I ran here, I realize my beautiful dress has grown short.

Never mind, I think, Mother is coming! Pushing myself up on my tiptoes, I rest my arms on top of the wall and look over—experiencing a familiar mixture of awe and apprehension. On the other side everything falls away precipitously. Below, the calm, green Loire winds past, giving way to the deeper and more varied green of the trees on its opposite bank. To the left, the river is traversed by a bridge as white as the wall I lean upon. My eyes follow the road across that bridge. I can see a long way, and just before the road dissolves into shimmers of light I see movement. Can it be Mother's party?

A motion closer at hand draws my attention. François followed me when I snuck out, and now he is trying to pull himself up onto the wall to see better. My stomach clenches. The drop from the top to the rooftops below would surely break his body to pieces should he go over. Grabbing my brother around the waist, I try to haul him back, but he clings tenaciously to the stone.

"Let go," I command.

Whether in response to my demand or under the pressure of my tugging, François' fingers release and we tumble backwards into the dry dust of the path. My youngest brother is slight of build, but at seven he is still heavy enough to knock the wind out of me. He scrambles up indignantly, heedless of the fact that he finds his footing in my skirts.

"I am not a baby."

"You are certainly behaving like one!" I shriek, looking at the dirty marks upon my gown. I can only imagine how the back of me—the part sitting in the dirt—looks. I feel like crying and my face must show it, for François' expression changes from defiance to guilt.

"I am sorry, Margot." He drops his eyes and nudges the path with his foot.

"Help me up." I reach out, unwilling to turn onto my knees and do further damage to my dress.

Taking my hands, François throws his weight backwards. For a brief, perilous moment I am lifted. Then my brother's feet slide from under him and I drop back to the ground as he lands there himself. At that precise moment, I spot my *gouvernante,* the Baronne de Curton, running toward us with my nurse and François' following. Madame's face is as white as my dress, or rather, I think, fighting the desire to laugh, considerably whiter given the state of my once lovely gown.

"What would Her Majesty say to see *une fille de France* in such a position!" Madame picks up François and sets him on his feet. He—wisely, to my way of thinking—scurries to his nurse, who has paused a few yards away, panting. "You are too old for such behavior."

This is a familiar phrase, and the only one that annoys me more is "You are too young"—something I seem to hear with equal frequency. I am too old to play the games I used to play with François. I am too young to join my mother and her ladies at Court. What, I wonder, am I of an age to do? I know better than to raise such a philosophical point under present circumstances.

I allow Madame to help me up. She circles me, shaking her head. "You must change. Her Majesty cannot see you like this."

A flurry of movement and burst of sound attract our attention. A group of figures emerges from an archway at the far side of the garden. The livery of the servants and the exceedingly fine dress of the handful of gentlemen and ladies proclaim the unwelcome truth. Whether we are ready for her or not, Mother has arrived.

The sight of her—gliding forth from amidst her companions, dismissing them by gesture—sets me trembling, and not merely because of the state of my gown. François, breaking from his nurse, takes refuge behind me. But I am too old for such behavior, and if I tried to dart behind Madame I doubt she would willingly shield me. I give a quick shake to my skirts and square my shoulders. Madame shoos François from behind me and urges us into motion. I try to walk smoothly so that I will appear to float as Mother does, but my sliding only stirs up dust, causing my *gouvernante* to hiss, "Pick up your feet."

Then I am face-to-face with Mother. Her eyes are as dark and as searching as those of the bird in my dream. And for a moment, while Madame and the nurses curtsy and murmur, "Your Majesty," I am frozen by her gaze. A none-too-gentle nudge from Madame frees me. I make my own reverence, then, straightening, take François' hand, not so much to reassure him as to fortify myself.

"Baronne de Curton"—the black eyes sweep over François and me from head to toe—"I presume from the grandeur of my children's attire that my courier arrived. Given that you knew I was coming, I cannot, then, account for the state of that attire."

Madame dips her head. I hear her draw breath. I wish I could find mine. Wish I could say that it is all François' fault for climbing where he ought not. But my voice has flown. So instead I bite my lip so hard that it hurts, to punish myself.

"Abject apologies, Your Majesty. I am mortified." My *gouvernante* bows her head lower still, and guilty tears prick the corners of my eyes.

Mother stands silent, perhaps to let each of us fully feel our faults. At last, when I do not think I can bear another moment of her scrutiny, she speaks. "I will see the children later. Make certain they are in better order." Then, without a single word to François or me, Her Majesty moves past our little party, to take a seat by the same wall we just left.

As the shadows lengthen, I am dressed once more in a selection of my best things. The time has come for François and me to be brought before the Queen. I am desperate to make a better impression than I did this morning. Madame is equally eager. As we walk to Her Majesty's apartment she makes me practice the Plutarch I plan to recite—twice. And when we stop before Mother's door, she straightens my necklace and wipes some mark that only she can see from François' face.

Satisfied, Madame raps and opens the door without hesitation at Mother's summons. Her step does not falter as she crosses the threshold, while my feet feel as if they are made of lead.

"Your Majesty, the Prince and Princess," Madame says, offering a nod to Mother's venerable maid of honor, the Duchesse d'Uzès.

Mother regards us with a look of appraisal.

"François, have you been obedient and applied yourself to your lessons?"

My brother makes a solemn little bow. "Yes, Madame." Our mother rewards his display with an inclination of her head. Then she turns her eyes to me.

"Margot, you are such a pretty child when you are not covered in dirt."

I feel my face color, and make a low curtsy by way of reply—far easier than finding my voice.

"It pleases me to see both children in health." Mother offers the Baronne an approving nod. "The thought of them here, safe, where the air is pure and free from both the infection of war and the creeping illness of heresy, was a great consolation to me while I attempted to talk peace with the Prince de Condé."

At Mother's mention of the notorious heretic commander Madame crosses herself. I mimic her gesture.

"I trust there are no French prayers here," Mother continues.

"No indeed, Your Majesty!"

"Good. I have rooted out whatever there was of that nonsense in my Henri." Her eyes shift back to me. "Does it please you to know that, when you see your brother next, there will be no need for you to hide your Book of Hours?"

I nod. I am pleased. Pleased to have Mother's attention, and pleased that my brother will no longer be inclined to cast my books on the fire. While we were living in company, he burned more than one. He gave me a book of Huguenot prayers to replace them, but I gave that to Madame and prayed daily that he would turn away from heresy. I was not sorry when his transgressions came to Mother's attention, though I was sorry for the beating he got as a result.

"The Lady Marguerite is very pious," Madame says. These are surely meant to be words of praise; why, then, does she shift from foot to foot? "But . . ." Her voice trails off and she clasps and unclasps her hands.

"Yes," Mother urges. The eyes upon me harden.

"Your Majesty," Madame's voice drops as if she will tell something very secret, "the Lady Marguerite *knew* you were coming. Knew it before the courier arrived." She crosses herself again.

"She knew?"

"Yes . . ." Madame's voice fades. I can hear her swallow. "During our morning lessons she told me she was waiting for you."

Mother's eyes sparkle. "So, Margot, it seems you are a daughter of the Médicis as well as the Valois."

I do not understand. Nor, it appears, does Madame. She looks entirely bewildered.

"I foresaw your father's death," Mother says, looking me in the eye. "I dreamt of his face covered with blood. I begged him not to enter the lists on the day he was mortally wounded. He would not listen." There is tremendous sadness in her voice, but then the corners of her mouth creep upward, almost slyly. "Some fear the gift of premonition. But I tell you, daughter, never fear what is useful to you." Mother intertwines her fingers before her and her smile grows.

"Mark my words, Baronne, I will find a crown for this one, as I did for her sister the Queen of Spain. There will be no need to settle for a Duc as we did for Claude."

I have but imperfect memories of my sister the Duchesse de Lorraine, but I know that she had a sweet temper and a deformed leg. Apparently the former mattered less than the latter when it came to making a match for her. I find this both surprising and interesting.

I wonder if this talk of my future means I will be allowed to return to Court with Mother. I am too young to be married, but surely I could learn many things—both from observing Her Majesty and from her retinue of great ladies. Henri is at Court; why not me? I open my mouth to ask, then close it again.

"Have you something to say, child?" The question stuns me. Nothing, not a breath, not a twitch, escapes Mother's attention.

"I . . ." The permission I would seek lies on the tip of my tongue. Instead I hear my voice say, "I have prepared a recitation for Your Majesty's pleasure."

"Well then, go on."

Frustrated by my own timidity, I will myself to ask the question, but the moment has passed. I have been bid recite. Obedience and training take over. Almost without volition, the well-rehearsed Plutarch pours smoothly from me like wine from a cask. My mother's glance never leaves my face. When I am finished, I stand, hands clasped, waiting for her verdict. Perhaps if she praises me I might raise the topic of Court.

But no words of praise come, at least not for me. Instead, the Queen's attention turns to Madame. "The effects of your tutelage show well in the Princess. I think, perhaps, she may be ready for more rigorous study."

"A tutor at her age, Your Majesty?" Madame seems mildly shocked, and her reaction rankles me. I know that I am clever.

"Yes. To secure a crown Margot's looks and family name may be enough, but to be useful to us once she is crowned, more will be required. To be a queen, a disciplined and developed mind is essential."

And like that our audience is over. Mother merely waves her hand by way of dismissal and, as Madame shepherds us toward the door, picks up a piece of fruit from a bowl on her table.

Well, I console myself as I am tucked into my bed, perhaps I will manage to find the courage to ask about Court tomorrow. When I awake in the morning and learn the Queen has gone—departed without taking leave of François or me—I hide and cry bitter tears.

CHAPTER 1

Winter 1564—Fontainebleau, France

"Dear God, the cold!"

It must be the hundredth time my *gouvernante* has uttered these words, or something very like, in the last three days.

"It was also cold in Amboise," I reply, trying to keep my voice cheerful while repressing an urge to kick Madame in the shins as she sits across from me in the coach. How can she think of the cold at a time like this?

"There were fires at Amboise, Your Highness, and chimneys that drew properly."

When we stopped at Nemours last evening, Madame was nearly smothered, thanks to an ill-maintained flue. Well, she can hardly blame me: I wanted to continue on to Fontainebleau, as it could not be more than another two hours' ride. Madame, however, insisted we stop. She wanted me freshly dressed and looking my best for our arrival at the château, for my arrival at Court.

Court—since word came a fortnight ago that I was summoned, I have thought of nothing else. I am going to join the Court, and the Court *ensemble* will depart upon the largest royal progress ever undertaken.

Drawing back a tiny corner of the heavy drapes that cover the window, so as not to seem disrespectful of Madame's comfort, I devour the landscape. The views on our trip have been dominated by rivers—first the Loire and then the Loing—but we are surrounded by woods now, the royal forest of Fontainebleau. Most of the trees are leafless in the gray winter light, but I can imagine them clothed in green, just as I can imagine a royal hunting party like those my brother Henri and I used to watch at Vincennes. I can almost see the riders in their dazzling attire moving between the trees; hear the snorts and pawings of the horses, and the barking of the dogs. I do not need to imagine the stag, for suddenly, *juste à côté* the road, a magnificent animal appears.

"Look!" I cry. But Madame and the other ladies are too slow. Before their heads turn, the stag is gone. Never mind—there will be more of interest to be seen, much more. I remain eyes out the window and mute, letting the conversation of my companions flow over me like water over stone. For a time I forget the scenery and think of my younger brother. How François cried when he discovered that he would not make the progress. He was told he is too young for such exhausting travel and too imperfectly recovered from a bout of smallpox that nearly killed him just short of a year ago. He insisted he was neither. Then, late on the night before he left for Vincennes, where he will stay, he woke me to say he thought the pox was to blame for his exclusion.

"It is because I do not look right," he said, tears streaming down his scarred face. "They are afraid I will scare the horses and ruin the pageants."

I told him not to cry, that no one would be frightened of him. To lie in such a situation cannot be a sin. In truth, the damage illness did to my once comely brother is shocking. Deep pits mark his face, and his nose remains misshapen. And part of me wonders, and feels guilty for doing so: Is he right? Has Mother left him behind because he would spoil the tableau that all murmur she wishes this progress to paint—a picture of the House of Valois triumphant and firmly in command of a France at last at peace? Surely one scarred little boy would not be the ruination of all her plans. No, I must believe he was left for his own good.

My sadness over separation from François cannot dampen my excitement for long. The trees give way to a more cultivated landscape. I spot a magnificent lagoon with an island in its center, then a portion of a château of white stone piped with delicate rose brick. It is long where Amboise was tall. I feel the wheels touch stone and my excitement surges. I am not alone: curtains on both sides of our conveyance are pushed open despite the rush of frigid air. The Baronne smooths her gown and then, reaching across, pinches both my cheeks.

We pass through a magnificent gate, stopping in an oval courtyard ringed by a delicate colonnade. Everywhere my grandfather's salamander greets us—carved in stone or worked in gold. Liveried figures and lackeys of all sorts swarm toward our coaches. Among the moving bodies and jumble of faces, I spy one I have been longing to see.

Without waiting for assistance, I reach out and fling the coach door wide. "Henri!" I hear Madame's gasp—a mingling of fear and disapproval—as I spring down, but I do not care. I haven't seen my thirteen-year-old brother in nearly two years. "You've grown so tall!"

"You have forgotten to say dignified." He takes my hand and makes a show of bowing over it. Then, pinching my arm, he turns and runs. I pursue as he weaves through the crowd in the courtyard and darts into the château.

Henri has the advantage. Not just because he is older and taller, but because he knows Fontainebleau. I pass through several rooms heedless of my surroundings, intent solely on closing the gap between myself and my brother. Then, suddenly, I am in a vast space. Winter light spills through enormous windows, causing the parquet floor to shine like ice, and swimming in this glossy surface I see my father's emblem. I stop and look upward, searching for the source of the illusion. There, among elaborately carved panels of wood touched with blue paint and gilt, I spy my father's device. Now that I have stopped, Henri stops as well.

"What is this place?" I ask.

"The *salle des fêtes,* you goose."

Ignoring the jibe, I turn slowly, admiring the room. Just behind my brother, frescos show hunting scenes like those I imagined this morning, only the figures are clothed in the ancient garb of myth rather than the grandiose fashions of the Court. I want to dance here. It is a ballroom after all. Without another thought, I begin an *almain.* As I rise to balance on the ball of one foot for the fourth time, Henri joins me. Humming beneath his breath, he catches up my hands and begins to lead me in a circle. I realize that we are no longer alone. A small dark figure stands just inside the door by which we entered. Mother! I pause, arresting Henri's motion, but not before he steps on my foot.

"Why do you stop?" Mother's voice is clear despite the considerable distance. "Come, let me see how you manage a *gaillarde*."

My brother does not hesitate. "We will do the eleven-step pattern," he whispers, and then begins to hum the more rapid music the dance demands. My brother is a natural athlete. And I, I am the stag, prancing and full of high spirits. As we execute the cadence and come to rest, Mother applauds.

"Henri my heart, you put gentlemen twice your age to shame! So elegant! It is pleasant to see you partnered by one whose looks and grace match your own. We must have a ballet featuring you both, now that Margot has come." Mother walks forward as she speaks, stopping just before us.

"As part of the Shrove Tuesday festivities?" my brother asks eagerly.

Mother smiles indulgently, offering her hand. "Ambition too," she says, stroking Henri's hair with her free hand as he bends over her other. "You are God's most perfect gift." Then, turning in my direction, her eyes harden and her lips compress. "Your *gouvernante* was at a loss to explain your whereabouts when I arrived in the Cour Ovale."

I feel myself blushing.

"It is my fault." Henri's voice surprises me. "I was waiting for Margot and whisked her away."

Mother's expression softens. Putting an arm around my shoulders, she says, "The King waits to receive you."

I imagined meeting Charles in his apartments—a gathering of family. So I am awed when a door opens to reveal His Majesty seated on a dais with dozens of courtiers in attendance.

A woman and a young man stand before him. I can see neither of their faces. Charles looks away from them at the sound of our entrance. He has become a man! A slight mustache darkens his lip. His face is not as handsome as Henri's, but it is kind. Does the King smile at the sight of me? If so, the smile is fleeting. Standing beside me, Mother gives a sharp nod and Charles' eyes return to the pair before him.

Taking advantage of his attention, the lady, who is exquisitely dressed, says, "Your Majesty, I appeal to your sense of justice. Surely a woman deprived of her husband by an assassin's hand is entitled to pursue his killer."

"Duchesse de Guise, Jean de Poltrot was put to death a year ago. Is that not justice?"

Charles' voice has deepened. If it is Anne d'Este who petitions, then the sandy-haired young man at her side must be her son Henri, Duc de Guise.

"Your Majesty, Poltrot may have struck the blow, but he was merely an instrument."

Mother sweeps forward. "Your Grace knows," she says, brushing past the Dowager Duchesse and ascending the dais to stand at Charles' side, "how dear justice and your persons are to His Majesty. But you must also know, Duchesse, how dear to His Majesty, indeed to all who care for France, is the present tenuous peace. It is not a year old. Would Your Grace kill it in its infancy with this lawsuit against Gaspard de Coligny?"

Mother's eyes are piercing. They seek an answer while making quite clear that only one answer will do. "His Majesty does not dismiss your suit, he merely suspends it," she presses.

"Three years is a very long time to wait for justice." The Duc speaks, drawing himself up. He is very tall for a young man Charles' age.

Mother offers him a smile—the patronizing type adults give children. But she does not answer him. Instead she speaks to the dowager. "Your son's feelings honor his fallen father, but also reveal his youth. You and I, Duchesse, have lived long enough to know how very short a time three years are when properly reckoned."

The Duchesse curtsys. "Your Majesties, we will be patient, since that is the King's will." She touches her son on his shoulder and he bows, then the two make their way down the aisle. I see a mingling of confusion and impatience in the Duc's eyes as he glances sideways at his mother. He is quite as handsome as he is tall.

My observations are arrested by the voice of a household officer. "Her Highness the Duchesse de Valois," he announces.

I look at Madame and she nods. Down the aisle I go to a general murmuring while the others of my party, announced in the same officious tone, follow. Stopping at the foot of the dais, I am aware that all eyes are upon me. I stand as straight as I can before executing my curtsy.

"Sister," Charles says, "we are pleased to have you at our Court. You will be a great ornament to it, we are certain, for we have received good report of your wit and of your dancing."

I am surprised. I supposed my education beneath Charles' notice. And if Mother is the source of Charles' information, then I am astounded to hear him praise me. There have certainly been very few words of approbation in the letters she sends Madame—or at least in those portions read out to me. Why, I wonder, if she is willing to speak well of me to my brother, can Mother not spare a word of encouragement for me? I have worked so hard this past year—applying myself to every lesson, whether with the tutor she sent for me or with my dancing master.

Turning to Her Majesty, Charles says, "Madame, the collection of beauties in your household is already the envy of every court in Europe, and here is another lovely addition."

I am to be a member of my Mother's household!

"As Your Majesty's grandfather King Francis was wont to say, 'A court without beautiful women is springtime without roses,'" Mother replies, smiling.

Late in the afternoon I get my first glimpse of the roses. Dressed in the sort of finery seldom required at Amboise, I am shepherded to Mother's apartment by the Baronne de Retz, who came with me from Amboise. The door of Her Majesty's antechamber opens to reveal at least two dozen young women. The colors of their fine silks, velvets, and brocades set against the room's brightly painted walls dazzle my eyes, and the smell of perfumes—both sweet and spicy—fills my nose. The entire scene is fantastical and made even more so by the arresting spectacle of a bright green bird flying above the gathered ladies.

"Here is the little princess!" The woman who exclaims over my arrival gives a small curtsy. Smiling, she reaches out her hand. I offer mine. "She is like a doll," she says, spinning me around. The other ladies laugh and clap in admiration.

"Something is missing." This new speaker has hair so blond, it looks like spun gold. She also has the tiniest waist I have ever seen. I simply cannot take my eyes from it. Stepping forward, she takes my chin and tips my face first this way and then that. "A little rouge, I think."

There is a ripple through the assembled ladies and someone hands a small pot to the woman before me. Opening it, she dips her finger then touches it, now covered with a vermillion substance, to my lips. *"Parfaite!"* she declares. "She will break many hearts."

The Baronne de Retz clears her throat softly. "Mademoiselle de Saussauy, Princess Marguerite is too young to think of such things."

The pretty blonde laughs. "One is never too young to think of such things."

I *like* Mademoiselle de Saussauy.

"Where is Charlotte?" the Baronne asks.

A girl with chestnut hair and carefully arched eyebrows comes forward. "Your Highness, may I present Mademoiselle Beaune Semblançay. She is the young lady nearest to your own age among the present company. Perhaps you would like to become better acquainted?"

The Mademoiselle holds out her hand. "Come," she says, "let us go where we can see the dresses better as everyone enters."

"This is not everyone?" I ask, amazed.

"No indeed, not by half," my companion replies. "Her Majesty has four score ladies, from the best and oldest houses."

My companion threads herself expertly through the crowd until we reach a spot that she adjudges satisfactory. As the door swings open to admit two ladies arm in arm, Charlotte screens her mouth with one hand and says, "The shorter is the Princesse de Porcien, the taller her sister the Duchesse de Nevers."

I can see the resemblance. Both have luxurious hair with tones of auburn. Both have milk-white skin. The Duchesse, however, has the better features, for the Princesse has a childish roundness to her cheeks.

"How old is the Princesse?"

"Fifteen." I detect envy in my companion's tone.

Wanting to make my new friend happy, I whisper, "You are far prettier than she."

Charlotte kisses me on the cheek. But her pleasure is short-lived and the look of jealousy creeps back into her dark eyes. "Ah, but the Princesse has been married already three years. I will be fourteen this year and have no husband."

For a moment I no longer see the door or the ladies who enter. I am lost in thought. At Amboise my companions did not speak of men. But here the topic seems to be on the tip of every tongue, from Mademoiselle de Saussauy, who said it was never too early to think of charming them, to the girl beside me, who worries because she does not have one.

"Her Majesty the Queen."

The pronouncement brings me back to my surroundings.

I do not immediately see Mother, but I do see a splotch of black against the colorful garb of the ladies-in-waiting. Working my way toward these somberly clad figures, I find Mother with the green bird perched upon her shoulder.

I wait to be recognized, but her eyes pass over me.

"We must not keep His Majesty waiting," she declares, clapping her hands and putting her feathered companion back in flight.

The room is so full of movement, talking, and laughter that it seems impossible anyone but those of us closest could hear. Yet the effect of Mother's declaration is immediate. The ladies part, allowing Her Majesty to precede them, then follow in her wake.

Charlotte takes my arm. "Hurry, before the best places are taken."

The best places are those with the best view of the King and the powerful men assembled about him. My brother Henri is already seated *tout proche* to Charles. He gestures to Charlotte and me, and we move to join him. A young man beside him rises at our approach. "François d'Espinay de Saint-Luc," Henri says, inclining his head casually in the youth's direction. Then, changing the tilt, he says, "My sister." Saint-Luc bows.

"Do not even think of asking her to dance," Henri continues, patting the seat beside him and forcing Saint-Luc to move down one by the gesture. "Now she is come, I finally have an adequate partner and I will not suffer to share her."

I blush.

I may sit beside him, but as the meal progresses I notice that another lady's eyes are constantly upon Henri. She has dark, curly hair and her dress is cut very low. "Who is that?" I ask Charlotte.

"Renée de Rieux."

"Is she one of us?"

"She is one of Her Majesty's maids of honor," Charlotte sniffs diffidently.

"But she is very wild and ambitious. Take care: she will use anything you tell her to her advantage."

I look back at the girl. Not far from her, the tall woman who spun me round earlier sits with her hand possessively on the sleeve of a man clad entirely in black.

Again I consult my knowledgeable friend. "Who is that gentleman, and whom does he mourn?"

Charlotte laughs. "He does not mourn. Why should he, when his Protestants have peace with the crown? That is the Prince de Condé. He and many of his sect favor dour dress, though why they think such drab colors are pleasing to almighty God, I cannot say."

I am stunned. This man with striking blue eyes and a well-groomed sandy-colored beard, who exudes an aura of importance, is the bugbear of my nursery? Good heavens. For most of my childhood I have known him as an enemy of the crown, yet here he is at Court dining and laughing as if there were nothing extraordinary in that. And perhaps there isn't. Perhaps this is peace. It seems I must reorder my thinking.

The Prince leans over and says something that makes the tall lady color.

"However severe his dress, the Prince seems to please that lady," I say.

"The Baronne de Limeuil? Indeed." My friend laughs.

The Prince reaches out a finger and runs it along the Baronne's cheek. A gentleman near to me scowls at the gesture.

"Poor Florimont." Charlotte rolls her eyes and tilts her head in the direction of the scowler. "He makes a fool of himself. He cannot accept being replaced by Condé. He doubtless reasons he is better looking than the Prince. And so he is. But with his patron the old Duc de Guise dead, the Queen has less need to know his mind than to know what passes through the Prince's. So the Baronne is in the proper bed, for the moment."

Perhaps I do not understand. It sounds as if Charlotte implies the Baronne has been both men's mistress. My face must show my dismay, for Charlotte, lowering her voice and pressing her mouth almost to my ear, says, "Do you think Her Majesty collects the most beautiful women in France solely to amuse herself? Some in her household serve her in ways that are less conventional than helping her to dress and guarding her against *ennui*."

Then, as if there were nothing shocking in her statement, Charlotte takes a drink of wine and speaks across me to another of Mother's ladies.

The balance of the evening passes in a blur. By the time I return to my chamber, I am utterly exhausted, thoroughly overwhelmed, and tremendously excited! There is *so much* of everything here—so much food, wine, dancing, music, and intrigue.

Sitting on the edge of my bed, I do not know which hurts more, my feet, my stomach, or my head. Yet, even as I rub my arches, I cannot wait for the sun to rise again, heralding a new day of discovery and adventure.

"Tomorrow," I tell my pillow, extinguishing my light and pulling shut the curtains of my bed, "after attending Mother and Mass, I mean to begin exploring this grand château."

I expected my grandfather's great gallery to be beautiful. I did not expect to have the breath sucked from my body by its majesty. It is unlike anything I've ever seen, unlike anything I have imagined—a vast, glorious eyeful with late morning sun spilling through its elegant windows. The carved wood of the wainscoting and ceiling is so elaborate, it makes the *salle des fêtes,* which held me spellbound yesterday, seem nothing at all. Frescoes framed in stucco and full of figures in classical dress cover the upper portion of the walls. A magnificent elephant wears my grandfather's regal F and a scattering of salamanders. Did King Francis own such a beast? How I wish I could have seen it!

Moving along, mouth open in wonder, I experience a growing awareness that many of the people and even the animals in the paintings are behaving unusually. A woman leans from a white horse, caressing an enormous swan. There is something about the look on her face that makes me uncomfortable in the same way that I was last evening when Mademoiselle de Rieux took a gentleman's hand and laid it in her lap.

Turning from this disturbing image, I cross the gallery but find little relief for my agitated feelings on the opposite wall. A pair of putti touch each other . . . in a very naughty place. Further along, I am confronted by a collection of men and animals contorted in face and form. How innocent the putti suddenly seem. I feel I ought not to see such things without knowing exactly what I *am* seeing. Yet I am fascinated. Glancing about, to reassure myself I am alone, I climb onto a bench beneath the fresco to have a better look. A door at the west end of the gallery opens and I freeze, hoping to remain unnoticed.

The boy who enters seems out of place in this gleaming and elaborate setting. His ruff is crooked; one leg of his breeches hangs lower than the other. The fabric of his clothing, while certainly suggesting he is a gentleman, is very plain. He does not notice me—or I presume he does not—because, without warning, he begins to run at top speed down the gallery. His arms pump. His footfall echoes on the wooden floor. A smile illuminates his unremarkable face, quite transforming it. Then he spies me.

Pulling up short a few feet from my perch, he bends, hands resting on his knees, and breathes heavily for a moment. Then looking up he asks, "Why are you standing on the bench?"

I do not feel I owe him an explanation. So I content myself with trying to mimic one of Mother's stern looks. "You ought not to run in here," I admonish.

"I know." The boy straightens up fully. He is not particularly tall and he wears his light-brown hair as haphazardly as his clothing. "But my tutor says it is too cold to go outside, and it is not as easy to sneak out as you would think."

Sneak out? I cannot imagine wanting to sneak out of the château, especially after weeks of wishing and waiting to arrive. "Can you not find amusement inside, in a court full of every sort of entertainment and attended by everyone of consequence?"

"I would rather look for frogs at the lagoon." He shifts from foot to foot. Slipping one hand inside his shirt, he gives his neck a scratch.

"You would get dirty," I say.

Again the shrug. "I like dirty."

"I don't." I smooth my overskirt in a gesture I've seen Madame do a thousand times.

"Best not let your mother catch you looking at that picture, then." He points at the fresco behind me.

My eyes rise unbidden to the naked men nearest me, their lips pressed. My cheeks burn. The boy's words come remarkably close to my own thoughts before I spotted him. How dare he make me feel guilty! Narrowing my eyes, I snap, "What do you know of my mother?"

"She is the Queen," he replies without hesitation. "You are Princess Marguerite. You've just arrived. I saw you at dinner yesterday." Then, as if he can hear the question I am preparing to ask, "I am your cousin Henri de Bourbon, Prince of Navarre."

"Why did you not say so at once? You are not very polite."

"No, I guess not. Or at least, people here tell me that I am not—often. I wish I could go back to Béarn." He shuffles his feet again. "My manners were fine there. And I was outside all the time—climbing, swimming, hunting."

I remember hearing that his mother, Jeanne d'Albret, Queen of Navarre, returned to Béarn after his father died of wounds suffered in the Siege of Rouen. I never gave any thought to where my cousin was. Or even, truth be told, to his continued existence since last we met as very young children. I wonder why he is here rather than at the court of his mother? But, more pressingly I wish him gone. He is singularly irritating.

"Why not go to Béarn, then?"

"Oh, I *am* going, if I have to slip away from the progress to do it. But I don't think it will come to that." He lifts his chin and looks me directly in the eye. "My mother will meet His Majesty during his travels, and I will go home with her then."

He reaches out a hand. "Would you like help down?"

I am not eager to accept his assistance, but jumping would be undignified, so I take his proffered hand and gingerly lower one foot to the floor.

"You are very pretty." The words are delivered more as a statement than a compliment.

"Thank you," I reply stiffly.

"I think I will kiss you."

"You will not!" I drop his hand and take a step backwards.

He shrugs. I swear, if I never see his shoulders rise and fall again, that will suit me very well. "Later, then."

"What?" I sputter. "I have no intention of *ever* permitting you to kiss me!"

"Not even if you marry me?" He tilts his head to one side and looks down his long, thin nose at me.

"Why would I marry you? You cannot even put your hose on straight."
I point accusingly to his right ankle, where his hose is badly twisted. He
does not seem at all discomforted.

"When I was little, His Majesty King Henri told me I was to be your
husband."

I have no idea if he is telling the truth, nor do I care. "My father is
dead," I say matter-of-factly. "And my brother, King Charles, would
never make me marry a boy who runs in the grand gallery and would
rather play with frogs than dance." Turning on my heels, I walk away. I
hope I have left my cousin mortified, staring at my back. But when I
turn at the end of the gallery to see what effect my pronouncement had
upon him, the Prince of Navarre is gone.

⁂ ⁂ ⁂

It is Shrove Tuesday. We will have one final magnificent entertainment
before such things give way to the solemnity of Lent. The meadow beside the lagoon looks like an ancient world. Delicate white columns—
some standing, others purposefully lying in pieces—are scattered among
the tables. It is as if we dine amidst the ruins of Ancient Greece.

Mother has outdone herself and she knows it. I can tell by the way her
cheeks color and her eyes shine. "The House of Valois," she declares, one
hand on Henri's shoulder and the other on mine as we ascend to the
King's table, "arrayed in splendor to remind all that we are the sole authority in France, and His Majesty will tolerate none who seek to undermine him or to undo the peace he has brought to his kingdom."

Taking my seat, my eyes are drawn to the island at the center of the
lagoon where a hundred torches illuminate a slender tower and its surroundings. *"Regardez!"* I say to Henri, clapping my hands. "Look who
guards the tower."

Henri laughs, for the pair are odd. While both are men, and both are
dressed in white flowing tunics topped by glowing golden armor, one is
enormous, a veritable giant, while the other is Mother's favorite dwarf. I
can hardly wait to discover what story will play out on the well-lit scene.

The House of Guise makes its entrance, the Duc at its head. His uncle the Cardinal of Lorraine walks with one arm draped possessively around the young man's shoulder. They are followed by the House of Montmorency, doubtless awarded precedence owing to the fact that the constable is charged with managing the royal progress. Finally it is time for the Princes of the Blood—the Bourbons. Louis, Prince de Condé, having bowed graciously to Charles, moves toward the table immediately to my right and nearly abutting our own and takes his seat at its center. A host of others connected to the Bourbons follow, my cousin, the Prince of Navarre, among them. I have not spoken to him since our encounter in the gallery, and that is just as well. Every glimpse of him since has reminded me of the moment he impudently threatened to kiss me. I pray he will not be seated near, but he is pushed down the table to be at my side.

I intend to ignore him, an effort that should be assisted by the fact that the riser supporting the Bourbon table is lower than the royal dais.

"Hello," he says, looking up at me.

I angle my body toward my brother as if I have not heard.

Despite the distance between us, I feel a tug on my sleeve. I cannot afford to be entirely rude while on display, and so, turning with an icy smile, I say, "Good evening."

Undaunted, he continues, "Are you performing?"

"My brothers and I have a pastoral later, after the sweets."

"Poetry." My cousin articulates the word as if in expectation of torture.

"The work of Monsieur Ronsard," I reply with some pique, "and very good."

"Not as good as yesterday's mock battle I'll wager."

"Then I suggest you run and hide after the sweets are served."

"That," he says, without the slightest touch of irony, "is an excellent idea. I fear I cannot fit many biscuits in my pockets and I do not wear a purse. So I suppose I had better limit myself to marzipans and candied nuts." He sighs as if this is a heavy sacrifice.

The thought of my cousin secreting treats on his person and slinking away merely to avoid seeing my brothers and I perform makes me furious. "Cousin, you may do as you like, but in the meantime, pray leave me unmolested."

"As you wish." The shrug reminds me of our last meeting. "So long as you do not accuse me of being rude later." He turns away, and I know by the knot in my stomach that it is I who have been impolite. I hate my cousin. He brings out the absolute worst in me.

As the meal progresses, those with roles in the theatrical slip away. On the island, musicians take their places. I stop eating to watch, surprised that the others around me can attend to their plates and their conversations. There is light inside the tower now. I glimpse the back of a man in a red hood and devil's horns at one of the windows. So transfixed am I by the actors getting into place, I do not even touch my last course.

Then, at my elbow, Henri says, "Come on! The best spots will be gone."

Looking around, I am startled to see the others already streaming toward the lagoon's edge. We join them. As we reach the bank, Charlotte runs up. Snatching my hand, she says, "There is a little rise under that stand of trees. What a view we shall have." We scamper off with Henri and Saint-Luc following.

Charlotte is right. The petite grove offers an excellent view. We are not the first to discover that. Édouard de Carandas, a handsome young Picard, sits upon the mossy ground, and as we lay claim to spots at the water's edge, Mademoiselle de Saussauy arrives. Without hesitation she drops down beside Carandas and, gesturing to his lap asks, "Is this place taken?"

The gentleman laughs. "I was saving it for you, Mademoiselle. Will you sit upon it?"

"Perhaps later, for now I will rest my head." She stretches out with her head upon the gentleman's padded slopes. Small clusters of ladies arrive arm in arm. I particularly notice the Duchesse de Nevers, but then, I always do. Over these last weeks she has become a subject of fascination for me—always wearing the best gowns and making the boldest statements. I find her thrilling.

Trumpets sound and music begins. The windows of the tower are filled with ladies close pressed by devils with swords and wicked leers. The ladies pantomime terror, holding hands before their faces to shield themselves and trembling exaggeratedly. Mademoiselle de Rieux leans from the uppermost window and, cupping her hands about her mouth, calls for help. The arrangement of things assures that her words cannot be heard, but one of my brother's dwarves trots out, carrying a placard spelling out the Mademoiselle's cry.

Liberators appear armored as Trojan warriors, the Marshals of France at their vanguard. The venerable Constable de Montmorency stumbles. My brother laughs and I shush him.

"I cannot help myself," he rejoinders. "It is ludicrous to see a man of seventy storm a castle—even when it is only made of silk."

The choreography allows the constable to bring down the dwarf, and then, his honor fulfilled, the elderly gentleman drops back to the rear of the knights.

A bell sounds. Armored devils spill from the tower, some dragging their captives. The Prince de Condé leads them. He is masterful with a sword, and though, given his presence among the demons, he must lose in the end, I cannot help admiring his ferocity.

One by one the devils fall twitching grotesquely under the blades of the Trojan knights. When only a few demons remain, the silken tower bursts into flame, and as fireworks light the sky, the last of the captives run forth to embrace their rescuers.

Next to me Henri cheers loudly. Others join in and everyone applauds. "Come on Saint-Luc, Margot, it is time for the sweets!" My brother sprints off, oblivious to the fact that his friend does not follow.

I have no intention of running like a child. I link my arm through Charlotte's. Standing, Monsieur de Carandas draws Mademoiselle de Saussauy to her feet. "The Prince de Condé wields a mighty sword," he says admiringly.

"Ah, but not longer than the one you keep in your scabbard. I could feel it where I lay," Fleurie replies.

Those standing nearest laugh heartily, as does the gentleman himself. He bows and kisses Mademoiselle's hand with an elaborate show of gallantry. Mademoiselle de Saussauy is all dimples and good humor in return and the two stroll off arm in arm.

"Fleurie is so beautiful," Charlotte comments wistfully. "That golden hair . . . And so *charmant*. If she does not snare a wealthy suitor in the course of our upcoming travels, I shall be surprised. Someone of more substantial rank than Monsieur de Carandas."

"Oh, but he is very fair of face," I remark. Under the influence of Mother's ladies, I have begun to notice such things.

"'Fair of face' is a fine consideration for flirting but of little import in marrying," the Duchesse de Nevers says, stepping between us and placing one arm around each. "Remember, girls, marriage is a matter of politics, finance, and family. Looks are for lovers." Then, releasing us, she disappears into the deepening darkness.

While we are standing there, looking after her, Saint-Luc approaches. "Ladies," he says, inclining his head. Charlotte and I look about and then realize he speaks to us. Are we to be the object of flirtation this evening as well? How delightful! If Mademoiselle de Saussauy may practice on a lesser noble from Picardy, why should I not try my skills on Saint-Luc? He is from an ancient and preferred Norman family.

"Seigneur"—I flutter my eyes as Mademoiselle de Saussauy does—"will you escort us?"

"It would be my pleasure." His voice squeaks a bit as he replies, and I notice there is color in his cheeks as he bows before offering one arm to each of us.

Charlotte squeezes my hand then lets it go. "You two go on." She scampers off, leaving Saint-Luc to me.

I take his arm and feel . . . nothing. What I expected to feel I do not know, but surely something, because I have observed the eyes of many a lady widen as she takes a gentleman's arm.

We walk in silence a short way. In the torchlight I can see Saint-Luc's Adam's apple move as he swallows. "I greatly look forward to Your Highness's performance in the pastoral," he says at last.

I cannot help but think of my cousin's scowls at the thought of my recitation. "More than the sugared fruits?" I ask, offering what I hope is a coquettish smile and wishing I had dimples like Mademoiselle de Saussauy.

"Of course! How can sugar hope to compare to the sweetness of your voice?" Saint-Luc is warming up to this game. We are two courtiers trading compliments. I feel very grand and grown-up.

"Would you believe there are some"—I lower my voice to a faux whisper and experiment with raising my eyebrows—"who would prefer a pocket full of nuts?"

"Impossible!" His attempt to sound shocked exceeds the mark a bit, but I appreciate the effort.

We have reached the edge of the dining area. Henri and Charlotte wait, already nibbling on dainties. A glorious table covered with confections of every sort, including a fanciful sugar paste fish decorated with golden scales, stands at the center of a ring of torches.

"I assure you, the Prince of Navarre confessed as much earlier." I give my head a sad little shake as if I am ages older than my cousin. "He plans to run and hide while I perform."

"Someone should thrash him."

"Would you? Would you give him a beating for me?" I press Saint-Luc's arm with my free hand. I can visualize him dressed in the golden armor of this evening's entertainment . . . and my cousin in the horns of one of the devils.

"Who is Saint-Luc going to beat?" Henri asks, sauntering up. He holds out a rolled-up sugared *crespe* so I can take a bite.

"The Prince of Navarre," Saint-Luc says, "for insulting your sister."

"Oh-ho, I should like to see that, Saint-Luc. Our cousin may be ill-dressed and ill-spoken, but I believe he is a capital wrestler, thanks to his upbringing, and handy with a sword."

A nice little group has gathered about us, drinking, listening. I want to say something clever—something capable of evoking laughter.

"Do not let my brother dissuade you"—I turn to Saint-Luc and offer him a kiss on the cheek—"for surely the Prince of Navarre has a short sword compared to the one which hangs in your scabbard."

My jest has the desired effect. Those around us titter appreciatively.

Suddenly I feel a hand upon my shoulder. It is the Baronne de Retz. She is not laughing. In fact, her face looks very severe. "Come," she says. Turning, she moves through the crowd. It is necessary for me to walk very quickly to keep up. By the time we enter the palace, I am breathless.

Rounding on me the Baronne says, "Mademoiselle Marguerite, I am shocked to hear you make a jest about a gentleman's intimate anatomy!"

I am flabbergasted. I did not say anything about Saint-Luc's person. Only his sword. I am about to say as much, but the Baronne presses onward. "What would Her Majesty think?"

The question stings. Mother has shown me precious little attention since my arrival. I certainly do not wish to garner maternal notice in a negative manner.

"What do you mean?" I stammer. "I only spoke as Her Majesty's other ladies do. I heard Mademoiselle de Saussauy use that quip this evening. She is a *dame d'honneur* from one of the finest houses in France. How can it be wrong for me to speak as she does?"

The Baronne gives a deep sigh. "You must conduct yourself with more decorum and aloofness than Fleurie de Saussauy. You may pass your time *with* the ladies of Her Majesty's household, but you are not *of* them. You must understand the difference."

"But I do not," I reply. "I see that Her Majesty's ladies behave differently than I have been brought up to do by you and Madame at Amboise, but theirs are the manners of Court. Why may I not adopt them?" I am warming to the injustice of my situation. "Why," I challenge, "may they wear their gowns without a partlet while I remain covered to the neck? Why may Renée de Rieux flirt shamelessly with my brother while I am made to feel ashamed for joking with his friend?"

The Baronne is silent, contemplating my face earnestly in the dim light. "Your Highness, every woman in the Queen's household has a duty to Her Majesty, a duty of obedience. If they are not content to serve the Queen as she will be served, they may leave Court. If they are derelict in their duty, they will be sent. The specific duties of Her Majesty's other ladies are not for me to say, nor for you to speculate upon.

"The duty you owe the Queen is different than that owed by the others. Yours is the duty of *une fille de France* and a daughter. The nature of your duty—to reflect well upon your royal house and to marry to the crown's advantage in due time—has been clear since your infancy. Such duty, set upon your shoulders by birth, cannot be declined. You may, however, fail in it."

My defiance collapses instantly. Tears gather in the corners of my eyes. "I do not wish to fail."

"Of course not. No more do I want you to." She places her hand upon my shoulder. "Her Majesty has not announced it yet, so perhaps I ought not tell you, but Madame is growing old. Her Majesty has adjudged it time for that lady to be relieved of her duties and allowed to enjoy leisure in recompense for years of service. As we depart on progress, I will take Madame's place as *gouvernante* charged, officially, with overseeing Your Highness."

I draw a sharp breath. I cannot remember a time when Madame was not with me. The tears which a few moments earlier merely stung my eyes roll down my cheeks.

The Baronne hands me a handkerchief from her sleeve. "My appointment gives me great pleasure. And I hope you will learn to view it as a positive good. You are lovely by God's gift, but if you will be more—if you will be a lady of refinement, witty and cultured—then you must take pains to develop the best qualities and eschew other less desirable ones. I shall endeavor to guide you, and I hope to see you flower into the first among Her Majesty's ladies. The one admired by all."

Dabbing away the last of my tears, I smile. To be thought capable of such attainment by a woman oft called "the tenth muse" is flattering. I mean to comport myself in accordance with the Baronne de Retz's direction from this moment forward.

CHAPTER 2

March to June 1564—On the Roads of France

We are a city in motion. Nay, larger than many of the cities we will pass. For weeks Henri and I watched the royal train assemble, but never could I have imagined the true enormity of our party. Leaning out of the coach, I regard with wonder the people and conveyances stretched as far as my eye can see. Litters, coaches, riders on horseback, pikemen, men-at-arms, foot soldiers, and a multitude of servants—the variety, colors, noise, and movement of the train are entirely overwhelming.

"Henri!" I call. "Can you see the end?"

Pulling up his horse, my brother allows the window at which I sit to draw even with him. "I cannot. I'll wager there are still riders inside the gates of Fontainebleau."

"Really? But we have come miles already."

"Yes, but we ride at the head of more than fifteen thousand souls." The pride in his voice is pronounced.

I have never seen fifteen thousand anything, let alone fifteen thousand people traveling together. I am jealous of my brother's view and of his relative freedom. "You are fortunate to be on horseback," I say.

"There will be plenty of time for you to ride beside me when the weather is not so cold. We will be on the road for months—for years."

Years. The thought of everything I will see and all that might take place on such a long journey excites me to the point of agitation. *How different I will be when we next see Fontainebleau! I will be a woman.*

I feel a hand on my arm and turn to the Baronne de Retz. "Your Highness," she says softly, "pray close the curtains, the other ladies are shivering."

Mortified, I cast Henri a longing look and then let the curtains fall.

"Your Grace, if you will be so kind." The Baronne inclines her head in the direction of the uncovered window beside the Duchesse de Nevers at the opposite side of the coach.

The Duchesse looses the curtains with a murmur of *"Bien sûr."* But I do believe her eyes, which seek mine, give just the slightest roll. I am shocked but that is not my only feeling. Her Grace and the Baronne de Retz are the same age but they are so different, and that difference intrigues me. Whereas the Baronne is steady and without question a paragon of female propriety, the Duchesse is all daring and dazzle. I know my duty is to allow my *gouvernante* to direct my behavior, but a little daring is surely not dangerous.

"Why do you pout?" My brother sidles up to me where I stand, watching Charles and Mother receive basins and ewers from the Cardinal de Bourbon. Nearby, a collection of Troyes' paupers—mostly women and children—sit on a long bench, prepared to be the objects of royal Lenten piety.

"I did not realize I would be left out of some of the grandest ceremonies of the journey."

Yesterday the King made a magnificent Entry into Troyes—riding beneath a canopy supported by dignitaries past elaborate set pieces and stopping to hear recitations of poetry written for the occasion. The residents of the city, from the wealthiest to the urchins roaming its streets, were permitted to witness it all. I was not. It seems the women of the Court, even the Valois women, are not included in the proceedings that constitute a Royal Entry.

"You did not miss anything worth seeing," Henri whispers. I know he is lying to make me feel better, and this pleases me. "Jean Passerate may be considered a great poet by the standards of Champagne," he continues, "but I was not the only one who snickered at some of his forced verses. I thought Ronsard would have a fit."

I blush at the word, knowing that Ronsard has better self-control than I. I threw an actual fit when I learned that the sights I was missing included a collection of exotic savages from the New World. I am very, very glad that Henri has not heard about my tantrum. The Baronne de Retz was aghast. "If this is how you will behave when disappointed," she said, "you will spend a great portion of your life stamping and scowling. To be a woman is to wait, to stand in the background, to accept that your life is governed by others."

When she was done with her reprimand, I cried and said I was sorry. But, watching my mother washing the feet of those selected for the honor, I am not certain being always in the shadows is a situation I wish to accept. It is not how she lives. Nor how the Duchesse de Nevers does. Then again, they are extraordinary women and I cannot fool myself into thinking I am that. Perhaps if I were a queen. Mother promised me I would be, back before France had peace. I must trust her, I must be patient.

Beside me, my brother shifts from foot to foot. He is never patient. When Henri wants something, he pursues it boldly, badgering Mother shockingly. "I cannot wait for Lent to be over," he mutters. "My stomach aches. It wants to feast, not fast. Let's go see the gift the city made to Charles."

"You saw it yesterday."

"But you did not and it's magnificent."

It turns out my brother's idea of magnificent is the stuffed body of an animal I do not recognize. It is like a salamander only much, much bigger, with a square snout containing fearsome teeth.

"It came back with one of the gentlemen who traveled with Admiral Coligny." Henri defies the warning look of one of the Swiss guards and reaches out a finger to stroke the beast's snout. "Feel the skin."

I ignore his instruction. "It does not look valuable," I remark. "Monsieur de L'Hôpital must be disappointed." L'Hôpital, Charles' chancellor, was assigned the first gift of the journey, doubtless because he gave Mother support for declaring the King of age a little early.

"Are you mad? This is far better than some golden statue! If I were Charles, I would not give it to L'Hôpital. I would pay him off instead."

"So would I." The voice from behind startles me.

Henri turns. "Cousin." His voice contains enthusiasm—something I certainly do not feel upon recognizing the Prince of Navarre.

"I wish I could have gone to the New World with Coligny. Or at least that they would make the savages stand here on display," my cousin says.

"Never mind," Henri replies. "We will soon have the English to gawk at. They have let Ambassador Throckmorton out of prison to sign the treaty. I guess I will have to keep an eye on you, Cousin. Was Throckmorton not arrested for conspiring with Huguenots against the crown?"

The Prince of Navarre shrugs. "I have never conspired with anyone, and I would rather see the savages or even the satyrs riding goats from yesterday's procession than stand around watching diplomats sign things."

Finally something my cousin and I agree on. Not that it matters. Given the size of our party, I am seldom in close company with him.

"Which would you rather see?" the Prince of Navarre asks as if he is quite content to have me settle the question.

"Neither. I want to see the Duchesse de Lorraine's new baby, just like Her Majesty."

"Girls! There is no accounting for them." And without waiting for a reply, he runs off, doubtless to look for savages.

"The city fathers of Lyon know how to impress." Charles sits on his horse gazing at the splendid boat waiting for him. Waiting for *us*. Not all of us, but for those selected especially by my brother and mother to accompany His Majesty down the Saône from Chalon-sur-Saône to Lyon. The rest of the train must go on as they have come this far: by horse, litter, coach, and foot. I cannot wait to get on the boat. As I am climbing aboard, I see the Prince of Navarre among those waiting to embark. Well, family is family, I suppose. I notice that the young Duc de Guise and his mother will also travel with the King. Unlike my cousin, the Duc is a fine-looking young man whose clothes hang easily upon him. He never looks out of place or discomforted whatever the occasion. And he is handsome, nearly as handsome as my brother Henri. His Grace's eyes catch mine for a moment and I feel a fluttering in my stomach. I wonder what he thinks of me. Apparently nothing, for his glance quickly moves on; he is merely, I decide with disappointment, taking stock of who has sufficient royal favor to be included on the voyage.

"Come, ladies," says the Duchesse de Nevers to Charlotte and me. "Shall we sit down before all the places furthest from Her Majesty are taken?"

Her Grace's quip is shocking but entirely accurate. The youngest and most adventurous of Mother's ladies generally try to keep the farthest distance, desiring the freedom that comes with less supervision.

We fall in behind the Duchesse, who makes her way along the deck briskly, then stops short and turns to cross to the other side. I notice Her Grace's sister, the Princesse de Porcien, walking in the direction we were originally going.

"You will not sit with your sister?" Charlotte asks.

"No, indeed, for did you not notice the Prince de Porcien beside her? I doubt even she will bear his company for long."

"Because he is a Huguenot?" I ask.

"Because he is a terrible bore," the Duchesse replies with a smile. "I know His Majesty wishes us to love the Protestants. How many speeches has he made en route urging the people to obey his edict of pacification?

I have lost count. But I do not believe I shall be found in violation of his decree merely because I snub my brother-in-law."

Charlotte and I both laugh appreciatively. Truth be told, I think being a Protestant a greater sin than being tedious, but I would never say such a thing aloud, as I wish to have a sophisticated air. Piety, it seems, is not particularly fashionable, and so I keep mine to myself as much as possible.

We settle into seats close to Mademoiselle de Saussauy. "What of scandal have you to tell, ladies?" the Duchesse asks the moment we are comfortable. "Come, I mean to be entertained, and I am not one to find scenery fascinating."

"Do you not wonder why the Baronne de Limeuil is left ashore?" Fleurie seems well content to begin the gossip. "Well, I have heard that, for all his stern looks and piety, Don Francisco de Álva has shown marked admiration for her."

"The Spanish ambassador! He would be a feather for her cap and increase her value to the Queen," Charlotte says.

The Duchesse de Nevers nods. "There cannot be another gentleman whose opinions are more important to Her Majesty as she wheedles for a meeting with King Philip."

I know that the diplomatic centerpiece of this tour, for all it is intended to show Charles to his subjects, is a rendezvous with my sister Elisabeth and her husband—the details of which have not yet been entirely agreed upon.

"Exactly!" Fleurie says. "He is the *plus important,* but when the Queen urged Isabelle to take him up, she refused."

"Refused the Queen!" I realize the moment I have spoken that my voice is too loud. But my shock is such that I did not think to whisper. Verily, I believe if Mother told me to jump from the ship, I would do so without question.

"She did." Fleurie leans in. "Her Majesty told the Baronne she could walk to Lyon for all the Queen cared."

"I wish I could have Don Francisco," Charlotte says.

"Ambitious." The Duchesse nods approvingly. "But do not overreach. You are too young and too unmarried for such a task. Do not insert yourself there thinking to gain royal favor; be patient and await the Queen's will. For obedience to Her Majesty generally comes with a wealthy husband."

"If you know so much about securing a husband," Fleurie challenges, "why do you not have one?"

"I am a different case. I have a title and wealth of my own. Those bring freedom. I must marry to be sure, and mean to do so before we return to Paris if I can."

"And what shall you look for in a husband?" Charlotte asks.

"A man of the Court who understands it thoroughly. Someone of importance. Oh"—she winks—"and a man without any gray in his beard, so that when I lie beneath him I am not kept awake by the creaking of his knees."

I give a little laugh, hoping that it sounds worldly. I am quite sure I have a far less complete understanding of what goes on when a man and woman perform the act of love than my companions, but would prefer not to seem the naïf.

After a cold dinner, the members of the Court begin to doze. Though my stomach is full and my head buzzing with all the wonderful if sometimes wicked things I heard at the Duchesse de Nevers' elbow, I have no intention of napping. Unlike Her Grace, I find the scenery we pass entirely engaging. Leaving my sleeping companions, I go to the rail for a better view.

My eyes are on a group of people on the bank elaborately saluting the King—little knowing that he dozes in his lavish chair—when my cousin joins me. I know it is him by the state of his hose and shoes, which I glance at surreptitiously. I have no intention of turning noticeably in his direction and engaging him.

"Shall I tell you a secret?" he asks without preamble.

"What makes you think I would keep it?" The last thing I want is to be the Prince of Navarre's confidante.

"I would not assume as much, but if you gave me your word I would trust it." I am considering my response but my cousin does not wait. "You are the only lady who does not find the sun too strong." He gestures to those under the elaborate canopy. "They are being silly because travel continues all summer and they are sure to get browned by the sun on horseback. They might as well enjoy the view as we do."

I was enjoying the view. I bite my tongue to keep from saying this. I know from past experience that, though my cousin provokes my incivility, I am never happy with myself once I have been rude to him. I begin to feel bad for even thinking such a harsh thing.

"What is your secret?" I ask, turning to look him in the face. The question is my penance.

He looks at me expectantly.

"I give you my word I will keep it."

"You know my mother meets us at Mâcon."

I do, and I have apprehended how excited my cousin is for this event. Henri and some of his friends have laughed over it, but, much as I do not like the Prince of Navarre, I could not join them. My cousin has not seen his mother in nearly two years. I know well how this feels.

He moves closer. "I will be going back to Gascony with her."

"I am happy for you." I am. My cousin, despite his long residence with it, seems continually out of place in my brother's Court. He fits in better on the road where he can ride all day. I've even observed him on foot, running in the dust with some of the pages. And he appears to enjoy adventure more than many in the train. Another thing we have in common. The thought of having multiple things in common with the Prince of Navarre is unsettling. Still, it cannot be denied. I simply do not understand the complaining that some do about the inconveniences of travel. They are, to my mind, entirely outweighed by the novelty of new places.

Yet even on tour the Prince of Navarre remains distinctly "other." Odd, I think: it is not his religion that makes him so—many Protestants travel with us and blend in until a Sabbath or holy day presents itself and they separate themselves for their odd worship. The Prince de Condé, who recently departed the train, never sticks out so, and he is a great leader of the Huguenots—something it is hard for me to imagine my cousin will ever be.

We dock close to Mâcon in ample time before Charles' planned *Entrée joyeuse*. As they are positioning the plank, I notice a woman with hair the color of Elizabeth of England's waiting, surrounded by half a dozen richly clad gentlemen. Their deference to her is clear. And her identity is made obvious to me by the agitation of my cousin, who nearly jostles the King in his attempts to move closer to where the plank meets the deck. This must be Jeanne d'Albret, come to receive us. A little forward of her, a young man in clerical robes also waits. The moment the plank is secured, he strides up it. On deck he kneels before Her Majesty, pressing a message upon her. Her face clouds as she reads it.

"Your Majesty, what is it?" the chancellor asks.

"Some of His Majesty's subjects insulted the host at the Corpus Christi procession."

I feel unsteady on my feet and not from the sway of the boat. Mother does not say the word Protestant, but what other sort of subjects could behave in such an abominable manner?

"They refused to remove their hats as it passed. Some heckled and others shoved those accompanying the Blessed Sacrament."

The Abbé de Brantôme, standing behind Her Majesty, mutters, "Heaven protect us from heretics."

Amen.

Mother looks past the messenger and my gaze follows hers to where the Queen of Navarre stands.

She offers her hand to the young priest so he may kiss it, then takes Charles' arm. "Let us not keep your cousin waiting. Where is the Prince of Navarre?" Spotting him, she says, "Come walk between my own son and daughter." Perceiving a number of incredulous looks, she adds, "Those who did not respect the Eucharist wish to divide France once more, and the King will no more permit such a division than he will allow their abominable behavior to pass uncorrected."

On shore the greetings between the Queen of Navarre, Charles, and Mother are gracious and formal. I swear I can feel every one of my cousin's muscles straining where he stands beside me waiting for the pleasantries to be finished. More than once, I catch Jeanne d'Albret's eyes wandering in his direction while others are speaking. The niceties at an end, Jeanne moves to stand before her son. He bows.

"My son, it has been too long. I have been glad of your letters."

My cousin looks into her face with eyes that are nakedly eager. I have the feeling that were they in private he would throw his arms about his mother. I wish away the hundreds of souls who must perceive as I do, and not because I am embarrassed by his lack of fashionable detachment—well, not entirely. His pleasure at seeing his mother moves me and I wish he could indulge in his impulse.

"I hope, Madame, you did not mind my spelling errors too much."

The Queen of Navarre smiles slightly. "We will talk of that later." Turning to Mother, she says, "Thank you for your attention to the Prince's studies and for your care of his person."

"*Ce n'était rien.* You are family and therefore he is as precious to us as he is to you," Mother replies without a hint of irony. "We endure this parting only because it is brief, and because we will see the both of you during the ceremonies that mark His Majesty's time in Mâcon." Mother watches as Jeanne puts her hand on my cousin's shoulder; then, just as the Queen of Navarre is about to lead her son away, Mother says, "Apropos such ceremonies, you will join us on Thursday next, I am sure, for an additional event. His Majesty is ordering the Corpus Christi procession repeated. We understand that the original was marred by some unbecoming conduct that I must ask you, by your sway among certain communities, to help ensure is not repeated."

It is clear that the Queen of Navarre knows what Mother refers to. Her lips compress. The gentlemen accompanying her murmur among themselves.

"Your Majesty knows that our faith will not permit us to walk in such procession," Jeanne d'Albret replies.

"Ah, but as His Majesty insists respect be shown to your sect, surely you and its other adherents can vouchsafe your Catholic brethren the same by attending."

"We will attend."

Mother lays her hand on my cousin Henri's other shoulder, closing her fingers. The boy is now between the two queens. There is an obvious tension and for one wild moment I nearly expect each to begin tugging upon him.

"Why, then you must sit beside me," Mother says. "And as he is but a boy and so accustomed to being with his cousins, you must give the Prince of Navarre leave to dress as an angel with my own children."

The two queens gaze into each other's eyes. Neither smiles, though the image of my cousin costumed as an angel ought to seem humorous to anyone who knows him.

"I suppose there is no harm in that," the Queen of Navarre replies at last. "It might do His Majesty's Catholic subjects good to be reminded that there are Protestants in heaven."

Heretics in heaven? Never!

"I hope such angels show better respect to their Catholic fellows than those of your sect in Mâcon." Mother releases my cousin's shoulder and the Queen of Navarre leads him away.

My cousin bore being an angel very well. He only stepped on his robe twice and on mine once. I tolerated being trod upon with equanimity because I knew that today we would return to our boat, while he would ride south with his mother. Twice in the course of the procession—which this time met with nothing from the Protestant inhabitants of the city but bowed and uncovered heads—he reminded me in a whisper that he would be back in the Pyrenees before long. It was not to be, however. Instead I stand watching Jeanne d'Albret take leave of her son.

There is pain in the Queen of Navarre's eyes. But nothing compared to the agony that transfigures my cousin's entire face.

"Why?" I whisper to the Duchesse de Nevers. "Why does he not go? Why would his mother take gold instead?"

Henri told me this morning that the Prince of Navarre would remain because His Majesty paid for the continued privilege of our cousin's company.

"She took the gold because she is no fool," Her Grace replies. "She would not have the boy in any event. Her Majesty made up her mind that his presence with the Court is necessary to the peace."

"How? He does nothing but race, ride, and wrestle like the rest of the gentlemen his age."

"Think, Your Highness. Think of the history of your own father. Did he not spend some years as a guest of the King of Spain?"

My cousin throws his arms about his mother, heedless of the snickers of some courtiers. My stomach tightens. My father was held hostage by the Spanish king—as a living guarantee that the French would give him no trouble. I do not believe I will ever like my cousin, but I cannot help feeling sorry for him.

"I should not like to be kept away from my family by politics," I whisper to the Duchesse. She looks at me oddly.

My cousin's tutor puts a hand on his shoulder and turns him toward the boat. The Prince of Navarre is not, I am relieved to see, crying. Charles and Mother move onto the deck with light steps, but my cousin, just behind them, trudges. Then he is lost to my view as the rest of the gentlemen and ladies in our party stream aboard.

***

The year is changing. Not from one to the next—that would be quite ordinary—but the very essence of what a year is. We are at Roussillon, and Charles has signed an ordinance proclaiming that henceforth each year will begin on the first of January instead of on Holy Saturday after vespers. This is monumental.

Something else monumental has occurred. This morning when I arose from my bed my linen and my shift were soiled. And though I was horribly embarrassed, and blushed throughout the Baronne de Retz's earnest instructions on the finer points of managing what will henceforth be a monthly event, my delight outweighs my distress. I am, at last, a woman. The words fill my head, but I cannot imagine saying them to anyone—not even Charlotte or the Duchesse de Nevers. The latter has become as close a companion as the former during these travels, and now permits me to call her Henriette. Will my friends know by looking at me? Will Mother? Surely Her Majesty will be told, for this development makes me marriageable. Will she say something to me? Will a prospective groom be mentioned at once?

I examine myself in my glass. Other than my cheeks being a little pink with excitement, I can detect no overt change. Disappointing. Well, at the very least I can make an alteration myself. Sitting at my dressing table, I unfasten my partlet at the front and open it, pushing the fabric back beneath the edges of my kirtle as necessary to achieve the desired effect. *That is better.*

I often feel as if my life, the real living of it, began when I joined Mother's household. I remarked as much to Henri the other day and he laughed. "By that calculation you are an infant too young even to walk," he said. Perhaps he has been out of the nursery too long to remember its limits. I remember them well—remember when the most exciting thing was the arrival of Mother, or catching a glimpse of some other person of import. Now I see important people every day, and Mother too. Yet, despite being the Duchesse de Valois and sister of the King, I am not an important person myself.

That is what I crave next.

CHAPTER 3

May 1565—Bordeaux, France

Mother's room is littered with things and with women packing them for tomorrow's departure. I assume I have been summoned to assist, but at the sight of me she claps her hands. "Ladies," she says, "the Duchesse de Valois and I have business."

As the others depart, I contemplate her statement. Business? To my certain knowledge, my mother and I have never had "business." As she passes me, my sister Claude, who recently arrived to join the royal train, offers me an excited smile.

When we are alone, there is no preamble. "You know we meet the Spanish next month."

"Indeed, Madame, planning for the event is all anyone speaks of." I might add: *or has spoken of for at least three months.* Unfortunately, the anticipated event is not as Mother envisioned it. Mother had been promised the attendance of King Philip, or so she thought. When she was told that the King refused to come—a show of his disapproval for the continuing peace with the Protestants—she went into a rage.

"May Henri and I dance in one of the entertainments?" I ask. "Our Spanish Pavane was much admired in Toulouse."

"Yes, there will be balls, ballets, and every sort of grand entertainment," Mother replies. "But, daughter, these are merely the trimmings, not the gown. When you are a queen, pray remember that agreements are more easily made in pleasant surroundings than in austere ones. And it is those agreements that truly matter."

"Queen?"

"Have you forgotten I promised you a crown?" She lifts her right hand and strokes a bit of hair at my temple.

I remember. Of course I do.

"This meeting with Spain is to be more than a reunion of family," Mother continues. "Much as I long to embrace your sister, I have other, more diplomatic needs. Or rather, France does. And the Spanish desire something more than to invest Charles with the Order of the Golden Fleece.

"I have summoned you because you are a marriageable young woman. I understand that your courses have come regularly for more than half a year."

I drop my eyes to the hem of Mother's gown and blush. Much as I wanted her recognition of this change when it happened—recognition that never came—her frank, offhanded mention of it now mortifies me.

"Yes, Your Majesty."

"Excellent. His Majesty the King desires closer ties with Spain. Beside ties of blood, ties of marriage are the surest. We will forward a match for you with King Philip's son, the Prince of Asturias. Then you can wear the Spanish crown when your sister is Dowager."

Queen of Spain! If my cheeks are pink now, it is with pleasure, not shame. I can hardly wait to tell Charlotte. No wonder Claude smiled at me.

"I, a bride!"

"Ah," Mother says quickly, "but you must not speak of it openly. Not until it is signed and sealed." Walking to the alcove of the nearest window, she brushes a pile of folded chemises from the seat as if they were inconsequential. Seating herself, she motions to the place beside her.

When I am settled, she leans in as if we are conspirators.

"I will do all I can to secure this match," she says, stroking my hand where it rests upon the bench between us. "And I will employ your sister Elisabeth in the business. Her letters and my spies indicate she is highly regarded by her husband and allowed considerable influence. But you must do your part as well."

I nod, eager to do what I can to please Mother.

"I have sent orders ahead to Bayonne for more than a dozen new gowns for your wardrobe. Every moment you are in company with the Spanish, you must be fashionable, you must be graceful, you must be modest. You have become a young lady of note based upon more than your birthright these last months . . ."

A compliment from Mother! I feel a rush of pleasure. I have been working hard to mold myself into a true lady of the Court, half Baronne de Retz and half—much to the Baronne's hinted displeasure—Duchesse de Nevers. How wonderful to think Mother has noticed the results.

". . . Display your natural wit, but never to the disadvantage of the Prince or any member of your sister's retinue. Display your piety at every opportunity, for the Spanish are as fanatical in their devotion to the Church of Rome as Admiral Coligny and his fellows are to their so-called reformed religion."

"Madame, I will obey you in everything."

A sharp knock sounds.

Mother takes both my hands and kisses them. "Do your duty to me and to the King and you will be a Spanish princess before the year is out. Now go—that will be your brother Henri."

"Henri?" I ask, rising. But Mother's mind has already left me.

My brother bows to me on his way in, but there is no opportunity to tell him my news. I burn to tell him. So, though I have packing of my own to attend to, I wait outside for his business to be finished. *Queen of Spain!* I turn the title over in my mind. *A queen like my mother.* And like my sister. True, the crown of Spain must wait for my sister's husband to die, but to be in line for such a crown is a mighty thing, and I will be Princess of Asturias in the meantime. If I must go to a strange land, it will be good to be part of my sister's court. I hardly remember her, but family is family.

My thoughts turn to my prospective groom. I long to ask someone what the Prince of Asturias looks like. I wonder if he likes dancing. If he is as spritely of step as Henri? Oh, why did my brother interrupt my time with Mother before I could ask such questions?

Henri emerges, the door falling closed behind him with a tremendous bang. He strides past as if I were invisible. Following, I grab his arm. "I am going to be a Spanish princess," I say. Only as he turns do I notice his black looks.

"Devil take the Spanish!" He gives a fierce shake to free himself of me.

"Henri, what is the matter?"

"Yours is not the only marriage being discussed. Our brother expects me to marry a woman old enough to be my mother." He gives a kick to a small bench along the wall and it skitters away like an animal.

"Who?"

"The King of Spain's widowed sister." He spits the words out. "She is thirty. Thirty! I told Mother no. Said that the very suggestion shows my happiness means nothing to her."

"You didn't." I am stricken that he would defy Mother when she loves him so dearly and when she has every right to expect his cooperation in the crown's arrangement of his marriage.

"You do not believe me?" It is he who grabs my arm this time, dragging me back toward the door. "Go in and see for yourself. I left her crying."

I have absolutely no desire to see Mother in such a state. Wrenching away, I run as hard as I can, not stopping until I gain my room. Charlotte is there. At the sight of her I forget Henri's bad behavior.

"It is Her Majesty's desire that I should marry the Prince of Asturias."

"A royal marriage!" Charlotte shouts. The servants folding and packing my things look up.

"Hush, I am not supposed to speak of it widely."

"Why not? If it is the Queen's will, then surely it will happen—"

I must admit I feel the same. My mother's will is strong, and, in all modesty I believe my personal appearance and attributes make me an attractive prospect as a bride.

"—and then I will be the only one of us without a husband." Charlotte's face falls. Henriette married Louis de Gonzague, Prince of Mantua, in March. She is not overly fond of the gentleman. But he is one of

Charles' secretaries of state and he is no graybeard, so, all in all, she declares him an unobjectionable husband.

"Not for long, I am sure. No woman as beautiful as you finds herself single at sixteen unless she wills it so," I reply, hoping this consoles her.

It does. She smiles. "I would still rather have been married before my thirteenth birthday, as it appears you shall be. Promise that I can help carry your mantle at the Mass. Or do you think the ceremony will be in Spain? That would be too cruel. Next to a wedding of my own, I will enjoy yours more than anything." She hugs me hard.

While she is squeezing the breath out of me, my sister Claude and the Baronne de Retz come in. Both are beaming.

"Here comes another bride to be," Charlotte exclaims, releasing me. My *gouvernante* is betrothed to Albert de Gondi, Charles' former tutor and a man much in favor with both the King and Mother. He has just been made *Premier Gentilhomme de la chamber du Roi,* but Henriette insists such titles can never erase the fact he was born a Florentine merchant's son.

"Felicitations!" Claude cries, hugging me. "It seems, of three sisters, two were destined for Spanish climes, and I can hardly regret being left behind when I have my dear Duc de Lorraine."

"And your pretty baby," I say, kissing her. The image of my chubby, pink nephew, whose baptism we attended near the start of our journey, fills my mind. How I would like a pretty baby of my own. "Tell me everything about the Prince! Her Majesty told me nothing . . . not even his name."

His name is Don Carlos. He is nearly twenty. They tell me he is tall. They say his father holds him in great esteem and that when he had an accident three years ago and all thought he would die, Philip asked for a miracle and promised to work one for God in return if the boy were spared.

My new gowns have been fitted. Today I wear the first. It is black, because, Mother assures me, that is the Spanish taste. It seems the wrong color for the weather. It is horribly hot. For this reason the Queen of Spain's entry into Bayonne takes place in the evening. But even though the sun has set, I can feel perspiration beneath my chemise. I sway slightly where I stand with Their Majesties, surrounded by a glittering array of courtiers and a hundred torch bearers. Is my unsteadiness a result of the heat or my nerves? Although we met my sister Elisabeth yesterday—receiving her quietly at Saint Jean de Luz and enjoying a private dinner as if we were any family and not a family in possession of multiple crowns—I have good reason to be apprehensive. Today I will meet my future husband for the first time.

My dear Henri is charged with escorting our sister into Bayonne. He rides beside her, springing from his horse to help her down from her stunning jeweled saddle. When they are side by side, it is easy to see they are brother and sister. Elisabeth's skin is pale, her cheeks are a delicate pink, and her eyes are dark. She is lovely. Everyone says so and I thrill at the thought that I have been told that I am better looking than she. I wonder if the Spanish prince will see this at once? I know my vanity is a sin, but can it really be wrong to wish my future husband to find me beautiful?

Henri leads Elisabeth forward, followed by a pair of gentlemen. The first is old. The second must be Don Carlos. He is tall, just as I was told. I wish I could say he was handsome, which I was also promised, but there is something out of harmony in his face. His chin juts forward oddly. Yes, that must be it. It is not so bad, really. His nose is good and he has shapely calves; I can see them quite clearly as he makes his bow. I try to catch his eye, but he shows no interest in me, and little interest in Mother or my brothers. Mostly, his eyes are on Elisabeth.

Mother offers Don Carlos a smile but seems more interested in the second gentleman, the one announced as the Duc d'Alba. She holds out a hand for him to kiss. "Your Grace, we are pleased to see you. We know in what high esteem our son, His Majesty King Philip, holds you." Her voice is pleasant, but every French courtier knows she is not pleased at all that Alba stands before her instead of Philip, and unless the Duc is an idiot he knows it as well.

"Your Majesty," he replies in clipped tones, "it was my honor to be entrusted with the Queen of Spain's safety, and it is my pleasure to reunite you with a beloved daughter." He calls forward the new Spanish ambassador for introduction and I transfer my attention back to Don Carlos.

His clothing, I cannot help but notice, while certainly not mean, is no-where near as fine as that of my brothers. There is an air of shabbiness about it that puts me in mind of my cousin the Prince of Navarre—my cousin who, like the rest of his coreligionists, is absent at the King of Spain's insistence. Periodically, Don Carlos' head seems to jerk ever so slightly. I wonder if he is tired and having difficulty staying awake.

Mother has a lavish Collation planned, the first of many entertain-ments costing hundreds of thousands of écus, all intended to impress upon the Spanish that France is as great a power as Spain. Because it is a fast day, all the courses that are not sweet will be fish—each rarer than the last. I am seated beside the Prince of Asturias.

"How was Your Highness's journey?" I start with the simplest of ques-tions as the first dish—lamprey with white ginger and cinnamon—is brought. I am utterly ignored. The Prince simply attacks the food before him. It is as if he has not eaten in a fortnight! I am transfixed and horrified. All the more so in the next course when he slurps the broth accompanying his eels so loudly that persons seated at the tables below look up.

In a desperate attempt to make him stop, and to please Mother, who keeps casting me pointed looks, I try again. "Your Highness enjoys eel, I see."

This time he raises his head and I expect an answer. Instead I get a belch. Then, without looking at me, he says, "Obviously." A moment later he rises and disappears. He returns as the next course is brought. There is a fleck of something that looks like vomit in the fur at the front of his short cape.

Servants set down salmon from the Bidasoa river cooked with orange slices.

"I suppose Your Highness has seen oranges on the tree in Spain, but I had not before we visited Provence where these were picked."

He looks at me from the corner of his eye, then takes a bite of fruit and fish together. He starts, clearly surprised. "They are sweet like those the Portuguese traders bring." He takes another bite. "You say these were grown in France?" He appears incredulous, an expression that makes his large lower lip jut out even further.

"Yes, I saw them in fields on the Mediterranean." Glad that I have fi-nally managed to start a conversation, I am willing to overlook his sour expression. "Her Majesty was so delighted that she bought property near Hyères so that she may have her own park full of orange trees."

"Such money would better be spent crushing heretics."

"We do not need to crush anyone. France has peace."

"Ha!" His laugh is loud and sharp. "Do not let the Duke of Alba hear you say that. His motto is *Deo patrum Nostrorum* and he is here to press the Tridentine decrees upon the King of France and *La Serpente*."

"Who?"

He curls his upper lip back but says nothing.

He must mean my mother. A white-hot anger burns inside me, an anger hardly compatible with making myself agreeable. I am well content to let the rest of the meal pass without speaking to the Prince. I keep my gaze elsewhere as well, not so much to punish him as to avoid observing his manner of eating. As the remnants of an exquisite sugar porpoise are carried away, Mother catches my eye. She narrows her lips sternly. I know what she is saying, though she does not speak. I wish I were as skilled at conveying my thoughts by looks. I would ask her what I am to do when the Prince is boorish and unwilling to make polite conversation.

It is time for dancing. The King will open it with our honored sister. As Charles leads Elisabeth to the floor, the Prince of Asturias mumbles something under his breath. I seize upon the chance to begin again. "What was that, Your Highness?"

He stares at the dancing couple and I fear my latest effort will pass unheeded. Then he turns his eyes fully upon me and I am almost sorry. They hold enormous anger though, excepting his own behavior, nothing untoward has happened this evening. "She was supposed to marry *me*."

"Who, Your Highness?" I ask, keeping my tone light and behaving as if there were nothing indelicate about his mention of former possible brides.

"Your sister. I wanted her. So, of course, he took her. That is my father's way. All the best things must be his, even what has already been promised to me." His voice rises. I shift uncomfortably in my seat. Surely he must know the impropriety of such statements. Imagine if the Duc d'Alba or my mother were to overhear such talk. I hold my breath, willing him back into the silence I was so eager to breach. But he continues. "She is just my age. Perfect for me. Yet she sat at his minion Alba's elbow this evening, while I am left talking to a little girl. And his decrepit flesh touches her in the middle of the night while I lie awake alone."

His hands twitch slightly in his lap as he falls silent.

"I am not a little girl," I snap. "I am only a year younger than Elisabeth was when she married." Don Carlos' eyes widen. "And as for His Majesty the King of Spain, unless I have been misinformed, he is a man in his prime."

Don Carlos grunts, then shifts in his seat so his back is toward me. He clearly has no intention of asking me to dance, so when Henri comes to claim me, I feel no guilt in leaving.

"Henri," I say, counting on our proximity and the cover of the music to allow me to speak frankly, "I think there is something wrong with the Prince of Asturias."

"You mean other than his table manners?" My brother laughs. "How he ate. Good Lord! I felt sorry for you, truly I did. Food was flying everywhere. It seemed a thing certain that your lovely gown would be spoiled."

He laughs again. I fear I will find no consolation with him in his present mood. Where can I seek it, then? I would not breathe a word of my concern to Mother. I may fear there is something odd about the Prince, but I fear Mother's displeasure more and she has made her desire very clear. She wants Don Carlos for a son. Besides, I tell myself, as I twirl in my somber black gown, Mother would not solicit his hand for me if there was truly something wrong with him.

"I cannot understand it!" Mother is frantic and she frightens me. We are alone in her apartment. It is Saint John's Eve. It has been more than a week since the Spanish arrived, and things are not proceeding in the manner Mother envisioned. It seems Alba came with a list of complaints as to how Mother and Charles rule France, and a list of demands—chief among them the repeal of the Edict of Amboise and all-out war to eliminate heretics. King Philip does not appear to care how that is done, by conversion or by death.

"Cosimo Ruggieri saw a crown in your stars," Mother says, pacing. I know that she has a great faith in her elderly astrologer. "But the Duc cannot be persuaded to discuss the match. He would rather complain about His Majesty's dining with the Turkish ambassador! And your sister—your sister says she sounded Don Carlos on the subject of your wit and beauty and he declared that he has hardly noticed you."

"Hardly noticed me," I stammer, "but I say something to him whenever we are in company. He even danced with me at the masquerade." My memories of that event are not pleasant. Don Carlos is no better dancer than he is company. He clutched my arm so tightly in the lifts that he left a bruise. The only time he smiled was when I cried out as he trod on my foot. I entertain a growing certainty that there is something very wrong with the Prince. At the *feux d'allegresse* on the evening of Charles' investiture into the Order of the Golden Fleece, I thought I saw him trying to urge one of the King's young spaniels into the fire. At this point, no one can be oblivious to his erratic behavior. Elisabeth clearly is not—I have seen her intervene to soothe him. Yet Mother mentions none of this, and her desire that I should marry him is unchanged.

"You will have to do better," she admonishes. "The Prince is the key. If he desires you, Alba will be forced to discuss the subject."

"Desires me? He told me I am 'a little girl.' "

"Show him differently. Flirt with him. Your beauty is the envy of my ladies. Use it. Today's entertainment will offer you opportunity to be apart with the Prince. I will keep the Duc d'Alba occupied on the barge." She stops walking and looks at me intently. "And I will instruct the Baronne de Retz not to chaperone you too closely. Perhaps when the Whale makes his appearance, you might grab Don Carlos' arm in your fright."

I shiver slightly. Am I to behave as Mademoiselle de Rieux and the others after all? And if so, I hope that Mother will at least tell the Baronne in advance so I am not chastised afterwards.

"Go and get dressed."

Charlotte and Henriette are waiting to ready me for the festivities. I need their advice, but I am less than delighted by Charlotte's first response to my entreaty.

"I do not envy you the task of bewitching Don Carlos," she says, rolling her eyes.

The image of the Prince hunched over his food, with some of it running down his chin, overwhelms me.

"It is hopeless," I groan.

"Not so," Henriette admonishes. "He is a man, and men are, for the most part, subject to seduction."

I am fastened into the most elaborate of my new gowns. No black for this occasion. It is silver and scarlet, detailed with countless pearls.

I have, I flatter myself, become rather good at the art of flirting over the past two years. Yet none of my tricks have worked to pique the interest of Don Carlos. Something more will be needed. "What must I do?" I ask as Henriette applies color to my cheek.

"Touch him," she replies without hesitation. "Take his arm. Let your hand brush his if he puts it on the table."

"Better still, let your knee brush his beneath the table," Charlotte adds.

I cannot imagine doing such a thing—at least, not with the Prince.

"And flatter him," Henriette continues. "I know what you are thinking: 'What is there to flatter?'"

"He is truly horrible," I say.

"*Ma pauvre chérie,* so he is." Henriette shakes her head. "How fortunate for you, then, that you must only arouse his desire, not satisfy it. Indeed"—she drapes a necklace of enormous pearls about my neck and fastens it—"remember that where marriage is sought, to surrender too much is to lose the game. Do not allow him to do more than kiss you."

Charlotte, who is arranging my hair, makes a face which I can see reflected in the glass.

"You sound like Baronne de Retz." I try to laugh, but the seriousness of my situation and the weight of the loathing I have begun to feel for the Prince defeat the attempt. "I would rather never be married than kiss Don Carlos."

"No, you would not." Henriette's voice is firm and practical. "But from the sound of things, there will be no match."

"Her Majesty will be furious, but if it is so, then why must I embarrass myself over the Prince?"

"Because you are likely right: Her Majesty *will* be furious, and you do not want her fury directed at you."

❈ ❈ ❈

I find Don Carlos as the barge slips its moorings and sets sail for the Isle of Aiguemeau. He is seated near one end. Not surprisingly, he is alone. I force myself to sit on the same bench. He does not acknowledge me.

"Your Highness, I believe we can expect to be serenaded by sea gods on our journey."

"More French poetry and preening. Do you never tire of showing off?"

"That is unfair, Sir; all that is done is done to honor and entertain Her Majesty the Queen of Spain, yourself, and your countrymen." Then, realizing that being peevish will hardly achieve the desired ends, I struggle to subdue my indignation and fold my hands, which were fluttering like angry moths, in my lap. "If you do not like poetry, what do you like?"

"To be left alone." The response is openly hostile. "You seem to appear wherever I am."

And yet, you told Elisabeth you hardly notice me. Dear God what a mortifying task this is. "I am trying, Sir, to be a good and attentive hostess."

For the first time since we began speaking, he turns fully to face me. His expression suggests he is about to say something caustic, and then, in an instant, his eyes change. "You look like your sister in this light."

Fine. If I must trade upon that, I will. "In the Court of France, I am often said to be very like her." Do I imagine it, or does he move ever so slightly closer? He is about to speak, when a small boat draws alongside and a musician begins to sing. Don Carlos winces. Without a word he jumps up and strides off, passing my cousin the Prince of Navarre as he goes. Before I can rise, that Prince settles into Don Carlos' place.

"I had a dog like that once," he says matter-of-factly, inclining his head in the direction that the Spanish prince went.

"What?"

"He got hurt in a hunt. He was struck by a glancing blow, but he did not die. At first I was so glad—he was one of my favorites—but later I was sorry."

"Sorry he did not die?" Comparing the Prince of Asturias to a dog is the sort of wholly inappropriate thing my cousin would do, but he is the first one to come close to discussing Don Carlos' oddity, so I remain where I sit without chastising him.

"Yes. I could never trust him after that. He did bad things. Worried the other dogs. Snapped without warning. His eyes were never the same after the accident, and I should have known from that that he was not the same dog. They had to put him down. I cried, but afterwards I was relieved." He pauses for a minute, thinking. "That is a major difference between people and dogs. I do not know what precisely you do when you look in a man's eyes and see he has changed . . . see he is not right."

Finally, someone has said it out loud, or nearly—Don Carlos is not right. The fact that it should be my cousin leaves me with mixed feelings. Mostly I am relieved, but my duty to my mother rises up behind that relief, so I say, "The Prince of Asturias is an important personage and will be King of Spain one day."

My cousin shrugs. "Will that make him well? I do not think so." He stands up. "I am going to the front so I do not miss the Whale. Have you heard? He will spout wine."

I have heard. I am eager to see. More than that, I ought to pursue Don Carlos so that I can clutch his arm at the right moment. Yet, when my cousin offers his hand, I decline. He shrugs again. "Your mother has made a bad choice. I think your father made a better one." And then he winks—he *winks*—before walking away. The nerve! If there is anyone I would less like to have as my groom than Don Carlos of Spain, it is the Prince of Navarre.

I creep along the other side of the barge and arrive near the prow in time to see the Whale. Though Don Carlos is plainly visible, I take a place next to my brother Henri, leaning upon the rail. While the beast is being attacked by courtiers playing the part of fishermen, Henri covers one of my hands with his. "That gown is marvelous," he whispers. "Not even a bevy of golden shepherdesses will be able to eclipse you."

The shepherdesses Henri alluded to greet us as we land, dancing gaily, each according to the portion of France she represents. On my brother's arm I sweep into a meadow such as I have never seen—a perfect oval framed by massive trees and punctuated with niches containing tables sufficiently large to seat a dozen courtiers each. Everything is decorated lavishly, particularly the dais where Charles, Elisabeth, and Mother will sit. If the feast is as splendid as the decorations, we will rise from the tables groaning. Or everyone but me will.

I am, of course, seated alongside Don Carlos, a situation which destroys my appetite. Even after so many meals, I have not become oblivious to the way he displays the contents of his mouth when chewing. I cannot look in his direction. And though I think of Charlotte's admonition about letting my knee touch his, I cannot do so, particularly because my brother Henri sits just to my other side. I should be ashamed for him to see me do such a thing.

By the time the last course is cleared, dusk is lengthening into darkness. Musicians enter, led by dozens of men costumed as satyrs. A hundred torches blaze at the large grotto meant to provide a stage. The light glints off the jewels studding the satyrs' horns and off their bare chests, which have been oiled. Looking at Don Carlos sitting perfectly still, the light reflecting from his eyes, I can clearly see that whatever he said about showing off earlier, he is impressed.

Henri perceives this as well, for he leans toward me and, putting his hand over mine where it lays in my lap, whispers, "I will wager the petulant Spanish prince has never seen the likes of this at his father's court."

The music begins. As if by magic a group of nymphs descends from the upper edge of the grotto while still more appear around its lip. They wear such an abundance of precious stones that they seem to light the night as surely as the torches do. "Look at his eyes bulge," Henri continues. "He is dazzled by their beauty, though why he should be surprised, I cannot imagine. The best-looking women among the Spanish party are French." He laughs lightly in my ear, tickling it.

I know he does not mean them to, but his words make me feel lacking. The Prince of Asturias can find French women attractive—just not me. I feel tears prick my eyes, but crying will certainly not make me more enticing. Pushing my brother's hand away, I turn slightly in my seat as if I would see better, consciously pressing my knee against the Prince's. I keep my face straight ahead as if all my attention is on the nymphs who have begun a ballet, but out of the corner of my eye, I see Don Carlos look at me. I hope it is too dark for him to perceive how my cheeks burn or he will know in an instant that I am, in fact, the inexperienced little girl he thinks me. A sudden cool breeze makes the torches quiver. The Prince leans toward me until his lips are as near to my ear as my brother's were moments ago.

"Alba told me of your mother's ambitions." I suddenly feel his hand upon my leg. I have succeeded, I think, though his touch gives me no pleasure. Then, with little delicacy, he forcibly pushes my leg away from his. "Perhaps Her Majesty has not informed you," he continues, "but the Duke told that lady that my father has no interest in a French bride for me. And as for myself, I would not have you if the King of Spain begged me." He removes his hand from my leg and leans back in his chair. As I gaze at him with horror, a giant drop of water lands upon his cheek. For one insane, confused moment I think someone has spit upon him—perhaps because I wish it were so—but then I know it is raining, for lightning splits the sky and drops fall everywhere. I jump to my feet, as do all around save the Prince. As I run past him, buffeted by sudden strong gusts of wind, trying to escape both my mortification and the storm, Don Carlos throws back his head and laughs.

I race for the bank where the barges are moored. Somewhere in my flight a hand touches mine. Charlotte has found me. Together we clamber onto the first boat. It is not the royal barge, but I do not care. I want to be back in Bayonne and I want to get there safely out of the company of Don Carlos.

The water is rough. A great many of the ladies cry out in fear. Some weep. I am not sorry for it. Under such circumstances, who will suspect that my tears are the result not of terror but of humiliation? Don Carlos was not to my liking and may well be as damaged as the Prince of Navarre's dog, but his assertion that he would not have me even to please his father is deeply wounding. And I am not only hurt, I am afraid. I have but one chief duty to Charles and Mother, and that is to marry where they would have me do so. I have failed in that duty. There may be a rapprochement between Spain and France, but I will not assist in it.

Henri is ill. A chill, he insists, nothing more. When Mother fusses, he calls her "nervous" and jokes to me that he will be well again once the Spanish leave and he no longer has to look at Don Carlos. He does not know precisely what happened between that Prince and I on the Isle of Aiguemeau, but he senses Don Carlos insulted me, and takes every opportunity to repay the favor. Unmoved by Henri's assurances, Her Majesty orders him to bed.

"Do not fuss," I say, pulling up a chair as he sits propped against pillows, looking restless. "I will help you pass the hours."

More than my great fondness for Henri drives me to his bedside. I have found myself unequal to telling Mother what Don Carlos said to me three nights ago. But if I cannot make myself confess, I am equally unable to continue the charade with the Prince—to beg for attention where I am so clearly an object of ridicule. So I seek to avoid Don Carlos until the Spanish depart in less than a week.

"Shall we play at cards?" I ask my brother.

Henri is a fierce card player, so I know that something is wrong when he begins to make silly errors—errors that allow me to win. Then my winning vexes him, so I begin to try to lose on purpose. To manage this without seeming to do so is not an easy thing. My brother lays down a particularly ill-chosen card and I resign myself to taking this particular hand. Strangely, he does not seem to mind, or even to be focusing on the game.

Rising, I place a hand upon his forehead. It is far too hot for my liking. Bestowing a kiss where my hand just lay so as not to worry him, I go in search of Mother. She does not even thank me, merely dashes off, calling for Castelan as she goes.

Unwilling to disturb Mother and her physician, I allow myself to be drawn into the afternoon's entertainments by Charlotte and Henriette. Yet my thoughts often go in the direction of my brother. When Mother does not appear to dress for dinner, I excuse myself. I arrive at Henri's apartment to find the antechamber empty. Have his friends, who always seem to linger, been sent away? This cannot be a good sign. Behind the bedroom door there is a murmur of voices. I press my ear to the wood.

"He has been bled three times but the fever still rises." Mother's voice is agitated.

"Yes, but it is very early, Your Majesty. This may be nothing more than a bad chill as His Highness insists." I recognize the voice of Castelan.

"'May' is not a comforting word."

No. It is not. Picking up my skirts I run to the chapel. I am a good deal calmer once I kneel before the blessed virgin. Her pacific expression puts me in mind of the phrase *Deo adjuvante non timendum*—With God's help, nothing need be feared. I will pray for Henri, and surely Mother will have the rest of her ladies and her collection of priests doing so before night falls. I stay on my knees until I can no longer feel my feet. Returning to Henri's apartment, I crack the bedroom door and find Castelan sitting beside my brother.

"Your Highness," he says, "you ought not to be here. There may be contagion."

"But I want her." Henri's voice is dry but still powerful.

I ignore the physician. "You want me, and here I am," I say, pulling a chair back to his bedside and drawing his hand into mine. Castelan shakes his head but says nothing more. Henri is bled and then dozes. I think of leaving, but I cannot seem to withdraw my hand from his, so tightly does he clutch me as he slumbers. I shift to make myself as comfortable as possible.

"No!"

The word jolts me from an uncomfortable nap. I open my eyes. The room is in semidarkness. Mother is at the other side of the bed with Castelan. Wishing to stay and listen, I close my eyes again.

"Your Majesty,"—Castelan's deep voice sounds solemn—"the fever is dangerously high and see how he sweats and shakes. I suspect the ague."

The ague. It is a disease of the heat and of the wet, and Bayonne—with its rivers and marshes—is both. Oh, why could it not have been a chill?

I wait for Mother to react. But there is a silence. Deep silence. When Mother's voice comes at last, it sounds very dry, putting me in mind of how my brother spoke when he demanded my attendance earlier. "How bad the case?"

"Your Majesty knows better than to ask at such an early juncture. I cannot even know the type of ague until we see the pattern of fever. Let us hope the case will be mild."

"Why?"

"Your Majesty?"

"Why does God test me?"

There is a pause. I pity Castelan: How can he possibly answer such a question? Finally he clears his throat. "Your Majesty, I will employ all my skill. Do not despair. The Prince is strong—"

"I am not a fool, Castelan. My children are fragile—from the twins I lost, to the King with his constant, worrisome respiratory ills." Strangely, Mother's voice strengthens as she recites these dire truths. "The only child with a decent constitution is Princess Marguerite."

I feel a certain pride, though I have done nothing to earn my general good health. Perhaps I take pleasure in the comment because, other than my beauty—another characteristic bestowed by God, not hard work— I am seldom praised for anything.

"You are lucky in that, then."

Mother gives a sharp laugh. "You call it luck? Sons frail, while a daughter is hale and hearty? I see no luck, only accursed fate. I have laid one son in the grave. I do not have so many that I can afford to bury another. A daughter I could spare. Do all that you can, Castelan, and then do more."

A lump rises in my throat and I squeeze my eyes even more tightly shut. I wish I were anywhere else, that I had not heard Mother's words. Wish that I were the one sick, not Henri. But most of all I wish I mattered as much as he did—to Mother, to the kingdom, to anybody.

Six days later we know that Henri has a tertian case. I can hear him calling out in delirium as I sit in his antechamber. Every third day he is gripped by fever. This is his third cycle, and Castelan expected improvement. Instead, the fever is so ferocious that my brother suffered a seizure this morning. I could hear Mother shouting instructions to those who held him so that he would not injure himself. And I felt a fear such as I have not known.

Mother is with Henri nearly continuously. She had some difficulty tearing herself away to discharge her duties in seeing the Spanish off when they went at last. This afternoon it is me Henri calls for. He has said my name so many times, I have lost count. But I must wait for the door to open—for Mother to summon me—and that does not happen.

I can think of no relief for my feelings of fear and helplessness but prayer. I send for my *prie-dieu* and Book of Hours. Arranging myself near the door to Henri's bedchamber, I hope that God will pay more attention to my petitions against the background of my brother's cries. I begin the Litany of the Saints. Looking at the faces of the martyrs, my eyes swim with tears. My blurred glance falls upon Saint Agnes, who resisted all suitors and every temptation. She is the patron of all young women yet chaste; surely she will help me. As I gaze at her lovely face, I become overwhelmed with a single thought—I and I alone can save Henri. Not by prayer but by sacrifice. I must offer something.

Father in Heaven, so many of your blessed Saints laid down their lives for your

Church. They are venerated by Christians everywhere and esteemed by you for their acts of sacrifice. Surely it is also noble to die for family. Accept my life in place of my brother's. The House of Valois needs its three remaining sons. It has daughters to spare—surely you heard Her Majesty say so as clearly as I did.

As these beseeching thoughts fly upward, a great calm settles over me. I turn the pages to the office of Compline. If ever there was an occasion to pray to the Blessed Virgin on behalf of the dying and for all those upon whom the night must soon fall, this is that occasion. I am deep in prayer when the door opens.

"Marguerite." I look up to see Mother staring at me. Then she nods in approval, as if she understands all. I feel warmed by her silent approbation. Walking forward, she looks down at my open book. "Yes, sleep. I must have some sleep; Castelan insists." She reaches out as if she might pat me on the shoulder but stops short of doing so.

"If Your Majesty does not require my attendance, I will pray awhile longer."

"You are very well where you are."

Over the days of Henri's illness, sitting in this antechamber, I have had ample occasion to observe the routine surrounding my brother. Generally, the physician leaves after a last bleeding, placing Henri in the care of the King's childhood nurse. She is steady but not young. Surely, I think, given enough time and quiet, she must slumber at Henri's bedside. Castelan leaves, nodding to me where I kneel. My wait begins.

Time passes slowly. My impatience—a failing indeed—keeps me from immersing myself as fully as I ought to in my prayers. I am sad to think that at such a serious moment, when the state of my soul is of the utmost importance, I fail to be as I should. The candles in the room burn down. I can no longer see my Book of Hours. The time has come.

There is relief in rising from my knees, for my legs are stiff. Is that why they tremble? As quietly as I can, I go to the door of Henri's sick chamber. I ease it open, thanking God that it is noiseless on its hinges. I slip inside. I see it is as I surmised: the nurse sleeps in a chair.

Henri lies with his handsome features composed, his form as still as one dead. Creeping forward, I put out a hand close enough to his mouth that I may feel his breath. When I do, I let out my own breath in relief. Perhaps feeling my hand hovering above him, Henri moves restlessly and then, as if the act of moving hurts, gives a low moan. The nurse shifts, but her eyes remain closed. Turning back the covers, I slip into bed beside my brother. I move close, turning to mold my body around his and laying an arm gently over him, hoping to somehow mystically draw his fever into myself. That same fever must make my arm jarringly cold, for my brother moans again and gives a convulsive shiver.

"Henri," I whisper, "it is Margot."

His body relaxes at the sound of my voice, then another fit of shaking takes him. Quietly I begin to hum, my mouth close to the back of his neck. A tune takes shape. It is a lullaby. Can it be as old as our time together at Vincennes? The shaking stops.

The warmth of my brother's body in my arms—though it is induced by the fever—soothes me. My eyelids grow heavy. I struggle to continue my song. And when I cannot, and realize that sleep is coming, I press my face against the back of my brother's neck and tell him that I love him and will miss him. My last thought is about heaven. Will it be silent like the grave, or will it be filled with music? I love music.

"*What goes on here?*" The voice is close and harsh. I am dragged from warmth and fall onto something hard.

Can I be dead? If so, I must be in purgatory, for it is hard to imagine landing in a heap in heaven.

As I am pulled upward and struggle to get my feet beneath me, I open my eyes. The hand is Mother's—in fact, she has hands on both my arms. Her face is close and it is livid. The nurse is awake too, standing at the bed with her hand on Henri's forehead. But she flees at a single imperious gesture from Mother.

Mother gives me a ferocious shake. "Marguerite, what are you doing in your brother's bed?"

When I hesitate, Mother shakes me again. I am puzzled by the obvious fury in her face.

"I love him so much," I blurt out. "I asked God to spare him and take my life instead if a life is needed." My stomach sinks. Have I forfeited my bargain by speaking it out loud? If so, I am a horrible failure.

"Fool!" Mother slaps me, wrenching my neck and sending me staggering back a step. Glaring, she shakes her head in disgust. "Did you really believe Our Lord would barter with you?"

The manner of her asking makes my already stinging cheeks burn. Why, I wonder, should I be ashamed of my good intentions?

Her eyes narrow. I cannot ever remember seeing her so angry—at least, I can never remember seeing her so angry at *me*. "If prayers were that reliably answered, do you think your father would be dead?" The question cracks like lightning. "That your brother, King François, would lie cold in a grave? God did not see fit to grant my prayers. Why, then, should he favor yours?"

I can think of no answer.

"Faith is a fine thing, Marguerite," Mother continues in a tone that belies the sentiment, "but you are not a little girl any longer, so you must temper it with reason and common sense. What if someone other than I had found you? What might they think? What might they say and to whom? The Prince of Asturias already will not have you . . ."

So she knows. The only thing that could make this moment worse is adding my rejection to it. My humiliation is complete.

"Will you render yourself unmarriageable entirely by notorious behavior?"

I do not understand. Perhaps my actions were foolish and my faith is childish, though I do not think it so; but even if I were beyond foolish— even if I were soft in the head—my royal connections must make me someone's bride. Don Carlos is proof of that. He is mad, but can afford to spurn me and be certain he will find another princess.

"Will you start rumors that you are a wanton at twelve and worse still that you sin with your own brother?"

Dear God, how could Mother think such a thing? How could she imagine that my behavior—motivated by the purest love and a desire to save my brother from suffering—is driven by impure thoughts? Or that being found with my brother could impute a damaging unchastity in any but the most twisted, unchristian of minds? I am horrified. I want to tell her she demeans me and herself by such inferences. But, of course, I have not the courage.

When I remain silent, Mother throws up her hands. "I have done with you. I am too tired to waste another breath on your stupidity. Go to your room. Tell no one of this. And let me be plain: if you repeat such behavior, your trip will be over and you will be sent back to Vincennes to join your brother François."

❀ ❀ ❀

I am not allowed into Henri's apartment again until he is declared out of danger—not even into the antechamber to keep a vigil. On the day I am admitted, Henri sits as he did when he was first ill, propped against a myriad of pillows. He holds out both arms to me and, when I stoop into his embrace, kisses each of my cheeks in turn.

"You may go," he says to Charles' nurse. She does not move from her place. "Do you not hear me, woman?" The tone of command in Henri's voice does my heart good. He must truly be on the mend. It also has the desired effect on the nurse, who scuttles out.

"You do not look happy," my brother observes.

"Oh, I am! Happy that you are past danger. I was so worried."

"I do not doubt it." He holds out a hand for mine. "You sang to me."

He remembers! Suddenly how angry my actions made Mother—a thing that has bothered me continuously—seems less important. "I did."

"And held me in your arms. Then you were gone. How I wanted you back. I asked Mother but she would not yield. She is angry at you. Why?"

I cannot say Mother is angry because I crawled into his bed. So I offer the easiest answer. "Don Carlos said he would not have me for a bride even if his father wished it. I have failed Mother and failed His Majesty."

Henri squeezes my hand tight. His face, transformed by rage, looks a good deal more like Mother's than it does under the influence of other expressions. Still, this rage does not frighten or chasten me: it pleases me, for I know it is directed at those who have slighted me.

"Devil take the Prince of Asturias! Devil take all the Spanish!" he exclaims. "They have offended the two most important ladies of the French court."

I begin to cry, my tears occasioned not only by his recovery but by the fierce affection he shows me. No one loves me more.

Henri's face grows gentle. He puts his left hand under my chin, tips it up, and wipes my tears. "Why should you care if you are rejected by a man whose head is full of trephination holes? You are *my* princess, not his, and I would not have you as far away as Spain however important the crown. Not even to please Mother."

PART TWO

Amour de Seigneur est ombre de buisson . . .

(The love of a great man is either momentary

or dangerous . . .)

CHAPTER 4

Late Summer, 1567—Montceaux, France

Henri sweeps into the room. "The Duc d'Alba has reached the Spanish Netherlands," he declares. There is a collective expression of pleasure from the ladies present. I am pleased too, of course—pleased that the Spanish have not set foot in French territories. Beyond that, I hope that Prince Don Carlos is apoplectic. I heard that he wanted command of the King of Spain's troops—that he had in fact been promised it—but Alba got it in the end, and the appointment as governor as well. It has been more than two years since I saw the Prince of Asturias, but I have not forgotten his disdain.

Henri pokes me where I stand lost in thought. He wants my attention and he shall have it. He is far more worthy of it than the Spanish prince. He is the center of my world.

"Her Majesty is on her knees giving thanks," he continues. He is trying so hard to affect a solemn look that I know something pleasant is coming. "After which," he pauses for effect, "she plans to shoot clay balls." His smile can no longer be suppressed. "You know what that means."

Of course I do. "Hunting! We are going hunting!" I dance about as I sing the words and end by throwing my arms around Henri's neck. The other ladies laugh and clap.

Picking me up, my brother spins me. "For a month at least! I mean to demand a boar for my birthday." Then, raising a hand to stop the objection he knows is on the tip of my tongue, he adds, "And I mean to demand you be permitted to join us in hunting it."

"Her Majesty will never allow that."

Henri's back stiffens at the challenge. "She will. And she will agree to come herself. Would you deny me my heart's desire for my natal day?"

"I never can deny you anything."

"Nor can Mother, and you know it. Besides, we go to Montceaux. That château always softens her heart by putting her in mind of Father. Just this morning she was remarking how much like him I have grown."

I think of the only portrait I have seen of my father as a young man—the one with him seated on a white horse, by Clouet. My brother has our father's nose and his mouth. But Henri's dark eyes and rich, dark hair make him altogether more pleasing to look at. "Duc d'Anjou, you are far more handsome." The appellation is a private joke. When Henri was invested last year, he became obsessed with being called by his new title—though why "Anjou" sounded so much better to him than "Orléans," I cannot say. I still poke fun at him for his vanity on the subject.

"Oh, to be thought handsome by the most beautiful woman in the kingdom." Henri tucks my hand over his arm. "How very politic of you to flatter me, Margot. Now, if Her Majesty says there can be no women at my boar hunt, I must choose some other type of game. For I would not hunt without you for anything."

❋ ❋ ❋

"Is that the Duc de Guise?" I ask Charlotte. We are in the grotto at Mont-ceaux, watching Anjou make quick work of several other gentlemen at a game of paille-maille.

"Where?"

Leaning forward, I point to the end of Monsieur de l'Orme's fanciful setting, where rocks built to look as if they were molded by nature cease, giving way to flat lawn bathed in strong autumn sunlight. A young man pauses at the entrance, half in light, half in shadow. It seems to me he would be the Duc de Guise's elder brother if His Grace had one, for he is far taller than the Duc was when last I saw him.

"Oh, goodness! I think it is!"

"Hearing he was back from Austria is not quite the same as seeing, is it, ladies?" Henriette gives one of her wicked smiles. "Regard how my sister looks at him! Her husband had best take care before he is cuckolded again."

I look for the Princesse de Porcien and find her farther up the court, turned entirely in the direction that I just pointed.

"Shocking!" Charlotte whispers. "She is too old for him."

"I see," Henriette responds. "But you are not. Perhaps it is the Baron de Sauve who needs warning. Poor man, in danger of being given a pair of horns when he has not been married half a year."

Charlotte, who long pined for a husband, was given one this spring—Simon de Fizes, former secretary to the King, and currently a secretary of state. He was not what she expected and she shed many tears think-ing, with good reason, the gentleman beneath her. For though he is a baron, Fizes bought his land and title not five years ago from the Bishop of Montpellier and by birth he is a peasant's son.

"No, indeed," Charlotte says. "Guise is not for me. Not because I fear the Baron, but I know my duty as a lady of the robes and maid of honor." My friend folds her hands primly and compresses her mouth into a dour expression—for a moment. Then, ceasing to play act, she smiles devi-ously. "When I cuckold my husband, it is with gentlemen of Her Majesty's choosing."

All three of us collapse into fits of laughter.

When I have enough breath to speak, I say, "Henriette, the Duc deserves better than to be painted in your sister's Book of Hours hanging from a cross." The Princesse has the odd habit of having former lovers thus portrayed, and every lady at the Court knows it, even as her husband seems pointedly to ignore the rumor.

"Does he?" Henriette looks at me sharply. "Could it be that *you* have an interest?"

"Why not?" Glancing back down the court, I observe that the Duc has taken a seat among the King's gentlemen and Charles turns to greet him. Guise is undeniably more handsome than when he left to fight the Turks, and when he smiles in response to some words of the King's, his face gains a liveliness that makes it more attractive still. As I am staring—and, yes, I must admit I am—the Duc's glance shifts and his eyes, unexpectedly, meet mine. My stomach trembles. He tilts his head slightly as if questioning me or perhaps taking my measure. Then a burst of applause breaks our gaze. The match is over. Anjou has won. My companions rise and the face and figure of the Duc are lost in a sea of skirts. By the time I reach my own feet and look again in his direction, he is gone.

I feel a certain disappointment, but it is swept away as Henri leaps the low wall dividing the alley from the gallery to be with me. "Ah, the day's victor!" I give a small curtsy.

"It takes very little effort to beat that lot," Henri replies. "Thank heavens, Guise has come. There will be decent tennis at last."

So Henri noticed the Duc. This should not surprise me: my brother has inherited Mother's sharp eyes. "Walk with me." He holds out a hand expectantly. "I have an idea for how we may bring all eyes to us at tomorrow's ball and make Mother proud."

I allow him to draw me through the crowd and across the lawn, toward the garden.

"It came to me last night in a dream," Anjou says, looking over his shoulder to assure himself we are out of hearing of other courtiers. "We must play Artemis and Apollo."

"But Henri, my costume is finished. You know I am Terpsichore. What shall the other eight muses do if I abandon them?"

"What care I for the other muses? And what should you? This is a sojourn dedicated to sport. We hunt nearly every day. Why, then, we must be the twins—the best pair of archers among the gods. Did you not tell me just the other morning how you thought you loved a hunt even better than a ball?"

"Yes, but—"

"But nothing. Are we not brother and sister as Artemis and Apollo were? And what brother and sister can be called more devoted to their mother's honor than we—except, perhaps, that ancient pair? The analogy will please the Queen, and to make sure it is brought to her mind, I've written a little verse recounting the tale of Niobe."

"And whose progeny shall we be threatening to slay?"

"Oh, I have kept it very general—nothing impolitic." He waves one hand, swatting my question aside as if it were a fly. "I merely wish to make clear that 'twould be the height of foolishness for any house to claim themselves the equals of the Valois."

I throw up my hands, for I am clearly defeated. The image of my brother and me hand in hand, declaring our devotion to Mother, is too pleasing to be resisted. "If you will manage the golden bows, I will see our tunics trimmed to match."

"Excellent. You must wear your new golden wig, curled in a Grecian style."

Ordinarily I would object, for wigs make me hot. But an image of the Duc de Guise's face stops my tongue. Perhaps a little suffering in the name of beauty is called for. Everyone says fair hair highlights my eyes and suits my pale complexion.

"And you must stop telling me how to dress and run to get your costume. Put it in my room and I will determine what is best to be done."

With a kiss on my cheek, he is off. Rather than returning at once to the château, I wander farther into the lush garden, eager to soak up the autumn sun. Sitting on a bench with the sound of distant conversations washing over me, I lean back and close my eyes.

A throat clears. If it is Henri back to disturb my peace with more instructions, I will strangle him. I open my eyes. The Duc de Guise stands over me. Goodness, he is tall, and even more handsome in close proximity than he was viewed down the length of the alley. His hair is golden without need of a wig. It waves and curls gently. A faint mustache rests on his smiling lips.

"Your Highness"—he bows—"I have just returned to Court and would present myself."

"To me?"

"You are the only one here, are you not?" His eyes betray an amusement that borders on insolence.

"Ah, that explains things, then," I quip. If he can be impertinent, so can I. "When others are absent, a princess of France must do."

"Not at all. Were the full Court present, I should still seek Your Highness's attention." He nods at the bench next to me as if asking permission to sit, than takes the place without waiting for my reply. Very aware of his proximity, I stand.

"And, Your Grace, were the entire Court present such a meeting might be proper, but alone in a secluded corner of a garden . . . Are these the manners of the Austrian court?" The Duc's expression shows no trace of embarrassment. Rather, he smiles at my challenge. His smile thrills me. I am flirting, but console myself with the thought that the Baronne de Retz would be proud of me for recognizing the impropriety of my situation. Never mind the amount of effort it takes to think of reputational niceties with the Duc's eyes upon me. I had best go before I lose my resolve to do so.

I take a step and the Duc is on his feet. Another bow. Utterly perfect. "May I present myself at a more appropriate time?"

"You may." Oh how I hope the Duc picks a moment when Charlotte and Henriette are with me. His attention, pleasing in itself, would be rendered more agreeable still by the notice of others.

"Until a more auspicious moment, then." He offers me another smile. "I shall leave you in peace." He walks away without looking back, which is just as well, for if he did, he would perceive that my eyes follow his figure. Peace, he calls it! Not with my heart pounding so. I run all the way back to my room.

When I burst through the door, my *gouvernante* is waiting. Beside her is a girl I do not recognize. At the sight of me, panting and flushed, both rise. The Baronne gives a sigh.

"Mademoiselle Marguerite, do you not get exercise enough hunting?" she asks. "Must you run about like a child when left to your own devices? Such is the behavior of the Prince of Navarre, not a princess of France."

The comparison stings. I've seldom thought of my cousin since his mother outwitted mine and took him from Court shortly after the New Year. Jeanne d'Albret told Mother she would show the Prince his patrimony. She had Mother's blessing for that, but then she rode onward to Poitou and Gascony beyond, without Mother's leave—or Charles'. Everyone says it is unlikely we will see the Prince of Navarre in France again, unless the peace breaks and he is at the head of an army. This talk vexes Mother. But while I recognize my cousin's absence is some sort of political loss, I find it entirely positive. I do not miss him and cannot imagine anyone else does. I certainly do not want my behavior compared to his.

"Anjou wishes me to make changes to our costumes and, given the short time before the ball, I was eager to start," I mumble apologetically.

"Hm." The Baronne gives me one last stern look, then says, "Here is someone who can assist you." She gestures to the girl. "Your mother has decided you are old enough to have your own attendant."

This is startling and pleasing news—a recognition of my maturity, even if the thus-far-silent gray-eyed girl looks very young.

"May I present Gillone de Goyon de Matignon, daughter of Count de Matignon and Thorigny." The girl curtsys neatly. "A cot has been placed in your wardrobe for the Mademoiselle." My *gouvernante* looks about as if determining whether there is other business to attend to. Apparently concluding there is not, she says, "I will leave the two of you to become acquainted."

I stand looking stupidly at this Gillone. She lowers her eyes under my gaze as I might under Mother's, stirring empathy in my breast. I've been made to feel uncomfortable sufficiently often that I do not wish to make this girl so. Looking about, I spot Henri's costume in a heap on my bed.

"Gillone," I say, "please go to my wardrobe and fetch my pale blue robe in the Grecian style." She curtsys again and departs without a word. While she is gone, I find my sewing and embroidery things and begin to pull the trim from Henri's costume. Head bent over my work, I start when a skirt comes into my field of vision. Gillone returned so quietly that I did not hear her. When I raise my eyes, she curtsys.

"Goodness, you move as silently as a shadow! It is not necessary to curtsy every time you come into my presence. You will exhaust yourself."

"Yes, Your Highness." She nearly curtsys, but catches herself.

Gazing at her standing with my robe over her arm, wondering what to do next, I realize that I am nearly as uncertain. I think of those among my mother's household who have been with her the longest. These ladies are not merely the women who dress the Queen or sit to embroider with her: they hear her worries and hold her confidences; they are friends. That is what I want.

"How old are you?" I ask.

"Twelve last January."

So she is older than she looks. Closer to my age, fourteen, than any member of Mother's household. Closer than either of my dearest friends, for Charlotte is seventeen and Henriette will soon be five-and-twenty.

"I was younger than you when I joined Her Majesty's household. The Court can be overwhelming. When I came, the Baronne de Sauve helped me to find my feet. I will help you, and we will be great friends." I smile broadly and am rewarded by just the slightest upturn at the corners of her mouth. "Now help me with these costumes. The Duc d'Anjou demands they be made over, and I do not like to disappoint my brother."

Henri is not disappointed. "Wonderful!" he says, putting his arm about my waist and examining our images in my glass.

"We do not really look like twins, for you are much taller," I say.

"I am sure Apollo was taller than Artemis. Men are always taller. And we are alike in a more important way. We each set the standard for our sex. We have no equal—not on the dance floor, nor in conversation, nor in looks—save the other." He puffs up his chest importantly. I feel a great urge to laugh, but know better. Henri's pride is a serious thing.

"I am pleased that you think me the loveliest woman at Court. Or perhaps you only flatter me to make certain I will continue to make over your costumes at short notice. After all, I see you looking at Mademoiselle de Rieux a great deal these days."

My brother blushes. "That is a different matter," he mutters. "Her face cannot compare to yours."

I might say it is not her face he looks at. But the observation would make me more uncomfortable than it would make him. Renée has been flirting with Henri for as long as I can remember, sometimes less, sometimes more. Presently more. Much more. I have never liked her and I like her less still when she sits upon my brother's lap or I catch him staring at her bosom.

Henri turns to look at himself from a different angle and the golden bow hung over his shoulder nearly catches me in the eye.

"Careful! If you blind me I will be in no state to perform." We head to the evening's festivities, Gillone trailing a few steps behind.

Henri looks over his shoulder twice as we descend the stairs.

"Does my little shadow unnerve you?" I ask.

"I am just wondering if she ever speaks. My gentlemen are far livelier."

"If by 'lively' you mean drunken, I concede as much." Henri's boon companions are some of the wildest young men. I wonder if the Duc de Guise will join them now that he is back.

The ballroom is full when we arrive. Henri likes it so. Whenever possible, we enter *en retard* so as to be seen by as many people as possible. Mother smiles at our approach.

"My dear ones," she says, holding out her arms.

"Can you guess who we are?" Henri asks. "I will give you a hint. By our costumes we make you Leto."

As my brother predicted, Mother is touched.

"I thought you were to be one of the muses." Charles, who sits beside Her Majesty, has apparently been listening.

"I've found a substitute to play Terpsichore," I reply. "Can you blame me for not wanting to be compared side by side with your Erato?"

The King smiles. His mistress, Marie Touchet, is dressed as Erato. She stands with a hand upon the arm of his throne. "I thank you for the compliment," she says, "and for sparing me a comparison which I could not hope to win."

Letting go of Henri's arm, I embrace the woman who has held the King's affections for nearly two years—ever since he first laid eyes on her at Blois during our return from the Grand Tour. "I love your golden curls!" she says.

"I will have some made for you," I declare enthusiastically. I like Marie. She may be only a petty noble, but her love for Charles is so obviously driven by her heart and not her self-interest.

"How very sweet, but pray do not trouble yourself, as I do not have your complexion and should look unnatural in them. I will leave it to you to be charmingly blond." Then, looking over my shoulder, Marie lowers her voice. "You appear to have charmed someone already . . . someone with fair hair of his own."

Turning, I see the Duc de Guise standing between his uncles, the Cardinal of Lorraine and the Duc d'Aumale. His eyes are definitely upon me. When he sees I perceive as much, he nods slightly, apparently not embarrassed to be found out. Will he present himself? I have no time to ponder the question, for Henri lays a hand on my arm. He clears his throat and raises his hand. A trumpeter I had not noticed before steps forward and sounds. Trust Henri to think of such a detail when he wishes to perform!

My brother begins to speak, "Seven arrows did Apollo use, and so many his sister, to honor the mother beloved of both . . ."

I hold forth my bow and draw back its string on cue, letting fly an imaginary arrow. Henri continues to recite and many pairs of eyes are upon me. Doubtless those witnessing my performance are thinking of Artemis. I know, however, that at the moment I would be Cupid. I have no desire to kill, not even to avenge an insult to Mother; I desire to captivate. I make certain to catch Guise's eye, but I am careful not to let my glance linger as I continue to pantomime. I have observed Her Majesty's ladies sufficiently to know that if one would entice, it is best to be arch.

When Anjou finishes, the assembled company applauds. Mother embraces us each, then retains Henri's hand to offer him words of praise. I take the opportunity to wander in the direction of my friends, keeping my back purposefully to Guise. Do his eyes follow me?

"So this is the reason you abandoned us," Henriette says. She is dressed as Thalia with her comic mask tucked under one arm, while Charlotte plays her counterpart Melpomene. "Not that we blame you," she adds, "but to offer Mademoiselle du Lude your role!"

"Was that meant to amuse us?" Charlotte asks. "Surely, you will cede that while the Mademoiselle has talents, dancing is not among them."

Fleurie de Saussauy covers her mouth in mock horror at Charlotte's remark, and the four of us laugh merrily. I feel a touch upon my sleeve and know from Charlotte's widened eyes who it must be. I turn.

"Your Highness, I am lately returned to Court and would take this opportunity to present myself." His expression is appropriately earnest, his bow perfect, but when he straightens an impish smile dances across his lips. "I trust this approach is more satisfactory than my last."

"Not entirely, Sir. You were going on well, but alas, you could not resist being flippant. By your last comment, you leave my friends with the impression that you have accosted me in some inappropriate way."

"An interesting impression," Henriette says.

"And now the Duchesse leaves me in an awkward position," the Duc replies. "For if I protest there was nothing interesting in our last meeting, I insult you in a backhanded manner. But if I say anything else, I fear compromising conclusions may be drawn."

"Oh, I hope they may," Henriette says. She, Charlotte, and Fleurie exchange looks.

"I must disappoint, Your Grace," Guise replies. "I happened upon the Duchesse of Valois in the gardens yesterday. Being a lady of the highest breeding and well schooled in propriety, she took herself off before anything sufficiently scandalous to divert you could occur."

"And what, Sir, would have happened had I remained?" I make my tone teasing, but my curiosity is real.

"Ah"—the Duc pulls a solemn face—"we will never know. Perhaps, however, if you will do me the honor, we may discover what will result of our dancing together. The music has started."

"So it has." Henri's voice behind me makes me jump. I turn to find him standing with Charles and Marie.

"Guise." Charles pulls the Duc into an embrace. Anjou's acknowledgment is less enthusiastic.

Turning his attention to me, Anjou says, "Come, let us dance."

I want to say that I have promised the dance to the Duc, but it is not the truth. Besides, I am used to complying with Henri's wishes. I lay my hand on my brother's arm. Looking at Guise, he says, "Tennis tomorrow, before the hawking party sets out?"

"If I win, I dance first with the Duchesse de Valois tomorrow."

Henri shrugs. "I am always eager to take a wager I cannot lose. And *when* I win you must forgo dancing with my sister entirely *demain soir.*"

I follow Henri to the floor. As we leave the others, I hear Fleurie say, "I will be your partner, Duc, I have the same hair as Her Highness and mine is real."

How vexing.

"Shall I come and cheer you at tennis?" I ask Henri as we execute a turn.

"If you are not too tired. I want Guise to admire the prize that slips through his fingers."

I want Guise to admire me as well.

As our dance ends Henri says, "Here comes the Duc. Shall I let him dance with you?" My heart beats faster. It never occurred to me that An-jou would monopolize me, though in truth he often does. Mademoiselle de Rieux moves past, throwing my brother a look that could light a taper. He colors. "I believe I will. Give him a taste of what shall be out of his reach tomorrow." Kissing my hand, he hurries after the Mademoiselle. Oddly, this does not vex me.

"Your Highness," Guise says, arriving beside me, "will you allow me to partner you?"

The dance is slower than the last, well suited to conversation. For the first pass, however, Guise merely looks at me. I am frequently told that I am beautiful. I hope the Duc finds me so. I am not intimidated by his stare. I meet his eyes with confidence, daring him to say what he is thinking.

Finally, as the second pass begins, he says, "Why do you wear that wig?"

This is *not* the compliment I expected. "Why do you wear that dou-blet? We both of us follow the fashion."

"Your own hair suits you better."

"You are very free with your opinions."

"I am," he replies. "Strong opinions make a strong man, as do strong convictions."

"That may be," I say indignantly, "but they are unlikely to make one popular when so candidly expressed."

He laughs. "Who is being forthright now? But you are right of course:

there are many ways to say the same thing. I will try again." He puts on a mild, courtly smile. "Your Highness looks exceptionally well this evening, but I would be so bold as to say that a wig cannot improve upon the hair God gave you, which is quite perfect."

My irritation vanishes, replaced by a stomach full of butterflies. To think that Fleurie hoped to beguile him with her honeyed tresses. I give him what I hope is an encouraging smile. As we turn and come together I ask, "How do you find the Court after your time in Austria?"

I expect a standard stream of praise. Instead Guise says, "Blessedly free of heretics."

Confronted again with the Duc's candor, I do not know where to look. I myself was chastised by Mother for comments expressing pleasure when Coligny and his confreres declined to come hunting. "Ah," I say, trying to sound clever, "they are not heretics when we are at peace. They are our Protestant brothers."

"They are *always* heretics," Guise responds quietly. "And I believe you know as much, for your jest is halfhearted."

"Indeed, Sir"—I lower my own voice—"I am not sorry they are absent." It feels thrilling to confess this fact, for which I was so lately punished. I hold my breath to see what he will say.

"I am glad to hear it." The earnest pleasure on his face makes him extraordinarily handsome. But it is more than his looks that quicken my pulse—there is something exciting about speaking on serious subjects rather than exchanging quips. So much of what passes for conversation at Court is merely cleverness and show, and when there are serious matters to be discussed, I am not wanted. I long to sound him on other topics, but our dance is over, and he leads me back to my friends.

"What a pretty pair you made," Charlotte gushes. "Half the women in the room—or at least those below the age of thirty—watched with jealous eyes."

"Including my sister," Henriette adds. "I think you should make a play for the Duc and then what a marvelous time we will have for the rest of the month!"

" 'We'?"

"Yes, we. You practicing your allurements and we, your dear friends, urging you on. With Guise as a conquest, your reputation will be assured.

Women twice your age will imitate your style of dress and manners if you bring the handsome Duc to heel."

An enticing prospect. More appealing still is the possibility that, while causing the Duc to fall in love with me, I might fall in love myself. I have never been, and I consider that a great scandal, given my age.

"She blushes," Charlotte remarks triumphantly. "She will play."

"It is not a game," I reply hotly.

"Of course it is." Henriette clucks her tongue. "The most pleasant game imaginable."

I arrive early for my brother's match, expecting little competition for the Duc de Guise's notice. Despite the hour, however, the galleries are crowded. The Duchesse de Nevers uses her most commanding look and I my rank to displace some of Anjou's gentlemen and claim seats worth having. Unfortunately, we have Mademoiselle de Rieux for a neighbor.

"Come to urge the Duc d'Anjou to victory?" she asks.

"Of course. Why else would I bestir myself so early?"

"I cannot imagine," she replies in a tone that suggests she can.

Henri and Guise arrive at the same moment, my brother at the center of a little knot of his gentlemen. Henri yawns openly, but I cannot tell if he is merely feigning boredom or if his sleep was deficient to the task at hand. Guise looks fully rested and entirely relaxed.

My brother salutes the gallery, then takes his racket from his newest favorite, Louis de Bérenger, the Seigneur du Guast. Guise takes his place for the first serve without glancing my direction.

Both men are marvelously athletic, so from the first the game is strenuous and engages the spectators fully. There is little of the ordinary gossip in the galleries to compete with the cries and grunts of the players or the satisfying thwack of rackets meeting a ball with force. My brother moves with his usual grace, but he is matched in elegance by his opponent—something that rarely happens. I watch the Duc extend his extraordinarily long arm and bring his racket forward in a smooth perfect arc. The neck of his shirt is open and a fine sheen of perspiration makes his collarbone shine like silk. Crouching to await Anjou's next, his calves appear carved of stone.

Leaning toward Henriette, I whisper, "I could sit and watch the Duc play at tennis the whole day."

"You and half the women of the Court. Observe: even *la belle Rouhet*—who might, by having married only slightly earlier than is currently fashionable, be the Duc's mother—sighs and leans forward now that he has begun to sweat, hoping to catch the scent of him."

The scent of him. What a thrilling and disturbing thought.

Anjou wins the first set and crows over it. Guise takes the second, a victory he greets with no more than the flicker of a smile. Both men are thoroughly damp now. Hair sticks to foreheads; shirts cling to chests and arms, allowing me to notice the musculature of both. Guast brings Anjou water. A glass is poured for the Duc as well.

"Thank you," Guise says, draining it in a single long swallow.

"*Ce n'est rien.*" Anjou shrugs magnanimously. "I will not have you blame thirst when I defeat you in the next." Henri looks in my direction and winks. Renée giggles. The Duc's gaze follows my brother's and meets mine. My heart pounds and my breath quickens.

The final game is fiercest of all. Guise wins, but Henri loudly claims the ball was out. All his gentlemen agree. A good number of spectators take issue and heated shouting begins. The Duc remains silent.

"It seems we must replay the point," my brother says.

The Duc glances in my direction for an instant. "Your Highness, I am tired. I cede the point and the match."

Henri's face goes slack and then becomes angry. "Come," he urges, "you can surely manage a short time more."

The Duc looks him straight in the eye. "I am sorry, I cannot. The victory is yours." He bows and begins to leave the court.

Henri takes a step to follow, his face livid. Guast catches him by the arm. "Come, there are better ways to celebrate victory than chasing after a man who cannot be bothered to properly finish a game."

"You are right. Let him go, the poor sport."

Does my brother not realize that he is the one who appears less than sportsman-like? Or am I the only one who sees what the Duc has done: he refused to replay the point because to do so would be to admit his fair shot foul. He knew he had won the game and knowing was enough. He needed no further recognition. *Or perhaps he did . . . perhaps he wanted mine and said as much with his last look.*

Anjou's friends crowd round him. He accepts their approbation and then heads toward the rail. He will expect my congratulations and I am prepared to give them, even if they feel hollow. Rising to embrace him, I am stunned when he quickly releases me and turns to Mademoiselle de Rieux.

She seems to make a point of breathing deeply before speaking. "You must be exhausted."

"Indeed, not," Henri replies. "I am barely winded."

Renée leans across the rail and puts her lips beside Anjou's ear. "I can remedy that."

I wonder if I misheard, but the laughter and leering looks of my brother's companions suggest not.

Anjou gives a nod and swaggers off, trailed by his friends. Before they reach the door, Mademoiselle de Rieux makes a hasty exit.

"Well, it seems Renée has succeeded at last," Charlotte says.

"I do not understand," I say. But I am afraid I do.

"Come, you are not a little girl," Henriette chides. "Men your brother's age have mistresses, and Renée has wanted to be a royal mistress since the moment your brother's voice broke. What do you think His Majesty does with Mademoiselle Touchet?"

"But Charles loves Marie!" The comparison between Marie, all modesty and reserve, and Mademoiselle de Rieux angers me.

"It appears he does," Henriette concedes. "What difference does that make?"

"A very great difference to the lady," Charlotte says.

"I think not," Henriette says. "In the end, both will be displaced, and will be left with whatever wealth and titles they manage to accrue during their tenure. If those be generous, the quality of their memories will be secondary. If those be deficient, then all past whispered words of affection will provide little consolation."

"I cannot believe Henri would choose a lady of such little refinement," I say, sticking out my chin.

"Do not believe it, then." Henriette shrugs. "Whatever you choose to credit, do not let it spoil your mood."

But my mood *is* spoiled. I break from my friends and head in the direction of my brother's apartment, telling myself I will speak to him about the hunt, but knowing that I truly go in hopes of proving Henriette in error. I am accustomed to being received in Anjou's rooms at all times. When I sweep into his antechamber, I breathe a sigh of relief. It is filled, as always, with a collection of gentlemen playing at dice, joking and drinking. Spotting Saint-Luc, I ask, "Where is Anjou?"

The others laugh, but Saint-Luc looks mortified. Leaping to his feet he says, "Resting."

This remark brings another burst of laughter.

"I wish I were resting as he is," Saint-Mégrin says.

"With His Grace?" one of the others asks, earning himself a cuff on the ears.

I feel my face burn. Saint-Luc offers an arm. "Come, I will walk you back to Her Majesty's apartment," he says.

I know he means to be kind, but the thought of him walking beside me and seeing my embarrassment mortifies me. "Thank you, no," I say, fleeing. Just outside, I lean my back against the wall and cover my face with my hands. I cannot tell which I am more, embarrassed or angry. One thing is certain: my desire to have the Duc de Guise's attention is made stronger. If my brother thinks he can have Renée on one arm and me on the other, he is much mistaken!

❈ ❈ ❈

The time to hunt arrives. As soon as I am in the saddle, I begin to look for Guise. The courtyard is crowded and every figure seems to be in motion. Mother, beside me with her favorite bird on her arm, is eager to begin. Falconry is a great passion, and when we go hawking, she sheds many years and many cares. As the gates open I spot the Duc, but I lose sight of him as we stream out. I see him next as we pause, and the men handling the dogs fan out across a meadow under direction of the *Grand Fauconnier*. The Duc sits with Charles, the tawny color of his doublet complementing his hair.

Courtiers break into groups. Anjou, moving past to join His Majesty, reins in his horse to salute Mother and me. I do not acknowledge the gesture.

"Come," Mother says. I follow in her wake, moving farther afield. When we stop near a wild tangle of underbrush, Mother unhoods her bird. I follow suit, carefully bending my neck and using my teeth to pull one of the laces. The dark eyes of my bird sweep the field and mine follow. I see the dogs standing at rigid attention, their handlers stroking their backs to keep them calm. The excitement of the women in our party is nearly as difficult to keep in check. We all know that we are but a moment away from heart-pounding sport. The leads come off. The dogs move into the brush. To my right, the first of the game birds is flushed. Mother's reflexes are quickest, her falcon released only an instant after the bird breaks cover. And suddenly the sky is full of birds—both the pursuing and the pursued. We put our horses in motion, dislodging still more game. All eyes are on the sky. I do not see Mother's horse stumble, but I hear it hit the ground. Pulling back the reins of my own mount, I am able to stop before I run upon the Queen's horse—or, worse still, upon the Queen.

Mother, focused on urging her horse to its feet, looks up. "Go on!"

Perhaps I ought to ignore her urging and wait to see that she is all right. But she has been unhorsed many times and, like hers, my blood is up. So I pull my horse hard left and charge off. Before I have gone twenty yards, Mother passes me. We ride, race, and give chase until both horses and riders breathe heavily. More than one rider besides Her Majesty goes down, and the Baron de Sauve gets stuck in brambles after enthusiastically following the dogs in.

We are gathered about the King before moving to another field when the sound of horses is heard. Shading my eyes, I leave off trying to maneuver myself closer to the Duc de Guise. Three members of the royal guard come into view. Riding straight for the Queen, they pull up sharply. The man in the middle leaps from his horse. "An urgent message."

Mother scans the page. Then, without a word, she hands the note to the Baron de Retz. "Your Majesty," she says to Charles, "we must return to the château. Ride beside me." She holds out a hand, beckoning the King as if he were a child standing too near a ledge. The King, by long habit obedient to Mother, does not question. He merely nudges his horse in the direction of the spot that has been made for him.

"You," she commands the guards, "stay close." Then with a sharp kick she urges her animal into motion.

Fear clutches my breast and ripples through the surrounding courtiers as we hurry to follow. Bad news has come—who can say of what sort?

Being an excellent rider, I reach the château not far behind the King. Anjou appears to help me down. The vexation I felt at him earlier is forgotten as I take the hand he offers.

"Come," he says, pushing through dismounted courtiers, dragging me along. We are not five steps behind Charles and Mother as they meet Her Majesty's secretary on the steps. Mother is speaking.

"Fifteen hundred horsemen did not worry me at Montargis. But when they are only a short ride from here, that is another matter. Who is at their head?"

"Condé," her secretary replies.

Mother walks on, drawing all the important men with her. "We need soldiers."

"The closest troops are garrisoned at Château-Thierry," the constable replies. "Most of them are Swiss—the same men who were sent to the border when Alba marched past to keep the Spanish from straying."

"Curse Alba," Mother says. "His maneuvers and his arrest of Coligny's cousin bring us to this. Are four years of peace to be spoiled by a Spaniard?"

There is an uncomfortable silence, during which I take the opportunity to gauge where we are heading—clearly to His Majesty's council chamber. When that destination is reached, Henri and I have no chance of entering. My brother must be thinking the same thing, for he grows bold.

"What is the threat, Madame?" he asks. "And how can I help the King, my brother, face it?"

Mother pauses and considers Anjou appraisingly. "Come," she says, decisively. "You are old enough to hear what will be said, and brave enough to be His Majesty's strong right arm." Then her eyes dart to me. "Margot? Why are you here?"

I have no choice but to go, but I am not happy about it. At sixteen,

Henri is not much older than I, yet he is included and I am dismissed. As I make my way to Mother's apartment, I wonder if I shall ever be permitted to participate in anything at Court more important than a pavane. I arrive to find a crowd. Apparently the fear of missing something important has caused at least two dozen women to overlook the nicety of changing after the hunt.

"A large number of armed Protestants have been spotted, with the Prince de Condé at their head," I say. The eyes of the others register fear at my pronouncement.

We wait for more news. We have been seated for some time, when the Duchesse of Uzès enters. Clapping her hands she declares, "We depart within the hour."

"For where?" someone asks.

"Meaux. Waste no more of my time or your own with questions. Pack only what is needed to carry you through tomorrow. Servants will see what we leave behind sent on. Assemble in the courtyard ready for the saddle. There will be no coaches."

The handwork, books, and instruments that were mere props as we waited are cast aside, and we run from the room. I am nearly to my apartment when I dash headlong into the Duc de Guise.

"Calmly, Your Highness," he says, reaching out a hand to keep me from toppling backwards. "Panic will not get us to Meaux more quickly."

"Why Meaux?" I ask.

"A fortified city is more defensible than a palace built for pleasure," he says matter-of-factly.

"Do we need defending?"

He considers for a moment. "That remains to be seen. If the Protestants stay at Rozay-en-Brie, then we will have given up our hunting for nothing."

"Do you think they will stay?"

"No."

"And when they come, what will be their purpose?" I hold my breath. It is the sort of question that Mother would never answer, but the Duc has thus far treated me as a person of intelligence.

He looks about to make sure we are alone, then draws very close. So close that I can feel his breath upon my face. "It is said they plot to kidnap the King."

Holy Mary! What stunning treachery! My body trembles slightly, and the Duc perceives it, regarding me with concern.

"Do not fear, Your Highness: there will be plenty of armed gentlemen to see you safely to Meaux." Then, placing a hand upon my arm, he adds, "And *I* will not let harm befall you." His hand drops as if he is embarrassed by the intimacy of the gesture. "Now go and make ready."

CHAPTER 5

Meaux, France

When we reach Meaux we take over the Bishop's palace—at least, those of highest rank do. Where those of lesser prominence go I cannot say. His Excellency was, of course, wholly unprepared for our coming. His Majesty's *fourriers* were not a quarter hour before our party. I feel sympathy for His Grace as he stands on the covered stairway of his own palace looking lost as courtiers stream past. Inside all is chaos. Servants, their arms full of linens, run in every direction. Space is tight. Henriette, passing me, tells me that she is crammed into a room with her husband—a situation not at all pleasing. I am led to a chamber where I find the Duchesse d'Uzès. The thought of sharing a bed with this very elderly woman is not appealing. Seeing me in the doorway, she says, "Come in, come in. Her Majesty is with the King, and I am making sure things are as she likes them."

I nearly gasp. For the first time in my life, it appears I am to share a bed with Mother. The dread of such auspicious lodgings adds to my state of agitation. I need a quiet place to collect myself, but where can I go when every corner is full? I hear a bell and my refuge is clear. Slipping out, I cross the courtyard to the Cathedral of Saint-Étienne. Entering the transept, I am greeted by graceful arches in pale, smooth stone and intricate carvings that give the walls the appearance of lace. I give a sigh of pleasure at the beauty. I can feel my heart slowing.

Drawing in the familiar smells of incense and candle wax, I move to the nave. The church is not deserted. Near the high altar a gentleman kneels, head bowed. I make my way forward quietly. I would not disturb the man's devotions. When I am a few yards away, I recognize the Duc de Guise. So he is a man of prayer—what a pleasant discovery. Looking up, he nods with a faint smile, then drops his head again over his clasped hands. Sinking to my knees and closing my eyes, I give thanks for our safe arrival and pray God will protect the King—protect us all. Then, though the subject is less exalted, I ask God to help me to show myself to best advantage while I am so closely in company with Mother. When I open my eyes, the spot where the Duc knelt is empty. I feel a certain disappointment, which is erased when I find him standing by the door. Silently he offers an arm and we step into the courtyard, now striped with golden light from the falling sun. Pausing he says, "You are a great deal calmer than when I saw you last."

"The walls of the city and my prayers bring me reassurance."

"I am glad to hear it."

"Did your prayers comfort you?" I ask.

"I did not seek comfort, but strength—the strength to slay Coligny." His voice is fierce.

"But I thought Condé headed the party we would evade."

"The heretics would never undertake such a plot without consensus. Their party is a many-headed monster and I expect more than one chief to be with them if we meet."

We are waiting for the Swiss. That is all I know. All anyone knows. Well, that is not precisely true. Those important enough to be on His Majesty's council doubtless know much more, but as they remain closeted with Charles, they are not to be seen or heard from. Last night I waited up for Mother, hoping to learn something. Day turned to night and still she remained absent from our room. Tucked in our bed, I left my light burning and tried to stay awake. Tried and failed.

As I pace the Bishop's great hall on this, the morning after our arrival, I wonder: Did she even come to bed? The hall is full. There was a certain excitement, albeit driven by fear, in our rapid ride here yesterday. Now there is nothing but overcrowding, boredom, and the disagreements that arise from those conditions.

I am sitting, made silent, stupid, and irritable by *ennui,* when I glimpse Anjou. I have not seen my brother since Mother parted us yesterday. He will have news. He always does. I jump to my feet but Henri moves through the crowd and is lost to my eye. Frantically, I search for him, spotting his back as he exits by another door. By the time I reach the next chamber, Henri has disappeared. I press on, in each room disappointed, until I reach what appears to be the Bishop's library. I could swear I hear Henri's voice as I enter, but I do not see him. Stopping, I listen closely. I hear whispering and breathing other than my own. The draperies by one of the long windows twitch. Why would my brother hide from me? This is no time for games. Walking to the curtains, I pull them aside. Renée de Rieux is against the wall, her legs wrapped around my brother, who pushes himself against her again and again. It takes me a moment to realize what I am seeing, and when I do I turn and run, the sound of Renée's laughter pursuing me long after heavy oaken doors should have killed it. I go straight to my room.

I am so angry. After the episode at Montceaux I had reason to know that my brother was involved with Renée, but knowing is far different than seeing. I close my eyes trying to banish the horrible proof that I have just had of their intimacy. It is no use—the image will not be banished.

Why her? Why? There are a dozen ladies in Her Majesty's household more refined, prettier, and less annoying. Nay, two dozen. I tell myself that I would be more sanguine had Henri chosen any of those, but I am not sure it is true. In verity I think of my brother as mine—my confidant, my dance partner—and it bothers me that he needs any other woman.

For hours I hope that Anjou will seek me out and apologize for what I stumbled upon. But by the time I send Gillone for a cold supper, I have given up. Unable to cheer myself, I retire. I dream of Henri and Renée. He is kissing the side of her neck as I saw him do and she is laughing— laughing at me. I call out to him and the next instant, in that strange way that only happens in dreams, it is I who leans against the wall. My neck he kisses. I wake with a start and sit up to find my flesh tingling strangely. Mother is at the dressing table brushing her hair in preparation for bed. I am glad to be in shadow, I would be mortified if she could see the excitement in my body. Thank God, neither she nor anyone else can see the content of my mind. Yet, even as I am mortified by my dream, I am also angry—angry at Henri.

"Anjou has taken up with Mademoiselle de Rieux," I blurt out.

Mother stops brushing and looks at my reflection—pale and wide-eyed—in the glass.

"I have remarked upon it," she replies.

Good. "And what will you do?"

She regards me curiously. "Nothing. Your brother is a man now and will behave as one."

"I do not understand."

Mother sighs. "And I wish you did not have to. This is an uncomfortable subject, but I will press it because a woman who does not understand men's needs will find herself a disadvantaged, heartbroken wife." For a moment her eyes lose their focus. Then, squaring her shoulders, her gaze sharpens again. "You will seldom be the only woman in the lives of those men most important to you. Whether you have only a husband or, one day, God willing, sons, you must reconcile yourself to sharing them with mistresses."

I swallow hard.

"You do not have to like this," Mother says. "You may even take revenge. Do you remember when you were a little girl how I took the Château de Chenonceau from Diane de Poitiers?" She smiles. "That was my revenge. But notice, I waited until your father was in his grave."

Of course I have heard this story—everyone has. Just as everyone, even his children, knows that my father kept Diane de Poitiers as his mistress. Still, to hear my mother state as much out loud is a difficult thing. I draw up my knees and wrap my arms about them in discomfort.

"I was polite to Madame while His Majesty lived, for the King's sake,"

Mother continues, "but also for my own. Had I harangued your father, pressing him to be rid of the lady, all I would have done was anger him and extinguish the power and influence I sought to cultivate.

"But I get ahead of myself. I would not merely tell you a story but give you a lesson—something you can use to manage your own future."

Coming to the bed, she sits and lays a hand upon my arm where it wraps around my knees. "It is to your advantage to permit and ignore those women who are least dangerous—those less clever than you, lacking connections, or with personal attributes which presage a short tenure. A woman who a man will soon tire of is no serious threat. In the case of your father, I did not have the opportunity to suborn such a liaison. Diane de Poitiers was in the King's heart before I came to France. Had I arrived and found His Majesty without a mistress, I would have made it my business to steer him toward a woman loyal to myself. One must be clever where there is a husband to be managed."

"But Anjou is not a husband. He is your son. If you chastise him, surely he will cast off Mademoiselle de Rieux."

"You fixate too much on the present situation," she replies with exasperation. "You are correct that the power of a woman over her child exceeds that of a wife over her husband. Sons are still men, however. They may be led from reason—from the good guidance of those who care for them most—by pretty eyes and easily opened thighs."

I look away. Thinking of Renée's thighs, which I so recently glimpsed, makes me feel sick.

Ignoring my discomfort, Mother proceeds. "Your brother is in the first flush of his manhood, and a glorious manhood it will be. He has been tutored in languages, in diplomacy, in combat. His education will not be complete until he is tutored in the ways of the flesh. I have weighed the Mademoiselle and think she will do quite well for that task. She will satisfy his desire for carnal pleasure, but I need not fear he will become so entangled as to be dangerously influenced."

Curious, I turn my gaze back to Mother's face.

She smiles. "Renée is not intelligent enough to entertain Henri's mind, nor graceful enough to please his aesthetic eye for long. He may lust for her but he will never love her. And he will never credit her counsel in place of mine."

I sense that she wants me to acknowledge her lesson. Not wishing to disappoint, I say, "Madame, I understand."

If she senses that I lie, she does not betray as much.

"Good," she says, patting my knee and then climbing into bed. "Now to sleep. When the Swiss arrive, we depart."

※ ※ ※

The sound is like thunder. Someone pounds upon the door. Gillone springs from her pallet, eyes wild like an animal's in the low light cast by the embers of a nearly dead fire.

"Hand me my *surcote*." Mother's voice is strong and clear. As she rises and pulls on the garment she calls, "Enter."

I have just enough time to pull the covers to my chin before the door swings wide.

The Duc de Nevers and Baron de Retz stand wreathed in light from lanterns they carry.

"The gates of the city have opened for the Swiss," Nevers says.

"What is the hour?" Mother asks, continuing to fasten her *surcote*.

"Just past three."

"I will rouse the King, you the Court. We depart as soon as horses can be saddled."

There is no panic in her voice. I wish I could say the same for my breast! To ride out of Meaux in darkness—never as I was drifting to sleep did I interpret Mother's words that we would depart at the arrival of the Swiss to mean a nighttime flight!

At the door Mother turns, claps her hands, and says, "Get dressed."

I scramble out of bed. Gillone hunts for a clean chemise. "Never mind," I tell her. "Help me into what I took off last night and have done with it."

Taking the steps two at a time, I arrive in the torchlit courtyard to find that the unseasonably warm weather has flown. The air is chill and moist. A stiff breeze off the river rattles shutters. My riding cloak is too light for such conditions but I do not have another. Climbing into the saddle, I lean over my horse's neck and say a little prayer of thanksgiving for the warmth of its body. I look for Mother, but see neither her nor the King.

I do spot Anjou beside a sleepy-eyed Mademoiselle de Rieux. He abandons her and rides toward me.

"Stay with me that I may keep you safe," he says.

"I am frightened."

I expect him to say something dismissive, to call me a goose. That is his way. But he merely mutters, "Accursed Protestants."

Charles and Mother emerge, causing a stir. We move to them, arriving as the captain of the guard does. In silence we move through the courtyard gate and find a line of mounted soldiers waiting. They are not very many and I shudder at the thought of what quick work fifteen hundred heretics might make of them. When we clear the city gates a much larger party awaits, thank God. We are placed at its center. Being surrounded by a forest of pikes, their metal tips gleaming in the torchlight, ought to reassure me, but the idea that such fearsome precautions are necessary only lends credence to my rising fear. I reach out and take Anjou's hand.

The captain of the Swiss gives a command and we begin to move.

"Do we not wait for the rest of the Court?" I ask, stunned. The party around us includes only my family and a small number of the highest-ranking gentlemen.

"We wait for no one," Mother replies.

The pikemen quick march, but we must still restrain our horses. As we stumble along at a stultifying rate my mind races. *How dare the men who pursue us threaten the King? They are his subjects and he was chosen by God almighty to sit upon his throne above them.* Perhaps, though, I ought not to be surprised: these are heretics, with no respect for God or his Holy Church. Why, then, should I expect them to respect God's anointed ruler?

After hours in the saddle, my nerves and ears continue to strain—alert for any sound of danger, and only briefly reassured when they perceive nothing but the marching of scores of feet and the thud of horses' hooves upon damp ground. Dawn breaks, but we do not. My legs ache from being so long in the same position.

Finally, we halt outside of the village of Le Pin. Turning my horse in place, I can see a party of courtiers riding behind our fortress of pikemen. Their number is small. I examine faces, but I cannot spot Gillone,

Henriette, or Charlotte. I wonder what has happened to the balance of our entourage. Did they remain at Meaux? Are they captured already?

My stomach growls, and as I climb down from my saddle, I am glad to hear riders ordered to secure something for us to eat. I wish to stretch my legs, but I have no desire to exit the safety of our living citadel. So I content myself with stamping my feet beside my mount. As I do, the Duc de Guise threads his way between riders to join me.

"How are you?" he asks.

"Wishing Paris were in sight on the horizon."

"We will see it before the sun sets."

"You do not think we will break our journey?" This possibility never occurred to me. The trip from Meaux to Paris must be in excess of fifteen leagues! While the horses might stretch to this, it is an extraordinary—nay, nearly impossible—journey in a single day with soldiers on foot.

"I know we will not."

"But the pikemen?"

"Those who cannot keep up will be left behind."

"We have not so many soldiers, I think, that we can spare any."

"Perhaps not. But we certainly do not have enough to be sure of winning should we give the Protestants time to catch us."

"Do not be an old woman, Guise." Anjou steps around my horse. "You will alarm my sister. We do not need equal numbers to achieve a victory when stout Catholics face rabble."

"Apologies, Your Highness," the Duc says to me. "It was not my intention to frighten you, merely to explain our actions." Then, turning to Anjou, he says, "I am as eager as you to fight in the next war—a war which must come, thanks to the heretic plot. We can both look forward to killing many Protestants, but I would rather begin with good odds and once His Majesty's person is secured." With a parting bow, the Duc makes his way back to his horse.

Anjou laughs. "I hope the Duc's dire predictions have not ruined your appetite. There is bread and cheese."

Bread and cheese? After nearly eight hours in the saddle . . .

Henri leads me to where Mother, Charles, and Marie stand. Mother is handing out our poor provisions. Chilled and hungry, I crowd in beside

Charles so that I can feel the comforting warmth of his body. There is something sad about the noble house of Valois gobbling such fare in a huddled mass. Sad and frightening. Henri can be as cocky as he likes, but no one else seems sanguine about confronting Protestant troops on our road home.

Shortly after Mother urges us back into our saddles, the sun disappears.

"Are we to have no luck at all?" Charles says with disgust. "Will it rain too?"

Mother shifts in her saddle. "Your Majesty, I would say we have been very lucky. We make good time and we have not seen a single Protestant soldier."

"Madame, you amaze me! The Protestants have us on the run whether we see them or not. It is undignified. It is maddening. They make me feel and look a fool. And I tell you, they shall pay!"

"They will pay, yes." The menace in Mother's voice cuts through my numb misery. "Dearly. We will pursue them even into their beds to extract satisfaction for this infamous enterprise."

"You—" Charles' reply is cut off by a shout.

We stop dead and the pikemen surrounding us turn to face outward. A murmured word—"Cavalry!"—rolls across the stalled party.

Anjou stands in his stirrups. "Perhaps we will not need to chase the Huguenots, Madame."

I burst into tears.

"Control yourself!" Mother snaps.

I clap a hand over my mouth to stifle my sobs. The commander pushes his way through the pikemen to Charles.

"Your Majesty, scouts have espied Huguenot cavalry not a half mile past that large hill. They do not seem to be lying in wait but, rather, move along the same road as we in the opposite direction."

"Looking for us," Mother replies.

"Looking but not yet finding. Inexplicably, they do not appear to be using scouts."

"They expect us to be at Meaux," the Duc d'Aumale posits. "They have no reason to imagine us where we are."

Thank God for small mercies. But what is to be done? I am nearly choking on my own fear.

"If we were still at Meaux, we would be able to defend ourselves," Anne de Montmorency says dourly.

"There is nothing to be gained in rearguing that decision," Mother says. "We are here. The Huguenots are there. What now?"

"Retreat. Take a different path," the constable urges.

"I will not be driven back like a rabbit harried by hounds!" Charles says savagely.

"Well said! Let us fight!" Anjou puts his hand on the hilt of his sword and my throat contracts.

"Not fight, but seem as if we are prepared to," Aumale interposes. "We have the advantage of surprise. If we march on at a blistering pace, we will cross the Huguenots' path not much after they apprehend the sound of our soldiers' footfalls. They will have no time to count us—no time to determine their advantage—and, being caught unawares, may be unwilling to engage."

The commander nods. "I will have my pikemen run at them. This fearsome sight alone may get us past."

" 'May.' I do not like 'may.' " The constable shakes his head.

"I do not like anything about our present situation, but the King says he will not retreat, and I agree," Mother says.

Aumale gives the constable a slightly triumphant look. "May I suggest, Your Majesties, you surround yourself with every armed gentleman and a score of mounted soldiers. Once past the Huguenot villains, such a group could ride for Paris with great speed."

"I will leave the balance of my soldiers to impede the Protestants and harry them as they go," the commander adds.

Mother looks from Duc to commander. "Quickly, then. Let everything be arranged."

As the soldiers make ready, I concentrate on controlling a nearly insurmountable urge to scream. I wonder if only my lack of breath, rather than my willpower, defeats the impulse. My stomach contracts into a ball as hard as stone. Mother is too focused on Charles to offer me a word of comfort, and Anjou is too excited. But as the King's gentlemen encircle us, comfort comes. The Duc de Guise draws his horse beside mine. Leaning toward me, he says, "You pray, Your Highness, I will fight, and we will both tell stories of this day to our grandchildren."

Then we are in motion. Pikemen quick march up the gradual slope in front of us. I am certain from the crest we will be able to see Condé's men. I clutch my reins so tightly that they cut my palms, wondering how many they will be. The pikemen disappear over the rise. I hold my breath. Nothing. From the top I can see nothing but the next, larger rise. Down we go into the dip between prominences, my stomach sinking as we descend, my hands still clutching. I do pray as the Duc bade me. Pray that by some miracle we will reach the top of the next hill and again see nothing— that the Protestants have turned off the road or been wiped from our path by God. I pray in vain. Reaching the next apex, our party stops abruptly though no command was given. A hundred yards from the bottom, scores of mounted men move along the road.

I spot Condé at once. As I do I hear Guise mutter, "Coligny," as if the word tasted foul in his mouth.

Two chiefs, and surely a thousand men. A stunning sea of horses.

Looking into the faces of the nearest Protestant riders, I observe that they are astonished as well. Like us they stare, gape-mouthed. I wonder if they know precisely who we are. Have they spotted the King among our number?

A sharp command. We move down the incline. Reaching the plain below, we pause. Another command. Lines of pikemen lower their weapons to charge position, and the drums, which have been silent all this way so we might be stealthy, begin to beat. My heart keeps time with them. The pikemen pick up speed, presenting a wall of points to the enemy. Ranks of soldiers with two-handed swords and a small number of cavalry follow.

It is a moment of decision—for the Protestants. Will they take the charge? Or will they part and let us pass? I feel light-headed and fear I will fall from my horse and be trampled in whatever comes.

When the wall of pike points is almost upon the first line of enemy riders, Condé shouts. He signals with his hand and his followers turn off the road, riding right.

Anjou gives a yell of triumph. Mother throws him a look that would freeze the Seine in August.

"Gentlemen," she barks, "do your duty to the King." Swords are drawn.

"Children," she continues, "once the pikemen pursue the heretics, ride as quickly as you can. Do not stop. Do not look back. And, Henri, do not engage our enemies—not even by mocking salute or shouted insult."

Anjou pouts but makes no reply.

We are impatient to be gone, but it takes time for the last of the Protestants to leave the road. As the final riders cross onto the flattened grass, Aumale cries, "Now!" He kicks his horse. Charles plunges after him. I dig my heels into my mount. He is not at his best, but he is willing, leaping forward at my touch. Run! I think. *Run.*

I love to ride, the faster the better, but there is no joy in this moment. No pleasure in the feeling of the wind rushing past or the thundering sound of my horse's hooves. The dust of the road swells in a brown cloud as every tired horse reaches a gallop. I wonder if the Protestants have turned and will charge, but I do not allow myself to look. When we have gone perhaps half a mile, my horse slows. I cannot bear the thought of slipping behind. I apply my heels once more, viciously. The beast gives a high-pitched whinny and jumps forward, galloping full out again, out of my control. We race past the others until I am alone at the front of the party. I hear Mother shout my name and desperately try to rein in my horse, but I cannot control or direct the animal, only cling to my seat. Gradually the beast winds himself, and when he reaches a trot I am able to stop him at last. I sit exhausted and shaking when two riders reach me at the same moment: Anjou and Guise.

"Magnificent madness," my brother crows. "I will wager not two among the Protestants ride so well."

I feel the compliment and seek to show myself as cavalier as Anjou by tossing off my fear and grinning.

"Madness indeed," Guise chimes in. There is no admiration in his tone.

The look on Mother's face as she arrives suggests she shares the Duc's lack of tolerance for reckless behavior. "If you cannot control that animal," she says, "you will have to double up with someone."

The glow of Anjou's praise is wiped away. "Madame, my horse merely reacted to the fear in the air. I do not believe he will bolt again. He has not the energy even should he wish to."

"We must have a change of mounts, Your Majesty," the Baron de Retz interposes, "if we are to stay ahead of Condé. I will ride ahead and see what may be done."

Having been reminded of the Protestants, Mother clicks her tongue and puts her horse in motion. "Pay what you must," she tells the Baron.

He salutes and drives his horse forward mercilessly.

I wonder how far the animal will go. Will we find the Baron on the road beside its carcass?

Perhaps our luck has turned, for we do not come upon Retz until we reach Chelles, where he is waiting with horses. There are not enough. Only a handful of the party can be re-horsed. Those who are not fall behind one by one. I worry for them. But I worry for us as well, for we begin to lose members of the royal guard as their horses are spent. The riders who remain are more tired than their mounts. My back aches, my arms too. We do not speak. Nor do we go above a trot until—oh, blessed sight!—the walls of Paris rise before us. The sun, beginning to set, gives the city a glow as if it were afire.

From that moment we run our horses hard, hoping only to be within the city gates before they drop. I watch in fascinated horror as the Cardinal of Lorraine's horse collapses. His brother Aumale stops to take him up. Several royal guards lose mounts. Unlike His Eminence, they are left to walk. I do not know if anyone would stop for me should my horse fail. I do not know who there is I would stop for. And I do not realize I am crying until we pass through the gates and I must wipe my eyes to see my way.

I am not the only one who weeps. In the courtyard of the Louvre, Marie becomes hysterical, sobbing on the ground beside her foaming, sweated mount. Charles tries to help her to her feet but stumbles, the muscles of his legs too fatigued to properly support him. I long to get down from my horse but feel powerless to do so. Again it is Guise who comes to my aid. Climbing the steps put in place by a servant, he half lifts, half drags me from my saddle. "You are all right," he tells me softly. "You are home."

I may be home but I am not all right. I will not be all right for a long time. Not until my friends who are God knows where between Meaux and Paris arrive safely. And not until the Protestants have been taught their duty to their King at swords' points.

CHAPTER 6

October 1567—Paris, France

"What will it take to move that man!" Mother looks up from the dispatch and slams her fist upon the table. The Baron de Retz, sitting opposite, jumps, but I am careful to hold still and stay quiet. Thanks to Anjou, I am hiding in a space I did not previously know existed, peering through a hole cleverly provided for such a purpose.

"More than a month has passed since we were driven hence in a frenzy by a galling act of treason," Mother continues. "Protestant demands make negotiations a farce. His Majesty has ordered those in rebellion to lay down their arms. That order has been ignored. And still the constable dithers!"

"He is too old, Madame." My brother Henri picks at something on his doublet sleeve and curls his lip disdainfully. "Montmorency thinks more upon his digestion than upon leading His Majesty's troops."

"The people grow hungry, thanks to the heretics' blockade," the Baron says. "You would not have them blame the King in their despair. Write to the constable. Press him to march to Saint-Denis and attack."

"I will do better than write. Since he does so little where he sits, let him come here. We will see if he is willing to mumble pale reassurances like those on this paper when he must look me in the eye." Mother crumples the page and casts it onto the table.

I cannot imagine anyone crossing Mother when she locks her eyes upon them. For a fleeting instant I feel as if she can see me, and I shiver.

"I will send for him." The Baron rises.

"Will you take the constable's command from him?" my brother asks the moment he and Mother are alone.

"Patience, son. You do not lack courage but could use more diplomacy.

Constable Montmorency was your father's good friend. More than that, he has served as a useful hedge against the houses of Lorraine and Guise since your brother François died with their talons in his arm. Those who have served well cannot be lightly cast aside."

"*Ventre-Dieu!*"

Mother holds up a hand. "When the constable sets out to do battle, I will surround him with younger, stronger men. You shall have a command and so shall others of your generation. I know war is a young man's meat and a king in his prime needs warriors of a similar age."

"I will make you proud, Madame."

"You always do. Now go and find some entertainment."

Moments later Anjou releases me from my hiding place.

"Happy?" he asks.

"Yes. And you must be too. You will command troops in battle."

"It is a beginning, but I will hound Mother until I have the prize I seek: command of all the King's armies."

"Can you never be satisfied?" I try to sound exasperated but I am, in reality, pleased. Anjou's ambition is laudable, and he knows I admire it. Perhaps that is why he stoops and kisses my cheek.

"I am satisfied when you are with me."

"Well, then, how shall we amuse ourselves?"

"Do you not wish to run off and report to the Duchesse de Nevers and the Baronne de Sauve?"

I do, very much. But I continue to wage a campaign to keep Henri from Mademoiselle de Rieux. So telling tales of what I've heard will wait.

"If you would rather I ran off—"

"No, indeed!" Henri smiles again. "Come watch me take exercise with my new small sword."

"All right." I take his arm. Charles presently is much engaged with final details for his royal *Académie des Maîtres en faits d'armes.* Anjou enthusiastically offers his ideas and support, swept up in the latest craze for sword work, but also trying to curry favor with the King to assist his ambitions.

We go first to my brother's rooms. I watch as he strips off his doublet and searches for something more suitable for fencing, wondering, as I admire the muscles in his back, if the Duc de Guise will be among the young men exercising. I have seen very little of the Duc since our return to the Louvre, and I realize wistfully it is highly unlikely he will be playing at arms this afternoon, as his uncles made sure he was quickly sent to the defensive lines lest the constable get all the glory. A fear that now seems very foolish.

Anjou pulls on a new shirt. As his head emerges he says, "By the way, I have something of interest to tell. In the letter Mother received from Elisabeth yesterday, our sister complains Don Carlos becomes more and more irrational. He has been aggressively paying court to her. Elisabeth does her best to conceal this, and his other signs of madness, from the Prince's father—out of what Mother calls a 'misplaced affection for the useless boy'—but fears the King of Spain will soon have her stepson confined for his own good."

Picking up his foil, Henri gives a few short thrusts, bending his forward knee more with each. "Are you not mightily glad?"

"Prodigiously!" Glad that Don Carlos is not my husband and, yes, glad his troubles of the mind overtake him. I know it is wicked to be cheered by such a thing, but there is a certain delightful vengeance in knowing that the man who sneered at the idea of wedding me has become a prating lunatic. Failing to win the hand of a madman is no failure.

And yet . . . the slight by the Prince still stings. Don Carlos, mad or not, is betrothed to the Emperor's daughter and I remain unattached. Even as I know thoughts of war dominate Mother's hours, and must do, I wish she would turn a modicum of her attention to finding me a husband.

"Why do you sigh?" Anjou asks.

"I do not!" I insist defensively. "Do you ever think of getting married?"

"No," Anjou replies, his voice oddly flat. "For I will not have my choice, and Mother's suggestions have been abominable."

If by his choice my brother means Mademoiselle de Rieux, then I am heartily glad he will be denied it.

He sheaths his blade. "Mother is not the only one to miss the mark. I swear to you, the Duc de Guise mentioned our brother's widow to me— never mind Mary Stuart has a husband already."

"When did you see the Duc?"

"At camp when I was last there to review the troops with Charles." Henri looks at me piercingly.

I fidget, then, taking his arm, say, "Come. I thought you were going to impress me with feats of fighting prowess."

He bends and kisses the top of my head, and as he does so I can hear him inhaling my perfume—his favorite. Straightening, he says, "I hope to impress you always and in every way."

"I am sure you shall. And I will relate tales of your gallantry and valor everywhere, as a good sister should."

I cannot sit still! There is a massacre going on and I am missing it.

Montmorency at last offers battle to Condé and his Protestants. The constable has a mighty force: more than fifteen thousand infantry, three thousand cavalry, and eighteen lovely new cannons. The Protestants have not a seventh of that at Saint-Denis. How those heretics must tremble at this moment—at least those not already dispatched to answer before God. How they must cry out as they are run through with pikes or felled by Catholic swords!

Anjou joined the constable last night. Charles rode out this morning to watch from a safe distance. Mother and I are left behind to wait for word of the battle's glorious result, word that must surely come soon, given that the fighting began hours ago. I bite my nails and pace from window to window, though there is nothing to see. This morning we heard the sounds of His Majesty's artillery, but no longer. We certainly have no chance of hearing anything else at this distance; yet, in my eagerness I strain my ears. Mother, by contrast, sits at her desk, writing.

"Marguerite!" she says, looking up. "If you cannot be calm, then you must be gone."

I freeze. The one concession made to me on the occasion of the day's battle is that I have been permitted to be with Mother in her study, along with the Duchesse d'Uzès, rather than being consigned to the room beyond with the other ladies. And though that larger party would doubtless be full of shared excitement and whispered speculation—all in all, a great deal more entertaining—Mother will have the news first. I make myself sit down beside Mother's chessboard and slowly set up the pieces, imagining each to be someone I know. Anjou for the Red King, though I suppose by rights that ought to be Charles. The pieces are finely carved with particularly dashing chevaliers. Perhaps that is why I imagine one to be the Duc de Guise. I run my finger along that piece before moving it. Then, turning the board, play the other side.

I am in my third turn as white when the door bursts open. A soldier no older than me crosses the threshold, breathing heavily.

"Your Majesty," he says, "Constable de Montmorency is felled. He is on his way to Paris, but all concede this effort is made merely so he may die at home."

Mother does not blanch. Not a muscle moves in her face. "Unfortunate, but what of the battle?"

"The Prince de Condé has the luck of the devil." The youth crosses himself as if Satan might be summoned by a mention. "He broke our line. 'Twas during his charge that Montmorency was wounded."

"Condé charged?"

"Before we could."

"*Incroyable!* Your brother was right"—Mother turns to me—"the constable was too old for the task set him." Returning her attention to the soldier, she gives him a sharp look. "I have had your sober news, now give me better."

I can see fear in the youth's eyes. Dear God, what if he has no better? At least, I pray he has no worse.

"We nearly had Condé. The Duc d'Anjou was screaming for us to take him. But Condé's men rescued him."

I can imagine my brother's curses at such a turn of events. Mother draws herself up fully in her chair.

"But we have broken their momentum," the messenger adds quickly. "There are not enough of them to carry the day, and surely the next report to Your Majesty will say the Protestants are on the run."

"That is the news we want, and woe betide the man who brings me other tidings."

I wonder if the soldier is thinking that he would rather die fighting than bring the next dispatch; that would certainly be my thought were I in his boots.

"With Your Majesty's leave, I will return to the field."

Mother nods curtly. The youth flees. As the door closes, Her Majesty stands, pacing to the same window that, just a short while ago, she made me leave. "God's blood!" she says, striking the sill, "was it too much to ask His Majesty's huge army to destroy twenty-five hundred men? I might kill so many myself, because I have the spleen for it. The constable did not."

"Will Your Majesty go to see him?" the Duchesse d'Uzès asks.

"No. Excuses from a dying man are no more palatable than those from one who will live awhile longer." Turning, Mother sits back down behind her desk and sighs. "But, as I am a Christian, I will send a note saying I am grieved by his injury and pray he will recover."

"Anjou has the spleen for fighting," I say.

Mother lays down the pen she has just taken up. I tense, ready to be told my opinion is unwanted. Instead she smiles. "Henri has all my best parts, and I shall see he has the opportunity to use them against the King's enemies from this moment on."

At dusk Anjou arrives, sweaty and angry.

"Men, animals, time—all lost," he says after briefly stooping to kiss Mother. "And for what?" Pouring himself a glass of wine, Anjou flops into a chair, heedless of the grime he imparts. "It will horrify you, I am sure, but I must report that our positions at darkness are changed insignificantly from what they were at first light—by a matter of yards, not miles." Throwing back the entire content of his glass, he wipes his mouth with the back of his hand. "I rode into the city with Charles."

"Where is the King?" Mother asks.

"Down in the courtyard, kicking a groom."

So Charles has surrendered to his black temper as a result of this reverse. I shudder at the thought of such a mood, which may linger for days and punish many more than the hapless groom.

"Have you word of the constable's condition?" Henri asks, kicking some mud off his boot onto the carpet.

"When he is dead, word will come from the Rue Sante Avoie," Mother replies with no discernible emotion. "And whatever you think of his conduct today, you will show appropriate respect at his passing. After all, it does no harm for he who comes next to praise he who went before where that predecessor is dead and no threat."

"Meaning?"

"Your brother will be naming you lieutenant general."

A broad smile illuminates Henri's face.

"And I will give the Duc de Guise a command under my brother." Charles stands in the doorway. Unlike Anjou's, his attire is pristine save for the toe of his right boot, where I distinctly detect traces of blood. I see also that the knuckles of his right hand are split and bleeding, though he appears entirely unconscious of the fact. "Guise fought splendidly, something which, sadly, distinguishes him from many. We may have God on our side, but Condé and Coligny have braver men."

I am sure he does not mean—cannot mean—to disparage our brother. But Anjou's smile fades.

Charles, having moved into the room, looks down at one of Mother's dogs curled up by the leg of her worktable, and I have the horrible presentiment he will kick it. Mother must think the same, for she says, "Your Majesty, if you need to kick something, pray limit yourself to furniture. I will not take kindly to violence against my animals."

"I do not need to kick something. I need to kill something."

"You did not kill the groom, then?" Mother asks.

"I do not believe so. Perhaps I should go and finish him."

"Do as you like." Mother's reply would horrify many but not me. She knows Charles and so do I—where he is opposed, there he will surely go. If he returns to the courtyard and kills the boy now, it will be in spite of Her Majesty's response, not because of it. The King remains where he stands and I begin to relax. And then, with a perversity I cannot understand, Anjou draws his dagger and offers it to Charles.

I sit perfectly still—so still that, but for my breathing, I might be made of stone, wondering if Charles will take the weapon. His eyes crackle with animosity, like a fire in a grate. His jaw clenches. I could swear I see his bloodied hand rise slightly, and at that very moment Henri pushes the dagger further forward, saying, "I will go with you if you like. We can make a bit of sport of it."

"Keep your dagger," Charles says, his voice so laden with disgust that one would think Anjou had suggested killing the groom, not he. "Use it to gut my enemies. Were the constable not already dying, you could begin with him." Charles raises both hands to his head, pressing them against his temples. "My mind races and my head aches." His voice is aggrieved and his body, rigid with anger since he entered, grows slack.

I hate to see him suffer so. I wonder, not for the first time, why God planted these violent rages within what would otherwise be the sweetest of temperaments. "Your Majesty," I say, "shall I come with you to your room, wrap your hand and bathe your forehead?"

"Yes." He beckons me and, when I arrive beside him, places one arm heavily across my shoulders, leaning into me so much that I nearly stagger. One would think he had been on the battlefield with the men who fought and had labored there to the point of exhaustion.

Mother gives me a look of praise. "I will send a draught to help you sleep," she says to Charles.

Slowly we make our way toward the King's apartment, my brother becoming more torpid with each step. Twice servants seek to relieve me of the burden of the King, each time to be waved off and followed by curses as Charles' agitation flares. When we reach his antechamber, his valet is likewise dismissed.

"Shall I send for something to eat and drink?" I ask, easing him onto a chair. "Perhaps it would revive you."

"I do not wish to be revived, only soothed."

I nod. Moving to his bedchamber, I fill a basin shallowly with water, then add oil scented with lemon balm. Snatching up a clean cloth, I return to find Charles head in hands. Pulling up a stool, I gently take one of those hands. "Sit back," I urge. "Put up your feet and let me apply a compress."

He arranges himself slowly, like a very old man, unbuttoning his doublet, putting his boots on the stool, and letting his head fall back as if that very exercise were painful. I tear off a strip of linen, then dip the rest, wring it out, and lay it across his forehead. His eyes close but his face does not relax.

Crouching beside him, I use the strip I tore to bind his hand. Finished, I ask, "Shall I send for your nurse?"

"No, sit with me for a while."

I shift from crouching to sitting on the floor beside him, basin in my lap.

Gradually his breathing slows. After some minutes, with his eyes still closed, Charles says, "You are an angel."

"No, Your Majesty, but I hope I am a good sister and a faithful subject."

"That, then, if you like. You are the only one who never asks for anything in return for kindness—at least, the only one who shares my blood." He sighs. "Marie is content to take what I give without asking for more. I wish . . ."

He lets his voice trail off and leaves me wondering what he wishes. That he could marry Marie? That there were fewer people around him whose ambitions made them greedy? I feel compelled to speak up for those closest to him.

"Charles, you are unfair to Mother. She wants what is best for you and for France."

"Does she?" He sighs again, opening his eyes and examining me curiously. "I suppose so. But there are times I find myself in doubt of it. And as for Anjou, he wishes he were the elder, of that there can be no doubt. And now he will lead my armies."

"For your glory."

"And his."

"As long as he serves both, where is the fault in that? Are not all the best men ambitious?"

"True." He sits up and drops the compress into my basin. Drops of lemon-scented water fly up, dotting my face. "But so are the worst men, dear sister. I have learned that since the crown came to me. You will learn it too. I pray not too painfully."

A knock sounds.

"Enter," Charles calls.

The Duc de Guise crosses the threshold, covered in dirt and sweat.

"We were just speaking of you," Charles says.

I wonder whether Charles means to imply Guise is one of the best or the worst men?

"Your Majesty, the Prince de Condé shows signs of breaking camp."

Charles springs to his feet. "After him! Or are you too tired to lead a portion of my army in pursuit?"

"I am never too tired to serve my king and will lead as many or as few as I am given anywhere Your Majesty chooses to send me."

"Excellent!" Two spots of color mark Charles' cheekbones. For the second time since his return, he appears on the verge of a frenzy—this time one of enthusiasm, not anger. I wonder if the Duc knows that such a fit of good spirits can be as capricious and dangerous. The King pulls the Duc into a clutching embrace, then releases him with equal violence. "On your way."

"Which companies shall I take, Your Majesty?"

This sets Charles back on his heels: he is not accustomed to making such decisions. Indeed, I suspect he has not command of the facts necessary to make such a pronouncement.

Seeing my brother's confusion, the Duc is quick to withdraw the questions. "Pardon, Your Majesty," he says. "I ought not to burden my king with questions better left to those under his command. To whom shall I report for orders?"

"Our brother, Anjou. Tomorrow he will be lieutenant general."

De Guise's visage registers surprise, but he recovers quickly and executes a smart bow before departing.

He is not gone a moment before Charles looks apprehensive. Scrambling to his *escritoire,* he pulls out a sheet and writes furiously upon it. "Follow the Duc," he commands, folding the note sloppily and thrusting it toward me. "Bid him give this to Anjou. I will not have our brother make a fool of me by countermanding what I have said."

I catch up with Guise when he is but a yard from the door of Anjou's apartment.

"Your Grace!" I call. He stops and looks back. "His Majesty sends this, by you, for the Duc d'Anjou."

"Has he changed his mind about my commission already?"

"Sir, I will not gossip about the contents of His Majesty's correspondence."

"Fair enough," he says, taking the note.

"Was the battle horrible?" I ask.

"It is always horrible not to win."

This, of course, is not what I meant; I wanted details, dying men lying in the mud, thrilling hand-to-hand combat.

"But we will win in the end. We must." I recall Charles' quip about having God on our side but not the best men—yet the man I see before me inspires confidence; Anjou inspires confidence.

"Your certitude is encouraging, Your Highness. I will keep your words, and your bright eyes, with me as I ride east."

My flesh tingles. I long to offer him something more concrete—a token. But that seems too forward. *A kiss might also do. For my part it would do very nicely. But how brazen would that be!*

He reaches out a hand. "May I?"

I give him my hand and watch with rapt attention as he dips his head over it. His lips are firm and smooth as they press against my knuckles.

"For luck," he says, straightening. I do not know if my cheeks color, but his do—color that is visible even through the dust of the field—and this surprises me.

"I will pray for you," I say in a low voice.

"I am honored. That you will think of me is enough."

When he is out of sight, I bring my hand to my own lips, kissing the spot he kissed as if by doing so I could take his kiss onto my own lips and return it.

CHAPTER 7

September 28, 1568—Paris, France

When Anjou marched from Paris at the head of the King's army nearly a year ago, I thought word of royal victory would come swiftly. I dreamt of welcoming the Duc de Guise back as a hero and perhaps allowing him to kiss something more than my hand. But, as with the Battle of Saint-Denis, the news that came was not what I expected. La Rochelle fell to the Protestants. My cousin the Prince of Navarre joined Condé, so that two princes led the heretics opposing the crown. I did not see my brother or my handsome Duc for four months. And when, at last, the Edict of Longjumeau ended hostilities and brought them home, they did not come as victors—not in their own eyes and not in the eyes of the people of Paris.

This was most unfair, as I pointed out to Anjou. For Mother said this new peace surrendered nothing to the Protestants that they did not have under the previous one. But my brother was no more persuaded by me than His Majesty's Catholic subjects were persuaded by broadsheets. Anjou strode around in a foul mood. And in the cities, Protestants began to die—murdered in the streets and even in their own homes. I did not celebrate these deaths, not because I was sorry for them, but because they angered Mother and I believed her when she said they must bring war yet again.

Today war comes, not by Protestant actions, but by ours. This morning Charles signed the Edict of Saint-Maur, revoking the rights of the heretics to worship, and now he walks through the streets of Paris behind the remains of Saint Denis. It is tradition, this procession honoring the Saint, before arms are taken up, and it makes the Court whole again for the first time in months.

I smile from my place behind the King at the sight of Anjou carrying a pole of the baldachin canopy covering the holy relics. He came from his vast camp at Orléans for this purpose. I say a special prayer of thanksgiving to the Saint for his return. And behind him, supporting the rear of the canopy, is the Duc de Guise.

People are out by the thousands along the procession route, enjoying the spectacle. I am waiting for it to be over, waiting for a chance to speak with the Duc at the banquet that will follow. I do not, as it happens, have to wait so long. When we are finished, he appears beside my horse to help me mount.

"Your Grace," I say, accepting his outstretched hand and wishing my own hand ungloved when it touches his. "I am surprised to see you smiling. When you were last at Court you were all scowls."

"My spirits were oppressed by that detestable treaty," he says, leaning a hand upon my horse's withers and looking up at me, "and by the company I was forced to keep."

"Condé and Coligny excused themselves from Court before you did, and yet still you were unhappy. Or do you refer to Valois company?"

"Never," he replies. "To be in the company of my king is an honor." Moving his hand from my horse to where my foot seeks my stirrup, he takes that foot in his hand and guides it in—failing to release it even as I twitch my skirt to cover my momentarily revealed ankle. "And to be in your company is my greatest delight."

"How long will you and the other gentlemen be with us?"

"I cannot say, but, regretfully, I doubt it will be long."

"Regretfully? Come, Duc, do not tell me a falsehood. When you leave, you go to chase the Protestants—an errand that will delight you."

"True. And yet I do not lie, for every pleasure requires sacrifice. I will have the pleasure of doing battle against the King's enemies but will sacrifice the happiness of being near Your Highness."

Does his hand move slightly upward? Yes, it rises to my ankle and I can scarcely attend to anything, so overwhelming is the sensation. For a fleeting moment I imagine what it might feel like for the Duc to press onward, sliding his hand over my calf and coming to rest on my knee. Then the Baronne de Retz arrives and the Duc steps back, taking his hand with him.

"Your Highness," the Baronne says, "we do not wish to be left behind." She turns her horse in the direction of Mother and I follow.

In the courtyard of the Louvre, Anjou lifts me down. "The first dance is mine this afternoon," he says.

"Indeed not. I fear you will have to give it to Mademoiselle de Rieux, for I have already promised mine to the Duc de Guise."

"Really? I hope Guise is as prompt in pursuing my orders once the fighting starts as he is in pursuing his interests." He offers an arm. "I am sure you promised him just to vex me, but you need not have: I am done with Renée. My time in Orléans has taught me she is not worth the trouble."

"Oh, Henri." Impulsively, I rise on my toes and give him a kiss. "I believe I must shift the Duc to later in the order and dance with you first after all."

Before he can say another word, I run off. I begin calling for Gillone as I open the door to my rooms. I look over at the garments laid out on my bed for the banquet as Gillone undresses me. They may have met with my approbation before I left for the Basilica, but I am no longer satisfied.

Stepping out of my farthingale, I say, "I have changed my mind about my gown. I want the rose-colored one, my new partlet with the rolled-back collar trimmed in lace, and the silver jeweled pomander the Duchesse de Lorraine gave me." These selections will surely increase my chances with Guise. The color of the silk will impart a glow to my complexion. And the partlet—well, I have learned from observation that when one seeks to attract the attention of a man as handsome as the Duc, it is wise to draw his eye to more than your rosy cheeks.

Gillone dutifully picks up the rejected items she so neatly arranged and heads for my wardrobe.

Going to my dressing table, I unstop bottle after bottle, searching for just the right scent. I wish I had some of the perfume just arrived from Florence for Mother. Her ladies passed it around and it was universally proclaimed to be enchanting. I certainly wish to be enchanting. I resign myself to a scent I already own, pour a generous amount between my hands, then plunge them through the neck of my chemise between my breasts. I finish by rubbing the last of the scent up either side of my neck to the base of my hairline.

Gillone returns. Moving in to lift off my chemise and replace it, she stops, sniffs, and looks at me wide-eyed.

"I am not a little girl," I say, "and tonight I want to smell like the other ladies of the Court."

I want to flirt like them too. And I desire help in doing so. So the moment I am dressed I go to the wicket to wait for Henriette. She spots me from her litter and motions for me to climb in as the conveyance comes to a stop in the courtyard.

"Marguerite, what is it?"

I look in the direction of the drawn curtains.

"Have no fear, I select my litter bearers and I pay them from my own purse. They are, therefore, willingly deaf, blind, and dumb."

"The game with the Duc de Guise begins again, and I know precious little of what comes next."

"What do you want to come next?"

"A kiss."

Henriette laughs. Then, sensing my mortification, she lays a hand over mine. "My dear, I am not laughing at your ambition. I am delighted by the moderation of your demands. It has been a long time since I have been in the company of such innocence in a woman of fifteen. It is utterly charming—and, I might add, precisely what will make you irresistible to the Duc. I have told my sister more than once that with a man of his sort, fervently pious, bound by tradition, and wishing to uphold all that is good in France, brazen availability will get her nowhere."

I am very glad to hear it.

"Surely you know how to kiss." She pauses and considers me. "Or if you do not, believe me, it is a thing entirely natural and you will need no instruction. So the only help you will need is in creating an opportunity. One may receive a kiss on the hand at a ball without raising scandal—even where one is a princess—but no more. Hm. Well, I will make an opportunity for you. Leave it to me."

She raps on the ceiling to put the litter in motion so that we may disembark near the steps. "But promise me, my dear friend, that we will speak again should you want more than a kiss," she says as we draw to a stop.

I do not know how to feel about her casual mention of things beyond kissing. My understanding of them is limited and the impressions I have received so disparate. The ladies Mother employs in seduction often joke about the burden of it, but clearly many enjoy their love affairs. Henriette certainly does. She is seldom without a lover and appears to relish each until she tires of him. Yet I have been made to feel that my value lies in my chastity and certainly it is a biblical virtue. Finally, the unfortunate glimpse I had of Anjou *in flagrante delicto* turned my stomach. I cannot imagine wanting a man to pin me against the wall and paw me. Perhaps I ought to admit all this to Henriette, but she is so much more sophisticated than I, and while she might find my naïveté charming, I wish to be perceived as knowing more than I do. So I merely toss my head and try to look bored and knowing.

We go in arm in arm. There is a different energy in the *salle voûtée* today, a very masculine one. Men seem to become more so as they prepare to go to war. They swagger more. They drink more—though in the case of Anjou's friends that is nearly impossible. They jest more loudly. Dinner is a boisterous affair. I sit next to Anjou and he reflects the general mood.

"How good it feels to be merry," he says. "We gentlemen must stock up on the civilized pleasures. In a few days we will be marching through autumn rains, looking to draw blood and cover ourselves in it. There will be no fine wine, no music, no soft forms and faces." Under the table his hand brushes my knee.

"I happen to know you take wine with you." I smile at him while trying to decide how I feel about his hand where it rests on my chair, next to my thigh.

"I wish I could take you."

"I would like that very much. Not the mud, but to see a battle—how exciting."

"It *is* exciting. But too brutal for your eyes, Margot. Would you like me to bring you a trophy? Perhaps Condé's head?"

"Oh, please! I could keep it in a box." I laugh at the idea and Anjou laughs with me.

"If I get his head, I suspect Her Majesty will wish to have it for a pike."

"Only return safely and that will be enough for me." I know it is a bit of a *faux pas* to turn things in a serious direction, but the danger my brother faces is real, and his life precious to me.

"Returning will not be enough," he replies, maintaining his own cavalier tone. "I must return victorious. I cannot bear to repeat the disappointments of the second war."

"My poor darling!" I lay my hand over his where it still rests against my skirts. "Do not even think of such a possibility."

He leans in to kiss my cheek and lingers there. "What is that scent? It is mesmerizing."

I am pleased to hear this. If my brother finds it so, then I pray the Duc will as well.

"Shall I send you my bottle to take with you?" I ask, looking for Guise. He is but a table away. His eyes are on me. I meet his gaze boldly, then half lower my lids and purse my lips slightly.

"Please."

"Consider it done." With my eyes still met by the Duc's, I imagine the hand resting on my chair is his and it suddenly seems to radiate heat.

I turn my gaze back to Anjou. "You may still have the first dance as well."

"I am favored indeed. Or do you do this only to anger Mademoiselle de Rieux? Jealous fool."

"Which of us is the fool, Mademoiselle or I?"

"Both, in different ways. You were a fool to ever be jealous of her, for she was nothing to me other than a means of exercise, just as my horse or my sword might be. I never loved her. She because she cannot accept being set aside with grace."

"She never does anything gracefully."

"Too true. While you are all grace. I will wager that your caresses are as graceful as your dancing."

I take my hand from his and, bringing it to the tabletop, play with my fork. "And who shall replace Mademoiselle?"

"I thought you would not want her replaced."

I remember Mother's advice back on that dark night in Meaux. "A man must have a mistress, is not that so? It is the fashion. Why not someone with the refinements Mademoiselle lacked?"

My brother swallows audibly, picks up his glass, and drains it in a single gulp. "Who would you suggest?" His voice drops.

I have not given the matter serious thought. Casting my eye over those dining, I spot Louise de La Béraudière. "If I were to choose for you, I would choose *la belle Rouhet*."

Anjou looks disappointed.

"She is polished, and such a pedigree. Has she not been the mistress of a king? That suggests she must possess a certain grace in the dance of *amour*. You deserve a graceful partner."

"As you wish me to have her, I shall obey." He takes my hand, fork and all, and brings it to his lips. "I will consider her training against the day when I next choose my own partner, because I aspire to be worthy of one so graceful she shames the muses."

Can he mean the Baronne de Retz? He will need luck there, to be sure, for I have never heard it rumored she strays from her husband.

Charles rises. "Come," I say to my brother, "shall we stroll before we dance? I am very full." We pause while the King, with Mother on one arm and Marie on the other, descends, then follow. As Charles makes his way to his seat beneath a canopy of cloth of gold, the other tables empty. I offer Guise a smile as we promenade past and my heart quivers when he returns that smile. I am eager for dancing to begin, for after Anjou I mean to dance with the Duc.

My brother, always attuned to my moods, senses my impatience. Stopping before Mother he says, "Your Majesty, the King may not be eager to dance, but some of us are."

She turns to Charles, who is whispering prettily with Marie. The King nods indulgently and tries to pull Marie into his lap.

On Mother's signal the music begins: a *galliarde*—perfect. Anjou's natural athleticism always draws eyes, and if I perform enthusiastically, I may offer a flash of ankle to Guise, who I very much hope is watching. We are not the only pair dancing with more than usual vigor. As I search among the moving bodies for the Duc, it strikes me that there is a general wildness about the dancers. People are breathless. Ladies glisten and gentlemen's eyes stray from faces to breasts rising and falling. The Duc partners the Princesse de Porcien. Hot anger fills me until I notice how often his gaze leaves her and finds me. Do I read longing in his looks, or do I merely imagine I do because I long to have him beside me?

As the dance concludes, Anjou holds out his hand. I cannot bear any more delay in my evening's plan. So, rather than taking it, I wave a chastising finger. "I believe you have a lady to seduce."

"As you command." He kisses my hand ardently and is gone, leaving me to look for the Duc. I need not look far. Turning to my right, I find him nearly beside me.

"Your Highness, will you dance?"

Oh, most willingly. I muster all my self-restraint to keep from responding with just that unfashionable enthusiasm, instead tilting my head in the affirmative very coolly. We wait side by side. His hand is so close to mine, they nearly touch. Nearly is dissatisfying. I will the musicians to begin. And as if in response to my will, and to my need to feel the Duc's hand, they strike up. *La volte!*

We separate but I do not mind. I have much to look forward to and anticipation will only make it better. As the Duc bows I notice the muscles of his calf, the neatness of his ankle. He comes toward me; I take his outstretched hand, not merely resting the tips of my fingers on it but letting him have the whole weight and flesh of it. The feeling is delicious and all too fleeting. We turn and separate. My breath quickens. When we meet next, he will lift me into the first series of turns. Just the thought of this causes unexpected sensations: I am conscious of my breasts in a way that I never have been before, my stomach tightens and, below, that place cloaked in dark seems to twitch.

His hand is on my waist. I raise mine to his shoulder and swear I can feel the heat of him through his doublet. As he twirls me, my other hand takes his other shoulder; it is as if we would fall into an embrace. Then his knee rises and I sit upon it, letting it lift me high into the air. I have done this dance before, but it has never felt like this. I am flying, my senses jumbled. Candles, faces, the silken and velvet fabrics of the other dancers' clothing, the ceiling of the room—all blend in a swirl of dazzling color. Every inch of my skin is strangely sensitive. I can feel the air upon me, caressing my face, as I turn again and again. When the five turns are done and I must retreat from Guise, I feel unsteady on my feet, as if I have drunk as much as one of my brother's gentlemen. I pass Henriette as I come around; she smiles a knowing smile and purses her lips into a kiss.

Again and again I return to the Duc's arms. Then, rather abruptly to my mind, the music stops. I must curtsy; he must bow. When I rise, his hand is ready: it draws mine through his arm as naturally as if the gesture had happened many times before. We walk without speaking to join those who make slow circles around the floor. My breathing will not return to normal. I do not know what to say. De Guise seems likewise struck dumb. Those around us laugh and talk gaily. But we move in silence, except for what the Duc can speak by looks. In his eyes I see unguarded admiration, excitement, even wonder—all the things I feel, mirrored back at me.

Henriette approaches on the arm of Bussy d'Amboise.

"Heavens, it is hard to believe we are nearly done with September." Henriette makes a great show of fanning herself. "I was just saying to the Seigneur that some windows ought to be opened before we are all stifled. Duc de Guise"—she steps forward, taking that gentleman's arm and drawing him away from me, much to my dismay—"perhaps you and the Seigneur could open a window for Her Highness and me so that we might be refreshed?"

"If you like," Guise says, not seeking to disguise his confusion.

"As we do not wish to chill anyone dancing, perhaps we ought to find a window in some convenient corner." She winks at Bussy.

"A window in the next room would be better still," the Seigneur says, his voice thick.

"Come, Duc, you would not, I think, be sorry to take some air away from this crowd." Henriette nods at Bussy, who offers me his arm. With Henriette and the Duc in the lead, the four of us stroll the length of the room. I see Charlotte standing in the far corner, beside a small door used by servants. When we reach her, she says, "The Baronne de Retz is not looking," and, as if it were the most ordinary thing in the world, she opens the door and we pass through. We are plunged into darkness and then another door opens. It takes me a moment to realize we are in the small red salon.

Moving to a window, Henriette gestures and says, "Gentlemen, do your duty." The two men quickly open the casement. "Oh, look," Henriette exclaims, as if she has never been in this room before, though she has passed hours in it, "Seigneur de Bussy, there is a *balcon*! Let us go out and take the air."

Bussy eagerly steps into the late afternoon sun. As she follows, Henriette says, "I fear it is too small for four. You do not mind, I hope, being left behind." There may be mischief in her heart but she manages to keep her countenance.

The Duc and I are left alone. Staring at each other. *Think, you fool. You have seen women draw men in numberless times. What would Fleurie de Saussauy say at such a moment?*

"Duc, for a man who earlier this day professed to be delighted in my company, you are very quiet." I try to say it teasingly, as Fleurie would.

"Apologies, Your Highness. It was the dance. It seems to have taken all my breath and my words with it." His voice is serious and so are his eyes.

I cannot make a careless reply to such a remark. "I felt so too."

"And do you feel this?" Taking my hand, he presses it to his breast firmly enough that I can feel his heartbeat.

"It races."

"Does yours?"

"Yes." I hesitate, then move our combined hands from his breast to mine. As his palm presses over my heart I feel the breast containing that heart swell with longing. He draws a sharp breath. Lifting his hand, with mine atop it, he kisses first my knuckles and then my wrist. I shiver all over.

He draws closer—so close that it would be an embrace if only our arms were around each other.

"Your Highness," he says gravely, "I am besotted. Since our eyes met at Montceaux one year ago, no woman save you has been worth looking at twice."

"Not the Princesse de Porcien?"

"She? She is not worth looking at once."

"Is looking enough, Sir?"

"It will be if you say it must be, otherwise no."

"I want you to hold me as you did when we were dancing."

He slips an arm around my waist. "Like this?"

"Not exactly." I put my hands on his shoulders as they were in *la volte.* "That is better."

He slips his other arm about me. "And this better still."

I give a deep sigh and relax against him until I can hear the heart that a moment ago I felt. It has not slowed.

The Duc drops his head beside my neck and inhales. I give a little start as his lips touch the place where my ear meets my neck.

Pulling back, he looks down into my face. "Do I offend?"

"No. My lips are only jealous of my throat." It is as close as I can come to asking for what I want.

"As a gentleman, I cannot have that." Gently he takes my chin between his thumb and first finger and tips it upward. His mouth descends, hovers where I can feel and, to my surprise, taste his breath. At last it presses into mine. His lips are softer than I expected for a man whose body is all muscle. They give beneath mine just as mine give beneath his. His lips part slightly and mine mimic them. A small breath leaves his body and enters mine, animating me in a manner I have never known. I believe I can feel, and even hear, the blood in my veins. When his tongue follows, I am overcome with sweeping pleasure. My hands tighten on his shoulders as my own tongue reaches back in answer to his. His fingers leave my chin and his arm slides behind my neck, supporting my head as I let it fall back in ecstasy. There is no other word for it. I hear light laughter and wonder if it is my joy taking on a form of its own, before realizing it must be Henriette on the balcony. I want to remain as I am for as long as possible, but a soft, insistent rapping separates us.

Henriette steps back into the room.

"I feel much better," she says. "And by the looks of it, you two do also. We had best return to the party before Her Highness is missed."

The Duc nods and reaches out a hand for mine.

"Your Grace, you and the Seigneur should go by the ordinary way. Her Highness and I will slip back as we came. If she has been missed, nothing can be suspected if we are not in the same part of the room."

As I move toward the hidden door, Henriette stops me with a hand on my shoulder.

"So?" she asks, her eyes eager.

"I got my kiss."

"I promised you it could be managed." She smiles indulgently.

"Oh, Henriette, I think I am in love."

"Every girl thinks she is in love with the first gentleman who kisses her. It will fade." She rolls her eyes. "Do not look so sullen and misunderstood. It is right that infatuation should fade. Unchecked, it is as destructive as it is wonderful. Enjoy the feelings of the moment—wallow in them—then bring them to heel. The sooner you have control of your emotions and urges, the sooner you may pursue them without danger."

I dare not tell her, but I like the feeling of being out of control. It is very much like being lifted in *la volte*.

Charlotte appears relieved as we slip into the room.

"Trouble?" Henriette asks.

"The Baronne de Retz was looking for Marguerite. I told her that I had just seen Her Highness leave with the Duc d'Anjou."

"Anjou is gone?"

"Slipped away with *la belle Rouhet*! Can you believe it?"

I can, but the thought kindles no spark of jealousy. Whatever they are doing, it cannot be better than the Duc de Guise's kiss.

"She is old enough to be his mother!" Charlotte continues.

"Let her have her fun," Henriette replies. "I have just reveled in Bussy d'Amboise's kisses. I found them sufficiently exciting to warrant an invitation to my little house this evening. There I intend to enjoy every inch of him, grateful throughout that he is only nineteen. I am a firm believer in the old adage 'young flesh is a great nourishment to love.'"

Charlotte laughs.

"Let us go and make ourselves obvious to the Baronne."

For the space of two dances I stand beside my *gouvernante* while she talks of the everyday. I do not hear a word. I am watching Guise across the room. My Duc returns to my side for a dance. Where we could not find our tongues before, now, as if loosed by the kiss, we both talk eagerly. He praises my dancing, my looks, my voice. We speak of the war to come and I profess my faith that he will be the commander most distinguished in it. We flirt in the customary way of the Court but it feels very uncommon to me, because underlying every quip and look is an attraction that makes mere proximity intoxicating. We dance three dances in a row without even noticing before Charlotte assails us.

"Your Grace, you have not danced with me and I am very vexed with you. I am sure Her Highness will surrender you, particularly as her *gouvernante* has been watching the two of you *closely* for some time."

The Baronne de Retz holds her tongue until I have almost convinced myself she will say nothing. Then, when I stand ready for bed, she says, "Mademoiselle Goyon, I will finish here."

Turning back my covers she says, "Your Highness danced a great deal with the Duc de Guise."

Sitting on the edge of the bed I busy myself removing my slippers. "His Grace is a good dancer."

"I suppose he is. The question is, is he something more?"

"He is a commander in His Majesty's army, a cousin by marriage, and a friend of my brothers. Is that what you mean?"

"No. I mean: Is he of special interest to you?"

Sliding beneath the covers, I am furious at myself for the blush that rises to my cheek. "And if he is?"

The Baronne sits down on the edge of my bed and looks at me earnestly. "Your Highness, you mistake me. I do not censure you. I merely wish to know your situation. It is the province of the young to fall in love—so long as that love is pure and the behavior it occasions blameless. It is my duty to make sure that your behavior is as it should be. Dance with the Duc. Promenade with him. Discuss music, art, even politics—quietly. I will be content."

I feel quite guilty for the way I snapped at the Baronne. Then she speaks again. "Only pray be cautious in who you seek counsel from lest an innocent flirtation turn into something worthy of censure. Remember *I* am the *gouvernante* Her Majesty selected for you."

"Madame, I hold myself ever open to your instruction. As for inappropriate counsel, I cannot pretend to know who you mean." If the Baronne will defame my friends, she had best be willing to be explicit.

Tucking the covers around me, she says, "We will speak no more of this . . . for the moment."

Good. I have more pleasant things to ponder—like the taste and feel of the Duc de Guise's lips. I have barely extinguished my light, however, when the very friend my *gouvernante* cautioned me against slips into my room.

"Henriette!" I cry, sitting up to be embraced. "I thought you were going to the Rue Pavée."

I am not embraced. Standing at the foot of my bed, her face illuminated by the light she carries, the Duchesse shakes her head. "And so I am. But I must keep Bussy waiting because you found it prudent to dance all night with Guise."

What? Is this to be my second lecture of the evening? "I let the Duc kiss me with your blessing," I say, confused.

"That kiss was not the problem. Your lack of common sense afterwards was. Discretion is Cupid's best friend, Marguerite." Walking around my bed, she sets her light on my table and takes the same spot where the Baronne sat to deliver her admonitions. "Do you wish to be able to steal the occasional kiss before the wars have the gentlemen and we do not?"

"Of course." I would be embarrassed if my friend knew how much.

"Then do not make a spectacle of yourself by dancing all night with the Duc, or, mark my words, you will be watched as you are not accustomed to being."

"Baronne de Retz has already made that clear."

"I am not surprised. She holds her honor very dear, and her position as *gouvernante* means she must hold your honor dearer still. Your maidenhead is coin of the realm, to be saved and then spent by the crown in pursuit of its interests. If she fails to keep you chaste and Her Majesty discovers as much, punishment will be severe."

"But a kiss—"

"A kiss soon leads to other things."

"Then why do you aid me?"

"Because"—the embrace comes at last—"I adore you. And because I believe in pleasure where pursued with caution."

"In other words, I may kiss Guise in secret but ought not to favor him too greatly in open court."

"You learn love as quickly as Latin." She smiles.

"All right, I will be circumspect. Only tell me, when can I see the Duc again?"

"Goodness, you are eager! And you are not alone. The Duc asked me the very same question."

How glorious to know that Guise too is smitten! "What did you tell him?"

"That tomorrow he ought to come to Anjou's wrestling matches, make certain he loses, and depart early."

❊ ❊ ❊

"Did it cost you very much to lose to my brother?"

"Not at all." Guise draws me into an embrace. "Let the Duc d'Anjou crow over his victory and the paltry sum he took from me. I am about to be richly rewarded."

"Shh," Henriette hisses from nearby. "Can you not make quieter use of your lips?"

The Duc dips his head to kiss me. Impatient, I rise to my tiptoes. His kiss is even better than I remembered.

Most of the Court—or at least those who are not old—are in Anjou's apartments for the evening's sport. Mother gave me permission to go with Charlotte. More than a dozen other ladies went, but not the Baronne de Retz, who doubtless felt safe staying behind because so many would be present at the event and because the Duchesse de Nevers had left the Louvre early, indisposed.

Henriette is no more indisposed than I. Clever friend, she merely sent her litter through the wicket empty and went to collect Guise once he had lost his match. I slipped away moments later.

The Duc's hands, which had been clasped round my waist, slide upward over my torso. I nearly cry out with delight as they come to rest on my breasts, but content myself with biting his lip as his hands tighten.

We are in the *Salle des Caryatides,* tucked into one of the columned recesses. It would be the perfect hiding place but for the echo. Henriette shushes us again from her place two windows away. Our only light comes from a sliver of half-concealed moon, so it is difficult to see Guise. I do not mind. I can feel him, taste him, and I find the darkness liberating.

His lips move from my mouth to my throat. I put my hands in his hair and pull his head down until his mouth reaches my breasts where they peek from the top of my bodice. He must kiss them through my partlet, and though it is very sheer, I wish it gone—wish I could feel his lips on my flesh.

"Oh, Henri," I whisper.

His head pops up. "You said my Christian name."

"Say mine."

He hesitates, though why he should be shy to do so under the circumstances I cannot imagine, then whispers, "Marguerite."

I kiss his neck. "Again," I command.

"Marguerite." There is urgency in his voice.

I put my lips back at his throat and run them down, past his collarbone, as far as the lowest point of the open neck of his shirt. I can taste the sweat of his recent exercise.

He groans. His groan brings another "Shh," and a few moments later Henriette clears her throat. "Your Highness," she whispers, "it is time for you to return to the sport, before questions are asked."

"No," I gasp, knowing she is right.

The Duc kisses me again then whispers, "As I love you, I would not see you embarrassed."

He loves me.

"I will dream of you," Guise says. Then he moves away through the moonlight.

I sigh. "He will dream of me."

Drawing me out from behind the columns, Henriette says, "He will do more than that." Then she laughs. "Ah, to be fifteen, and to have a seventeen-year-old lover again."

I slip back into Anjou's apartment and press into the crowd circling the wrestlers and shouting encouragement. Anjou, who has not yet lost a match, is still on the floor. He pins Saint-Luc and, his victory declared, springs to his feet, shouting, "Enough. I have had enough. It is time for wine." Someone hands him a glass and he moves in my direction. "Sister, you have a pleasing flush upon you. Can it be my wrestling has stirred your blood as well as my own?"

"I have no doubt wrestling accounts for my color," I reply, unable to resist the *double entendre*. "Your luck was certainly in this evening. What about last?"

My brother takes a seat and pulls me onto his lap. "Are you asking about my amorous fortunes?"

"Indeed. Have I chosen better for you than you chose for yourself?"

"As for my past choice, yours bests her easily. As to my future choice, I will be so bold as to say I have faith she will eclipse Louise de La Béraudière."

"You intrigue me."

"I hope so." He offers me what is left in his glass and I finish it.

"When do you leave?"

"Before the week is out."

So few days. So few moments left with Henri. It is delicious to think of the Duc by his Christian name, but even better to whisper that name to him.

My brother looks at me closely. "It pleases me to see your face fall at the mention of my departure. Mother will come part of the way; perhaps you can travel with her."

"Oh, I hope so." Closing my eyes, I can see Anjou at the head of His Majesty's army, beautifully armored and mounted, a royal banner waving at his one side and the Duc de Guise, handsome in his battle dress, at the other.

❈ ❈ ❈

"Please, Henriette," I whisper. "It has been three days, and they leave to-morrow."

My friend looks in Mother's direction before replying. "I may not be the Baronne de Retz, Margot, but nor am I foolhardy. Better no meeting than a meeting discovered." She takes another stitch. We are hemming a few last shirts for the departing gentlemen, she for her husband and I for my brother. "I am no friend to you if you are compromised."

Finished with her shirt, Henriette folds it neatly and picks up another. Charlotte lets out a mild oath as her thread breaks. "Perhaps the gentlemen will not be long absent."

"Oh, dear God, I hope they are." Henriette pulls a face. "The Duc de Nevers is the best husband when he is the furthest removed."

Charlotte laughs. "Paris is not large enough for the both of you?"

"Generally, yes, but I fear the Duc 'fortifies' himself for an absence of some months. Very tedious, particularly as Bussy will be leaving as well."

"Je comprends," Charlotte replies, threading her needle. "The Baronne de Sauve is in a most attentive mood as well. Fortunately, I have been able to allude to some business of the Queen's and thus keep myself out of my house and out of his way. But tonight I suppose I must give him a proper send-off."

"Oh, you are a good wife," Henriette laughs. "And a good liar too! You have no royally sanctioned *amour* at present."

I have wanted a husband for years. Listening to my friends, I begin to wonder why. But surely where a lady has a husband who suits her heart as well as he suits the interests of her family, she does not view him as a burden.

"Henriette," I say, "if you are with me, you cannot be with the Duc de Nevers."

"Nicely played. But what excuse could I have for being at the Louvre this evening? Every family dines at home to bid farewell to sons, husbands, and brothers. A certain someone will be with his mother. She has come from Annecy to see him off."

"And to remind him to kill Coligny," Charlotte adds.

Exasperated, I rise, taking Anjou's finished shirts. Mother looks up as I place them beside her. If my friends are not sorry to see their husbands go, it is clear that Mother will miss her son.

"Can I not go with you to see off Anjou?"

"Marguerite, we have discussed this. It is not a pleasure trip. I go to make certain the King's orders and Anjou's commands are obeyed as the army heads to Estampes."

Everyone seems determined to thwart me. Scooping up the entire pile of shirts, I say, "I will take these to Anjou." Mother nods. I am in no very good mood as I make my way toward my brother's apartment. Then I hear voices and one in particular—the Duc is nearby! Sure enough, I open the next door to find Charles, Guise, and several other gentlemen laughing and talking as they walk toward me.

"Sister!" Charles says jocundly. "Does Her Majesty have you carrying laundry about now?"

"They are shirts for Anjou. He is packing." Guise looks at me and my cheeks grow warm. I hope the gentlemen will think I am embarrassed by Charles' jest.

"Nonsense, his *valet de chambre* is packing. Find a servant to take those shirts and come with us to the armory. I will show these gentlemen how I wield a hammer."

"Ought you to exert yourself so?" Charles still looks drawn from his bout of illness this past summer. Mother has been planning special menus for him and seeking to curtail his exercise, even his hunting—a restriction Charles has not accepted gracefully.

His Majesty smiles indulgently. "Here, gentlemen, you see true sisterly devotion. If only my brother's concern for my health were as genuine."

I am glad Mother is not here to hear him speak so of Anjou, but his words can hardly surprise his companions, all of whom know there is increasing rivalry between Her Majesty's sons.

"If you would rather, sister, we can go see the new stallion that has arrived for me. He was bred at Her Majesty's farm."

"I will meet you in the stables, after I have found someone to deliver the shirts."

The Duc speaks up, "Your Majesty, shall I accompany the Duchesse de Valois?"

Clever, clever man.

"Yes, do." Charles nods.

I move past the gentlemen. The Duc falls in behind me. When the next chamber is empty, I half hope Henri will stop me and take me into his arms. But of course that would be the height of imprudence. Instead he moves to walk beside me.

"I am glad of this chance to see you privately," he says. "I came to the Louvre hoping for such a moment."

"I am thankful you did. I feared we would have no opportunity to make our farewells." I do not like the feel of that last word on my tongue: there is a possible finality in it which evaded me in the past. Quite unexpectedly I begin to cry.

"Marguerite, don't." He puts a hand on my arm and we both stop. "Do not send me off with tears but with smiles—they are luckier."

"You will not need luck," I say. "I know you will acquit yourself bravely, and I will wait for news of your gallant deeds, and thrill to them. But I will wait even more eagerly for your return and, though I know you will enjoy being in battle, will pray daily that the fighting is swiftly concluded."

"I should not have thought so even a week ago," he replies, "but I too will be glad if the prosecution of this war can be counted in weeks rather than months. So long as I have victories to enhance my reputation, and Coligny's death to my credit, I will be very happy to be back at Court." He lowers his voice. "Back in your arms."

The attraction between us is nearly suffocating. I curse the daylight and the very public nature of where we stand. How can a château so large have so few private corners?

"I wish you could be in my arms now, that I could send you from here with a kiss to remember me by."

"Can you imagine I will forget you?" He seems genuinely distressed. "Your image will rise before me every time I draw my sword. I fight for my King, for my Church, and for you."

"That is august company, Sir, and I am honored by it. If you will fight for me, then you must have something of mine to carry, as you would colors into a tournament." I have been clutching Anjou's shirts against myself, a poor substitute for clasping the Duc. There is one I took particular care with, painstakingly embroidering the neck and wrists with black-work. Pulling it from the pile, I hold it out.

As he reaches for it, the door closest to us opens. A serving girl with a ewer bustles in, humming. In my surprise, I drop all the shirts.

"Your Highness, I am so sorry." The girl looks for somewhere to set down her pitcher so she may collect what I have dropped.

"Never mind," I say, "I will get them. But hold a moment."

I stoop and Guise crouches beside me, helping to collect the fallen shirts and taking the one I meant for him in the process.

"Here"—I hold the linen out—"fold these and deliver them to the Duc d'Anjou with my compliments."

The servant takes them with a curtsy. As the door closes behind her, the Duc throws back his head and laughs.

"What is so funny?" I ask.

"We are. If we are going to be this nervous, we might as well risk a kiss. Stolen ones are the sweetest." He leans in. The kiss is brief, but the Duc is right: its urgency and the fear of being discovered make it intensely exciting. "Now," he says with a smile, "I am ready for battle."

CHAPTER 8

October 20, 1568—Paris, France

"Your Majesty"—the Baronne de Retz enters at a run—"the King is on his way with the Cardinals of Lorraine and Bourbon. Their expressions are grim."

Mother rises.

"A battle?" I murmur to Henriette. *A loss?* My mind immediately goes to the two who matter most to me among the hundreds in His Majesty's army. My heart pounds.

"Impossible," my friend murmurs back. "Her Majesty is barely returned from seeing the troops out of Orléans. They cannot have reached the Protestants. The sides must come face-to-face to fight."

I wonder then what the news can be? Charles enters. "Grim," the Baronne said. "Grim" may describe the faces of the two cardinals, but the word scarce suffices for my brother's looks. He is stricken.

"Madame"—he stops before Mother, taking her hands—"I would rather anyone else could have brought this news, yet I could not allow them to do so, for it is such as must be related by blood."

Mother blanches.

"Our sister Elisabeth is dead in childbirth."

A collective gasp rises up from the assembled ladies.

"No," Mother insists, "she cannot be. She is not halfway through her time."

"That may be so, but her time has run out." Charles begins to weep, lifting Mother's hands and pressing his mouth against them.

Mother looks past him, to the Cardinal of Lorraine.

"Your Majesty," he says. "Word comes from Spain that the Queen was taken to childbed far too early and died shortly after the infant daughter she labored to bring forth."

"Not Elisabeth! Not Elisabeth!" Mother cries in anguish. She and Charles collapse into each other's arms, both wracked by sobs.

I am frightened—more frightened than sad. I barely knew Elisabeth, but I know Mother. She is all stone and strength. To see her in such a state is overwhelming and terrifying. Apparently, not only to myself. Around me, ladies begin to weep. This general falling apart attracts Mother's attention. Her head rises from Charles' breast. Taking a step back, she wipes the tears from her face with a nearly vicious firmness.

"Ladies"—she claps her hands—"this behavior is not seemly." I wonder if she means merely ours, or if she is embarrassed by her own collapse.

"Your Eminences, I rely upon you to plan a Mass honoring the Queen of Spain. I am sure that will give all in the Court a measure of comfort."

She touches Charles' arm. "Come, my son, we will seek God's comfort now, in my chapel." Leading the King as if he were a child, she retreats. At the door she looks back and says quietly, "Let none disturb us."

Charles reemerges before long. He says nothing, but acknowledges me by stopping to kiss the top of my head. The Queen remains in her chapel. Slowly the sun moves through the sky, sweeping the scene outside the windows with warm autumn light, yet I feel cold. Mother and Elisabeth may have parted at Bayonne on less-than-perfect terms, but in the intervening three years that unpleasant meeting with the Spanish seemed to be forgotten between them. Watching a little bird pulling the seeds from a pod on the windowsill, I think of Mother's last letter to my sister—gone no more than two days; of how Her Majesty worked on it, consulting with her physician and several cooks, trying to compose the best diet for Elisabeth, who was strangely large for her stage of pregnancy. This mark of caring made me envious. Now I feel guilty over my petty jealousy.

At last, when I begin to wonder if we will all sit through the dinner hour, the door opens. Mother steps into the room looking so composed that, had I not witnessed it, I would never guess at her earlier distress.

"Margot," she says, "come with me."

I follow as she moves briskly. By the time we arrive at our destination—His Majesty's council chamber—I am out of breath. Without knocking, Mother walks in. Men all around the table rise. Charles alone remains seated, his face melancholy, his eyes swollen.

"Gentlemen"—Mother strides to where the King sits and puts a hand on his shoulder—"the house of Valois has suffered a loss. A personal tragedy, must not, however, be allowed to become a political one. The death of the Queen of Spain may, if we let it, impact our war against the Protestants—a holy war I have sworn to prosecute with vigor. I here declare that I will not let it."

The men are utterly attentive. Mother looks about, meeting every eye.

"Make no mistake," she continues, "the Protestant chiefs have heard of the death of my daughter, or soon will." There is murmuring: clearly more than one man present has considered this point. "Doubtless they whisper that her death will loosen the ties between France and Spain. Such talk represents their wishes, not fact. Philip of Spain is bound to us by a shared devotion to the Holy Church in Rome."

"Your Majesty," René de Birague says, "the Spanish king thinks himself the better Catholic. His contempt for our efforts to suppress the heretics has been plain. If he has been so outspoken when ostensibly muted by ties of kinship, his language will doubtless be more strident absent such ties."

Heads nod, including Mother's. The Superintendent of Finances has always been a favorite.

"Indeed," Mother says. "We must find a reason for Philip to be no worse a critic of French policy than he is. I have an idea on that score. Philip must marry again. That is certain. His only son is dead three months. If he loved one Valois princess, he ought to be eager for another. I wish the King of Spain's fourth wife to be the Duchesse de Valois."

I am not sure that I understood properly until every eye in the room turns to me.

"The Princess Marguerite is as pretty as her sister," Mother continues, gesturing to me as if I were merchandise in a market stall. "She is young and her health has always been good, so she can be expected to bear sons."

Mother means to send me to Spain to take Elisabeth's place! Heads nod and men smile. I ought to feel the same pleasure I see on the councilors' faces. I have often lamented my status as the longest unmarried of Mother's daughters. But at the moment I can only think of two things: the face of the Duc de Guise, and the fact that I will be expected to kiss a man who begot children with my sister. Now that I know what kissing entails, the thought of tasting lips my sister has held between her own turns my stomach.

"We cannot openly propose a match while the Spanish king is in mourning," Jean de Morvilliers says, letting his fingers tap idly on the table. "But we may make more subtle moves."

Mother nods approvingly at the chancellor. "I wish Philip to know of our proffer within the month. And"—she looks around the table meaningfully—"I wish to hear no mention of this beyond those assembled here." Moving back down the table, she takes my arm. "I will interrupt your business no further."

As she draws me out of the room, I expect some discussion of the match. Instead, Mother moves off, leaving me standing outside the chamber door. I was a prop in the scene that just played out, nothing more.

"Madame, have you no instructions for me?" I call after her.

Without turning, she says, "Work on your Spanish."

The service for Elisabeth draws to a close. Charles' violet-clad shoulders shake as he cries. His attendance is a testament to how deeply he feels Elisabeth's passing. As king, tradition dictated he absent himself, but as brother he could not bear to do so. Reaching out, I offer a hand, which he closes tightly in his. A lump rises in my throat, not for Elisabeth, for Charles. He has a tender heart.

Another brother reaches for my remaining hand. After living largely apart from the rest of the family since I left him at Amboise, François arrived yesterday. I had not seen him since Charles' "Assembly of Nota-bles" in the winter of 1566, when he was invested as Duc d'Alençon. François seemed a stranger as he climbed from his horse rather awk-wardly. Then his eyes met mine and he gave a little smile. Whatever else had changed about him over the intervening years, that smile had not. He was the little boy who played with me in the nursery, and I sensed we would be friends as we were then.

Filing from the chapel, we proceed to our waiting horses. Mother, in her grief, needs to see the son absent from this morning's ceremony, so we are setting out for the army's winter quarters at Saumur. Watching Her Majesty climb into her saddle, I wonder how it is that Anjou alone should have the power to console where the rest of us do not. I love my brother, but the unevenness of our mother's affection rankles. He is first among her children. And I . . . I fear I am last. And now I have been given an opportunity to raise myself in her estimation by a prestigious marriage. Yet I find myself balking.

In the days since Mother laid her matrimonial hopes for me before the council, her plan has seldom been from my mind. Time and again I have told myself Philip is the most powerful king in Christendom and there-fore the most desirable husband. But such bright thoughts are haunted by the shadows of every mocking story I have ever heard from Her Maj-esty's ladies about the elderly gentlemen they have been obliged to seduce. And I have been having nightmares about King Philip—or, rather, the same nightmare over and over. In the dream I am in the *Salle des Caryati-des*. Henriette stands guard as she did on the night the Duc and I first kissed. A gentleman holds me in his arms, but I know by the way he does so that he is not my Duc. Pushing back, I look up and I am horrified to see Don Carlos of Spain—or rather a gray-haired man with Don Carlos' jutting chin and haughty eyes. He must be Philip. As he stoops to kiss me, I struggle. But he only laughs and says, "Be still, girl, your sister never made such a fuss." I always wake shaking and utterly repulsed. But when I related the dream to Henriette and Charlotte, neither showed any sympathy.

"You cannot blame the real King of Spain for the behavior of the incarnation of him that your imagination creates," Charlotte said.

"I know," I replied, "but I fear my mind creates him as it does because it seems wrong to take my sister's place."

"Do not be silly," Henriette admonished. "I would lie with my sister's husband even as he molders in his grave if I thought by doing so I could wear the crown of Spain. This nightmare is not the result of anything substantial. In all likelihood it comes from your silly fancy that you are in love with Guise."

Silly fancy! I think as my horse moves along beside François' in the late autumn sun. What I feel for Henri is more than fancy. But I will concede this much: it does not follow it is wise to allow my *amour* with Guise to keep me from doing my duty to the King and my mother.

"You are very pensive," François says. "Are you thinking about the Queen of Spain?"

"Yes." I lower my voice. "I am thinking about whether I would like to be the next queen of Spain."

"Why wouldn't you?" my brother asks. "A crown—what is better in all the world?" There is absolutely no doubt in his voice. "If I were a king, no one would shy away when they saw me. No one would talk behind their hands about my scars or the fact I do not seem to be getting any taller. Or if they did"—his face is suddenly vicious—"I could order them killed."

I am sure he jests, and I am about to reply that a queen does not have such power, but Mother does; Elizabeth of England too. This realization gives me pause. Could I have influence as Queen of Spain? I cannot say for certain, but Mother more than once remarked that Elisabeth held sway with her sovereign husband. At very least, as a married woman I would be my own mistress. That would be something—something marvelous. A wife must be obedient to her husband. But Philip would be only one master. Presently I am under the thumb and the eyes of so many more.

I smile at François. He may be younger than I, but he speaks wisdom. I have made up my mind. I will be the Queen of Spain. If I must kiss King Philip, so be it. After all, I may surely kiss others as well. Both Henriette and Charlotte indulge in romances with men who please them more than their husbands. Perhaps a Spanish lover is in my future.

The Queen's secretary bustles into Her Majesty's apartment at Metz. "A letter from Madrid." He holds out the sealed packet. Like the Queen's other ladies, I rise, but Mother puts out a hand to stop me.

"You may stay," she says with a slight smile. "I hope for good news in a matter that concerns you."

My stomach feels odd. For more than four months, whatever Mother may have heard about my prospective marriage, I have heard precious little. Left in ignorance of the negotiations, I have done what I can to prepare myself to be a Spanish queen—working diligently on learning the history of the House of Habsburg and the language. Now perhaps the moment has come for me to know my future. As I watch Mother open the ambassador's dispatch, I try to remember the Spanish word for seal.

Mother's smile fades first. The color in her cheeks follows. "The father has no more interest in you than the son did."

I feel as if I have been slapped. "I do not understand."

"Philip's happy marriage to your sister may cause him to mourn her, but not to look favorably upon her family. It seems there is nothing but ill will for France at the court of Spain."

Her eyes return to the page but do not move, so she is thinking, not reading. I am not thinking, only feeling. The embarrassment of another marital rejection is horrible enough, but there is something especially brutal about being spurned by a man who adored my sister.

"God's blood!" Mother's words interrupt my pitiful reflections. "Spain has urged us again and again to dissolve the peace and bring the Protestants into submission. But when His Majesty goes to war, rather than aiding us, the Spaniards are but another obstruction."

The color begins to return to her face in angry red splotches.

"Philip is less interested in the preservation of faith than he pretends," she continues, her anger making her more candid than I am accustomed to. "His real interest is power, and he doubtless reckons that the impoverishment of France by war strengthens Spain. I prefer the German princes. They may be heretics, but they are plainspoken in their positions and their hostilities."

Mother's face is nearly purple. I can see the blood pulsing at her temples. Rising to her feet, she opens her mouth and then, quite suddenly, sways as if she were aboard a ship. She reaches out to clutch the chair she just left.

"Madame!"

The Queen falls back into her seat. For an instant her eyes reflect the same panic that imbued my voice. Then she says, "Get hold of yourself, Marguerite. Is it not bad enough that I must deal with treachery abroad and a depleted treasury at home? Must I be saddled with a hysterical daughter who appears destined to remain unmarried?"

She puts her head in her hands. "Go."

I run to my rooms. François is there. He often is lately. Without a word I rush past him, snatch up the Spanish I have been working on—books and all—and cast it onto the fire with such force that sparks fly out. One lands upon my skirts. Before I can reach down, my brother is beside me beating at the spot with his hand, then stamping the small glowing fragments that litter the hearth.

"Margot, you might have been burned." Looking up from extinguishing the last of the embers, his eyes widen. "Who has made you weep?"

"The King of Spain and our mother. Neither loves me, nor do they find me useful."

"The more fool them." François takes my hands in his.

I am surprised by this response. I expected protestations that Mother cares for me. I stop crying, catch my breath, and look more closely at François. "You think Mother does not love me, then?"

"Not as I do. Not as she ought. Not as she loves Anjou." There is bitterness in this pronouncement, but even more noticeable is the certitude.

Is this what being left so long alone at Amboise did to my brother: made him sure he is unloved? If so, is that horrible or fortunate? I waver between believing Her Majesty indifferent to me, and grasping at gestures which suggest she might care. My striving to secure her approval and her love is constant, and can be crushing. Would believing—truly believing—I was unloved free me? No. It would destroy me. I know that by the nausea that wells at the thought of being nothing to Mother, and by the need I feel to prove to François he is in error.

"Mother loves all her children."

"Convince yourself of that if you wish," he replies. "But I refuse to be duped. She does not love me and I do not care." He does not care, but his voice shakes. "The day will come when she will be sorry for thinking so little of me. When she will not be able to look over me or past me. When she will need me and wish that I needed her."

I think of my brother as a boy. After all, he is just on the cusp of fourteen. But in this declaration—in his clear, angry eyes and fervent expression of ambition—I glimpse the man in him. Like Charles, there is something frightening in that man. This is knowledge worth having. It also makes me vaguely sad. It seems that, among my brothers, Anjou alone has been spared a dark side. I can see that prince in my mind's eye as he was at Saumur, striding about, all muscle, grace, and authority, showing His Majesty the troops. Is it any wonder Mother loves Henri best? He has earned that place by never disappointing. Can I say the same? Not if I am being honest. Anjou once called me his equal. I must try harder to make it so.

François is stretched out, head resting in my lap, eyes closed when it happens. Pausing to turn a page in the book I am reading aloud, I glance in the direction of the window just as a bird flies into it with a sickening thud—a black bird. My body starts involuntarily.

"What is it?" my brother asks, eyes still closed.

"A bird struck the glass and fell away. I fear it is dead."

"There are birds enough to fill the March sky without that one."

François is right. Why should the death of a bird leave me feeling uneasy?

I begin reading again, but my apprehension lingers. More than lingers:

it grows. The door swings open. Charlotte stands on the threshold, her face blanched of color.

"The Queen has collapsed!"

François sits up, catching the book with his cheekbone and knocking it from my hands. It lands with a thud very like the black bird made.

Dear God, was that the sound Mother made as well when she collapsed?

Clutching his face, François asks, "What happened?"

"I do not know. I do not know," Charlotte replies in panic. "She was with the King and his advisors. They carried her to her rooms." My friend's hands twist in her skirts. "I saw them. The Queen was insensate and hung in their arms as one . . ." She stops, covering her mouth with both hands.

As we did as children, François and I go together. Arriving outside Mother's apartment at a run, we find a crowd. I push my way through until I am at the door. Marie is there, eyes filled with worry. Embracing me, she says, "Charles and Castelan are with her."

Turning the handle, I push. The door opens slightly, then comes to rest against the sturdy body of a royal guardsman. He turns prepared to upbraid whoever has tried to make entry. But at the sight of François and me, he steps back, allowing us to pass.

Mother's physician is beside her bed. Charles stands at the foot with several others. The King acknowledges us by look but says nothing. Straightening up, Castelan comes to join him. "It is the strain of the war," he murmurs. "Her Majesty would not rest after the death of the Queen of Spain, though I more than once urged rest upon her. She would not believe the war could proceed without her. Now nature does for her what she would not do for herself: puts her to bed."

"I blame the Duke of Florence," Charles says angrily. "Word came yesterday he was delaying the loan he promised."

I glance at Mother, her eyes closed, her face white, her stillness a stark contrast to the fury that animated her when I saw her last. And I know I am to blame. Ought I to tell Castelan of this morning? Of how Mother's anger was disrupted by the sudden swaying? I find I cannot, so instead I say, "I fear, Your Majesty, that the letter from your ambassador in Madrid also upset her."

The men around me look perplexed. "What letter?" Charles asks.

So Mother kept the news of my rejection to herself.

"Howsoever Her Majesty came to be reduced to such a state"—Charles' chancellor clearly feels a discussion of diplomatic points can wait—"the question must be asked." He pauses. We all know what question. It trembles in the air as if it were a living thing. But it seems only he has the courage to speak it aloud, so we wait for him to continue. "Is there reason to fear for Her Majesty's life?"

"It is too early to say. I will know better when she is again conscious."

"Is it certain she will regain consciousness?" the chancellor persists.

"Enough!" Charles commands. "Such pessimism has no place at Her Majesty's bedside. Out!" The gentlemen retreat, leaving only Castelan.

Charles' moment of regal self-possession fades. He seems to shrink as he creeps along the side of the bed. By the time he kneels beside it, he looks more like a boy of eight than a man of eighteen.

"Mother . . ." The voice so stern a moment ago is a whisper, choked by tears. "You must not leave me. I cannot rule alone."

"I could."

Does François really mutter this beneath his breath?

Moving to Castelan's side, I repeat de Morvilliers' question, "Will she wake up?"

"I am of the opinion she will. Other than being as one asleep who cannot be roused, I detect no symptom of illness. It is my belief that once her body is fully rested, she will rejoin us."

"I will be here when she opens her eyes," I say.

The King looks up. "As will I."

"No, Charles," I say gently, "you must manage your kingdom and direct your commanders in the field. That is the duty of a king. Waiting and watching are my duties as a daughter."

He nods. "As I know you will do your duty with care, I cannot stint in mine." Rising, he approaches me with eyes burning. "Do not leave her. You are my eyes and ears in her sick chamber."

François brings me my book and my embroidery. I send for Henriette and Charlotte. They are glad to come. After acquainting them with the Queen's condition, I turn to the subject most on my mind.

"The crown of Spain will not be mine." I can feel my eyes prick as I say it.

"That is a great shame." Henriette shakes her head.

"I hope it is not more. I hope Her Majesty's disappointment over the matter is not what felled her."

"Do not be absurd. Her Majesty is made of stronger stuff. She has laid a husband and a son in the grave. Left with a boy king, she managed to keep him on the throne in a time of war. If the King of Spain has put her in this bed, it is not by his failure to marry you."

I pray Henriette is right. But I do not feel relieved.

Nor, apparently, do I look it. For Charlotte says, "I know it is selfish of me, but I am glad you do not go to Spain. I would have the three of us together awhile longer."

"I can tell you someone else who will be cheered by the Spanish king's decision," Henriette adds. "The Duc de Guise would rather have you on French soil, and he has made that quite clear."

"To whom?" I did not see the Duc when we were in Saumur, as he was quartered at Chinon.

Henriette winks. "I will not say. But I trust my source. The Duc does not like the idea of your marrying."

A sudden movement from the bed keeps me from replying. Mother has half raised herself. Her eyes are open but they do not seem to apprehend us.

Jumping to my feet, I say, "Madame! We thought you left us!"

"I did. I have been to Châteauneuf to see your brother." She looks about wildly as if searching for something recognizable.

"You are at Metz, Madame. You have been for weeks."

Rather than calming her, my pronouncement agitates her further. "Foolish girl, I have been with Henri."

I lay a hand on her shoulder. She burns; I can feel as much through her chemise. "Henriette, find Castelan. Tell him the Queen is awake and feverish."

Charlotte crosses herself.

Turning my attention back to Mother, I gently ease her onto her pillow. "Rest. When you next wake, Henri will be here."

A lie but it serves its purpose. Murmuring my brother's name, she closes her eyes. I wonder, has word been sent to Anjou? Surely it must have been.

Castelan seems to think it a good thing that Mother spoke, no matter how nonsensically. He bleeds her for the fever, which he assures me is neither high nor serious.

As the light fades Mother begins to thrash. Her eyes open, again bright but seemingly unseeing. Touching her, I am sure that her fever worsens. Shouting for a servant, I send again for the physician.

You said she would not die. I long to fling the words at Castelan when he arrives. He does not look sanguine as he did hours ago. Watching him bleed Her Majesty, I have the sudden urge to go out and see if I can find the body of the bird that struck my window. Perhaps, if I cannot, I can believe the creature was only stunned and, having awakened, flew away. But I will not leave Mother, and besides, what chance would I have of finding a black bird in the dark?

"If Your Highness wishes to retire," Castelan says, "I will watch over Her Majesty."

I cannot be persuaded to leave. I am roused from a fitful sleep in my chair by Mother's voice.

"Alexander, my Alexander," she croons. "I knew it would be so." The words are perfectly clear but I do not understand them. Opening my eyes, I see a bleary-eyed Castelan standing at Mother's bed. She is sitting up, looking into the darkness of the room.

"Your Majesty, you have a fever; you must rest," the physician says.

"Yes, the battle is over. I can rest. But not before I see my Henri—"

I am not certain if she means my father or my brother.

"—see the Prince's head."

A great wave of fear rolls over me. Has something happened to Anjou?

Castelan moves to where he has arranged the items of his profession. Quickly he mixes a draught while Mother continues to stare at nothing, a smile on her face.

"This will calm her," the physician says. Mother is perfectly calm, her expression nearly pacific. But I know what he means—the draught will make her sleep, and that will surely relieve his obvious discomfort. Will it lessen mine? I wish it were so easy. Even after Mother sips the liquid and closes her eyes, I feel frantic. I am sure Mother has seen something. Not in her room but in her mind's eye. It could be merely a memory. Or it could be a premonition. She is known for them. Is my brother Henri safe? Who has lost a head?

※ ※ ※

"Henri! Oh, Henri!" I know it is unseemly, but I do not care: the instant my brother is off his horse, I throw my arms around him, heedless of the gentlemen who accompany him and of the grooms rushing forward. Standing on my tiptoes, I kiss his cheeks again and again. I have known since yesterday, when Monsieur de Losses arrived, that my brother was safe. But knowing and seeing are two very different things.

Henri laughs, waving his companions on and picking me up from the ground. "What is this? You like me better when I win battles, eh?"

And Henri did win. Monsieur de Losses brought that news as well—how, at a place called Jarnac, Anjou and Marshal de Tavannes surprised the Huguenots; how the Huguenots were defeated; how Condé was killed. Mother, awakened from a sleep far less troubled than the night before, had no patience for the tale, merely declaring, "Did I not know of this victory yesterday?" But I listened to every word.

"I love you always!" I declare.

"I know, I know." He embraces me again. "What were those lines Ronsard wrote for you?"

I finger the buttons on the front of his doublet. " 'My sweet affection, my garden-pink and rose, thou canst take all my flock away, and of myself dispose.' " The words, last delivered in performance at the army's camp, seem entirely different spoken softly looking up into my brother's face.

There is something odd about the moment, but it passes as Henri releases me and asks, "Where is Mother?"

"Sick. Did Charles not tell you?"

A flash of anger moves across Anjou's face. "He did not."

"Perhaps his message did not reach you. You were on the move."

"Perhaps." He does not look appeased. "Is she very ill?"

"She had a fever but it is gone. Yet she is very weak. She cannot hold a pen to write—she tried this morning."

"She tried to write? Then her mind is clear."

"Yes, and her opinions as strong as ever."

"Take me to her."

Charles is beside Mother as we enter. At the sight of Anjou, Her Majesty's face is transfigured.

"My Alexander!" she cries, extending trembling hands.

They are the same words she said the night of her fever. This is more than coincidence! I believe that she did see the victory as she insisted to Losses last evening.

Anjou moves forward, drawing me along. After taking Mother's hands and kissing each, he turns to Charles and says, "Your Majesty, we have crushed your enemies."

Charles looks less than enthusiastic.

"I would have brought you Condé's head, but the whole of that gentleman's remains are being paraded around Jarnac, tied to the back of an ass while your loyal Catholic subjects cheer."

"Is it true Condé surrendered before he was killed?" Charles asks.

I had not heard this.

"A nicety." Henri does not flinch. "I assumed you wanted him dead."

"I did." The admission sounds grudging. "But I wonder: If you are captured, will you consider such honorable traditions niceties?"

"I will not be captured."

The two regard each other with animosity, then Anjou turns back to Mother.

"Are *you* pleased with me, Madame?"

Tears well in Mother's eyes. "You know that I am. All of France will be when news of the victory spreads. Your brother is gratified as well, just as he would be by the success of any of his commanders." She looks meaningfully at Charles. "Anjou rode from the field of battle to offer you his victory. Will you not extend to him your approbation?"

Charles rises. "We are pleased with your victory at Jarnac."

Anjou bows.

As he is straightening, Charles adds, "But it would have been better still had you not allowed Coligny to escape with a large part of the Huguenot forces."

This is another fact of which I was unaware.

Anjou attempts to look uncaring, but one corner of his mouth twitches.

"Your brother will pursue Coligny when he leaves us," Mother says.

Charles tilts his head. "Perhaps I will go after the admiral myself. Now the fighting has begun in earnest, I would not mind some field experience. I had no desire to live in a tent all winter, but spring in the saddle—yes, I believe that would suit."

Anjou darts a glance at Mother. She offers him a look of warning in return.

Neither is lost upon Charles. He smiles. "I leave you, Madame, to be entertained by our brother's stories of the fray. I myself will await Marshal Tavannes' account. He is the more senior military man."

Anjou's face is livid. As the door closes behind the King, Mother's voice is soft. "Calmly, calmly."

Henri is not soothed. "I would rather die cruelly and be tied to an ass myself than cede my command to my brother," he says with vehemence.

"There is no question of that," Mother replies. She closes her eyes. "I wish you and Charles would not provoke each other so. It has been thus since you were but babes."

I find Mother's wish odd. Whatever rivalry there is between my beloved brothers, she planted its seeds.

Anjou's face is all concern. "You are ill and we have tired you."

"I am not too tired to hear all you have to tell of the battle."

"Soon."

I am surprised to hear my brother deferring. There is nothing he loves better than to entertain Mother; nothing he enjoys more than basking in her admiration.

"I am hungry, and dirty," he says. "You know that I do not like to be dirty."

Mother smiles without opening her eyes. "Go and make yourself as handsome as you are brave. I will wait."

"Sleep. When you next open your eyes, I will be beside you."

Anjou motions for me and together we creep from the room. We are not two steps outside before his temper flares. "Do you see? Do you see how His Majesty treats me?"

"Charles is jealous." I can understand how Charles feels, so surely Henri should be able to. "The King is not being styled the next Alexander. He will not be the talk of the Court as the gallant commander who led royal troops to a glorious victory."

"Will I be so celebrated? Or will he see that Tavannes gets the credit?"

"Mother would never allow that."

"Not if she were in full health . . ." He pauses and his face falls. "She looked so weak. Are you certain Castelan said we need not worry?"

"I am. I promise you I am with her constantly, trying to do every little thing for her so that she will not exert herself. The last two nights I slept beside her bed."

"Charles is there a great deal too, is he not? Whispering to her." His brow furrows.

"Is it not natural he should care for her as you and I do?"

"Natural or not, it gives him opportunity to discredit me. While I am away fighting, he has hour after hour to work against me with Mother."

"*C'est absolument ridicule!* You always have Mother's heart, even if Charles has her ear. Can you believe her devotion to you will be shaken?"

"No, because I will not allow that. Come, I have a proposition that will be of advantage to us both."

Henri's apartment is crowded. Men who rode in with him mingle with those who, hearing he has arrived, have come to share his wine and hear his stories. Several embrace him. Released from their arms, Henri puts up his hands. "Gentlemen, my time in Metz is short but not too brief for a mighty revel this evening. In the meantime I would be at Her Majesty's bedside. Therefore, I must make myself presentable. Out, out." My brother's *valet de chambre* moves forward to help him but Henri says, "You too."

When we are alone he says, "You do not mind playing the *valet,* do you? I know you have no experience undressing a man, but it is not hard." He unbuttons his doublet and removes it. I hold out my hands. It smells of him. A scent as familiar to me as my own, and one I have missed.

"Here is the crux of the matter. Among our siblings, I trust you alone. You are my own Princess, as faithful to me as man can ask woman to be."

I feel my cheeks warming at his praise, and turn to lay aside the doublet and pour water into his basin that I might hide my blush. Shirtless, he comes forward to use the basin.

"You see how it is?" He offers a blinding smile. "You anticipate me. I can rely on you." He begins to wash, the muscles in his arms and chest showing with every motion. Battle, it seems, has further developed his fine, sportsman's figure. "Will you assist me?"

"Only tell me how."

"Be my eyes, my ears, and my voice. Send me news and seek ever to influence the Queen so that I retain my present fortune."

I watch him sit down and remove his boots. While his eyes are thus turned, I find the courage to raise an embarrassing point. "I will write to you every day, but as for influencing the Queen, you credit me with a power I do not have. Why should Her Majesty listen to me?"

Looking up, he replies, "She will listen because I will tell her to do so. I will point out that you are no child but a woman grown—a woman of sense and as devoted to me as she is. I will advise her that I hold your opinions in highest esteem and weigh them heavily."

"Do you?"

"Of course."

"Oh, Henri . . ." That he should value me so moves me.

"Will you pledge yourself to be my partisan? Will you make certain that I am in our mother's thoughts and favor though I be leagues away?"

"It will be my honor to serve you so."

"Good. And I urge you to set aside your timidity and speak to Mother as you do to me."

"I will try."

"You will not find it hard, I assure you, once you apprehend that she will listen graciously. Mother has the ability to make one feel like the very center of the world."

I doubt I will ever feel her regard to that extent, but do not say so, merely turning while Henri removes his trunk hose and puts on new ones. I fetch him a clean shirt, and as I hand it to him he says, "Such service shall not be without reward."

"Your regard is enough."

"But you will have more. As you have promised to safeguard my fortunes, I pledge to raise yours. Be assured that, as you are the person in the world whom I love most, you will always be a partaker of my advancement."

He begins to button his fresh doublet. I push his hands away playfully. "Be still and let me do that. After all, I am the *valet* here."

CHAPTER 9

May 1569—Metz, France

Today I am sixteen—sixteen, beautiful, and happy; utterly, blissfully happy. It is all as Anjou said it would be. Shortly after he rode away in March—gone to chase Coligny—Mother called me to her and said, "Your brother has related the conversation you and he had and how he wishes me to see you through his eyes. By his account you are a woman worthy of his trust and mine. And so you shall be treated. It will be a great comfort for me to converse with you as I would with him while he is away."

How those words changed my life! All that was shrouded in mystery before—the business of the King's council, Mother's hopes for her sons and her fears for them, her dealings with diplomats from every land—is suddenly laid bare before me. I pass hours in Her Majesty's company, listening and learning.

Generally, I am with Mother from the moment she awakes, but I took special care in dressing today, so by the time I slip into the room, her breakfast tray is being removed.

"Margot!" she says, looking at me with bright eyes. "Come sit beside me. I have been waiting for you."

Mother's ladies know of my elevation in importance, so a place is quickly made for me. Reaching beneath her pillow, Her Majesty draws out something small, wound in velvet. "I did not like to give you this until things were certain, but I heard yesterday that Fourquevaux was received with grace by the King of Spain." She hands me the packet. *"Joyeux anniversaire."*

Charlotte and the Baronne de Retz, who sit on either side of me, press in as I begin to unwind the velvet. A small, gold, heavily engraved oval is left in my hand. A necklace? No, the back of a miniature portrait. I turn it over in my palm. A young man gazes out with piercing eyes. He is clad in full armor of the finest sort.

"Il est beau!" Charlotte exclaims.

He *is* strikingly handsome—or he would be if he did not have hair as red as flame.

Carefully I lean forward to read the inscription: *Sebastianus I Lusitanor Rex*. "The King of Portugal?"

"Yes." Mother smiles. "Portugal is not Spain, but it is a crown worth having. And it comes with a handsome groom near your own age."

Can she mean . . . She must!

"Madame, I am delighted!"

"Ladies," she says, "you may congratulate the Duchesse de Valois."

I rise and the women surrounding me take turns offering embraces.

"And, ladies," Mother continues, "you may gossip about this match as much as you like. King Philip will find it hard to disavow arrangements that are spoken of widely."

"Why need the King of Spain be involved?" I ask. "The King of Portugal is a grown man and sovereign in his own right. Surely he can select his own bride."

Once such a question might have gone unanswered, but no more. "All young monarchs have advisors," Mother replies. "Dom Sébastien's uncle, the Spanish king, takes a keen interest in him. So, I understand, do a pair of Theatine monks who Dom Sébastien's grandfather, King John, charged with his upbringing. But as I have reason to believe that His Holiness Pope Pius will promote the match, I do not believe any of these men will be a serious impediment."

Fingering the miniature, I look again into Dom Sébastien's eyes, imagine calling him "husband," and smile. "Your Majesty thinks of everything," I say. I wish I might say more—might tell Mother that her care, her efforts to secure my future, constitute a birthday offering that moves me beyond any object she might have gifted me. But in front of so many—never. Leaning in, I kiss her on both cheeks.

Mother is flustered by this display. Perhaps I am her daughter in my reticence as much as in any other way.

"Go along. Go and show off your portrait to the Duchesse de Nevers."

I do not wait to be urged twice: grabbing Charlotte's hand, I nearly drag her from the room. Our friend is never an early riser unless called upon by duty, so she is not difficult to locate. She is in her room, though not in her chemise as I thought she would be when—upon hearing our knock—she called out, "A moment." No, she is fully dressed and sitting, slightly flushed, quite at her ease.

"Ah, this is fortuitous. I have a gift for you!" she says as soon as she sees me.

"And I have news."

"Gossip or news?"

"Both," Charlotte teases. "Margot has news that will soon be *the* great gossip of the Court."

"Well, then, she must go first."

"His Majesty negotiates my marriage to the King of Portugal."

"He does?" The voice is male, and familiar. Without warning, the Duc de Guise steps out of the adjoining cabinet.

"My gift," Henriette says, as if no other explanation were needed for the sudden appearance of a gentleman I have not seen in more than half a year. I freeze, the miniature portrait of Dom Sébastien clutched in my hand. The Duc is thinner than when I saw him last. And taller, if that is possible. I thought him a man when he held me in his arms at Paris, and perhaps he was, but he is somehow more so now.

"Perhaps, Your Grace, our surprise is not entirely welcome." The voice is serious. The eyes meet mine only for an instant, then pull away.

"Say something," Charlotte whispers, nudging me.

"Your Grace"—*Is it odd that after so many months I do not use or even think of him by his Christian name?*—"please do not mistake astonishment for displeasure. I simply cannot account for seeing you are here when I thought you with His Majesty's army."

"I brought a message to the King."

"It must be a very important dispatch if they send a duc."

"Oh, for heaven's sake!" Henriette rises and, moving forward, plucks Dom Sébastien's likeness from me. "He *sought* the errand."

I glance back to the Duc. It must be true, for he colors. I feel rather than see Henriette retreating, taking Charlotte with her. My emotions are in a jumble. Last autumn when he left I thought of Guise so often. But lately, I realize, my mind has seldom moved in his direction. Is this because I have had so much to think about as Her Majesty's confidante? Or is it because I no longer care for him?

His Grace takes a step forward and I catch my breath. *No, it is not the latter, for that single step closer has made my heart race.*

He looks me straight in the eye. "Perhaps I should have stayed at Cognac."

"I would rather have you here."

"Would you?" He takes another step.

"Yes."

"What need can you have for me if you are to marry the King of Portugal?"

"It is not certain. I only just learned that His Majesty pursues the match."

"He is eager for you to have a foreign husband."

"He is eager for me to wed a king," I reply, vaguely irritated. Charles loves me and wants what is best for me. So does Mother. Why should the Duc make it sound as if they wish to be rid of me?

"I would rather you did not."

"Henriette told me you did not wish me to marry the King of Spain. How did she know that?"

"I told her."

"You write to her?"

"Are you jealous?"

"Of course not." I do not believe I sound convincing.

"You have no reason. It is I who have rivals, not you. I have been gone seven months and already you are offered to two kings."

I do not wish to speak further about Dom Sébastien or my marriage; the topic is making me increasingly uncomfortable. As is the Duc's proximity. I wish things were as before he marched away—that he would simply take me in his arms and kiss me. Yet he stands without so much as raising a hand to touch me.

I try to turn the subject. "You have come from Cognac. How goes the siege?"

"You wish to talk of the war?" He smiles wryly. "Fine. We will raise the siege. We make no progress, and so will go instead to intercept the Duc de Zweibrücken's German soldiers before they can reach the main Huguenot force." He shakes his head. "Satisfied?"

"No."

"Nor am I. I left the fighting to other men and rode halfway across France so that I could see you"—he pauses—"touch you."

"Why do you not?" I whisper, but he hears me. His hand rises and caresses my cheek. His skin is rough. I like that.

"Because in the first moments I thought we were strangers again."

"I do not believe we will ever be strangers, Sir."

"What, then?"

I do not answer because I do not know.

"I would devote myself entirely to you," he says. "While I have been away, I have seen many gentlemen do things that will require confession. I did none."

My heart leaps. "Whatever sins I have confessed during these long months, Sir, the type you allude to are not among them. I may have failed in my duty as a daughter, a sister, and a Christian, but my lips have trespassed with no other."

He takes me in his arms at last. "If I considered our embraces sin," he says solemnly, "I would abstain from them even as they are my greatest desire. But I know that my feelings for you are honorable, and that my desire to preserve your reputation unbesmirched is stronger even than my baser longings." He lowers his lips to mine. The kiss is just as I remembered: utterly, overwhelmingly wonderful. When our lips part, he looks down into my face with eyes that no longer show doubt. "I leave tomorrow."

"No!" Having been reminded of everything I feel for him, it seems cruel that he will be gone again so soon.

"It is my duty and it presses upon me, for I have not yet sufficiently distinguished myself."

"Were you not commander of the royal scouts before Jarnac? That battle was won through surprise, doubtless permitted by good scouting."

He smiles. "It pleases me to hear you argue my valor. Knowing that you follow what I do makes me eager to perform feats worthy of your admiration. Your brother has Condé to his credit, and your mother Andelot. Shall I kill the latter's brother for you before I see you next?"

That he would kill for me is thrilling. But Coligny will not be an easy man to slay: he is a seasoned fighter. I want a brave lover but also a living one. "I understand your need to avenge your father. But pray remember that, even as that gentleman looks down upon you from heaven, he would not want you to lose your own life in doing so. So kill but do not be killed."

"I will do my best. You must make me a promise in return. Try not to be married when next we meet."

"That is an easy promise to make, for I will see you at dinner."

"Do not make light, Marguerite." There is a sudden sharp pleasure in hearing my name from his lips again. "Tell me that I have your heart and that you will not be too eager to give your hand to a foreign prince."

"You have my heart."

He kisses me again, gently. "I must go and change. I told the King I would be at his disposal."

"But I will see you later."

"Of course. We shall stroll arm and arm, or dance, properly chaperoned, and all will think 'There goes a handsome pair.' "

"Will I see you again like *this*?" I know the question is immodest, but the feel of his arms about my waist is so good.

"In this very room. I have the Duchesse de Nevers' word."

Mother looks up from her desk. The fact that she is strong enough to sit for hours—opening correspondence, replying, receiving advisors and diplomats—seems miraculous. Soon she will be well enough to travel and we will go to see Anjou! Mother and I both long to see him. And I hope that this time I will find the Duc de Guise at the same camp.

"The Portuguese ambassador at Madrid tells Fourquevaux he only awaits instructions from Lisbon to conclude your match."

"Oh, I am so pleased." I work to match my expression to the sentiment, even if the contents of my heart are not in accord. The Duc's visit—so brief—changed much. The clandestine correspondence that Henriette has facilitated between us since altered things even more. For while an embrace may permit the confusion of lust and love, surely words alone do not. Henri's notes are infused with such nobility and piety and convey such a depth of feeling that they cause me to admire him more with every line. This must be love—true, holy love. It is a feeling so precious that I have not spoken of it even to my friends. Let them think I still play a courtier's game. I cannot bear for them to laugh at me as Henriette did the first time I proclaimed myself in love with His Grace. Besides, Henriette might cease to help me if she knew I am in such earnest.

"Perhaps you will be a bride even before your brother Charles takes one." Mother is keen to have Charles wed the Emperor's eldest daughter, Anna.

Try not to be married when next we meet. The words sound so clearly inside my head that Guise might be in the room.

"You think negotiations will conclude so quickly?"

"I pray so."

Who will God listen to, I wonder, if I pray the opposite?

There is a commotion just beyond the door. Mother and I both hear it. "Do not be alarmed," she says. "My guard is outside." But I notice she surreptitiously unsheathes the dagger she keeps on her worktable. I rise just as the door bursts open. My brother Henri stamps in—Henri, who we last heard was on the move below the Nièvre river. He is scowling. I am struck dumb by both his unexpected appearance and his expression. Mother too seems at a loss for words. Anjou is not.

"I have disbanded the army."

"I pray," Mother says, eyes wary, "that you have done so because you have won such a victory that it is no longer needed. But if so, why do you not greet us with smiles?"

"Your prayers, Madame, have not been efficacious as of late. Did you not pray that Zweibrücken's men would never meet those of Coligny? Yet they did. Well, now those forces have met mine at La Roche-l'Abeille and I did not emerge the winner." He kicks the nearest chair so hard that it topples over.

"Were many lost?"

"Most of two regiments of foot soldiers, including the men sent by His Holiness. They dress better than they fight, the Italians. Philippe Strozzi was taken captive and I ransomed him, though given what a miserable commander he was, I ought to have left that cost to the Pope. The Duc de Guise—"

"Was the Duc hurt?" I do not realize I've spoken until Anjou looks at me with mouth agape.

"No. I should have been glad if he had been, vainglorious idiot! His disregard of my orders was the cause of my embarrassment. Wherever he has gone, I pray I do not see him. Should he cross my path, I have a mind to thrash him or worse."

"If the Duc is to blame," I say, seeking to soothe Henri but not willing to unequivocally admit my love's fault, "then surely he will be branded with it. You will not be held culpable for the defeat."

"Sister, I adore you, but you know very little of war if you believe that. I am lieutenant general; all that goes ill is laid at my feet. If by no one else, then by our dear brother." He looks pointedly at Mother.

Moving forward, I reach up and push back the hair at his temple. "You must know that we never believe anything ill that is said of you, not even by Charles."

He puts an arm around me and pulls me against him, burying his face in my hair.

Raising his head once more, he addresses Mother. "Do not worry, Madame, I did not lose more than the King could afford. But I was so disgusted with those who remained and felt so little chance of success that I decided to let the men wander away to their homes. Tavannes was of the opinion that this might be the best way to pull apart Coligny's army. For if they do not have us to face across a field, they may well disband and give us time to think."

"And if they do not?"

"Then I will be back in the saddle and headed south posthaste. But for now I am going to my rooms to get drunk." He releases me.

"I will walk with you." Mother rises.

I am left behind, but I do not begrudge Mother time with Henri. I find myself drawn to Her Majesty's desk, wishing to see for myself the words of our ambassador in Madrid—hoping that Mother is more optimistic about the negotiations than he. But Fourquevaux appears to believe Dom Sébastien will accept my hand. I am about to lay the pages down when a passage catches my eye: "I would be deficient in my duty if I did not report that I have heard, and from more than one source, that Dom Sébastien may be of little use in fathering children. So while an alliance between Portugal and France may be effected by the marriage, it may well last only as long the Princess and her husband survive."

Of little use in fathering children. I am not certain what that means, but it troubles me. I long to have children, and more than this, since I first kissed Guise, I have had undeniable urges to act in a manner that produces children.

❀   ❀   ❀

"He has a perfect horror of women—that is what the nuncio's secretary says." Henriette keeps her voice low, though we are in my rooms. The Louvre is a place where anything one would keep confidential should be spoken softly.

"I cannot believe Mother would seek to wed me to a gentleman who prefers—"

"Boys?" Henriette offers.

"*I* cannot believe you seduced a priest!" Charlotte says.

"Why not?" Henriette replies. "I like novelty. And as His Holiness has been heavily involved in the negotiations for Margot's marriage, I felt certain the nuncio's secretary would be abreast of matters." Turning to me she adds, "As for Dom Sébastien's preferences, it is not entirely clear that he likes men any better than women when it comes to acts of love. What is clear is that he has been taught by the monks who have him in their thrall that every woman is unclean and the origin of sin. To such a man boys may be the lesser of two evils." Refreshing my glass, Charlotte's, and her own, she says, "Poor thing."

I am not entirely sure who is the object of her pity, but I am feeling very sorry for myself at the moment.

"Thank heavens not every man feels as he does," Her Grace continues, raising her glass. "Let us drink to men with a taste for women. Men we can enjoy and use to our own ends."

What about love?

Charlotte sips, then smiles sweetly at me and says, "Men like the Duc de Guise, defender of Poitiers."

My brother was not at Metz long when word came that the Huguenot army had gathered outside of Poitiers. A siege was anticipated. Henri rode off to reassemble the army. We returned to Paris, Mother being well enough to travel at last. And while we waited for word that Henri had reached Poitiers, other reports began to arrive—telling of the brave actions of the Comte de Lude and his garrison, and revealing that my beloved Duc and his brother Mayenne were within Poitiers, fighting to defend her. The Duc's eagerness to build a soldier's reputation may be gratified at last. If stories from that city continue to be so favorable to him, Poitiers will be his making.

I raise my glass, happy to acknowledge His Grace.

"When word arrived in the capital yesterday of the daring party Guise led to destroy the bridge over the Clain, my sister ordered a Mass to thank God for his safety and success," Henriette says.

Alas, my happiness in the Duc's achievements is not perfect. I am not alone in my admiration of him. Nearly every lady at Court swoons over each arriving dispatch. Besides ordering masses, the Princesse de Porcien writes bad verse in the Duc's honor. I have seen it.

Then there is my brother's equally unsettling reaction. From the moment Anjou got word of the Duc's doings, his letters to Mother have been filed with vituperative tirades against Guise. Anjou seems to believe everything that is done by the Duc is done to make him look less.

I sigh. "I would rather marry Guise than the King of Portugal."

Henriette and Charlotte are immediately serious. "You had better not say that to anyone else—not even in jest," the Duchesse says.

"I know. But there must be some way to defeat this match. I do not wish to be married to a man who will hate the sight of me. I will be unable to sway such a man, and if I am to be a queen I long for influence."

Both ladies nod.

"The Monsignor mentioned that Dom Sébastien's mother wishes him married to an Austrian archduchesse," Henriette says. "So perhaps, if you can delay the match, fate will intervene."

"I have very little faith in fate, at least where it comes to it obliging me."

Henriette rolls her eyes. "Yes, your life is quite blighted. You have two gallant ducs twisted about your little finger—one of them royal. You are an extraordinary beauty. You possess a pair of friends as loyal as can be found anywhere and you have lately become exceedingly close to Her Majesty. Obviously fate and fortune hold you in low esteem." Dropping her mocking expression she continues, "But, as you are in your mother's favor, perhaps you may depend on your influence rather than fate, and speak with her about the Portuguese?"

"I will see how Poitiers goes. If Anjou has a victory, perhaps I will plead my case with him. For now I am tired of thinking of the matter. The sun at last shows itself. Let us go enjoy it in the gardens."

"Not before I finish my wine," Henriette says. She picks up the half-full glass and drains it.

My glass is on its way to my lips in imitation when Mother sweeps in, beaming.

"Anjou sends word. Coligny's army has been reduced by disease and is in the direst condition. He expects victory at Poitiers any day and wishes, before the need to pursue those Protestants who flee is upon him, to hold counsel with the King and his advisors. We leave immediately!"

We. I am not being left behind!

We receive word as we ride that my brother, not wishing to tax Mother's health, has come north as far as Plessis-les-Tours and waits for us there. By the time we see that comfortable old château on the horizon, all in our party are exhausted by the rapidity of our travel. Anjou runs from the building like a young boy to meet us—lifting Mother from her saddle and embracing her with vigor. I am the next to receive a welcome, and as I am clutched in his arms, a figure emerges from beneath an arch into the sunlight. It is Guise! Have the two of them made amends?

Charles comes forward to greet Anjou. While they pretend to be happy to see each other, I gaze at my Duc where he stands with a group of other officers. Even among such company—the flower of French manhood—he stands out, and not only on account of his height. There is something about the way he stands, grave, attentive, and yet entirely at ease, that draws the eye.

"Who are you looking for?" Henri's voice surprises me.

I turn to him, smiling. "No one. I am only eager to be inside and take some refreshment."

Anjou offers me one arm and Mother the other, drawing us past the assembled noblemen. As he does, Guise smiles—just that, nothing more, but the curve of his lips fills me with a rush of feeling that must show on my face, for the Duc's smile grows. In the moment before we are past the gentlemen, I realize that Guise is not the only one to notice my reaction. The Seigneur du Guast peers at me thoughtfully.

Henri escorts us to Mother's rooms. She brought so few ladies that I have no chance of sneaking away. Not that I would abandon my duty to Her Majesty. Henriette did not make the trip, but as Charlotte and I carry away some items of the Queen's clothing I whisper, "I must see him." She knows whom I mean.

We dine in the King's apartment. Henri is in the highest of humors. Charles tries on several occasions to bring up plans for the conclusion of the siege and the war beyond it, but each time Anjou says, "Tomorrow. Tomorrow I shall lay all before you until you and your advisors can see it as clearly as Tavannes and I do." And if turning His Majesty's questions aside in such a manner is unseemly, who will upbraid Anjou? Certainly not Mother. She looks at Henri with such worship-filled eyes that, even without being thwarted, Charles would doubtless have fallen into the sulking expression he soon wears.

Mother is chary enough to remember she is only recently over a long illness. As we push back from the table, satiated, she says, "I will retire."

"Shall I go along with you and lie at the foot of your bed?" Henri asks.

"If your men can spare you."

"They shall be made to, and any who complain of it will feel my anger. But I expect no protests, for all my friends know that you are the center of my world."

Does Charles snort?

"Margot, come along and undress me."

"Shall I come too so that you have all your children?" Charles asks. Then, without waiting for a reply: "I thought not. I have a headache, in any event. As Marie is not with us, you can at least leave me Margot to massage my temples."

"Why does everyone like him better?" Charles asks, flopping into a chair once we are alone.

"They do not."

"You do."

"I love all my brothers." Moving behind him, I place my fingers on his temples. Reaching up, he pushes my hands away.

"Get out."

"But I thought—"

"What? You thought we were companions and confidantes? So did I. In you I thought I had a true heart and keeper of secrets. But you are Anjou's creature."

Moving around in front of him, I crouch down and place my hand on his knee. "Charles, please do not do this."

He puts a hand over mine. "I cannot blame you. I may be king but it is Anjou who has elevated you. Draw what conclusions you like from that, and then censure me for my anger if you dare."

"I do not fault you. It is not my place to judge you. You are my king, and a beloved brother. I only remark that letting Anjou nettle you tires you and emboldens him."

"Could he be more bold?"

I fear the answer is yes. Henri has more confidence than anyone I know. Yet position he does not have. "Audaciousness cannot make him king," I tell Charles. "You look more powerful when you resist the urge to swipe at him."

"It is instinct, bred into my bone. The stallion nips at the fly, does he not? Well, though our brother bites me, I will not let him have my crown. You may tell him that . . . and Mother too." He lifts his hand from mine. "Go."

Standing outside my brother's apartment, I feel sad and tired. Slowly, I walk in the direction of my chamber. I do not notice Charlotte until she says my name.

"There you are! My goodness, you are very stupid this evening, wandering in a daze when you might be using your liberty to better advantage."

I blink at her.

"Did you not tell me you wanted to see him?"

All my *ennui* dissipates. "Yes!"

"Come, then. Her Majesty told me you were with the King. She will not be looking for you. In case anyone else should, Gillone will say you have retired."

"Where are we going?" I ask as she pulls me down a narrow set of stairs.

"Into the dusk, where things that ought not to be seen are less likely to be."

We emerge into what must be the kitchen gardens. I smell rosemary as our skirts brush the plants along the narrow path. Ahead, a figure stands silhouetted against the last sliver of burnished copper glowing upon the horizon.

"I will wait inside," Charlotte says, stopping.

I need no urging to go on. I cannot see the Duc's face until I am some yards closer. He does not smile as he did in the courtyard, but his eyes are warm, as is the hand he reaches out to me.

I move in to be kissed but instead he says, "There is a bench against the wall."

There is indeed, wreathed by dead and withered vines. We sit side by side. Henri collects my other hand and kisses both.

When he raises his head I say, "Since we last met, Sir, you are the talk of the Court. You must be pleased."

He gestures away his accomplishments as if they were nothing. "You are not married. So I am pleased."

"I do not know for how much longer. Every letter Her Majesty receives suggests the Portuguese will close with her ambassador."

My love's handsome face becomes solemn. As I have so many times these last days I think that I am too young to be married—whatever my contrary thoughts were before. I must have more time for love first, for the love of this man.

Leaning forward, he kisses me tenderly.

"You must keep me informed of the negotiations," he says as our lips part. "It is not a good thing to be distracted when fighting."

"I will try." I am thinking of how quickly I lost track of him once the army disbanded after La Roche-l'Abeille. And of the imposition our improper correspondence places upon Henriette.

Henri, it seems, worries about something different. "I understand. It is a risk for you to write to me. I would be mortified if anyone should become suspicious. Your honor is more important even than my peace of mind."

"Not to me," I murmur. "Your peace of mind and your person are dearer to me than my own."

He kisses me again. That is when I hear it—the snap of something dry underfoot. Henri hears too. Releasing me, his hand goes to his side, where he must have a dagger. He peers into the semidarkness.

Nearer the château I can make out a figure stooping to pluck something from a plant.

Fearful of discovery, I gasp slightly without thinking. The figure straightens and for a moment looks outward into the garden. Henri and I sit perfectly still. I would not draw breath were it not absolutely required. After a minute the person—whoever he is—places what he picked into his mouth and turns back. A crack of light grows into a doorway as he reenters the château.

"This is what I fear," Henri says quietly. "Whoever that was might have walked forward and, finding us in this compromising setting, spread gossip or worse. Your brother Anjou harbors a grudge against me. He works to damage me in the eyes of others, including the King. He would love to ruin me."

"Whatever Anjou says ill of you can only raise you in His Majesty's esteem," I reply. "But surely it is not so serious betwixt yourself and Anjou? Can a single battle two months past have done such damage?"

"Things between the Duc and me have never been particularly amicable. He likes me very well as an adversary—at tennis, in wrestling, in the competition for glory that so often accompanies war—but I do not believe I should ever have called us friends."

I shift uncomfortably. I can think of nothing I have observed to belie his statements, and I only wonder that I never reflected on the point before. "To ruin you with your conduct here, Anjou would have to ruin me. He would not do so. He loves me too well." And, I think, as he loves me, surely he will come to love the Duc better when he sees that I do.

"I love you well too, and therefore I cannot take such a chance. I should like to pay open court to you"—my heart leaps—"but now is not the time.

Let the matter with Portugal be settled first." Then, perhaps sensing how I tense, he says, "Settled to our liking."

"And in the meantime?"

"In the meantime we will be as careful as mice in a kitchen when the cat is about. Perhaps a diversion. I might court another."

I shake my head no.

"Think about it, Marguerite. It is the surest way to keep the attention I pay you from being discovered."

"It is the surest way to make me despise another lady."

Leaning forward, he whispers in my ear, "Your jealousy excites me." Pulling me to him once more, he kisses me until I cannot remember where we are. All thoughts are of him. All of my body throbs and aches unbearably.

"God give me strength," he murmurs as he releases me.

Now it is my turn to whisper. Putting my mouth against his ear, I ask, "If I let you create a diversion, will we be able to continue to snatch moments such as these?"

His breathing seems labored. His hand rises to my breast and squeezes through my gown. "To be alone with you . . . truly alone . . . is my greatest temptation and my greatest fear."

Again I move my mouth to his ear. I feel his entire body stiffen. "Why fear what is such a pleasure. Though I am a maid and ought to fear the unknown, when I am with you I would run where I have never walked. I fear detection only, nothing else."

His mouth moves to my throat, kissing lower and lower. I have visions of reclining on the bench, of letting him . . . I do not know what, for in truth I am aggravatingly naïve of the details of such things. But it is as I said to him: I am not afraid. I lean back, pulling on his shoulder, willing him to follow me. I feel him hesitate. "The Duchesse de Nevers' sister pines for you," I say. "I have never had any fondness for her. Let her be the object of your feigned pursuit. Send her letters. Kiss her hand." I pull him toward me again. "Only, for mercy's sake, kiss me before the fire your last kiss ignited consumes me."

He hesitates. "I will kiss you," he says, "so long as I feel sufficient self-control to be certain that I do nothing else." Then, leaning forward, he presses his mouth to the cleft where my breasts meet above the line of my bodice. I give a soft moan and in response he darts his tongue into that crevice, making my back arch with pleasure. I bury my hands in his hair, clutching it so that he cannot escape me. The Princesse de Porcien is forgotten. All is forgotten save the sensations of my flesh and the faint smells of the garden wafted over us by the late August breeze.

CHAPTER 10

Autumn 1569—Château of Plessis-les-Tours,

La Riche, France

"Shut the window." Mother looks up from her embroidery. I hurry to comply. The warm breezes of summer are flown, as are all the men. I wonder if the nip of fall is in the air where they are. For that matter, I wonder where that is, precisely.

Each day Mother and I wait for two things: word that the war is over with Anjou victorious; and a letter from His Majesty's ambassador in Portugal declaring me betrothed. We both anticipate the first with genuine impatience. When it comes to the second . . . I continue to feign enthusiasm, but it taxes me. Two weeks ago Her Majesty had a report blaming an outbreak of the plague in Lisbon for the delay of my betrothal. I found myself thinking—though it was unchristian—that Dom Sébastien might succumb. Since then we have had word the plague recedes, without the King even catching it. Death, it seems, cannot be counted on to extricate me from my situation. I must exert myself to do so.

"Shall I bring you a wrap?" I ask Mother.

"No, I will adjust my chair a little closer to the fire." Settling in with her work again, she pauses to smile at me. "What a companion you have become."

"Nothing pleases me more than my closeness with you and my brothers, Madame. Truth be told, I am not eager to leave the bosom of my family to become Queen of Portugal."

"No girl is eager to leave what she knows for what she does not know," Mother replies. Then, after a moment of consideration: "I may have been the exception, for though my uncle the Pope was good to me, he was not as a mother or father. Your grandfather François was much more of the latter to me."

"The King of Portugal delays matters. Might we not do the same? He and I are both young. Surely another year with you, Madame—which would give me the greatest pleasure—would be nothing to the Portuguese?"

This time when she looks at me Mother's eyes are more searching. "It means so much to you not to be parted from me?"

"It does, Madame. Serving you . . . I feel it is my life's work. Serving you, and being always here for Anjou."

"You miss him as much as I." She nods understandingly.

"If only the sentence of death pronounced by the Parlement upon Coligny were enough to kill that gentleman!"

"Have faith, daughter. Someone will claim the fifty thousand écus, or your brother will do the deed without expectation of reward and come home to us."

"The Duc de Guise would surely also kill the gentleman without recompense."

"True, but we must not hope for that. After all, if His Grace were to have credit for the admiral, your brother would return to us all scowls and curses."

"However he returns, I wish to be here, Madame," I say, endeavoring to turn the conversation back to my impending marriage.

"And you shall be. Even if you were married tomorrow by proxy, some months must pass before your journey to Portugal. The gowns alone would take so long."

"I of course stand ready to do my duty, Madame. I only ask you to consider if I might be dutiful from a lesser distance. If I were given a French husband as my sister Claude was, I could be ever close to you." There, I've said it. The thing I have longed to say but been afraid to.

"Margot!" Mother's face is not exactly angry, but neither is it pleased. I swallow hard, waiting for a lecture, balancing continued resistance against quick capitulation.

A heavy knock sounds. The door swings wide, though Mother has not yet commanded the knocker to enter. Anjou's close companion the Seigneur du Guast crosses the threshold, covered in dust. In a single instant my thoughts of the King of Portugal are gone and I doubt my mother could remember his name if pressed. This man comes from the field of battle. He comes with news of my brother . . . and of Guise.

"Your Majesty, Your Highness. I have ridden from Moncontour. There has been a mighty battle."

"And?" Mother demands.

"His Majesty's troops, under the Duc d'Anjou, were victorious. Eight thousand Huguenots surrendered. Coligny flees south but is badly injured, and surely, once cornered, he and those with him must fall."

"Praise be to God," I say, crossing myself adamantly.

"Praise be to your brother," Mother responds. "He is a warrior prince to match any alive. How is my son?"

For the first time I notice that Guast's face does not entirely reflect the triumph he reports. "Your Majesty"—he licks his upper lip as if he is nervous and my stomach clenches—"the Duc was unhorsed at the height of the battle."

"Oh, dear God!" Mother's face blanches and my stomach flips. If something has happened to Henri, how shall either of us bear it? "Is he hurt?"

"Scrapes and bruises only, Your Majesty, I give you my word, and I was with him after the event."

"You are certain?"

"Quite certain. Be assured, Your Majesty, the Duc is more distressed in spirit by his unhorsing than damaged in body. His personal guard, devoted to him as all who know him must be, fought ferociously to protect him until he could be mounted again and withdraw from the field. His Grace charged me particularly with telling you not to distress yourself on his account, for he holds Your Majesty's peace of mind too dear to bear the thought of worrying you needlessly."

I see a muscle in my mother's cheek move slightly, and her hands on the arms of her chair are rigid. "Seigneur, we appreciate the speed with which you brought this news and the solicitude of your delivery. I pray you will tell the Duc we showed as much bravery in receiving word of his peril as he showed during it."

"Of course. But Your Majesty will have an opportunity both to show fortitude and examine the Duc for signs of his fall. Even as he pursued Coligny, the Duc bid me beseech Your Majesty, and His Majesty the King, to follow him south and meet him *proche de* Saint-Jean-d'Angély. He means to siege that city and would have the wise counsel and approbation of you both."

My heart, a minute ago pounding in fear, soars. We will go to Anjou. I will see with my own eyes that my brother is safe. I will soothe and cheer him with a report of all that I have said and done on his behalf while he fought so valiantly.

"Sir, I will take your report to the King. Pray, if you can bear to be apart from your friends in arms so long, rest with us a day. Then I must have you back in your saddle with a message for my son: Tell the Duc that though I must move many and cannot travel with the same speed as you, the Court will soon be in sight of his tents."

Guast, having bowed to Mother, passes me as he withdraws. As he does, he darts me a look I do not quite understand.

The flurry of packing begins while Mother is still closeted with Charles. A journey of more than forty-five leagues lies ahead, and it will take us three days. I can hardly bear to wait so long to embrace and congratulate the hero of Moncontour, as Anjou is being called.

As I move briskly about, giving instructions, I pray the fine autumn weather will hold. Wet roads could double the time it takes to make our journey. I try not to think of other events that might slow our progress; with the country at war no road is guaranteed to be safe.

Gillone sidles up to me carrying an armload of folded chemises. "Your Highness"—her voice is low—"the Seigneur du Guast is at the door."

My surprise is complete. I cannot imagine why the Seigneur calls upon me rather than resting after his long ride.

"Make sure to pack my new gown, the one the color of golden autumn leaves," I instruct as I head for the door. I do not immediately see du Guast, then I realize he is standing to one side of the opening, close to the wall.

"Seigneur." I incline my head.

"Your Highness." He does not move.

"Will you come in, Sir?"

"No, I thank you." Looking in either direction he lowers his voice. "I have a message, *un message privé,* for you from the Duc d'Anjou."

My heart flutters. I wonder what my brother would tell me alone? Perhaps some details of his injuries? Or perhaps he tasks me with some action? I reach out a hand expectantly.

"It is not here"—he taps the pouch at his waist—"but here." He lays two fingers alongside his temple. "Can you meet me?"

"Meet you?"

"Alone."

I look behind me once more to make certain I was not followed. Confident no one's eyes are upon me, I press through a slender opening in the row of hedges at the back of the garden. The space between the hedges and the stone wall was left so that gardeners might trim the massive border. It is like a small *allée.* I discovered it in the month since our arrival. How I wish I had known of it when Guise and I might have walked it together.

The Seigneur du Guast is waiting. At the sight of me, he moves forward and executes a bow. I notice, with some confusion, that he is dressed like a gallant—as if he were attending a court festivity, not meeting furtively to deliver a message.

He offers his arm and, not knowing what else to do, I take it. We walk in silence, passing from light into the shadow of the tall wall before us.

"I have heard," Guast says, "that after the siege of Poitiers the Duc de Guise came here."

"He did." I am utterly confused. Why is the Seigneur speaking of the Duc? "As one of that city's chief defenders, he wished to make a report and receive the royal approbation that was his due."

"I hear also that the King was not alone in praising him; that all the women of the Court offered him their admiration."

"His bravery did him no harm with anyone at Court, including those of the fairer sex." The thought of how jealous I have been over the other ladies' praise of the Duc causes my ears to burn.

"He has your admiration, does he not?"

I stop walking and drop his arm. "What has this to do with my brother or his message?"

"You fail to answer my question," he replies. "Interesting. Yet I do not need an answer. I saw how you smiled at him when we were all gathered here to hear the Duc d'Anjou's plans. And I saw more as well."

"I do not know what you mean."

"I had an upset stomach the night of your arrival and came out to the garden to find some mint to chew on."

I remember the shadowy figure that evening, my gasp, and the long moment he peered toward where the Duc and I sat. Knowing that the figure was Guast makes my mouth dry. I decide that any protest will only make him more certain, so I say nothing.

"Again silence." He shakes his head as if this means something. "Would it please you to know my spies say the Duc is mad for you? That no amount of flirting or flattering words from other ladies can divert his attention?"

It does please me, but I have no intention in confiding in this man. None of this is in the smallest part his business. "Nonsense, Seigneur. All at Court know that His Grace woos the Princesse de Porcien."

Guast actually has the temerity to laugh!

"Sir," I say sharply, "I had some difficulty in arranging to meet you and I must return to the château with all possible haste. You are wasting time."

"I am, indeed." He steps forward until his breast touches my own. He runs an index finger along the side of my cheek. "Is this how he touches you?" The smell of his breath, its warmth on my face, makes bile rise in my mouth. I realize with a sudden, horrifying certitude that there is no message.

I step back but my retreat is stopped by the hedge, and Guast follows. I am trapped between his body, so close that I can feel its heat, and the branches behind me, which press my back through the silk of my gown.

Leaning in further so I can feel his beard against my face, he says, "You accept the caresses of Guise, do you not? Mine may not be the hands of a Duc, but they know how to give pleasure." Without warning, his right arm goes around my waist, pulling me to him, and his left hand fondles my breast.

"Seigneur! You forget yourself," I gasp.

"No, indeed, Your Highness, I know who I am—the proud son of an ancient family and a close friend of your brother, Anjou. I would be your close friend as well." His mouth closes over mine. The thrust of his tongue between my lips feels like a violation. I clench my teeth against its further intrusion and shove with all my might against his chest, twisting and turning in an effort to escape him.

My mouth breaks free of his. "I will tell my brother you importune me."

I expect Guast to release me. Everyone knows Anjou adores me. But instead Guast says, "Better not. I can make trouble for you, Lady— whisper in your brother's ear what I know of your dalliance with Guise. He has no love for the Duc. Yes, I can hurt you, but I would rather please you." He pulls me more firmly against him and I can feel his arousal. I am gripped by fear such as I have never known. We are at the very corner of the garden, cut off from view. If I break free of him, can I outrun him? Can I even escape the hedges? If I scream, will anyone hear?

"Please, you must let me go."

"Must I?" His mouth closes over mine again. As I struggle, the branches behind me scrape at me like the claws of angry dogs.

"My mother," I gasp as he breaks off his violent kiss. "I will tell the Queen of these forced attentions." Surely, if he does not fear Anjou, he fears Her Majesty. Everyone does.

"And I will tell Her Majesty that you made me willing proffer of your charms. Tell her that you slipped from the château, away from your *gouvernante,* intent on seducing. If it were not so, why come alone to this deserted spot?"

"You told me you had a message from my brother!"

"Did I?"

"You are evil."

"You drive me to threats." That hand that was on my breast goes to my hip. It begins to gather my skirts. I can feel my hem rising. "I am a captive of your beauty, just like Guise."

"Not like His Grace," I say, frantically trying to arrest the work of his hand with one of my own. "The Duc would never impose himself upon me. He is an honorable man, and I am chaste."

Guast inhales sharply. "Chaste?"

I realize I have made a terrible mistake. Far from inspiring pity or honorable behavior, my confession appears to have excited Guast further. "Here is an unanticipated pleasure."

Heedless of the pain, I press farther back into the bushes. "Sir, my chastity is meant for the King of Portugal. If I am found not to be virginal on my wedding night and accuse you—"

"No one will believe I, rather than Guise, took your maidenhead, except the gentleman himself. And I shall enjoy lording that over him. Just as I shall enjoy having what is meant for a king." His voice is thick with lust. Grabbing me by both shoulders, he swings me away from the bushes. I know instinctively he means to push me to the ground. If he succeeds, I am lost. With all my might I throw my weight toward him, pushing against his breast with the palms of my hands. He is thrown off balance, releasing me as he struggles to remain on his feet. It seems that he will, and then a miracle happens. The Seigneur's foot, touching a patch of damp and matted autumn leaves, slips and is lost from under him.

As he falls to one knee I turn and run like an animal pursued by the pack toward the gap in the hedge. I am through it, scrambling across the parterre. I dare not look back. Such a glance would steal precious moments. *Holy Mary, mother of God, give my feet wings.* And then, oh, second miracle, I am inside the palace. My immediate, urgent need to escape the Seigneur gives way to a need to reach my chamber without attracting attention. For the plain fact is I did slip out unaccompanied, and to be seen returning with my clothing asunder and my face white as ashes could be the start of damaging rumors.

At last I slip into my chamber. I want to weep. Indeed, the first tears of what would be a torrent slip down my cheek. But, turning from fastening the door, I find Gillone looking at me.

"Your Highness, what has happened? Are you crying?" She hurries forward.

"Help me undress." I seldom use a tone of command but I employ one now, hoping to arrest further questions. I turn so that Gillone can unfasten my bodice.

She gasps. "Your Highness, your dress! It is slit and torn as if by animals."

"You imagine things, silly girl. I only slipped trying to return from the gardens and fell against a hedge."

"Slipped?" Gillone does not sound convinced. She removes my overskirt and fingers a gash in the silk.

"Yes. If the dress cannot be discreetly mended, destroy it." Then, seeing that her look has become even more incredulous, I add, "Her Majesty had little tolerance for spoiled gowns when I was a child. Do you imagine my age would spare me from a tongue-lashing now?"

Dipping her head, Gillone gathers the ruined gown into her arms. "Perhaps you should tell Her Majesty what happened." We both know she does not mean the story I just told her. She senses that was a lie and urges me to tell another the truth if I will not tell her. Admittedly, she appears to do this out of kindness, but my temper flares.

"Out!" I order. *Tell Mother what?* She would think me both disobedient and a fool for going to meet Guast. And she might think worse. She might think me lascivious. Guast certainly did. I thought my conduct toward the Duc de Guise innocent—or, if not precisely innocent, harmless. What were a few stolen kisses? I see now that they were sin.

Going to my *prie-dieu*, I kneel and allow myself to weep—swept with both relief and guilt. *Oh, Holy Virgin, it is clear to me that I am lust-filled, and that my wicked desires were plain enough that the Seigneur du Guast perceived them. Help me to purge myself of my sinful thoughts and feelings. Give me the resolve to keep the Duc at arm's length and accept only such attentions as might be paid me before a chaperone.*

The moments in the garden come rushing back to me. Even as my lips burn and my skin crawls at the thought of Guast's hands on me, I cannot help concluding that I brought his attentions upon myself when I let the Duc touch me in similar ways. I must, therefore, be forever silent about what has happened, not only because I might not be believed, but because my silence is my penance for past transgressions.

Saint-Jean-d'Angély is on the horizon at last. The past six days have been a misery. The Seigneur du Guast lingered with the Court after our encounter. Though he spoke not one word to me, his insouciance and the bold way he looked at me added to my mortification. His departure should have been a blessed release. But those moments in the garden are never long from my mind. I am having nightmares. I cannot eat.

I've ignored Henriette's pointed questions and Gillone's looks. Faithful to my self-imposed pledge, I've told no one what passed. Praise heaven, Mother attributes my lack of appetite and the circles beneath my eyes to concern over Anjou. After all, she also looks haggard, and Anjou's unhorsing is the cause.

As my brother's camp comes into sight through the drizzling rain that has punctuated our journey, she places a hand over mine. "Not long now. We will see your brother sound and whole and will ourselves be so for the first time since the Seigneur brought us word of his fall."

Oh, Henri, how I long to see you! If I am your champion you are also mine, and I will be safe once I am in your sight. Perhaps I may find a way to get Guast banished from your circle without telling you what he has done.

When the carriage stops, Anjou is there. Charles climbs down. There is an awkward exchange of bows, then His Majesty hastens to the shelter of a tent bearing the royal standard. Henri does not follow. He stands, rain streaming from his hat onto the shoulders of his doublet, waiting for us to descend. As soon as Mother's feet are on the ground, he pulls her into an embrace.

"My darling"—she pushes him to arm's length so she can examine him better—"what a relief to see you well. Here we are, the women who love you best in all the world." She embraces him again, then steps aside to make way for me, and I quite willingly follow her example, throwing myself upon my brother, my tears at seeing him mixing with the rain.

Henri's arms do not close around me. Instead he turns and offers an arm to Mother. "You should not stand in such weather. How could I bear it if you became ill on my account?" He leads her toward a tent and I follow, lifting my gown, hopping over puddles and wondering why my embrace was not returned.

Inside, Henri takes Mother's cloak. I try to catch his eye as a servant removes mine, but he is busy pouring Mother wine, waving away a second attendant in order to do the task himself. Anjou's eyes seem to touch on everything but me. Dismissing the servants, he beckons to Mother. "Come to the brazier."

Henri rubs Mother's hands between his own. "I hope you find the arrangement of your tent satisfactory. I supervised it myself *tout proche* to mine."

Anjou speaks rapidly. There is high color in his cheeks. He is clearly agitated. That likely explains my being slighted. Like Charles, Henri has a propensity to become fixated on a single thing, worrying it as a dog does a bone. I wonder what he is fretting over. Is he dwelling on some event from his last battle or anticipating his next? Flattery, I think, should revive his spirits and gain his attention.

"We heard much of your magnificent victory," I say, coming forward to pour myself a glass, since no one has offered me one, "but no one can match your descriptive powers. Tell us: What was it like to see the Swiss shatter the Huguenot Landsknechts?"

Anjou's eyes meet mine for the first time. They are surprisingly hard. "I have no wish to speak of such things. You must rely on others to tell the tale. There are those who can be satisfied by an incomplete victory, but I cannot."

"My Alexander"—Mother lifts a hand to his shoulder—"how can you call it incomplete? Prisoners in the thousands, Coligny injured . . . That is a glorious victory, to be certain."

"Ah, but, Madame, I had thought to make Coligny ride the ass as I did Condé. A dead man cannot flee south and take the remnants of his armies with him."

Here, then, is the reason for Henri's ill humor: Coligny's escape.

"The admiral has the devil's own luck." Mother shakes her head. "But it cannot last forever. You must tell me about this Maurevert you mention in your letters. A man with so few scruples could be useful, provided his aim improves."

"Madame, I am happy to give you my opinion on that subject, but later . . ." Anjou looks at me, his lip curling back oddly.

Something is wrong, and it is not merely the escape of Coligny.

". . . Some stories are best kept close, and our sister has *friends* only too eager to know every detail of our actions."

I am perplexed by his reference to "friends." But if Henri's meaning is ambiguous, his hostility is clear. Mother does not miss it—indeed, how could she? "Henri, what goes on here?"

"Here?" he replies. "Nothing. Elsewhere . . . well, we shall talk of that later. When you are out of your wet things and we are alone."

A handful of women tumble in, laughing and shaking the rain from their cloaks. Henri kisses Mother's hand. "I will leave you to the ministrations of your ladies." As he goes, he throws me a last look—filled with both anger and pain.

Has Guast said something to Anjou, and what precisely? *If he claims I have fallen to him, I will defend myself! Surely he is not such a fool.* I must find out what is amiss here. But the usual entertainments stand between me and that opportunity. Thankfully our long days of travel have left everyone tired. By the time we share a cold supper, yawns are frequent, and Her Majesty declares her intent to retire early. Good. Henri will surely come to see her once she is tucked into bed. He always does. I will try to have a word with him while he, Mother, and I are closeted cozily together.

Charlotte mixes Mother's wine while the rest of us undress Her Majesty. As Mother slips into a velvet nightgown lined in sarcenet, Anjou enters. The cluster of bodies surrounding Mother parts for him and he kisses her on both cheeks.

"You may go," she says, dismissing the others. As they pull on their cloaks, I mix glasses of wine for my brother and myself.

Anjou leans in and says something in Mother's ear.

She hesitates, then says, "Margot, you as well."

Oh, no. Henriette, at the tail of those departing, glances back. Trying to seem unruffled, I take up my cloak and bustle to join her.

I stop just outside. Henriette and Charlotte do as well. The three of us stand silent in the circle cast by the lantern in Henriette's hands. Only when the others are out of sight do I speak. "Something is wrong."

"Nonsense!" Charlotte squeezes my arm. "You know how they are, Her Majesty and the Duc: they have merely been apart too long and each craves the other's undivided attention."

Henriette, however, clearly believes me. Raising the lantern so that she can see my face, she asks, "Can the reason you are dismissed be the same that sees you off your food and out of looks?"

"I believe so." My mind races. I fear more than ever it is Guast. But how can I be entirely certain without speaking of my encounter with that gentleman directly? Because if I am wrong I would not have either Anjou or Mother know of Guast's attack.

"Come away and tell us all. We will devise what is best to be done," Henriette urges.

I shake my head no. "Leave me." Standing in the rain, I resolve to probe the cause of Anjou's pique first with Mother, who, loving me as she does, will surely tell me. I must wait for my brother to depart.

Henriette shrugs, knowing I can be as stubborn as she. She offers me the lantern. When I make no move to take it, she slips an arm about Charlotte's waist and the two move away. Charlotte looks back before they disappear, her pale face a mask of concern. I am sorry if I have hurt her. She and Henriette are my dearest friends, but this is a Valois matter.

Left alone in the dark and rain, I cannot say how long I stand, only that it is long enough for my shoes and cloak to be soaked through, long enough for me to feel as if the rain will drown me. Then a shaft of light cuts the darkened ground. My brother, lantern in hand, turns back to the interior of Mother's tent. "*Bon nuit,* my beloved." He hurries off as I stand perfectly still so that he will not see me.

Mother does not look up when I enter. Likely she thinks I am a servant. She sits calmly before her brazier, arms crossed over her chest, lost in thought. I clear my throat.

"Marguerite, what do you do here?" Her use of my full name is telling.

"Madame,"—I hasten forward—"I would speak with you."

"Speak, then. I am tired. This day has been more trying than expected." She looks at me as if I ought to know why and my heart skips a beat.

"For myself as well, Madame. Can you tell me why my dearest brother disdains me? Why you break our comfortable habit of spending a few quiet moments together before you retire? I cannot account for the coldness on either of your parts." *Or rather, I will not if I do not have to.*

"I well believe that, daughter, for you are young and foolish."

"Young I may be, but this past month you have praised me many times for my clarity of thought and maturity of action. To my knowledge I have done nothing to alter your opinion."

Her face softens. "I am willing to believe that what you have done you have done unwittingly—"

This confuses me, for if Henri reports to Her Majesty that I have flirted or worse with Guast, how could such immodest behavior be unwitting?

"—but the plain fact is you have attracted the amorous attentions of the Duc de Guise. Do you deny it?"

For a moment I am relieved. I am accused of Guise, not Guast, and here I may defend myself without mortification. Then a darker thought intrudes: for the second time in less than a fortnight my flirtation with the Duc brings unpleasant consequences.

"The Duc admires me, Madame, but how can that affect your opinion of me?"

"I cannot permit the House of Lorraine to use your ears to hear matters of state. They held sway over your brother King François. They will never have such influence with another Valois king while I draw breath."

"Madame, I assure you, my ears are my own and my lips know better than to repeat matters important to my king or my kin."

"Lips forget their restraint where kisses are involved, daughter. When you are older you will know the truth of this. Your brother says you have been flirting with Guise. There is nothing unusual in a girl your age playing at love, but if you will make your lips available to the Duc and others for amorous enjoyments, can you blame me for making certain they have nothing of political significance to whisper?"

"Others"—the word stands out in Mother's accusation. I am so angry that for a moment I cannot see. My face burns and angry tears sting the corners of my eyes. "Who else does my brother accuse me of?" I know the answer, but the question must still be asked. *Oh, Henri, after all my devotion, how can you be so willing to believe and speak ill of me?*

"Anjou asserts you tease the Seigneur du Guast and make a fool of yourself in pursuit of him."

"I detest the Seigneur and would rather have no lips than kiss him!"

"That is well, but I fear it is at odds with what your brother tells me."

"My brother has been misled!"

"Why should the Seigneur spread rumors about you?"

Because I spurned his advances. I want to speak the words, to shriek them, but they simply will not come out. The thought of where they might lead stops my tongue. How can I bear to describe my encounter with du Guast to Mother? The mortification would crush me. And if she should not believe me . . . in that event, I think I would die.

After a moment or two of silence, Mother rises and, putting a hand on my arm, turns me in the direction of the door. "Go to bed, Margot."

"Madame, I beseech you, have more faith in me. Do not distrust me on Anjou's word alone."

"You forget that I trusted you first on his word. If he has withdrawn his confidence, that is sufficient to shake mine."

"And everything that passed between us is to be forgotten? All the good service I did for him set aside because someone tells him lies about me or he tells them himself?"

Mother slaps me. "Never call your brother a liar."

I can taste blood, but I stand my ground. "Betrayer, then. Strike me again if you like, I will not take it back. I have offered Anjou nothing but loyalty and he defames me mightily in a manner calculated to cause me injury. I will not forget it." I lift my chin defiantly, eager to see what Mother will say. Without a word she turns her back. It is worse than the slap.

"You are getting water on my carpet." Anjou's voice is maddeningly calm.

"Is that all you have to say?" Rage and disappointment rise like twin fountains inside me.

"What else should I say?"

"You might tell me why, though I have honored our pledge in every particular since Plessis-les-Tours, you have slandered me to Mother."

Henri rises with his ordinary fluid grace as if nothing were wrong, and moves forward until he is very close. "You know why. The Duc de Guise. He moons over you. Everyone says so." He reaches out his right hand and runs the back of it along my jaw in a caress before taking my chin between his thumb and first finger.

"And if he does? Do you think a little flattery is sufficient to make me forget my duty to you?"

"Ah, but it is more than flattery, is it not? You have fallen in *love* with the Duc." He gives my chin a vicious squeeze, then releases it.

"No." I raise fingers to my face where it aches from his touch.

"No? Come, Margot, your blush tells the truth that your lips will not."

"If I admire the Duc, so do half the women of the Court," I reply defiantly. "Where is the betrayal in that?"

"You are not the other women of the Court. You are as far above them as I am above Guise. How can you debase yourself with him?"

"I do not debase myself! The Duc is not"—I struggle to make myself say the word, to contradict directly what I am sure my brother has heard from Guast—"not my lover. I do not take lovers. You cannot say the same."

"My mistresses have meant nothing to me. But Guise means something to you." Anjou leans in until his lips brush my ear. His breath makes me quiver. "Does he mean more to you than I do? Will you torture me by embracing my enemy?"

I take a step back. "The Duc is not your enemy. He serves the King under your command."

"He serves himself, and ignores my commands whenever it suits him. Or have you forgotten La Roche-l'Abeille?" My brother's face is fierce. Despite months and intervening battles, the embarrassment of that occasion clearly remains a fresh wound.

"I have not, but surely everyone else has. It is time you do too. Your many victories since are spoken of throughout France."

Anjou does not appear placated. I cannot understand why he fails to see any affection I have apportioned to Guise leaves plenty for him. "The

Duc is an ambitious man," I continue. "It would be unusual if he did not husband his own interests. But I have promised to safeguard yours and you can trust me to do so because I love you."

"Do you?"

"Can you doubt it? Can you doubt it when I have sung to you, danced with you, hunted beside you, and taken your part in every quarrel since we were reunited at Fontainebleau five years ago? Can you doubt it when I offered God my life in place of yours when you were ill?"

"I do doubt it." His eyes blaze again, but not with anger. This is something else. He moves close once more. "But you can put my doubts to rest. Swear you will not see Guise alone."

It is difficult to imagine such a pledge, but not as difficult as it would have been a week ago. My brother merely asks me to give voice to the promise I made on my knees the night of Guast's assault. Yet my voice is a whisper as I speak. "I swear it."

Anjou exhales audibly. His left arm encircles my waist. He bends and I expect his customary kiss on the forehead, but his lips do not stop their descent until they meet mine. It is a lover's kiss. My mind spins and settles upon one thought—Henri's anger was rooted in jealousy! I am confused both by this fact and by my lack of revulsion at his lips against mine. Here is sin greater than any the Duc and I have committed, yet my heart races as it does in Guise's embrace. My tongue seeks Anjou's and my flesh thrills at the touch of his hands.

Then, in an instant, attraction turns to disgust—not at my brother but at myself. I must be the most wanton, lustful woman on God's earth; a monster so openly licentious that every man around me succumbs to base passion, even my own flesh and blood. Worse still, my passions respond to such sin-soaked caresses. Tearing myself from Anjou's embrace, I stoop, hands on knees, retch, and vomit.

Henri recoils. Doubtless cognizant for the first time of the evil nature of what we have done. I put up a hand to shield my face so he cannot look at me.

"I see how it is. I disgust you! I repulse you but Guise does not."

I look up, stunned. *This* is his concern?

"And to think I believed you when you said you loved me best. You are

all artifice, just as Guast said, captivating men for your own cruel purposes. Unwilling to fulfill the promises your lips and your actions make."

I cannot breathe. Cannot believe what I am hearing. I retch again, but
nothing comes up.

Grabbing me roughly, Anjou drags me toward the entrance of his tent.
"Well, the Duc can have you, then, and welcome. I want none of you. From
this moment your beauty and your pretty words have lost their power over
me. Get out!" Opening the tent, he shoves me into the rain. I stumble and
fall to the ground, shaking uncontrollably, in the wedge of light shining
forth from behind my brother. Then the flap closes, the light is gone—all
the light in my world. I am abandoned by Henri, distrusted by my mother. I am wretched, guilty, and alone.

I have no will to move. Will Anjou do me better justice, I wonder, if he
emerges in the morning to find me dead on the ground? Resting my head
on my knees, I cry. When I run out of tears, I cannot think what to do.
Then it comes: confess. I must have forgiveness of my sins, and then I
must avoid repeating them. My pledge to distance myself from Guise,
given to Anjou, may not restore my brother's or mother's trust, but it is
worth keeping nonetheless. Putting my hands down into the muck, I
struggle to my feet. I will write to my Duc. Tell him that when we are
together next, he must not come near. I will not see him alone again, and
that thought nearly drives me once more to tears.

The lanterns in my tent burn low. Gillone has fallen asleep, her head
thrown back and my nightshift on her lap. Relieved not to have to explain where I was, I move cautiously so as not to wake her. Catching a
glimpse of a face in the glass on my makeshift dressing table, I gasp. I turn
this way and that, looking for the madwoman who has stolen into my
tent before realizing the image is my own. My eyes are wild. Portions of
my hair have come undone. Wet hanks hang about my face and cling to
my neck. My skin is so pale, I might be mistaken for dead.

Removing my cloak, I let it fall to the rug. I strip off the sodden dress
underneath, tearing myself free when I cannot reach the fastenings. I
crawl into bed in my damp chemise, clutching my writing box.

How difficult my task is. The very act of writing to the Duc is inappropriate. If my letter should be intercepted, I must at least take care that

it does me no further harm. Perforce, then, there is no room in it for the type of sweet words that might act as a balm to the sting I must deliver.

"Your Grace." The salutation will seem a slap to a man who has heard me whisper his Christian name. I bite back such thoughts and continue. "I fear our friendship, though innocent"—it would be cruelty to share the guilt I feel over our conduct; unnecessary too, since there will be no more—"occasions talk at Court." My blood heats as I recall the nature of that talk. The balance of the note is brief, but bound to cause as much pain in the reader as it costs me to write it. I sign myself "Duchesse de Valois" and hasten to fold and seal the missive before more tears, like the one that bleeds the letters of my title, can fall upon the page and spoil it. Then I place the letter beneath my pillow. It is difficult to imagine sleeping on such a cruel object. But I am exhausted, and the thought that I will not sleep is barely formed before it is betrayed.

I wake sneezing. My cloak is gone, as are the remnants of my gown. My head aches dully. My limbs feel like lead. But I must rise. I have duties. I do not expect a warm welcome in my mother's tent, but I will attend her, belying the words my brother has spoken against me by my diligence. Besides, I must give my dreadful note to Henriette. Gillone eyes me questioningly as she dresses me, but whatever thoughts she has or conclusions she drew from the torn and ruined garments she whisked away while I slept, she keeps them to herself.

Mother is in the final stages of her toilette when I reach her tent. Though the other ladies greet me warmly, I receive no acknowledgment from her. It is too late to insist on the honor of holding out her shoes, but as she moves to her dressing table I press forward. It has lately been falling to me to arrange Mother's hair. Taking up a comb, I find my hand shaking. As a result the comb catches.

"You are clumsy this morning." Mother's eyes in the mirror are sharp.

"I am sorry, Your Majesty."

"Give the comb to someone else before I am pulled apart."

As I pass the comb, it is I who feels pulled apart. I have come to do my duty, but if I am to be snubbed publically it will be very hard to bear.

As Mother's hood and veil are fastened in place, Anjou enters.

"Madame"—he brushes past me without a glance—"I see a good night's sleep has refreshed you." Anjou's eyes catch mine in our mother's glass. "Which is more than I can say for our sister. Such tired eyes, Margot. What disturbed your rest, I wonder?"

"A guilty conscience, perhaps." Mother's words as she passes me are low, but even so, I am surely not the only lady who hears them.

"Or perhaps she misses absent friends." Henri winks obnoxiously. "But we have no time for such trivial worries. Come, I am eager to discuss my siege preparations."

When they are gone, the other ladies begin to straighten Mother's things. I move to Henriette's side.

"You do not look well," she says.

"As my brother cruelly pointed out."

"No, not tired: ill. Come, I will walk you to your tent."

I let her guide me outside, then stop. "I will go and lie down, but need your assistance in a matter far more important than seeing me to bed." I draw the note from between the front of my bodice and my partlet. "We both know that you have ways of conveying messages that ought not to be sent."

Henriette laughs. "I should object to being depicted as devious, but I own I delight in it. Give me the letter." Taking it from me, she turns it over in her hand. "No address, but I know the recipient." My note disappears into the bodice of her gown. "Is love the cause of all this pallor? I would be very disappointed to hear it. If I have taught you nothing else these years, I hope I have taught you not to make a fool of yourself over a man—even a very handsome one." She crosses her arms expectantly.

"No. I am not pining for Guise. I am mourning my loss of favor on his account. He is the cause of the rupture with Anjou, and through Anjou with my mother. They think I spy for the Duc."

"Do you?"

"No."

She nods, satisfied. "Then consider your letter delivered."

I find myself wondering if, had my answer been different, I would have been left without a messenger?

CHAPTER 11

Autumn 1569—Saint-Jean-d'Angely, France

I own that I expected my mother to send for me. Each of the three mornings since she snubbed me, I've dressed and waited for my absence to be remarked upon. Waited for a summons. But my mother, it would seem, is quite contented to go about her business without me. I've taken my meals alone, pleading indisposition, but even this raises no alarm in Mother. I am in fact ill—listless and feverish by turns—and have little appetite. Gillone entreated me to let her go for the physician yesterday, but I would have none of it. As the third afternoon of my self-imposed exile wanes, I change my mind. The flashes of heat I have been suffering give way to a constant fire beneath my skin and a pain such as I have never known in my head. I send for Castelan. Gillone returns with Henriette instead.

My friend's eyes are full of concern. "She burns! Listen," Henriette crouches beside me, "a fever most terrible has taken hold of the camp. It began with a half a dozen gentlemen and now there must be fifty lying with parched lips, covered with purple sores." She turns to Gillone. "Have you seen such sores upon her?"

"No, Your Grace."

"There is a mercy, then. We must get her to bed."

Hands are upon me but I cannot imagine that they will be able to lift me. I am as heavy as one of my brother's iron cannon. Yet, despite my conviction, I am raised. I open my eyes and the room spins. I try to walk, but fear I am of little help as Henriette and Gillone bear me the short distance to my bed.

"I am going to the Queen," Henriette says.

Gillone reaches out a hand and catches Her Grace's sleeve. "Are they dying?" she whispers.

"Yes."

I let my eyes fall shut. *So while I have been hiding, Death crept into the camp. Is he coming for me?* I want to ask but my tongue is too dry and cleaves to the roof of my mouth. Gillone, murmuring a string of unintelligible words, places a cloth on my head. It is like ice! I struggle to push it away. "Can you not see I am freezing?" I say testily through chattering teeth. I close my eyes and, when the cloth returns, have not the strength to resist it.

Time no longer exists. I fade in and out of consciousness, uncertain of much of what I see or hear in those moments when my ears and eyes are open. Of only one thing am I absolutely certain: Mother is here. It is night. It is day. It is something that I do not recognize as either. Yet Mother remains. Once I think I hear her singing to me in Italian. Is it a dream—all of it save the fire that burns me and the aches in my joints and head? If it is, I would not wake, for in my feverish delusions I have proof Mother cares.

My eyes open. Something is different. The pain is gone. Things around me are no longer shadows that fade in and out of focus. I can quite clearly see a lamp burning on a table near the foot of my bed. Mother dozes in a chair next to it. I find I have the power to turn my head, and discover Charlotte sitting beside my bed. I lift a hand and beckon her—a mighty feat. She comes and, lifting my hand to her lips, bursts into tears.

"Why do you weep?" My voice sounds loud in the silence and strange as well—cracked, as if I were aged.

"Because two days ago none thought to see you open your eyes again."

A dry cough on my part causes her to drop my hand and offer water. I drink deep, letting the liquid soothe my parched throat, then ask, "How long have I been ill?"

"More than a fortnight, and each day worse than the last. Her Majesty has been quite desperate. She would not leave you even to see Castelan when he called for her as he lay dying."

"Castelan is dead?"

"Chappelain too. Ambroise Paré rode from Paris lest the King be left without a physician. Scores of others succumbed—from foot soldiers to gentlemen we have dined and danced with . . ." Her words trail off into a small sob.

So our Lord has, in His wisdom, left me to live while gathering others to Him.
"Has Anjou—"

I mean to ask if my brother has been here, crying and begging my forgiveness, but Charlotte interposes peremptorily. "Be assured, *both* your brothers were untouched by this pestilence."

Mother shifts and opens her eyes. Seeing Charlotte sitting upon my bed, she springs to her feet.

"Is she gone?"

"Where should I go when you have cared for me so tenderly?" I say.

Relief sweeps across Her Majesty's usually inscrutable features. "God be praised," she says, coming to lay a hand on my forehead. Then, as if embarrassed by her unguarded behavior: "I ought to have known it would be so—whatever the doctors said—for I did not see you in your grave."

Mother gestures for her chair and Charlotte draws it up. Sitting down, Her Majesty momentarily rests her hand upon mine. "You gave us many hours of worry. His Majesty and Anjou asked after you until I could no longer bear to answer their inquiries. They would both have been at your bedside had prudence not made me forbid it. I am sure you will see them in the morning. Think of what a balm that will be."

Anjou lies at the foot of my bed, gazing at me as if I were the sun in the sky. Seeing me reach for a book on the table beside me, he says, "Will reading not tire you? Shall I read aloud to you?" Without waiting for a reply, he leaps up, snatches the book from me, and resumes his position.

Mother, who sits nearby embroidering, gives him a doting smile. Her Majesty is delighted with Anjou's devotion to me as I make my slow recovery. My brother begins to declaim dramatically. I try to ignore the faces he makes at me when Mother's head is bent over her work, and try to lose myself in his words. I am not entirely successful. Beneath my covers my hands clench. After perhaps a quarter of an hour Mother says, "The light is fading: it is time for me to dress to sup with the King. Will you come with me, my son?"

"I will follow. I can still see well enough to entertain my sister a little longer."

Mother places a hand on Anjou's shoulder and stoops to kiss the top of his head. "Do not strain your eyes. Good night, daughter."

The ruse continues only briefly once the tent flap has closed. Tossing the book onto the bed, Anjou says, "Finish it yourself if you are inclined. Or do you have more interesting reading? Come, Margot, do you hide Guise's letters under your mattress?" He slides a hand beneath the ticking, heedless of how he jostles me.

I do not bother to deny such correspondence. "Do you not have a city to siege?" I ask bitingly.

"Oh, things go well enough. I can spare some time for you."

"I do not desire your company."

"True. But I desire to make certain you do not tell poisonous falsehoods to our mother."

His attendance is not what keeps me from speaking out against him. Saying unfavorable things about Anjou can only rebound to my detriment. I learned that when I called him a liar and received a slap for it. I have been reminded of it throughout my recovery as I see Mother praise him for his false attentions to me. But I will not be the one to enlighten Anjou, even if by showing him the truth I might be rid of him. His fear of being degraded in Mother's eyes is the only weapon I have in the war begun between us.

"I will bide my time," I say. "One day the city will fall and battle will take you elsewhere. In your absence Mother will see by my virtuous conduct that her fears of me are misplaced. She is too clever to be fooled by your lies for long."

"Not lies!" Anjou looms over me. "I only wish they were lies," he says bitterly. He draws a deep breath and something in his eyes changes. "Prove to me they are. Tell me that you love me and I will rebuild what I have destroyed."

"Tell you that I love you! When you have defamed me? When you torture me with your teasing and insinuations even as I struggle to regain my health? I thought God spared me because my illness had made you repent of your cruel treatment. I see now that he spared me because he would not give you the satisfaction of my death."

"I wept when they said you were dying."

"Mother must have been impressed."

He raises a hand as if he will strike me, then lets it drop. To my surprise he falls to his knees and tries to take my hand. I quickly snatch it out of his reach.

"I did not want you dead. I only wanted you to be mine and mine alone. Is that a thing so wrong?"

"I was yours—your ally."

"That was not enough."

I remember the kiss: his lips on mine, the heat between us on that chilly, rainy night.

"Why?" I ask, trying to push the image from my mind. "Is it my fault?" I whisper the question.

"Your fault or God's. You are the perfect match for me, and he made you that way. Only your beauty is equal to my own. Only your wit can divert me. I told you when you chose *la belle Rouhet* for me that I would make my own choice next, and she would put all others to shame. You are that choice. You draw me to you by every action and every breath."

I swallow hard. It is as I feared. However unwanted, the ardent attention I have received is somehow of my own creation. "Brother, I do not mean to tempt you to wish for more than we can, as siblings, have. I swear it."

"You protest that you do not knowingly entice me. That may be so. But having been made aware of my attraction, you do most deliberately spurn me." His voice, though soft, brims with fury. "I have my pride, Margot. As you are superior to every other lady of the Court, I am superior to every other gentleman, yet you prefer another."

"I have foresworn the gentleman." My voice cracks. "You have my solemn oath."

"Then finish what you have begun and give your love to me." Leaning closer, he takes a slow, deep breath, and I shiver, knowing he inhales my scent as a hound would the aroma of his prey. "Think careful before you answer, Margot." His lips are so near my ear that I can feel them moving. Truly I am as a cornered animal, and my heart races accordingly. "This is your second chance; there will not be a third. Say no and make a sworn enemy of one who stands ready to adore you." His lips touch the place where my ear meets my face. The kiss is tender, and chaste, but I know the kisses that will follow, should I offer any encouragement, will be far from innocent. I force myself not to move—not until I've come to a decision.

My brother will make a dangerous enemy. He is unscrupulous. His power with Mother is vast. During these weeks of recovery I have tasted his rancor. The thought of months or even years of such treatment makes me feel hopeless and exhausted. I do not know that I have either the courage or the strength for a prolonged struggle with Anjou.

If I give myself over to him, my horrible sin cloaked by the gathering dusk, what will I gain? Peace with Anjou; a restoration to Her Majesty's good grace; and, as my brother guards his possessions jealously, protection from Guast. These are not insubstantial benefits.

"I am waiting," he whispers.

I hope God is looking elsewhere. Turning my face to my brother, I take his hand and put it upon my breast. He needs no further urging. His mouth closes on mine and for the second time I feel his tongue slide between my lips. Bile rises in my throat but I swallow it down determinedly. The hand that was on my breast travels upward, unties the neckline of my shift, then slips inside, making first contact with my bare flesh. I feel panic very like that I felt in the garden at Plessis-les-Tours. It takes all my self-control not to scream. Using his free hand, my brother yanks the pillow from behind me so that I fall back flat against my bed. He lies beside me.

"Oh, Margot," he murmurs, kissing my collarbone, "tell me that you love me."

Forcing myself to put a hand into his hair, I focus my eyes on a seam in my tent. "I do." The words sound choked, and I pray Anjou thinks they are so as a result of passion, not fear and disgust.

A hand runs along my thighs where I have pressed them together. I begin to pray, though I do not know what I am praying for, and though I am certainly not worthy of God's attention in this moment. Miraculously, Anjou's hands are gone from my body. *Perhaps he is satisfied. Perhaps my ordeal is at an end.* The thought is barely formed when my brother opens the neck of my shift wider to reveal both my breasts. "So perfect. So white," he murmurs in obvious delight. "Like Venus. That is what you are, goddess of love. My own goddess."

His mouth grazes the flesh of the breast nearest him. His hand returns to my legs, trying to push between them. I am drowning in my own terror. I know that I should open my thighs, but I cannot. I am desperate to keep my brother's hand out, as desperate as the citizens of Saint-Jean-d'Angley are to keep him from their city.

"Do not be afraid," Anjou croons. "I mean to give you pleasure. All the pleasure that a goddess deserves."

I try to focus on the burdens that will be lifted once I capitulate. I manage to relax my muscles slightly.

"That's right," Anjou urges, slipping his hand between my legs and running it upward until it comes to rest against my crotch. "The first time is the hardest. Soon you will spread your knees willingly, I promise. And I will make you sing my praises even as I sing yours."

The first time! Suddenly it dawns upon me that this coupling—such an abomination to all that is holy—will not be a one-time event. Letting my brother take my maidenhead will bring peace, but to keep that peace I will be forced to lie with him again and again. My sin will be perpetual until he tires of making me a sinner. Here is a thing worse than anything I can imagine—worse than death; certainly worse than loss of the Queen's favor or my brother's enduring enmity.

"No!" I cry out. I grasp the hand that would violate me and wrench it from me.

Anjou laughs, as if my struggle were a game. Plucking his arm from my grasp, he wraps it around me and pulls me against him. "I can be patient," he says. He moves in to kiss me and I bite his lip. I can taste blood. I know by his cry of pain and surprise that it is his. He releases me to put his hand to his injured lips and I use the moment to my advantage, shoving him as hard as I can. He falls off my cot and lands with a satisfying thud on the floor.

Grabbing the bell from the table beside my bed, I ring it violently. "Gillone, I need you!" I cry.

Anjou jumps to his feet. The look he gives me is so hate-filled that I wonder if even the arrival of Gillone will keep him from doing me violence. But he exhibits a cold self-command reminiscent of Mother. Touching his lip, he removes his hand and looks at the blood upon it. "Those who draw blood from me always regret it. I meant what I said—I did not wish you dead—but after this, you may yourself wish it." Casting a glance in my glass, he straightens his doublet, then draws back the flap of my tent to admit Gillone. "Your mistress has suffered a relapse," Anjou says. "I fear the effects of her illness may be lifelong."

❧ ❧ ❧

When Saint-Jean-d'Angely capitulates we set out for Angers. I am too weak to ride. Charles gives me his litter, placing me in it himself each morning. Henriette sits beside me as we arrive in Angers. Heedless of the cold and of Henriette's disapproving look, I open my curtain to see the stout, round towers of the fortresslike château. Tonight we will dine and sleep indoors for the first time in a long while, and such simple pleasures will be delightful. "Do you think Ambroise Paré will permit me to bathe?" I ask my friend. I would dearly love to wash away the last traces of my fever—and the lingering feeling of uncleanliness left behind on my flesh by Anjou's hands.

"Why need Monsieur Paré be consulted? Leave it to me."

"Then perhaps I can go to the chapel." I would be clean in spirit as well as in body. Closing my eyes, I imagine kneeling before the splinter of the true cross brought to Angers by Saint Louis, asking God to make my soul new again.

As we draw into the courtyard, my spirits are the highest they have been since that dreadful day when the Seigneur du Guast began my undoing. Charles dismounts and makes his way through the throng toward my litter. I smile at him, but in the next instant less welcome faces come into view—the Duc de Guise and his uncle the Cardinal. Why are they in Angers? My mother's eyes ask the same question as she stands beside Charles.

I glance past the Queen to the Duc. His face is stricken. He takes a few steps forward and then draws back. *Good.* I pray that he will keep his distance. To approach me now would confirm everything Anjou has said. Anjou glides to Guise's side, speaking to him, pulling him forward even as Charles offers an arm to help me from my litter.

"Here is a gentleman particularly desirous to inquire about our sister's health." Anjou nearly shoves Henri forward, smiling unctuously.

"Your Majesties." The Duc bows. "Your Highness." He inclines his head without meeting my eyes. His obvious pain wrings my heart, but not sufficiently to make me regret wishing him elsewhere.

The Cardinal de Lorraine, on his nephew's heels, bows as well. "Your Majesties," he says, "we were in the greatest apprehension when we heard of the illness in the royal camp, and prayed continuously that His Majesty and all dear to him would be spared."

"We were, praise God, entirely untouched," Charles replies without appearing to sense anything is amiss. Perhaps Mother has not related to him the rumors brought to her by Anjou.

"Your Majesty," I say, laying a hand on Charles' arm, "I am fatigued. May we go in?"

"Of course. Duchesse de Nevers, where is my sister's cloak? Throw it about her shoulders lest she take a chill."

Henriette moves in, giving me a pointed look. Having placed the cloak about my shoulders, she takes the Duc's arm. "Will you help me find my sister, Sir? I am sure you are eager to see her."

Bless her! As Charles leads me in one direction, Henriette and Guise go in the other. Yet the damage is done. I hear Anjou say to Mother, as they walk behind me, "How singular. Here waiting for her is just the balm Margot needs. I wonder: Did the fair Duchesse summon Guise or did our sister?"

Gillone is in my room. I sit on the edge of the bed and she kneels to remove my shoes. Mother lingers. We both know why.

"You look tired," she says. "I know we spoke of your dining with the Court, but perhaps it is best I have something sent up."

I should be disappointed, but instead I am relieved. I do not need to be in company with the Duc. "I appreciate your solicitude, Madame. I am well content to keep to my rooms." My dream of visiting the chapel fades; any foray outside this room would only provide Anjou with fodder for gossip that I rendezvous with Guise. Even staying shut in may not be enough, my brother may insinuate the Duc waits on me.

"I would be happy for some company, however, if Your Majesty would be so kind as to send someone." I deliberately fail to name a choice of companions, hoping to impress upon my mother that I have no fear of spies.

Alone, I try to think what is best to be done. I cannot send a note to the Duc. Yet, as long as he does not know Anjou makes trouble, Henri is likely to unwittingly provide fodder for my brother's wicked campaign. I would warn him, yes, and more than this I would reassure him that my health is no longer in danger. The pain in my breast when I recall his face as it looked in the courtyard reminds me that resolving to give up the Duc did not render me suddenly unfeeling toward him. I must be pitiless with myself in rooting out the unwise affection, but to feel no pity for Henri would be both impossible and unchristian.

A knock announces the arrival of the Baronne de Retz, always Mother's first choice when I must be spied upon.

She greets me with a kiss before settling down in a chair. "Shall I read to you?"

She has barely begun when Henriette enters with Charlotte and followed by a dozen servants bearing a copper tub and vessels of steaming water.

Baronne de Retz gives the Duchesse a questioning look. Without missing a beat, my darling friend says, "Her Highness's physician recommends a bath." How glibly Henriette lies. Someday I hope to be able to equal the feat. It is a marvel, and very useful. The room is filled with bustle as the tub is screened from the door and filled. Relaxing into the water, I seek an excuse to send my *gouvernante* far enough away to converse with my friends.

"Baronne, if you would be so kind as to continue reading . . ." The moment the lady returns to her chair on the other side of the screen, Henriette whispers in my ear, "Is it true you are quits with Guise?"

"It must be so," I whisper back.

"Madame de Sauve," Henriette says more loudly than necessary, "will you bring those last pitchers." Then, dropping her voice to a level certain to be masked by the sound of the pouring water, she says, "I am glad you recognize that no man is more important than your own fortunes, but surely the appearance that you have given him up would be sufficient. The Duc is heartbroken."

The Baronne de Retz pauses to turn a page. I sit silent, a lump rising in my throat. When the reading begins again, I take Henriette's hand and whisper, "I am sorry for it. Tell him so. But my sorrow changes nothing. Tell him that as well."

"And I thought you were falling in love with him." I avert my eyes. "Well, my sister will be glad to hear you are done with him."

My glance snaps back to Henriette and she nods. "I thought so." She lets the topic die and I lie back and close my eyes, struggling to keep from crying. Why is it so painful to do what is right?

Her Majesty comes to collect me for Mass in the morning. The walk to the chapel is the longest I have taken since I fell ill. I find myself revived by the sight of the altar and the colored light streaming through the windows that tinges my flesh with a holy glow. Charles is delighted to see me and fusses over my comfort. I do not see my Duc. And that is good. Then the Cardinal de Lorraine climbs to the altar—a jarring sight. His face is too much like his nephew's. Once His Eminence opens his mouth, however, his words and not his looks become my focus.

I know that God is everywhere, always, but while often I must take that on faith, this morning I feel His presence. A great calmness comes upon me. Even Anjou, only a few places from my own, cannot spoil the hour. Fortified by the Blessed Sacrament, I find I am able to catch sight of the Duc as I leave the chapel without undue inquietude. This is just as well, for while I have forsworn any inappropriate contact, I will surely need to meet with him on common occasions. If only he will not accost me, I believe all will be well.

I am taken back to my room and arranged, semi-recumbent, before the fire. I am reading in company with the Baronnes de Retz and de Sauve when Anjou swaggers in. Guise is with him.

"My dear sister," he says, "look whom I have brought to you. How fortunate we do not find you in bed, for that would breach propriety." He winks horribly and my stomach lurches. My brother is a veritable demon.

Charlotte begins to rise to make way for the gentlemen. I make a desperate, darting grab for her hand and pull her back down beside me.

I am not so fortunate with the Baronne de Retz. Before I can turn in her direction, she says, "Will Your Highness sit?"

"Oh, I must insist my friend take the seat." Putting an arm around Guise's shoulder, Anjou draws that gentleman forward. "He is as dear as a brother to me—would he were one—and he has been in agony over the Duchesse de Valois' illness."

Henri is clearly perplexed by Anjou's show of affection. Warily he takes the proffered chair. My brother stands behind, putting a hand upon Guise's shoulder. It is a position of dominance, and I can see by the Duc's eyes that it is not to his liking. But what can he do? He can hardly shake off the hand of a royal prince.

Looking at me, Anjou gives a chastising shake of the head. "Sister, it was unkind of you not to receive His Grace last evening. You left him to suffer a sleepless night."

"I assure you, Your Highness, I slept," Henri says. I am not certain whether he addresses me or my brother.

Anjou replies: "I am glad to hear it. But you would have lain down more comfortably had you seen Marguerite."

There is insinuation in both what Anjou says and how he says it. Perhaps only I perceive it, but my stomach tightens further and my face flushes.

Anjou cannot let this pass. "Observe the color in her cheeks, Guise. The sight of you does her good. If only Her Majesty were here to see as much.

"Well, I must go," my brother says brightly. "Her Majesty expects me."

The Duc begins to rise. "I should go too."

Yes. You should.

"No, Guise, stay where you are. I insist. If anyone is looking for you, I will tell them where you can be found." Passing the Baronne de Retz, Anjou says, "Madame, I believe your husband seeks you."

Clever. I take hold of Charlotte's hand and mouth the words "Do not leave." She looks puzzled but nods.

Charlotte's presence will, I pray, be sufficient to guard me against evil rumors, but she is no impediment to the Duc. The moment the others are gone, he leans forward, hands on knees, and says, "I have been mad with worry. We heard that you were ill but then nothing—nothing but the daily report of who had succumbed. I had no recourse but to hold my breath and pray your name would not be among the dead, for I have no claim that would have permitted me to inquire about you."

"I am sorry I worried you."

"Are you?"

"Of course."

"How can I believe that after—" He stops short. "Surely, Baronne, you might withdraw a little further. Please."

Charlotte looks at me.

I am at war with myself.

"If you would sit by the door," I say at last.

The Duc releases his breath in a single long puff. "Why did you write me that terrible letter?"

"Your Grace—"

"Henri."

"Your Grace, it has been brought to my attention most forcefully that our . . ." I pause. *Our what? What word can I use?* "Affair" suggests more than we have done. "Dalliance" trivializes our encounters and they were anything but trivial to me. ". . . that our *amour* has led me to transgress, to behave in a manner unbefitting a princess of France." I look at my lap. "I must ameliorate my ways before I embarrass His Majesty."

"*I* am an embarrassment?"

Glancing up, I find his eyes as full of pain as they were in the court yard last evening. How I wish I could stop hurting him. "No," I say. "You are a gentleman of honor and well-earned reputation; I am not embarrassed of my admiration for you. But it has led me into sin."

"A kiss is a sin?"

"Not one."

"How many, then? How many does it take to make a sin?"

"Sir, we have surely exchanged enough kisses to cross the threshold wherever it lies. And not all kisses are equal." I feel myself blushing.

"I consider myself a devout man, and yet I do not believe anything we have done is sin," he replies earnestly. "Not the embraces we have exchanged nor the professions of love." Taking a hand from his knee, he runs it through his hair.

"Others think our flirtation less innocent." I lower my voice. "They mistake me for another sort of *dame de la cour.*"

"Who? Who thinks such things of you?" He springs to his feet. "I will call them out and run them through!"

His fierce, protective tone, the angry tilt of his jaw—I believe I have never loved the Duc more. I ache inside.

"I cannot say." I drop my head. For a moment nothing happens. Then the Duc sits down. I feel his fingers upon my chin, drawing it upward until we are eye to eye once more.

"Such gossip is poison, but you must not let it fell you. You know that you are not such a one. I know it."

I wish I felt the confidence he so obviously does on the point. But Anjou's words blaming me for his attraction—and Guast's wolfish glances—are not so easily dismissed.

"There is more. The Duc d'Anjou believes I spy for you."

"He is a fool!"

He is far worse.

"Is this why you distance yourself from me—to silence unjust gossip?"

I nod. He smiles. I am stunned.

"What can there be to smile about?"

"I thought you had ceased to love me." He takes my hand. I know that I ought to retrieve it, but his touch, unlike that of the other men who have lately sought my hand and more, comforts.

"I kept telling myself it could not be so, for you cried when you wrote that dreadful letter—"

"You noticed."

"Of course. But the stain was so at odds with the prose, and soon I saw only the latter. Again and again I asked myself why you would demote me by the term 'friendship' and call me by my title. The only explanation I could find was terrible—that I had lost your love."

"You have not. But can we not love from a greater distance?"

He draws the hand he holds to his mouth and grazes my knuckles with his lips. "Can I do this from a distance?"

"No." I sigh where he perhaps expected me to laugh, and his face falls.

"I distress you. That is not my intent—ever. If you will not let me fight in defense of your reputation, then I will live in defense of it. What must I do?"

"I have sworn I will not be alone with you."

"Then you will not be: I will renounce the pleasure of unchaperoned moments. And in public not a word, not a look, shall escape me which would raise an eyebrow of the Baronne de Retz—at least, not when there is anyone nearby to hear or see it."

At this I do laugh. "And when they are not?"

"Why, then I shall say I love you and call you Marguerite. And you will smile and whisper, 'I love you too, Henri.'"

"I do."

"Knowing that will make all our new cautions bearable."

CHAPTER 12

Spring 1570, Paris

"No, no, no!" Henriette's voice is strident enough to bring Gillone's head popping out of the adjoining chamber. I wave my shadow back.

"How can you be so cruel?"

Henriette's expression is hard. "It is you who are cruel—to yourself and to me, a friend who only tries to safeguard you from your own foolishness."

"But you have relayed messages between us before. Many times."

"I was trying to help you to be discreet, but that is no longer possible. The whole Court talks of your romance with the Duc and speculates on where it will end. I do not need to speculate. I can predict the future as clearly as Her Majesty claims she can—at least in this instance." She shakes her head. "Your mother will crush this *amour,* and you will be even further from her favor than you are now."

"I do not believe that. Nor does Henri," I reply defiantly. "Her Majesty grows frustrated by the lack of progress in the Portuguese match—"

"And you think her current short temper favors you? Unbelievable!" Henriette throws up her hands.

"We do not! Why do you think Henri has left Court? We *know* we have engendered a dangerous level of talk, and this is not the time for him to press his suit. But it does not follow that such a time will never come." My friend's eyes do not soften. And her expression might, without stretching too far, be called mocking. I am in no mood to be ridiculed. "The House of Lorraine is one of the greatest in France," I say with all the hauteur I can muster. "Henri may be from a cadet branch, but he is clearly Lorraine's future. He is a hero of the wars and all France is in love with him."

"All except those who matter: Madame Catherine and Anjou."

"Neither is king," I snap. "Charles and I are close. I understand him. I soothe him in his moods. When Anjou rejoins the army, Henri and I will approach the King. As he loves me, he will want me to be happy."

"You are seventeen, Margot, not a child. Stop behaving as one! Is His Majesty happy himself?"

Henriette's question makes me think of the last hours I passed with Charles. He had another of his headaches and required the ministrations of both myself and Marie. Mother had just delivered a blow to him: Anna of Austria, to whom he was betrothed, had married Philip of Spain by proxy despite my brother's prior claim. This was, of course, neither Charles' doing nor his fault, but in her fury Mother made him feel as if it was.

Henriette moves to fill my silence. "If the King does not have the power to make himself happy, manipulated as he is by Her Majesty, how can you believe him capable of giving you what you want in opposition to the Queen?"

I will plead with her no more. I will find another way to correspond with Henri. And I will not be cowed. "I have faith in His Majesty," I reply, lifting my chin. "And faith in the Duc. They will not disappoint me, even if you do."

Henriette gives a short laugh. "Will it shake your faith, I wonder, when I ask where Her Majesty is this morning?"

"I do not know." It is the truth. Mother is secretive in her comings and goings. She could be with her astrologer or Maître René, who mixes her perfumes and her poisons as well. She could be meeting with foreign envoys privately. Or perhaps she walks to examine the work at her beloved Tuileries with Jean Bullant, who has taken charge of the project. I was merely glad to have this free time to seek a word with Henriette, and gave no thought to why we were at liberty.

"Her Majesty went to see the Cardinal of Lorraine in his sick bed," Henriette tells me.

"So? That is very Christian of her and, if anything, proves that even she cannot ignore the House of Lorraine."

"Your argument might have more force if she went to see him openly. That she did not suggests she will deliver more than polite well wishes. I have reason to believe she will confront him with his part in spreading rumors you will marry his nephew."

What a horrible thought. That I cannot dismiss it makes me furious. "You have reason? You mean you have spies!"

"Everyone has spies—everyone who can. You have been grateful for the information I gathered in the past. When you do not like the message, will you condemn the messenger? You are your mother's daughter. Fine: Be blind, then. Be deaf. Neither choice makes it more likely you will be happy." Henriette pauses and takes several deep breaths. "As I love you, I had better leave before more harsh words make rapprochement between us difficult."

When she is gone, I sit down and have a good cry. In the half year since my rupture with Anjou, Henriette and Charlotte, always dear to me, have become yet more important. Mother remains distant. More than this, she shows a level of distrust absent from her manner before I gained her favor. Then I was merely overlooked. Now I am observed most warily. And this has complicated things. For though Henri and I foreswore all unchaperoned contact at Angers, when winter broke, so did our resolve. It was surprisingly easy to ignore my conscience—nearly as easy as it is to discount the reproachful lectures the Baronne de Retz favors me with daily. It is harder to disregard Henriette's words. I know she loves me and she is among the most astute courtiers. Still, I must believe she is in error and that Henri's hopes are not without reason. To do otherwise would break my heart. For no man but he can ever make me happy. I simply must be his wife. And while he is away, I simply must be able to exchange a line or two with him.

Wiping my eyes, I turn my thoughts in a practical direction. Who among Mother's ladies might correspond with the Duc? I remember that the Comtesse de Mirandole is a friend to Henri's mother. She is of an age where she might write to anyone without being suspected of something immoral. She will do nothing to oblige me for my own sake, nor can I say we are friends and therefore that I can trust her as I do Henriette. But if I can bribe her to act for me, then I can, I believe, count on her self-interest to keep her from betraying me. She would certainly be sent from Court if we are caught. And the risk of being banished even if she goes to Mother with my proposition rather than acting upon it is high. Mother is happy to have tales of her children, but she will protect even the less favored of us from the repetition of such gossip to others.

Going to my wardrobe, I open the box containing my jewelry. It is nothing compared to what Mother possesses. But I am a royal princess, and so I have some pieces with stones of value. My eyes light upon a ring Anjou gave me. A token of our former *amitié,* it means nothing to me. Concealing it, I leave my room in search of the Comtesse—in search of a new accomplice.

"Your Highness." The voice that awakens me is urgent. A single taper reveals Gillone's pale face. "Her Majesty sends for you."

I struggle to a sitting position. The sheer difficulty with which I opened my eyes suggests that I have not slumbered a full night. "What hour is it?"

"*Cinq heures et quart.*"

The apprehension coloring Gillone's voice fills my breast. Something is wrong; there can be no other explanation for my being roused at such an hour. *Has something happened to Charles?* "Quick," I admonish. "I must dress." Under such circumstances I have no patience for all the accoutrements of proper attire. When I join the Baron de Retz, who waits to escort me, I do not even wear a farthingale.

I am ushered to the apartment of the King. Charles, Mother, and Anjou stand in a little knot. I am relieved to see them all, for this means no one is dead—at least, no one at Paris. I say a silent prayer that neither Claude nor her children at Nancy have been taken from us. Unlike myself, both Mother and Anjou are perfectly dressed. Charles on the other hand wears only his nightshirt. As he turns to face me, the King's eyes are wild either with fever or anger.

"Charles." I move forward. "What news?" My hands touch his for a moment before he pulls away. His are cool. Not fever, then.

"News?" He laughs. "What disturbs our rest this night may be news to us, but I am quite sure it is not so to you." A muscle in his check twitches.

I am being called to account. I tremble, not because I know myself guilty of anything, but because reason and my brother's temper are quite often strangers.

"Show her." Charles spits the words.

"Do you know what I have here?" Mother holds up a single sheet of vellum and my mouth becomes dry. I do know—a letter of the Comtesse de Mirandole, doubtless the very one to which, only two nights ago, I lovingly added lines to Henri. Perhaps I ought to feign ignorance, but my mother surely recognizes my handwriting.

"How did you get that?" I ask. I see Anjou smile and I know—though how precisely he intercepted the letter I cannot say.

"Let us say"—my mother rests a hand on Anjou's arm, confirming my suspicion—"that some at Court care more for your reputation than you do yourself."

"Madame, surely a few lines are not so serious. I swear I have done nothing worse—nothing to compromise my reputation."

Mother's hand moves so quickly that, before I realize it has left my brother's arm, I feel her palm strike my face.

As I raise a hand to my stinging cheek she glances calmly down the page. "'I long for you by the light of the sun and dream of you by the light of the moon.'" The words I wrote so lovingly are defiled by her cold voice. "'Come back soon, that we may enjoy such words as cannot be trusted to a letter.'" I spring forward, reaching for the page, but Anjou grabs me and pulls me back sharply, tearing my sleeve as he does. There is nothing I can do but watch as Mother touches the corner of the page to one of the tapers, then drops the sheet to the stone floor. When the page ceases to burn, she calmly grinds the remnants to ash with her foot. Anjou releases me with a shove.

"Do you realize," Mother asks, "that, before I bid him hold his tongue, the Cardinal of Lorraine boasted his nephew will have you for a bride? Perhaps the Duc de Guise has *had* you already."

"Whore!" This time it is Charles who slaps me, so hard that I stagger backwards.

"No! Charles, I swear I have no sin of that type upon my conscience. The Duc's intentions have been honorable. He does wish to marry me; in this his uncle is not mistaken." This is not the ideal time to approach my brother with my hopes, but I have no other defense. I reach out to Charles, but he recoils.

"I have no doubt that the Duc wishes to marry you." Charles' voice is filled with venom. "He is wildly ambitious. But what Guise wishes for and what he will get are two different things."

"Very different." Anjou's voice is menacing.

"It is not only the Cardinal of Lorraine who speaks of your marriage to Guise." Charles circles me slowly, coming to a stop behind me. Leaning in, he hisses, "My court hums with talk of it." I tremble. "But I was willing to believe the rumors arose solely from your beauty and the Duc's avarice, even when our brother told me things were otherwise." I feel his hand in the hair hanging down my back and then, in a single, violent, twisting pull, I am drawn back against him. "I thought you an innocent"—he twists harder, until I fear the hank of hair he holds will be ripped from my head—"and you made a fool of me."

"Charles, please," I beg, trying to reach behind and free myself from his torment, "I swear that I have consented to nothing. I have promised nothing. We meant to come to you when Henri returned to Court. To come to you together so that the Duc might ask for my hand."

Charles snorts in disgust, but he releases my hair and pushes me away. For a single instant I consider running, but I am like an animal cornered with the King behind me, my mother before me, Anjou to one side, and the door, which I know to be guarded by the Baron de Retz, to the other.

"Why should I condescend to have the Duc as my brother when I expect to call the King of Portugal by that name?"

"Because he loves me, and I him." The moment the words are spoken I wish them unsaid. The mocking looks of Mother and Anjou are painful proof that my confession makes me ridiculous in their eyes.

"Charles, you know what it is to love, even if others do not," I plead. "You love Marie."

"But I do not think to marry her. I must consider my duties as a monarch and you must remember your duty to your monarch."

Moving to stand beside the King, Mother says, "Daughter, you do Mademoiselle Touchet ill by comparing her to Guise. She is utterly devoted to Charles. Can you really be foolish enough to believe that *you* are the Duc's object?" The curl of her lip is like a knife upon my flesh. "Let me disabuse you of that notion. You may be a fool in love, but the Duc is a practical man, a man of power who hungers for more. When he whispered pretty words to you in the dark, it was a connection with the royal House of Valois he sought."

"That and a cozy place for his cock," Anjou sneers.

Anjou's words sicken me. And Mother's—I do not credit my mother's assertion. I cannot. Yet it enrages me. And, at the edge of my mind, it occurs to me that some part of the anger I feel is directed at myself and at Henri. Am I a fool? If not for letting Henri speak love to me and loving him in return, then for failing to heed Henriette when she foretold this? And ought not Henri to have kept our hopes to himself instead of filling the mind and the mouth of his uncle with them? The doubts my mother causes make me hate her as I never have before.

"Why, Madame," I ask, advancing on her with fury, "can you never believe that I might have value to someone in and of myself? Why can you not conceive that anyone could love me? Is it simply because you yourself do not?"

"Do not speak nonsense. My children are my life! France is my life. Of course I value you—better than you value yourself—for I know the worth of a woman's honor." Mother's face is fierce. Her hand rises; then, just as I expect her to strike me again, she lets it drop. I watch with fascination as she takes control of her temper, rearranging her face into a look of deliberate calm.

"You will not hurt me, Marguerite, though you try."

The idea that she would paint herself as the aggrieved party in this situation is beyond comprehension. I want to attack her, to tear at her as she and my brothers have just torn at me. I take another step, but Anjou catches me easily and restrains me.

"You will not hurt me," Mother continues, "and you will not endanger your brother's reign. This folly stops now. From this moment all communication with the Duc, save the words required by politesse in open court, will cease. Resign yourself to that or risk far more serious punishment than the few blows you have endured here. And know this: you will never be permitted to marry the Duc." Her tone has a finality to it that sucks the air from my lungs. I look at Charles. The sight of his face—entirely unsympathetic—causes my knees to give way entirely.

Anjou supports my weight for a moment and then, giving a high, brutal laugh, releases me and lets me fall to the floor. "What about Guise?" he asks. "Blighted ambitions seem too small a price to pay for deflowering our sister. Your Majesty must have a better revenge."

"Guise is hunting, is he not?" Charles looks down upon me with pitiless eyes. "I will send Angoulême hunting as well and ask him to bring down more than a stag. He shall strike the Duc and bring the House of Guise down a peg and back to its senses."

No, no, no! The voice inside my head screams in terror. If Charles gives such a command, our half brother will obey. His fortunes and his very life depend on the King. He has no friend in Mother, who sees none of her husband in him and too much of the lady who seduced that husband.

"Excellent." Anjou laughs. "Shall I take our sister back to her room?"

"Get her out of my sight," Charles says, averting his gaze.

"Let me make her presentable first," Mother says. "We do not need talk that might further compromise her."

Do you not mean talk that would reveal you to be monsters capable of beating your own kin?

Anjou takes me beneath the arms and draws me to my feet. At the King's dressing table, Mother brushes my hair and tidies my face. She can do nothing to conceal the tear in my sleeve or stop the bruise rising along my right cheekbone. Looking in the glass at Anjou, who hovers behind us, she says, "Go quickly, before the whole palace is awake."

I rise with as much dignity as I can muster. Anjou takes my arm. I try to shake him off but he shows me by a shake of his head that he will have none of it. Swinging the door to the hall open, he pushes me before him. The Baron de Retz stands aside, his face impassive. Whatever he heard, whatever he observes, he will keep my mother's counsel.

Anjou pushes me through the door to my apartment, nearly into the arms of the waiting Gillone. Her face reflects the shocking sight I present as clearly as Charles' mirror did. We are not alone. The Baronne de Retz sits on one of my chairs.

"How did it come to this?" she asks sadly, shaking her head.

"It is the province of the young to fall in love. You once said so yourself," I reply, disentangling myself from Gillone.

"That is not what I am talking about and you know it."

"I have done nothing else," I snap. I am tired of protesting my innocence.

The Baronne stares into my eyes as she never bothered to in all the lectures she delivered on appropriate behavior—as if she would see my soul. Perhaps she does, for she says, "I believe you."

"Help me, then."

"I cannot."

"Then you condemn the Duc to death."

"Surely that is an exaggeration."

"The King is in one of his rages," I reply. "He means to arrange a hunting accident and none around him have any reason to dissuade him. There must be some way to get word to the Duc so he will be on his guard."

"The Duchesse de Nevers." The Baronne's tone is resigned. She knows, of course, that much of whatever passed between the Duc and me beyond the eyes of the Court must have been managed with Henriette's help. She has for some time viewed the Duchesse as her adversary and my corruptor. How I love her for putting aside her personal feelings. I only hope Henriette will do likewise. It has been a month since we argued, and though, on the surface, we appear to be as we were, there remains a reticence between us.

"They will be watching for the Duchesse at the wicket," I say. "If my mother has not thought of this precaution, Anjou will have."

I send Gillone to the Hôtel de Nevers to tell Her Grace that, if she loves me still, she must put a man in the saddle on his way to where Guise hunts. A man she can trust who will warn my Duc that there is more of danger in the woods than the chance he will be thrown from his horse, and that he would be better returned to Paris and safe behind the gates of his *hôtel*.

I watch my shadow go, then sit down and put my head in my hands and cry. If Charles has fixed on my beloved's death, surviving his hunting excursion is only a first step. Must Henri live always looking over his shoulder for Angoulême? One attempt, even more, may be survived. But where my family is determined to be rid of someone . . .

After a few moments of sobbing I feel a hand on my shoulder. "Is the crown of Portugal such a terrible fate?" the Baronne asks softly. "You fell in love with the Duc because he is handsome and brave. We have it on good authority that the King of Portugal is both. Allow yourself to be guided by duty and all will be well."

I look up at her, incredulous. How am I to stop loving Henri and begin loving a man I have never met? A man with the red hair of a devil? "If I am forbidden to marry where I love, I would rather not marry at all."

"Those are very dangerous words—particularly for the Duc de Guise."

CHAPTER 13

Summer 1570, Paris

Three days later I hear that Henri has returned to the city. Word comes first from Henriette, who in light of my situation has forgiven all, and who has even refrained from reminding me that she warned it would be so. She mumbles "He is *en ville*" as she breezes into Mother's apartments. And her information is soon confirmed by the gossip of a hundred tongues as well as by the black looks of my brothers.

In the afternoon, while the King and his gentlemen are playing at tennis, Angoulême arrives. I see him pass the wicket from my seat in an open window. He moves with hesitancy and I delight in that. *You failed,* I think. *I wonder what Charles will say.* I must know. Folding my hand of cards, I look across at Charlotte. "I am bored; let us go and see who has beaten whom upon the court."

My friend springs up eagerly. Baronne de Retz, who has been at my side nearly every waking moment since the fateful night on which I was beaten, begins to rise as well; then perhaps recollecting that I will be going to the very place Her Majesty is, she settles back with her embroidery.

As soon as we are out of Mother's apartment, I take Charlotte's hand and begin to run. We arrive breathless and giggling, looking like two young women eager to be entertained. Mother, after shaking her head at our frivolity, pays us no mind. Anjou is seated beside her, in the King's usual place, dripping with perspiration. Charles is playing Bussy d'Amboise. Monsieur de Carandas, the most tennis-mad of the King's gentlemen, yells advice to each in turn from the sidelines, but most other spectators appear more interested in their private conversations. Henriette waves from the other side of the court, where she is consuming grapes from the outstretched fingers of her latest conquest, Charles d'Entragues, or "*le bel Entraguet,*" as most of the Court calls him. Though I am sure she expects me to join her, I take a seat near my family.

"Come to cheer your brother?" Mother asks.

"Who else should I cheer?"

"Indeed," Anjou snipes, "Guise is absent."

"Let that be, now, Henri," Mother says. "Margot knows it is finished."

"Not quite, apparently," he says. "The Duc has returned to Paris, or am I misinformed?"

Mother gives him a stern look.

"Hardly surprising, considering that he lives here," I reply, with a shrug.

"For the moment." Anjou gives a wicked smile. "But I suspect him to be keeping company with his father before too long."

"Henri!" Mother's voice has none of its customary fondness. "Enough."

I long to snap that the day Anjou tries to put my beloved in a grave will likely be the day my brother finds himself mortally wounded, either at Guise's hands or at mine.

Bussy misses a return, giving Charles the victory. Racket over his head,

Charles turns to one gallery and then the next to receive the cheers of his courtiers. Charlotte and I rise and shout like the rest. Mother applauds. Anjou alone does not stir himself until, as everyone is returning to their seats, he raises a hand to point down the gallery. "Look who has come to make excuses."

Angoulême moves through the young men who roughhouse good-naturedly courtside. They have no reason to be sobered by my half brother's arrival and so slap him on the back and jostle him, but the sight of Angoulême alters His Majesty's expression. The light of triumph disappears, replaced by a flush caused by a less pleasant emotion.

"Who will Your Majesty play next?" Bussy asks.

"You play in my stead," the King replies. "Perhaps you will play better against the next opponent than you did against me."

Leaving Bussy puzzled, Charles drifts toward Mother. "Out of our place," he says to Anjou with a wave of his hand. Anjou avoids rising and bowing by slipping from chair to floor and leaning against the leg of Mother's seat as if to say to Charles, *You may have the throne but I will always come between you and our mother.*

Angoulême, having broken free of the knot of noblemen, makes his way toward us.

"Remember, Your Majesty, your business with the Chevalier is private. I urge you, therefore, to keep your displeasure private as well." Mother speaks low. She tries to catch my eye to dismiss me, but I am careful not to see her.

Reaching us, Angoulême makes a bow, clears his throat, and says, "Your Majesty—"

"Please," Charles interrupts, holding up a hand, "do not tell us you have brought us back a boar or a stag. You knew the tribute we wanted, and, failing that, nothing will satisfy."

"The man has two score eyes and twice as many friends."

"And you have too many excuses."

"If Your Majesty desires it, I will continue my pursuit."

"We do desire it, but if you could not bring down the beast in the forests, why should your luck be better in the streets of Paris? What might pass as an accident where many are shooting will hardly look like one in the Rue du Chaume."

Mother puts a warning hand on Charles' arm, apparently thinking his mention of the street in which the Hôtel de Guise stands too explicit.

"There are ruffians about everywhere, Your Majesty. A man may be set upon for his purse and lose limb or life instead," Angoulême says.

Unwittingly I give a little gasp. Turning in her seat, Mother says, "Baronne de Sauve, would you and the Duchesse de Valois return to my apartment and tell my ladies I will be there soon to dress for dinner."

I am loath to go, and have my own lack of self-possession to blame. As we make our way out, I console myself; it is beyond imagining that the details of whatever my half brother plans next would be discussed beside the tennis court. It is enough for the moment to know that Charles' anger is not spent.

That is what I tell Henriette later in the afternoon while all the ladies of the Queen's household are in the gardens of the Tuileries. Henriette and I have retreated to Monsieur Palissy's grotto. It is an excellent spot for privacy, as the ceramic frogs, snakes, and lizards he fashioned, which I find delightful, repulse most of the ladies. As an extra precaution Charlotte sits outside, prepared to sound a warning before any can overhear us.

"Leave it to Entragues and me," Henriette says confidently. "We will keep the Duc one step ahead of the King's men. I will see Guise this evening."

"How I wish I could go with you."

"I know. I know too that the Duc would bless me a thousand times over were I able to transport you secretly to the Rue du Chaume. But, alas, such subterfuge lies outside even my considerable powers." She seems genuinely regretful, though whether at disappointing me or at being forced to admit there are limits to her machinations, I cannot be sure. She begins to leave, then stops short. "Why not?"

"Why not what?"

"Help you see your Duc, of course."

Rushing forward, I take both her hands in mine. "Do you think it possible? Do not raise my expectations cruelly without hope of fulfillment."

"I never raise anything cruelly." She laughs. "I have planned to meet Entragues at that little house in the Rue Pavée that I have taken expressly for the sort of rendezvous my husband cannot know about. But instead I shall give up my hours of *amour* so that you can steal one with Guise. I will bring him here."

"Here?"

"The weather is warm. The moon will be nearly full. All the Court will be at the Louvre, and these gardens deserted. You have only to contrive to be here."

Henriette was right. The moon is very bright, though not so bright as to justify the care with which I dressed. I have not been so fastidious in my toilette since my love left to hunt. Removing my cloak, I lay it on a bench, pinch my cheeks, straighten my necklace, and wait.

Henriette has arranged for Henri to give a long, low whistle before entering the grotto, and never has my ear been more eager for a sound. When it comes, and before it stops reverberating from the rock around me, I am in Henri's arms. His lips close over mine. His hands caress my cheeks, where they find moisture. He breaks off our kiss.

"Are you weeping?" He draws me into the moonlight so he can see me better.

"Only a little, and nothing compared to the tears I should have shed had Angoulême found the courage to take aim at you in the forest."

"Angoulême? Pfft!" Henri wipes my tears with his thumbs. "Pardon me, love, but he has neither the courage nor the aim to make me take him seriously. When I arrived at the Hôtel de Guise, I heard that you took far more punishment at the hands of your brutish brothers than I ever feared from your half brother. It was only with the greatest difficulty that I subdued my urge to ride for the Louvre and make them pay."

"You must not even joke about such actions. My brothers are your sworn enemies. Charles wants you dead and you must not give him any opportunity to see his wish fulfilled."

"He can hardly have me killed in open court. I would have more respect for him were he—or Anjou—to challenge me openly. In trial by combat I would thrash either soundly, and perhaps in future they would remember that a man who attacks a woman is not man at all." He pulls me against his breast and strokes my hair. "They have not enough honor between them to equal one true gentleman. But forgive me, I forgot they are your brothers."

"There is nothing you could say of Anjou that I have not myself thought. Charles . . ." I push back from him and seek his eyes. ". . . I believe Charles left to himself would be a good man and a good king."

"Ah, but he is never left to himself."

"Oh, Henri." My tears begin again. "You have fought and bled for Charles. There are none braver or more worthy among his gentlemen. Why can he not let you have my hand as your reward?"

"Your mother wants to stop my influence. She fears the sway of even healthy friendship upon him. But will you give me up so easily?" His voice is earnest. "Will you consent to marry Dom Sébastien?"

"To save your life, yes."

"It will not come to that, I swear it." He kisses the side of my neck. The effect of his touch, his scent, is overwhelming. The strong yearnings I felt before he went away—the very urges that, along with a need to lessen gossip, drove him to the cool of the forest lest we fall into sin— surge through me. I know that he feels them as well, for as he moves his mouth to mine his kisses are frantic, the arms that hold me are tense and, when my hand strays to the front of his *haut-de-chausses,* his arousal is clear. I am nearly delirious with desire. *I have already been accused of having Henri and he of defiling me. Why should it not be so, then?* The offer of myself stands on the tip of the tongue I thrust into his mouth.

Then I remember the rage on Charles' face as the cry of "Whore!" rang from his lips. If there is to be even a feeble hope of calming the King's hatred, I must retain my trump card—the ability to offer myself up to a physician's examination to prove my virginity.

I push against Henri. Rather than being confused by my action, he releases me entirely, takes two very deep breaths, then paces away and takes a seat on the low bench. He knows as well as I how close we are to committing an act that can never be undone.

"We must have a plan," he says at last. "Just as we would if we sought victory in battle."

"You have won so many battles; do you believe we can win this one?"

"I must believe. To think otherwise is to be defeated at the outset. And the prize"—despite the low light I can see him shake his head—"the value of the prize nearly within my reach is beyond any city I have ever taken."

A joy equal to the desire that a moment ago consumed me fills my breast.

"I am not a patient man, but I know how to besiege a city—how to play a waiting game. The King will cool. He has not the temperament to maintain a heated and active grudge. There is a royal ball just shy of a fortnight from now. I will keep to my *hôtel* until that occasion and then, as I am called upon to do by my position as *Grand Maître de France,* present myself with an outward show of deference befitting a loyal subject and dutiful officer."

"And I?"

"You will spend the next two weeks being the most obedient sister and daughter in Christendom. Or appearing so. Reassure the King and your mother that you stand willing to marry the Portuguese as soon as it can be arranged—"

"But such a marriage, or even a betrothal to Dom Sébastien, puts an end to all our dreams!"

"And for that reason the marriage must be prevented, but not by you. You must appear blameless when it comes to nothing."

"How, then?"

"Philip of Spain thinks your brother too lenient with the heretics."

I know my love thinks this as well. Any tolerance for Protestantism in France is wholly unacceptable to his pious nature. I think again how fitting it would be that we should marry and Henri become the King's chief counsel in seeing France entirely Catholic again.

"While Admiral Coligny draws his men closer to Paris," Henri continues, "perhaps word will reach the Spanish that Charles thinks of peace."

"Does he?"

"Who can say? He thinks whatever Madame Catherine thinks for him at present. No matter. My uncle wants your hand for the House of Lorraine nearly as much as I want it myself. He will be happy to see the right words home to the right ears.

"Now come." He holds out a hand. "Kiss me again without tears."

I hesitate. Not because I do not wish to be kissed, but because—as I was reminded so recently—my will to stop at a kiss is severely to be doubted. Henri senses the hesitation.

"Marguerite, I swear to you, on my honor, that as I revere you and hope to have you for my wife, I will not take the rights of a husband until I am bound to the duties of one."

I need no further reassurance, for I wish to be upon his lap as much as he wishes to have me there. "Do not show too much restraint," I urge an instant before I offer my lips. Without further thought of the kings of Portugal, Spain, or France, I surrender to the sensations of my body. Until I hear a noise—a low whistle.

Henri hears it too and, springing to his feet, unceremoniously drops me on the floor of the grotto. Moving his hand to his sword, he carefully unsheathes it. The whistle comes again. "Who goes there?" Henri's voice is almost a growl.

"Put up your sword, fool, who do you think?" Henriette slips in. "Are you so besotted that you forgot I accompanied you here?"

I blush in the darkness, wondering where Henriette was while Henri and I wrestled lustfully.

"Time to go," she says matter-of-factly. Henri nods. "But first, here." She removes her cloak and holds it out. "You must act the part of my maid, and I will take you home in my litter."

"Surely I can slip back on my own."

"You cannot. While the two of you exchanged pretty words, Entragues found me. It seems one of Anjou's spies reported that you left the Hôtel de Guise, though he could not, praise God and our luck, tell the Prince your destination."

"No!" I put a hand on Henri's arm.

"Entragues heard your brother say, 'Never mind where he has gone: he must come home again and I shall set Angoulême to wait for him.' So, Duc, you will play my maid."

Henri takes the cloak and ties it on. I draw up the hood for him. "Take care, Henri. If anything were to happen to you . . ."

"Nothing will happen. I will feel humiliated but nothing worse." Turning to Henriette, he says, "I do not see what this achieves. Assuming

I am taken for your maid, how am I to get from your litter to my home? You are well-known, Madame."

"I should hope so."

"And well-known as a friend to the Duchesse de Valois. If Angoulême recognizes your litter arriving at my *hôtel* and a woman is seen exiting it, will not a rendezvous with Marguerite be suspected?"

"Not when that woman can be clearly seen to be my sister the Princesse with a servant trailing a step behind. And that is what you shall appear to be: a servant come to make her late-night visit to a man look somewhat less scandalous. We will stop to retrieve Catherine en route. I've sent a message telling her you are eager to see her and that we will make a merry party."

I am far from happy with this development, but how can I object? Henri's safety is paramount. As he stoops to kiss me one more time, I ask, "When will I see you again?"

"At the ball."

My breath catches. "Not before?" I know his decision is wise. After the events of this evening it is clearly not safe for him to venture from the Hôtel de Guise. But my need for him is such that the thought of a fortnight without sight or touch of him seems unbearable.

"We are at war, remember." The arm he has slipped around my waist tightens in an almost violent manner. "Sacrifices must be made."

The night of the ball has arrived! Trailing behind Mother with the other ladies, I attempt to check my excitement, or at least the appearance of it. But it is difficult to look calm when tonight my love returns to Court. So much depends on his reception. When we reach the *Salle des Caryatides,* the musicians are on the balcony playing softly. Charles is seated beneath his velvet canopy with a number of gentlemen gathered about, basking in his momentary favor while Anjou keeps his own court in a corner.

Charles rises, acknowledging Mother's entrance. Those we pass bow. All eyes are upon the Queen until they aren't. The disturbance—a murmur: *"C'est de Guise."* Heads snap round. Eyes, not the least among them those of His Majesty, look down the length of the room. At such a moment I need not fear attracting attention by looking as well.

Henri is immediately distinguishable thanks to his height. He is dressed magnificently and makes his way by confident, unhurried steps toward the King. Charles moves in the Duc's direction with Mother behind. Guise has been absent from Court long enough, and his absence given so many explanations—all of them whispered and few of them true—that those present naturally close in upon the spot where my brother and my beloved must meet. When they are nearly upon each other, Henri stops, bows deeply, and says, "Your Majesty."

Charles' hand moves to his sword. I take a step forward, but Henriette grabs my arm. "What is your business?" Charles' voice is shrill.

"I have come to serve my king as I have in the past, in fulfillment of my office and my inclination." Henri bows again.

"Did you serve us in the past? Or did you serve yourself?"

"Your Majesty, I protest that I have served you faithfully, often in arms and with no thought either for my aggrandizement or my life."

A voice behind me says, "Poor Guise, I think he must be telling the truth. For if he cared for his life, he would not have come tonight." It is Anjou. Hatred surges through me. Were I not necessarily transfixed by what passes between Charles and Henri, I would fall upon Anjou, scratching and biting like an animal until removed by force, heedless of the spectacle I was creating.

"You serve at our pleasure, do you not?" Charles asks bitingly. "Well, you have misapprehended our pleasure if you believe we looked for you tonight, or that you are welcome." Henri stands steady and proud before the King. Yet I who love him perceive a slight flexing of the muscles along his jaw. Charles takes a step forward, his hand still on the hilt of his sword. "We forswear your service, Sir, and caution you to keep yourself out of our eye and the reach of our sword."

The crowd, which was all this time silent, begins to buzz like a nest of angry bees. The slight could not be more public nor the warning more clear. A tinge of color rises on Henri's cheekbones. He bows again with perfect correctness. When he straightens, his eyes meet mine for a single instant. I see worry in them. Then he turns and makes his way through the crowd toward the door.

"As you love him and trust me," Henriette whispers, "do not follow." She slips from my side as the courtiers surrounding us come to life. Some surge to the King. Others turn to their neighbors. A number follow the Duc. What was a buzz becomes a cacophony. The sound and the movement overwhelm me—or is it my raw fear? Charlotte slides to the place Henriette vacated and slips an arm about my waist.

"Come," Mother says commandingly, "this is a ball. Your Majesty"— she must touch Charles' arm—"will you open the dancing with your sister?"

Me? How can I dance when I do not trust myself to stand should Charlotte's arm be withdrawn?

"Disappointed, Margot?" Anjou asks, stepping beside me. "Madame," he says to Mother, "I believe our sister thought to have another partner."

The Queen throws him a look that would cause any save her favorite to quake. "Margot." Charlotte releases me and I, quite miraculously, stay on my feet and give my hand to Charles. Courtiers part. The musicians strike up the first chords of a new piece. "Smile." This last admonition is hissed at us both as Her Majesty backs away. There is nothing for me to smile about, but at the sight of Anjou's sneering face I do. To be crushed is one thing. To let my brother see that I am crushed is another. As the King and I complete our second pattern, others join the dance. Charles asks quietly, "Did you summon him here *ce soir*?"

"I? I wish he had not come." The words are true and, apparently, Charles can read their veracity in my tone.

"I take no pleasure in paining you," he says. I believe him. In this he is entirely unlike Anjou. "But I cannot permit Guise's grasping insolence. As Mother said, it is over, Margot. And make no mistake"—the momentary regret in his voice vanishes—"I will see the Duc dead before I will let him into this family."

"I have given him up, Charles, I swear it!"

"You will have to do better than that. You will have to prove it."

How does one prove such a thing?

Looking across the formation of dancers, I see the Princesse de Porcien and I know with dreadful certainty. With certainty comes despair. I might cease to breathe, sink to the floor and turn to dust, did not my pride demand I get through this dance, and did not one vital, horrible task remain to me.

When the music stops, I look for Charlotte. She knows without my saying anything that the room, full of swirling bodies and laughter, is no place for me. Taking my hand, she leads me toward the door. We are a few feet from making our escape when the Baronne de Retz appears. I do not wait for her question.

"I am going to my room. If you believe my misery needs another witness, you are free to follow."

Charlotte must have expected me to collapse as soon as we are out of the sight of the rest of the Court, for she casts me curious sidelong glances as I press on rapidly toward my apartment. When we are nearly there, we come upon Henriette. "He is safely away but he is shaken," she says. There is none of the delight in her eyes that usually accompanies narrow escapes.

"We are all of us shaken," Charlotte says as we enter my anteroom. "Whatever people imagined about the quarrel between the Duc and the King, I will wager none imagined His Grace being turned away from the Louvre."

"Yet now they doubtless imagine much worse," Henriette says.

"Because of me," I say, at last finding my tongue.

"No!" Charlotte replies. "You are not to blame."

"What use is there in assigning or accepting fault?" Henriette asks impatiently. "What is to be done?"

I open my mouth but no sound comes. I take a deep breath, which catches, then try again. "Henri must marry. He must close the matter with your sister at once." The words come out broken, like my heart. Part of me hopes Henriette and Charlotte will express disagreement, but while both look stricken, neither raises an objection.

"He will need persuading," Henriette says. "Likely more persuading than I alone am capable of."

I hope so. Dear God, I hope so. If Henri is not as horrified by the idea of his marrying the Princesse as I am, I will be inconsolable.

"I will write to Claude. Henri is not alone in his danger; the entire House of Lorraine should care deeply what befalls him."

"Yes!" Henriette nods approvingly. "The Duchesse's husband will wish this disgrace resolved quickly. Ask the two of them to come to Court."

A lump rises in my throat at the thought of what I must say. I must reveal much that is painful—not only the depth of my own love and loss, but the betrayals and cruelties of my family. There is a small measure of consolation in the fact that such Valois sins will be confided fully only to another of my bloodline.

I am as nervous as a cat. I have counted and recounted the days until Claude could be expected in Paris. She did not come yesterday, so this day must certainly see her arrival. True sister, she replied at once, saying that she would rescue me from my disgrace and put my beloved on the path to his salvation. I care nothing for myself. I am content to be ruined so long as Henri is no longer in peril.

Mother knows that the Duchesse and Duc are coming. How could it be otherwise? A leaf does not drop in the garden of one of the great châteaux without her knowing. She goes about whistling softly, anticipating the company of a daughter more satisfactory than I—one who married where she was bid and lives blamelessly. I wonder, watching the Queen clicking her tongue against her teeth, then smiling as she feeds her parrot, whether she has guessed in part the purpose of Claude's visit. I suspect she has. It would be unnatural if the Duc de Lorraine did not come to counsel his kinsman.

The door opens. I glance in that direction with anticipation. It is only Anjou. Doubtless he comes to borrow Mademoiselle de Rieux. He has taken her up again and is very indiscreet. I turn back to my embroidery.

"Look who I found making her way from the courtyard," Anjou says.

My eyes rise again. Claude!

"Daughter." Mother offers my sister both her hands and both her cheeks in turn. "Did you bring the children?"

Claude now has six little ones.

"No. Charles thought it best they stay at Bar-le-Duc, as our visit will be short."

Mother puts an arm around Claude's waist and guides her toward the settle across from me. "He is right, of course," Mother says. "Coligny and his ilk make the roads less safe by the day. I received word this morning that he closes on La Charité-sur-Loire. But let us not talk of the war. I spend nearly the whole of my time considering it, to the detriment of my health and, I fear, without substantial benefit to your brother's kingdom."

"Madame," Claude replies, "you are too modest. The conduct of the war may not progress as quickly or as definitively as His Majesty's most devoted subjects would wish, but the King and his troops would be lost without your good counsel." Then, looking across at me, she says, "Sister, I hope I find you well."

Mother gives me a chastising look. "Your sister has been involved in a bit of folly—not uncommon in the young—and suffers from low spirits in consequence."

Her trivialization of my heartbreak grates, but I bite my lower lip and keep silent.

"I am sure Marguerite is chastened whatever her transgression, Madame. She has a true Valois heart." She rises.

"You are going?" Mother asks.

"I must. I have not yet been to our *hôtel*. I was so eager to see you that I persuaded Charles to part company with me. But if we are to return and dine, I must unpack and rid myself of the dirt of the road." Claude takes a few steps toward the door, then stops. "I wonder, shall I take Marguerite with me?"

"Do. Your influence will do her good, and in her present humor she is of no use to herself or anyone else here."

Anjou moves aside to let us pass. "There is no use beating her; we have already tried."

Claude throws him an icy backwards glance, then whispers, "Courage." We sweep to the courtyard where her litter stands. Climbing in beside me, she says, "The Hôtel de Nemours."

I gasp.

"I am sorry I could give you no warning, but from the moment I read your letter it has been my opinion that the sooner this thing is settled, the better. Charles and I stopped to see the Duchesse de Nemours before I came to the Louvre. Her Grace understood our plan at once, but she fears her son will be difficult to persuade. He is, after all, a most determined man and used to having what he wants."

"But what can I tell the Duchesse that you have not?"

"You misapprehend me. While I have been here, Charles rode to get his cousin."

Henri! Henri will be at the Hôtel de Nemours! Here is a thing I never prepared for—to argue personally for a marriage that will destroy me.

Claude looks concerned. "Have you the strength to see him? I believe you may have a power over him that exceeds that of any other."

Do I have the strength? At this moment I fear not. I fear that, much as I have told myself ceaselessly since the night of the ball that I would do anything to save Henri, I will not be able to push him from me. I close my eyes. *Please Lord, grant me sufficient self-abnegation to do this terrible but necessary thing. In the name of Your Son who gave up His body to be beaten and His life so that sins might be forgiven, help me offer up all my hopes for the future to save my beloved.*

When I open my eyes, Claude still looks at me. "Shall I turn the litter?"

"No. The Duc must go from Court and not return until it is time for him to wed the Princesse de Porcien. This and this alone will stop the mouths of his enemies and mine. This alone will save the life so precious to me. If I am necessary to this result, I will do what I can."

She takes my hand and kisses it. "You do have a Valois heart, or perhaps better say a Médicis one."

I am startled to realize what she means: my mother is known by all to have the strength to do what others cannot, the strength of her sons combined. Could there be something of my mother in me that is useful rather than hateful?

When we arrive at the Hôtel de Nemours, the Duchesse waits just inside. She embraces Claude and curtsys to me. There is wariness in her eyes. I cannot blame her. She must hate me at this moment, for her sons are her life and I have endangered the eldest and dearest of them.

"Has Charles begun?" Claude asks.

"He will not hear reason," the Duchesse says. "He knows he is in grave disfavor, and accepts even that his life is in peril, but turns from the remedy."

Her Grace leads us into the next room. My brother-in-law stands, hands on hips, interrupted in midsentence by the opening of the door. Henri sits before him, looking more bored and vexed than terrified. At the sight of me he leaps to his feet.

"Marguerite!" The way he says my name, the light in his eyes—I am nearly undone before I begin. In a few strides he is at my side, slipping an arm about my waist and pulling me against his hip in a protective manner, heedless of the impropriety of these actions. "These fools do not understand how I love you."

"We do," Claude replies. "But we also understand that love will not lead to happiness, nor will it restore you to your place at Court."

"The King has publicly turned from you, son," Anne d'Este says. "There is talk of negotiations with the heretics. Do you wish the houses of Guise and Lorraine to be absent from such talks?" I feel Henri stiffen.

"The devil take the King and the Huguenots!"

"That is precisely what I fear," his mother presses. "Think of the harm that may come to France without the staunch Catholic voices of Lorraine at any conference for peace. Will you surrender the souls of your countrymen because you are crossed in love?"

"If my countrymen and my king have not enough sense to look to their own salvation, why should that concern me? I have executed my duty to both faithfully. Fought for both. And my recompense has been ill use. I am through being His Majesty's loyal servant."

Even though we are just five in the room, both Anne d'Este and my sister glance around nervously at this pronouncement.

"Are you through too with all ambition?" Henri's mother asks. "Content to be a ruined man and stay one? Are you ready to cast all that your father achieved for this house aside and live—if you are allowed to live—at Joinville in obscurity?"

My beloved starts as if slapped. His arm goes slack for a moment as if he would release me, then tightens again. "Surely matters are not so serious." He tries to laugh but fails. "Or at least not permanently so."

"Your Highness," the Duchesse de Nemours appeals to me, "speak to him."

"Yes. Marguerite, speak," Henri urges. "Tell them what we mean to each other."

"Henri, you know that I love you"—I am surprised at the calm of my own voice—"but my sister is right: Charles will never allow us to be happy. He has set his mind against us and the only person who could turn it, my mother, wishes us ill."

This time he does release me, taking a step away so he can see my face. The pain and confusion in his eyes wrings my heart.

"Will you urge me to marry another? For that is what the Duc de Lorraine proposes. He wants me to set the Princesse de Porcien in the place you thought to occupy." His voice is urgent, but still tinged with confidence. *Oh, Henri, how I love your boldness, but this is, sadly, no moment for bravado.*

Impatiently he takes another step away, rounds on me and, with eyes as sharp as swords ever were, lowers his voice and demands, "Will you say you no longer wish to be my wife?"

"I need not give voice to a lie to urge prudence upon you. I want to be your wife more than I have ever wanted anything, but my experience of life tells me that what I want does not matter—it has never mattered. The King told me the night of the ball that he will see you dead before he will consent to see us wed." I notice the Duchesse de Nemours put a hand out to steady herself at these words. "Do you believe that if I cannot have you I would wish you dead? Can you ask me to carry your destruction on my conscience?"

Henri hangs his head. And I know we are close to prevailing. Success has never seemed more unwelcome. The first tear rolls down my cheek and I brush it away angrily. I cannot afford to give in to my own emotions until I have finished.

"Henri, look at me."

He does not look up.

Slowly, as if I were a woman of great age, my bones brittle, I move forward and get to my knees before him. I can see him watching through lowered lashes. "My love," I plead, "you must save yourself. You cannot be my husband but you can yet thrive as one of the greatest and most powerful men in France. Do not let my brother take your future as he has taken mine." My voice shakes and, despite my best efforts, tears continue to fall. Henri looks at me squarely.

"What would you have me do?" he asks, his voice breaking.

"Solicit the hand of the Princess de Porcien."

"You condemn me to a life of unhappiness."

"I condemn myself to one as well. And yet I think it a good bargain, for while you may despair of domestic contentment, I believe you will find purpose and satisfaction in other realms. I pray it may be so." I mean what I say, but saying it takes the last of my strength. I collapse to the floor and, heedless of my dignity, lay on my side weeping.

Falling to his knees beside me, Henri gathers me to him so that he cradles me against his breast like a child. "Help her," he says to my sister.

"Only you can do that."

Henri rocks me gently, putting his lips first against my temple and then close to my ear. "I will marry her," he whispers. "God forgive me for the lies I will tell at the altar when I do, and for the pain I have caused you." Raising his head, he says to the others, "Make your plans. Seek the lady's hand on my behalf and I will take it."

I feel a tear drop from Henri's face onto mine. Looking past my beloved, I see that the Duc de Lorraine has turned away—either moved or horrified by his cousin's display of emotion. Claude and the Duchesse de Nemours cling to one another. Their eyes are wet, yet they shine with triumph. I ought to feel the victory as well—Henri is saved—but I am conscious of nothing but pain, my own and Henri's.

My sister takes a step forward and reaches out a hand.

"No!" Henri's voice is adamant. "Leave her. You have succeeded in separating us, but not yet. Not yet!"

I bury my face against his chest.

I sense rather than see the others retreat. A click of the great oak door marks their passing. I am seized by the sudden horrible thought that this is the last time Henri and I will ever be alone together.

Henri's hand is on my hair, both catching and caressing it. He is shaking, not with desire, but with grief, and so am I. Tipping my face up, I see in his eyes a mirror of my own heartbreak. "We haven't much time," I sob. *No, we have no time at all.*

"Do not forget me," he says, "when they send you to Portugal."

And as painful as the thought of seeing him as someone else's husband is, this sudden idea of not seeing him at all, of being away from Court, is worse. "Never," I say, reaching up to touch his cheek. "My heart is yours; it cannot be recalled. It stays with you wherever my hand is given."

Lowering his mouth, he kisses me. I taste the salt of both our tears. Our kiss is deep but neither springs from nor ignites passion. It is a kiss entirely spiritual, the union of two hearts and souls soon to be torn from each other.

"Come," Henri says, "let us go out of our own accord before they come back to take you away."

I understand what he means. Nothing is left under our control but the manner of our parting, so we must not cede that. Wiping my tears with both hands and rising, I ask, "Is this what it is like to ride from a field of battle defeated?"

"Yes," he replies with a nod of his head. "We cannot, it seems, carry the day, but we can surrender with dignity rather than begging for mercy where we will get none."

We walk out together, heads held high, hand in hand, but I wonder as we go: *Why was there no mercy to be had, either at the hands of our king or our god?*

PART THREE

La mort n'a point d'ami . . .

(Death hath no friends . . .)

CHAPTER 14

March 1571—Paris, France

"Close the shutters. I do not intend to rise."

Gillone moves back toward my window but Henriette stops her. My friend comes to the bed where I lean back against the headboard, a look of determination on her face.

"Enough!" She takes me by both shoulders and shakes. "For months you have been listless and fading."

I know it to be true, but make no reply. This seems to exasperate her further. "You were present in body only at the King's nuptial celebrations at Mézières. You crept around Blois as a ghost." Releasing me so that I fall back against my pillows, she puts her hands on her hips. "At last we return to Paris and all the city enjoys the spectacle, save you."

Shrugging, I close my eyes.

"Today you will rise and dress to dazzle."

"Why should I?"

"Why should you not?" my friend challenges.

Tears well beneath my closed lids. "You know why."

"Because the Duc de Guise is married nearly half a year and has lived away from Court that long? Well, in case it has escaped your notice, he returned two days ago for the Queen Consort's upcoming coronation." My eyes snap open at Henriette's unfeeling words, loosing the tears that had gathered.

She shakes her head angrily. "Is the sight of him what prostrates you? Have you not observed that, despite his long looks in your direction, he is a picture of health. You, on the other hand, are a shadow of that princess he fell in love with."

I push myself further upright. "I am certain Henri expected to find me thus," I snap, "and sees my condition as a mark of a faithful heart. Why can you not respect it as such?"

"Why should I respect a woman who has given herself over to grief and forsaken all pleasure at an age when there is much joy and pleasure to be had? You behave as if you are a hapless leaf tossed upon the storm-swollen Seine with no power to take matters in hand."

"Because I have no such power. I am nothing but a point in a treaty, offered to one groom and then another in the manner most likely to bring benefits to the crown. I have accepted that in the past but . . ." My voice trails off as my mind travels back to the terrible day of my beloved's nuptials. The wedding felt like a funeral—my own. I survived it, but was so thankful when at last we departed the Hôtel de Guise. How could I know that the cruelest twist of the day was yet to come?

As we entered the Louvre, His Majesty was accosted by his secretary with a letter from Portugal. Dom Sébastien declared himself too young to marry and declared me well able to wait. Tears I had held in check all day, through every sort of agony, began to fall. Not because I wanted Dom Sébastien, but because I ought to have been wanted by him—by someone. At seventeen, I was the most beautiful woman in France and yet also three times spurned. My heart staggered under that blow. It was nearly stopped by the next. As I wept into my hands, Mother and His Majesty pronounced that they were done with Dom Sébastien. That instead they would use my hand as a seal upon the *Paix de Saint-Germain-en-Laye,* forging an unbreakable bond between the Catholic and Protestant branches of our family by marrying me to Henri de Bourbon, Prince of

Navarre. My cousin, the ill-kempt and ill-mannered pest from my girlhood. A notorious heretic.

"But what?" Henriette challenges. "You are unhappy. You have been denied your heart's desire. How will you fight back? *All* women are pawns of their families—bartered and bedded for the aggrandizement of their houses. I was so myself. Yet you do not see me weeping, waiting for my beauty to fade. I am the Duchesse de Nevers, not by marriage but in my own right; I have money, I have looks, I have love—and on my own terms. I engage in the battle for my fate by living as I like.

"You must rise and do the same. You want Guise in your bed. Have him. He is someone else's husband. My sister's, in point of fact. You will be another man's wife—possibly the Prince of Navarre's. But all this only makes it easier."

"Easier?" I bristle. "How can marriage to a heretic make anything easier?"

Henriette leans in toward me. "Who is more chaperoned, the maiden or the wife? The maiden, of course. You know that to be true by your own experience. When you are Princess of Navarre, unless you are caught *in flagrante,* who is to know if the gentleman who makes you sigh and sweat is your loathsome husband or another?"

Here is an unexpected thought. For a moment I am stunned—but I am also awakened from the torpor that has held me fast in its grip since last October. "You urge me to embrace a match with Navarre so that I may take Guise as lover?"

"That is what I ought to advise, but I look at you and despair that you will fade to nothing before that. The time for caution is past and you were never very adept at it anyway." She smiles slightly for the first time since she began speaking. "So I urge you to live again, without waiting for your marriage or any other event. The Duc is at Court after months of absence. Instead of pining for him impotently, remind him why he loves you."

A sense of power and purpose swells in my breast. I throw off my covers and swing my legs out of bed. Stalking to my mirror, I examine my figure. I am thinner than I was last fall, but I know I am still an object of Henri's desire. I saw as much in his hungry eyes when he first entered my presence two days ago. Felt as much in the lips that brushed my hand during our brief greeting. And I still want Henri—God, yes. At the thought of him, my stomach quivers.

Turning to my friend, I say, "I will have the Duc. I have been accused of him and beaten on account of it. Let me have the pleasure now; I have been punished for it already."

"Bravo!" Henriette's eyes sparkle. The color rises in her cheeks as it has in mine. "I think you must dine with me at the Hôtel de Nevers this week." She beckons Gillone forward with a clean chemise.

"You mean . . ."

"What could be more natural than that the Duc should also be my guest?" Henriette pulls my shift off and drops fresh linen over my head. The fabric soft and crisp against my skin is delightful. "He is my brother. My sister will not come. She can scarcely keep a mouthful of food down since the Duc put her with child, and she cannot bear to watch others eat."

I wince at the mention of the Princesse de Porcien's condition. The thought of her carrying my beloved's child—something I hoped to do myself—remains unbearable, though it is no longer news.

Henriette, sensing my discomfort, takes my hand. "Let me arrange it all. It will be my little gift."

I draw a deep breath. Henriette's tone is light but the gift she offers is anything but little. "Make it soon," I plead.

Henriette gives a delightful laugh by way of reply.

"And now," I say, inclining my head as if I do her a great favor, "you may make me as dazzling as you like."

Never has the ride to the Hôtel de Nevers seemed longer. From behind my kidskin mask I see men working on the monuments for my sister-in-law's entrance into Paris. *Bless Elisabeth and her coronation.* She is the reason my beloved is in the city. Without her I would not be riding to see him, anticipating his strong arms around me—and so much more. My very flesh is alive with anticipation of the surrender of my virginity. I quiver. I could not eat this morning.

Henriette greets me, drawing me to her comfortable and familiar apartments. Covered dishes are in place and wine has been poured.

"For appearances," she says. "And you may be famished after."

My throat constricts and my heart beats inside my ribs like a caged bird. Lifting a glass from the table, I take a gulp. A knock sounds.

"The Duc is prompt," Henriette says with a smile. She takes the glass from my trembling hand, sets it back on the table, and then calls, "Enter." A servant swings open the door to reveal Henri. His eyes meet mine. For a moment he is motionless, staring at me as if I am the very queen of heaven.

"Brother, come in. Your meal awaits." Henriette smiles at Henri. Then she turns to the servant. "That will be all," she instructs.

Henri moves to me, taking my hand and bringing it to his lips. "Margot." His voice, usually so sonorous, is low and broken. He pulls me into his arms, his lips close over mine. After five long, lonely months I taste him once again. His breath is my breath. I am engulfed by his delicious smell.

"Ahem." The sound of Henriette clearing her throat has an immediate effect. Henri and I pull apart, staring at each other, dazed. His cheeks are flushed and I imagine that mine are as well.

Glancing at the Duchesse sheepishly, Henri bows, then says, "Forgive me, sister, but a starving man has little use for manners."

"Ah, but, Your Grace, I must insist on decorum." Henriette's look of mock severity causes us all to laugh. "Have a glass of wine. I will prepare your beloved for bed."

I cannot seem to get enough air. My stomach spasms, and something else as well, as if those lower lips which man has never parted have come alive.

It appears that Henri is also affected, for as Henriette draws me away, he picks up the nearest glass and drains it.

In Henriette's chamber the bed is turned back and flower petals are strewn over the sheets. Soon I will slide between those sheets with Henri beside me. We are, strangely, almost reverently silent as Henriette undresses me down to my silken chemise. When only that remains, she leads me to her dressing table. Opening a case, she draws out a necklace of enormous sapphires and fastens it around my neck. "The effect against your skin is beautiful," she says, beginning to take down my hair. When she has finished brushing my tresses, Henriette loosens the neck of my chemise. Unstopping a bottle on her dressing table, she pours some perfume into one of her palms, rubs her hands together and then, quite unexpectedly, reaches over my shoulders and runs her scented hands beneath my chemise and over my breasts. I am both embarrassed and fascinated to see my nipples harden though the fine silk of my garment.

I climb into the bed, allowing her to arrange the pillows. Standing back, she nods her head, satisfied. "Beautiful. One more thing." She bustles to her dressing table and then to a decanter of brandy, opening the libation for no purpose that I can ascertain. "I fear from the Duc's looks that you, my dear friend, are the undoing of his much-vaunted self-control. We must take precautions that, if it is so, your womb will not be quickened. There will be time enough for the Duc to give your cousin an heir once you are wed." She laughs as if delighted by the thought of my cuckolding the Prince of Navarre.

She holds out her hand. In her palm I can see a small piece of sponge. "It is doused in brandy," she says. Her explanation means nothing to me.

"What am I to do with it?"

"You must push this past your *dame du milieu,* do you understand? It will hurt, but it will offer your womb some protection."

I look away as I part my *babichon* and push the sponge inside. It stops momentarily and then, in a single, swift thrust, it is gone. I yelp with the pain of it and my eyes water.

"Good," Henriette declares, satisfied. And then she is gone.

A moment later Henri enters. He stops just over the threshold to stare. "*Mon Dieu,* you are a thing too beautiful to be real," he says. Slowly he walks to the foot of the bed, unfastening his doublet as he comes. As he undresses I finger Henriette's sapphires, arching my neck, hoping to look my best. Henri's eyes never leave me.

When he stands in nothing but his shirt—a garment as fine as my chemise—I summon him. "Come to me," I say, opening the neck of my chemise even further. "Lay claim to what should have been yours. To what *is* yours by my own volition. For I swear to love you always and no other."

He eagerly complies. Lying beside me, his hands run over me—cupping breasts, caressing my waist and belly, slipping between my thighs. "I have dreamed of this since first you caught my eye as a slip of a girl," he murmurs, kissing the side of my neck. As he pulls me against him I can feel the organ of his manhood pressing against my belly. It is as a rod of iron. Fascinated, I reach down to touch it. As my fingers meet his flesh—surprisingly soft—he cries out in delight. His delight emboldens me and I stroke him again and again. His hands fall to my hips and begin to gather up my chemise.

Rolling on top of me, he asks, "Shall I make you mine, then?"

The tenderness in his face makes my heart ache. I draw up my knees, rubbing them along his haunches. The smoothness of his skin sliding against mine causes me to moan.

"Yes."

I have not a moment to prepare myself. Like a warrior charging into battle, Henri gives a mighty thrust and disappears inside me—stopping only when his loins collide with mine.

In all the months we feasted on stolen kisses, all the evenings he fondled me and crooned words of love, all the frustrated moments I longed for this and could not have it, never did I properly imagine the exquisite feeling of his flesh inside me. As he draws himself in and out, covering my face and neck with kisses, nipping and teasing my nipples with his lips and teeth, I am overcome. I want to touch every part of him. My hands run along his back beneath his shirt. My legs entwine behind his buttocks. I cry out in pleasure and the sound of my own voice excites me further. I want to shout to all the world that he is mine.

Harder and harder he presses me, his face growing fierce. I wonder if he will go through me and touch the silken sheets I rest upon. I close my eyes, helpless in the face of my own sensations. Without warning, the tunnel of my flesh, which he occupies so fully, begins to spasm. I keen his name, and as I do his voice joins mine, joyous, strangely strangled and shouting. Collapsing on top of me, he rolls onto his back, taking me with him. With my head resting on his chest, I can hear his heart racing faster than horse ever galloped. I can feel his hand stroking my hair.

"Dear God," he murmurs, "I must have you night and day. Must dwell inside you. I swear your body was made to please mine."

He is pleased! The thought fills me with pride and thanksgiving. He loves me, he has taken me and I have pleased him. Should my heart stop beating in this moment, it would be enough.

CHAPTER 15

January 1572—Paris, France

Another year has begun. I am to be painted by Clouet. It has been more than ten years since he made a portrait of me, dressed in cream. This time I will wear black. How fitting. Jeanne d'Albret has left Pau and moves ever northward, bringing with her a will to come to terms, and my detestable cousin.

After a year's delay I felt certain the Queen of Navarre had no real interest in a marriage between myself and the Prince of Navarre. I started to feel safe. But I underestimated Mother. When wheedling and bribing failed, she turned to her favorite method: threats. Her Majesty intimated she would seek a papal investigation into the validity of Jeanne's marriage to Antoine de Bourbon. Such an examination would call into question my cousin's standing as First Prince of the Blood.

Who can say if there was any true defect in Jeanne's union? The Queen of Navarre, as a member of a reviled sect, may simply have despaired of a fair hearing from the Holy Father. Whatever her reasoning, Jeanne wrote saying if His Majesty would confirm her son's position, the Prince of Navarre would wed me. Without a miracle, I will be my cousin's wife before we see another autumn. So my heart is as dark and heavy as the gown I am fastened into for my portrait.

I am not the only one in a black mood. Ruggiero *il vecchio* predicts Mother will die near Saint-Germain. All work on the Tuileries has been halted because it lies in the diocese of Saint-Germain l'Auxerrois. And even such a precaution does not lift the pall that has settled on Her Majesty. I am not sorry. Mother has blighted my life. I am glad that her happiness has been taken by this prophecy, even though I am not quite wicked enough to wish her dead.

If delight in another's distress were all I had to sustain me, mine would be a miserable existence. After another prolonged absence, however, my love, my Duc, has again returned to Court. He has been au Louvre daily—letting his wife, pregnant again, languish at the Hôtel de Guise, clutching a basin and heaving, while he flirts with me. Mother casts us warning looks but seems willing to tolerate the renewed attention we pay each other. I cannot understand this indulgence on her part, but I do not care to delve too deeply into it.

When Henri and I are together—dancing, stealing a glance across a room or a kiss in some darkened corner, exchanging witticisms—I feel alive as I have not since he left Paris last. But only when he moves inside me is the cause of my soul's oppression blotted completely from my mind. Henri jokes that I have become insatiable, but he relishes it. And I relish finding new ways to leave him breathless in my power.

The first thing Henri gave me when he returned was a small ladder of a length to reach from my window to the dry fosse below. It is remarkably light. I laughed when he told me it could support his weight and allow him to be with me in secret. But the first time I saw his face appear above my windowsill, I stopped laughing. That night Henri gave me the string of pearls that I am wearing for my portrait. I wear it now as well—it and nothing else—as I wait for the signal to lower the ladder. The blessed low whistle sounds! I swing open my shutters, the cold winter air meeting my skin and invigorating it. Moments later Henri climbs over the sill and drops to the floor. Without a word I take his icy hand and press it to my breast. He tries to pull me to him but I use my other arm to hold him off. I draw his hand up to my mouth and begin to gently bite his palm. He gives a deep groan. Again he reaches out and I swat his hand away.

"Patience," I murmur. "You made me wait and now it is your turn."

"I made you wait?"

"It must be an hour since you took leave of the King." I reach up, draw his head down, and run my tongue over his lips before releasing him.

"I had to allow time to make sure the King's other guests were safely away and most of those who live au Louvre were abed," he says pleadingly.

"I thought maybe you'd gone home to your wife." My tone is teasing but, in truth, I continue to think of the Princesse as a rival.

"Why would I do that?"

I lead him to the bed. "Sit down," I order. I remove his ruff, his doublet, and then his shirt—all very slowly—pushing his hands away again and again as they seek to help, allowing him only brief caresses of my flesh. Once he is naked from the waist up, I kneel and draw off his boots. As I do so, I can feel his hand in my hair, twisting. I unhook and roll down his hose, then begin to unfasten the front of his *haut-de-chausses*. As soon as there is a large enough opening, his prick pushes out. I slide my mouth over it—something Henriette advised me to try.

Henri cries out. I feel the hand in my hair tighten into a fist. Without warning I rise and lower myself onto him. His head snaps up and his arms close around my waist. Leaning in, I bite his ear, his neck, and then plant my lips on his, kissing him violently. When we are done, we are both exhausted. We lean against each other, our sweat and heartbeats mingling. Then he falls back onto the bed, looking with undisguised admiration at me where I sit upright, his member still inside me.

"God, I will miss you."

The lingering glow of my pleasure is extinguished like the flame of a candle snuffed between wet fingers. "Miss me? You are not coming to Blois?"

"I must wait for the child."

Climbing off him, I look for something to put on. "The Princesse has months before her confinement." Finding a *surcote*, I wrap it tightly around me.

"But the doctors make a great deal of the delicacy of her health. It is not like when she carried Charles—"

"A perfect excuse to leave her here, but no excuse to stay yourself."

"Marguerite! Would you have me look a monster before the whole Court? I may not love my wife, but I am still a gentleman and value my reputation." He reaches for me but I take a step back.

"I gave up my reputation for you."

He has no easy answer for that. "Let us not make this about your honor or mine," he says uneasily. "I concede you mean more to me than my honor. But the plain truth is Her Majesty would hardly allow me to stand about the halls of Blois while your marriage is negotiated."

"How can she prevent you coming when the rest of His Majesty's gentlemen attend him? What reason could she possibly offer?"

Henri sighs. "When has your mother needed a reason to do as she will? She is too subtle to say, 'Duc, you may not come to Blois, I forbid it.' Rather, I will be charged with some matter that takes me elsewhere." He looks up to see if I will yield, but I allow neither my face nor figure to soften. "Or if she cannot be bothered to find a pretext for keeping me from Blois, I will meet with an accident."

How different this Henri is from the one who nearly refused to leave me, to leave Paris, to save himself before he married. I push the thought away. Of course he is different. So am I. Ought I to begrudge my love his caution when we sacrificed so much to make certain of his safety?

"Enough." He holds his hands out, palms up in resignation. "I must be mad, but I will follow you—whatever others say and whatever the risk."

His willingness to put me before all else assuages me. "You must not," I say, rushing back to him. Taking his face in both hands, I tip it upward and kiss his forehead as a mother might kiss a beloved child. "Though I cannot bear the thought of being parted from you again so soon, I will not sacrifice your honor and safety to satisfy my selfish needs."

"My beautiful, beautiful love," he says. "I will write to you every day. Unless the receipt of my letters will put you in peril . . ."

"Not at all. Nothing would please me more than for Jeanne d'Albret to find me reading one—except, perhaps for her to see us as we are now. I want no man but you. And I wish my cousins to know I am yours so that the Prince's honor will demand he reject me."

The motion of my horse reminds me of Henri—both the rhythm of the animal and the slight soreness I feel after being several hours in the saddle. My beloved made love to me more times than I could count during my last days in Paris. So often that I am left tender as a virgin after her first encounter. I am riding silently beside the King, thinking of the frenzied hours Henri and I passed last night, when Mother maneuvers her horse into the place at my other side.

She waves my brother on. "I have decided to put your cousin in rooms near to yours," she says without preamble. "I will place the Queen of Navarre *près* to my own apartment on the pretext that this will permit us to interact without interference from the multitude of royal advisors on each side of this matter. And I will give the rooms adjacent to Jeanne's to her daughter. Such actions will seem natural while providing you with an opportunity."

"An opportunity, Madame?" I ask disingenuously. "You have impressed upon me repeatedly that the Queen of Navarre is strict in matters of morals. Surely then you do not wish me to flirt openly with her son."

"Of course I do, just not when his mother is looking." She looks me up and down. "Your color is healthier since a certain Duc returned to Court. And even at your worst you are likely the most beautiful woman your cousin has ever seen. My spies tell me Jeanne comes with a long list of conditions. I do not want to waste months wrangling."

I, of course, wish to waste years.

"Fortunately," Her Majesty continues, "Jeanne's son has inherited her strong will. He is not a man to be entirely led by the nose, or so I am told."

I am surprised at the admiration in her voice. After all, Mother requires malleability in her own sons.

"Dazzle your cousin," Mother says, "and I think we may dispense with many hours of negotiations." She lowers her voice. "And remember, while I reward dutiful children, I punish those who defy me—and sometimes their friends as well."

The sinister underpinnings for Mother's toleration for my flirtation with Guise are revealed. She desired a way of twisting me to her will, and he—or rather my love for him—will become the rope by which I am led or hung. Whatever I do to scuttle this match once the party from Navarre arrives will have to be done subtly. I cannot sacrifice Henri.

"I will be agreeable."

"Be more than agreeable. You know what it takes to capture and hold a man. Even as the Princesse de Porcien works to provide her husband a second son and thus herself with twice the security, she remains jealous of you, with good reason."

I am about to protest, but Mother raises a hand.

"You need not waste either of our time in denials. Provided you wrap your cousin around your finger and lead him to the altar, I do not care how much you upset the Princesse."

I remember years ago when Baronne de Retz admonished me that my standards of conduct must be above those other ladies who served the Queen. I wonder what my former *gouvernante* would think to hear what Mother asks of me.

"Madame, I will do all that I can to charm the Prince without engaging in conduct that might demean the House of Valois."

"You were not so fastidious in the past." Mother snorts in disgust. "If you were, they would not call you 'Guise's whore' in the south. Yes, I have heard it."

"From Anjou."

"Does it matter where? Just be advised that if you give credence to the name in front of the Queen of Navarre, the consequences will be unpleasant." She says the last word as if it were "deadly." "As for the Prince of Navarre, I shall count on your looks if I do not have your enthusiastic cooperation. And who knows, perhaps your cousin likes a difficult chase. He is an avid hunter. But make no mistake: you are a quarry that cannot escape. When terms are reached, Henri de Bourbon will have you if I have to truss you up and deliver you myself."

Everyone expected the Queen of Navarre to arrive at Blois in grand state shortly after we did. As days slip by with no sign of her party, Mother becomes increasingly testy. I count the days with mixed feelings. Each is a precious sliver of freedom. Yet, just as pleasant anticipation can increase eventual pleasure, the anticipation here increases my dread.

When we have been at Blois a week, Henriette bustles in as my hair is being dressed. I know by the way she moves that she has something important to tell. Has my cousins' party been sighted? Does she have news from Paris?

"A representative of the Holy Father arrived this morning," she proclaims. "And not just any diplomat: the Pope's nephew, Cardinal Alessandrino."

Dear God! Can it be the dispensation? Henri assured me it would be difficult to obtain and I have taken solace in those words, considering the Holy Father the final bulwark against this detestable match. If a dispensation has been secured this quickly . . . . I can barely breathe. Then it dawns upon me: Henriette is smiling. She would never delight in news abhorrent to me.

"And?" I ask, clutching the edge of my dressing table.

"He brings a letter from the King of Portugal—"

I believe I have stopped breathing entirely.

"—avowing that he is so eager to have you, he will take you without dowry and without delay."

"Oh, Henriette!" I jump to my feet and pull my friend into an embrace. "I am saved." Three years ago, when the Portuguese match was first pursued, I would not have celebrated such news. But now, with no hope of marrying my lover and faced with a marriage to a heretic, Dom Sébastien seems an attractive groom indeed.

"Margot, you are too hasty! I fear the Cardinal comes too late. My husband, from whom I had this news, asserts it is so. He says both King and Queen Mother firmly believe Navarre the more desirable husband."

"An opinion easily held when he will be someone else's spouse! It is not they but I who must subjugate myself to a heretic. I who must spread my legs for a man who, when last I saw him, smelled and looked always as if he had passed a long summer day in the saddle. How shall I bear such a thing?"

"You can hardly say *that*. But you may choose to say something to sway matters. That is why I bring the news expeditiously."

"I will go to the King at once."

When I arrive at Charles' apartment, I am not surprised that it is Mother who calls "Enter." Her Majesty, on the other hand, is entirely astonished to see me. "Margot? Your brother and I are engaged in business of state."

"I have come on a matter of state."

She looks faintly amused. "The only matter that need occupy you is the order in which you will wear your gowns when we entertain your future husband."

"I believe, Madame, there is something more serious to be considered."

Mother narrows her eyes. Her fingers drum on the arm of her chair.

"I have heard Dom Sébastien of Portugal renews his suit."

Mother's fingers stop but she holds her tongue, perhaps not wishing to confirm the news.

"Is it true, Charles?" I ask. "Has the King of Portugal sent word that he will have me?"

"Yes. In fact, he sent pages of them in his own hand. But those words do not move us. Why should they?"

Charles is prone to feeling slighted. I pray my understanding of that fact will assist me. "The King of Portugal comes late to a proper appreciation of the glory and advantages that a connection with the royal house of France brings," I say, shaking my head. "I feel that to be so, as, doubtless, you do. But though his former coldness toward the match deeply offended my dignity, I am willing to look beyond that to factors that might matter more to you and to France." I bow my head as a sign of submission.

"You would forgive Dom Sébastien's insult?" Charles' voice betrays curiosity. Mother must hear it, for she jumps in.

"It is not only your sister who was insulted—"

Charles holds up a hand—a rare occurrence. My hopes rise. If I can be heard, I have some chance, at least.

"Why?" he asks, looking at me searchingly.

"Because I care more for the Holy Church than for myself. My marriage to Henri de Bourbon would be an anathema to our faith, Charles. If I marry the King of Portugal, then the great Catholic powers stand together undivided and unsullied."

He waves a hand dismissively. "I am more interested in the peace and prosperity of my kingdom."

I must tread carefully. I swallow, afraid I will anger him by repeating what I have heard from Henri and Henriette. But he must certainly have heard the same from others, so I press on. "On that score too you should hesitate to wed me to Navarre. The idea is unpopular with your subjects, particularly those in Paris. They see our cousin as an enemy to the crown and part of a sect that has been too liberally treated."

"Why should the opinions of common men intimidate His Majesty?" Mother asks. "He knows what is best for them."

Charles nods.

I stand on the edge of failure, but I am not willing to give up. Not when my entire future hangs in the balance. Pragmatic arguments are not moving Charles, but there is another plea I can make: that of a sister. Advancing to my brother's chair, I kneel. Looking into his eyes, I say, "Charles, as my King, you have every right to rule over me as you do your people. But as a kind and loving brother, will you not consider my desires? I beseech you to give me the King of Portugal for my husband."

"Dom Sébastien is not the only one to discover his feelings *en retard*." Mother's tone is sardonic. "In this you make a pretty pair. He did not like you for a wife but is now desperate to have you because Pius the Fifth tells him so. You had no desire to marry him, yet now you beg on your knees to have him. Who, I wonder, has instructed you? Could it be a duc, not a pope?"

Does Mother truly think Henri counsels me, or does she merely want to convince Charles he does? She has told the King that my marriage to Navarre will help to counterbalance the influence of the House of Lorraine. If Charles sees the hand of Guise in my plea, my fate is sealed.

"No, Madame! 'Tis my conscience that instructs me. My own and no other's."

Mother gives a dry laugh, as if she doubts I have a conscience. Anger nearly blinds me.

"Madame, I am a good Catholic! You have *every* cause to know that. When your other *enfants* said their prayers in French, I was entirely faithful to the Church of Rome. Nor have I strayed since. How can it surprise you that the thought of being yoked in marriage with a notorious heretic is abhorrent to me?"

"Margot! Do not speak of your cousin in such a manner," Mother admonishes.

"How should I speak of him, then? Was he required to abjure as part of the peace? If he was, I have not heard it." I know that I am doing myself no good by losing my temper, but I am powerless to stop. "I did not complain when you sought to bind me to a madman. No, I bowed my head and said, 'As you wish.' Nor did I object to an old man, one who was already in my imagination as a sister's husband. The King of Portugal was not to my liking, but at least he—and those who came before—were Catholic gentlemen. It is bad enough that we have to sup and dance with heretics; that they return to the King's council. I thought the peace an edict of toleration—live and let live—but I see now it is an edict of submission. Not for the Huguenots, but for your children who you will suffer to be corrupted by the Huguenot taint."

Mother gives a triumphant smile. "Your sister protests that her words are her own, but she sounds just like that idiot Anne d'Este and her son.

"Margot, have you learned none of my pragmatism these last half dozen years? Pity. You ought by now to be able to take any situation and turn it in a useful direction. If you do not like the idea of a Protestant husband, then once you have him, make Navarre Catholic. I assure you neither I nor the King will object to that. In fact, it is what we hope for. Now, get up."

Ignoring her instruction, I look to Charles. When he will not meet my gaze, I get to my feet, defeated.

"You have been heard," Her Majesty says. "Now hear me. The papal delegate requests an audience with you. You will grant it, but I will be watching. Do anything to thwart the match with Navarre, and I will reward the religious fervency you have just exhibited with a cloistered stay in an abbey at the edge of your brother's kingdom."

I bow my head, knowing I could not bear to be locked away where Henri could never find me. I have no choice but to tell the Holy Father's representative that my faith requires obedience to my king, not just to my god.

※ ※ ※

There is grace in this place—grace and pain. Pain for my mother and soon, I suspect, for me. The papal representative had barely left my apartment at Blois when it was decided we would come to Chenonceau and Jeanne d'Albret would be redirected to meet us here. A short time ago a rider in royal livery galloped up. Surely the party from Navarre has been spotted. I walk back and forth before the windows in my apartment, looking at the frozen river Cher as I wait for the Prince of Navarre and his mother to arrive. I am dressed extravagantly, and to all eyes appear entirely ready to play my part. Only I know that beneath my gown, over my heart, I have secreted a letter from Henri, a reminder to continue to resist this match.

The door behind me opens. A summons, no doubt. I do not turn.

"If you are not the death of me, Jeanne d'Albret will be."

Mother!

"The Queen of Navarre is only a short distance away," Her Majesty says, motioning me toward her. She ought to be elated, but her face is angry. "She has her daughter with her but not her son." Her voice bristles. My breast fills with relief. "Come. We will greet the infernal woman with smiles and see if we can discover where she has left the Prince."

We descend to assume positions in a carefully arranged tableau in which the widowed Princesse de Condé is prominently placed, as are the other Protestant ladies. Someone shoves a puppy into my arms. It is from one of the King's litters and has a bow around its little neck. I am to give it to Catherine de Bourbon in a sisterly gesture. Fine, I have no objection to pleasing a thirteen-year-old. The animal wiggles in my arms. I nuzzle its ear.

Jeanne enters. She is not as pretty as I remember her being when I saw her years ago. And she holds her mouth in a pinched manner, as if she disapproves of everything and everyone. Good. A woman with such an expression will be predisposed not to like me. She and the Princesse of Navarre are surrounded by an impressive entourage. As the group sweeps forward, the Baronne de Retz identifies key noblemen in a whisper. I pay no attention. I see no point in learning their names. I shall doubtless be afforded little contact with them and do not care who they are so long as they go away dissatisfied.

We exchange the formal greetings etiquette requires. Then, as I hand the squirming puppy to the Princess, Mother says, "Cousin, we hoped also to welcome your son. Where is the Prince? Not indisposed, I hope?"

"Have no fear on that score," Jeanne replies. "He was in excellent health when I heard from him three days ago. I have charged him with managing my kingdom in my absence. Such training is invaluable for a man who will be king."

Mother nods understandingly and I nearly laugh out loud. She has no interest in training or allowing my poor brother Charles to rule without her and he is already king.

The Queen of Navarre turns to me. "The Prince sends his greetings. He looks forward to receiving you at Pau when the little details that must precede your marriage have been resolved."

Married in the Navarre? This is no little detail. The wrangling has begun before the horses are unsaddled. "Your Majesty," I say, "when you write to the Prince, thank him for his salutations and tell him that, although he remains in the south, I have memories from our childhood to rely upon in forming my opinion of him. Perhaps he can likewise recall when last we were together." There is nothing whatsoever wrong with this little speech from Jeanne d'Albret's perspective, but Mother's ladies must see its unflattering meaning plainly. My attitude toward the Prince when we were younger was hardly secret. I do hope that the Prince of Navarre remembers vividly every occasion on which I corrected his behavior, avoided him, or teased him. And most particularly that he remembers my vow never to allow him to kiss me.

"I wonder, would the Duchesse de Valois escort me to my rooms?" Jeanne asks.

"We will share that honor," Mother replies. "It has been too long since we saw each other. I am eager to be reacquainted even as you get to know my daughter better."

In other words, Mother has no intention of permitting Jeanne and me to be alone, as neither of us can be relied upon to proceed according to her script. I have the sense the Queen of Navarre is not used to being managed. I might feel sorry for her if my future did not depend on her being thwarted.

"The Queen of Navarre is so frustrated that she becomes ill," Henriette says. She and I are huddled in one of the chapel confessionals. With the château full of spies for both sides of the negotiations, it seems the only truly safe place to report on such matters. Henriette has one of her own spies kneeling in prayer at the back of the space, near the door.

"I have noticed her coughing," I reply.

"She has night sweats and fever." Henriette pauses for a moment, listening intently. "Where is Charlotte?"

We expected the third of our circle to be with us, reporting on what she has learned about Jeanne's letters since she enterprisingly bribed one of the servants to bring her the Queen of Navarre's blotter. "Never mind Charlotte," I say. "What else?"

"The Queen complains that your mother says one thing in the morning and another in the afternoon." Henriette shifts slightly, inadvertently stepping on my foot. "And that she is observed everywhere, even in her rooms."

"Doubtless she is. Holes and cracks are not just for mice where Mother is concerned. How I wish my cousin would give up. Instead of coming back to Blois with us, she could as easily have headed south to Navarre."

"I am sorry to report that, despite the arduous nature of the negotiations, those who give odds on such things still favor resolution."

"There are odds given on my future?" *Is there no embarrassment I will be spared?*

"Among the gentlemen, yes."

In a strange contrast to the two dour queens locked in endless rounds of quibbling, the gentlemen Jeanne brought with her and those in Charles' suite appear rather easy with each other. His Majesty has found a favorite among them, the Comte de La Rochefoucauld, who despite being much older is always willing to join in entertainments from tennis, to cards, to playacting.

The curtain parts and Charlotte's face appears. She is exceedingly pale.

"You look as if you have seen a ghost." I expect her to laugh but she looks down at her feet.

"It is worse: I have been with your mother."

"Are we caught?" Henriette asks.

Charlotte shakes her head. We make way for her. Pushing past Henriette, she sits upon the bench and pulls her feet up on it as well. She looks very sad.

"Come, you will feel better when you tell us," Henriette urges.

"I have been given a frightful task." Charlotte looks up mournfully.

"Who?" Henriette asks. "The gray-bearded, unsmiling Baron de Rosny?"

"Would that it were." She covers her face and from between her fingers says, "The Queen Mother has asked me to stand ready to seduce the Prince of Navarre should Margot fail to beguile him."

Henriette gives a low whistle. I reach out and steady myself on the confessional wall. I ought not to care. I have no desire to sleep with my cousin—ever. But the fact that Mother personally arranges an infidelity for the man she thinks to make my husband galls me. It is savage. Particularly when undertaken by a woman made deeply unhappy by her own husband's dalliance.

"Margot, say something."

"I hate her."

"But not me?"

"Never you!" I touch Charlotte's shoulder.

I exit the confessional first. Rather than returning to my room, I kneel to pray. The silence left in Henriette and Charlotte's wake is a balm. I drink it in, staring at the crucifix above the altar.

"I was Catholic as a young woman."

I scramble to my feet and turn to face the Queen of Navarre.

"So I have heard."

"In fact, until I was nearly thirty."

"But you are not Catholic now, Madame, so I cannot account for your presence in this chapel."

"I do not believe that."

"You wish to speak to me alone."

She smiles slightly. "I have told my Henri you are quick. Do you know what he replied?"

I do not, nor do I care.

"He replied that he remembers as much from when you were children; that you were always the brightest of his Valois cousins."

"Very flattering."

"I have no concerns about your mind, only about your character."

"Madame! Have I not shown you every *politesse* since your arrival? How, then, have I earned such discourteous speech?"

"I do not mean to be rude, only forthright. In fact, I am surprised to find you as unspoiled as you appear—and told my son so—given the atmosphere of this court. Whatever our religious differences, as you are a woman of sincere faith, you must know the Court of France is rife with sin."

My cheeks warm. "If you have such concerns about my upbringing, I wonder that you are still here."

"Your past is not my primary interest. There are good reasons for me to consider this match despite it. But the merit in all of them falls short if I do not have some assurance of your future conduct."

"If you ask if I can love your son, I tell you plainly, no."

"So it is your turn to be forthright." She nods. "Good. I do not particularly care if you will love Henri. I married Antoine de Bourbon for affection. Such an act can have as many pitfalls as pleasures. What I wish to ask is: Can you obey my son?"

"Madame, if the Prince of Navarre is made my husband, I will be obedient in all reasonable things."

This does not appear to satisfy. Jeanne looks at me intently. "But who shall be the judge between you of what is reasonable? As husband, Henri must lead. Can you let his conscience be yours? Will you follow the religion of your husband?"

I straighten to my full height and touch the cross I wear round my neck. "Madame, I would not set aside my conscience for your son, nor switch religions, if he stood to inherit the crown of the whole world and not just a kingdom much smaller than the one my own family rules."

"Might not your own conscience counsel a change? A church, like a court, can become corrupt. What, then, is the point of clinging to it?"

"What comes from Our Lord cannot be corrupted by man and is unchangeable. Men may ignore God's word through sinful action, or trespass it through heresy, but that changes nothing. It remains the only truth."

I brace myself for anger. I have come perilously close to calling the Queen of Navarre a heretic to her face. But she merely looks at me for a moment through her cold, unflinching eyes, then nods as if deciding something.

"It is the way of the young to speak with a certitude they have not earned by experience. I have often cautioned Henri about it. But I encouraged you to be candid, and I am not sorry to know your mind. Will you be sorry, I wonder, to know mine? I believe I have traveled a very long way for naught. You are not the bride for my son, however lovely you are and however advantageously connected."

"What did you say?" Mother is furious.

I expected to be called to account for my conversation with the Queen of Navarre earlier. The day it happened, in fact. But clever Jeanne d'Albret waited until she could speak to Charles alone, maneuvering around Mother for a second time.

"I told Her Majesty I would obey the Prince of Navarre in all corporal matters, but not in matters of faith. Nothing more. And I will swear to that upon any holy thing you like."

Mother looks at Charles where he paces before the windows of her study. "And what exactly did the Queen of Navarre say to you?"

"That there will be no wedding and that, by the affection she bears me, she will not trespass longer on my hospitality to no purpose."

"That sounds like her." Mother moves to where Charles stands. "She is cleverer than I thought." There is grudging respect in her tone. "But I will not be bested so easily." She looks out the window. Whatever she finds there I pray it is not inspiration. I have just dispatched a letter to Henri telling him I believe I have escaped the match.

Mother turns. "We must do something bold, Your Majesty."

"What would you suggest, Madame? I will not beg for a husband for Margot. That would be demeaning to us both."

If Jeanne has offended Charles' dignity all will be well.

"The matter of the marriage was settled in principle before Jeanne left Nérac," Mother says. "Since her arrival she has been fixated upon a thousand little details of the ceremony."

"Ancient history," Charles replies. "For now it appears she rests her refusal upon Margot's unbending Catholicism."

"Perhaps, but she will have a hard time sustaining that objection if it is all she has, for she knew your sister, and indeed Your Majesty, to be firmly Catholic from the beginning."

"So?" Charles looks as genuinely puzzled as I feel.

"We cede everything at once—everything save your sister's faith and the requirement that Henri de Bourbon travel to Paris to be married."

I gasp.

"And you make the proffer publicly—at dinner *ce soir*."

"That will set our cousin scrambling." Charles chortles, and in that laughter I hear loss. Charles likes to win just as much as Mother or Anjou. He seldom gets the chance, so the opportunity to outplay the Queen of Navarre appeals. "Oh, yes, I will do it, if only to see her face. She is so controlled, so in command of her every expression, but I believe this may discompose her."

"More importantly, it will leave her with nowhere to retreat," Mother says. "Her advisors are nearly all in favor of the marriage, and have Coligny at their elbows urging. One of her chief defenses—beside her slew of objections to details—has been the claim that our word cannot be trusted. Well, this offer will be made in front of a hundred souls. There will be no going back from this pledge, at least not with honor."

Mother smiles as if she has won already.

The breeze through the window is warm and playful. Birds are riotous in the budding trees. No one could be insensible to the glorious signs of spring. I part my lips slightly and believe I can taste it. Closing my eyes, leaning on the open casement, I allow myself to forget why I am here. I allow the April weather to trick me into thinking myself reborn. And truly my whole life should lie ahead of me.

"The documents are ready."

My eyes open at the sound of Mother's voice. The blue skies over Blois have lost their power to delight. The twittering of the birds seems suddenly the cackling of diplomats. For three months my hopes of avoiding a marriage with Navarre rose and ebbed. In a moment I will sign my marriage contract. There is no hope left.

Turning from the window, I see the King, with the Cardinal de Bourbon and Admiral Coligny on either side of him. I cannot read Charles' face; the admiral smiles; the Cardinal looks solemn. I wonder if this is because, unlike Coligny, who merely worked for this match, His Grace must pay to achieve it. He has been made to renounce all rights and recognize my cousin as sole heir of the House of Bourbon. On top of this, he will turn over one hundred thousand livres to my groom.

Opposite His Grace, Mother stands with Jeanne d'Albret. The two queens, in their dark attire, stand out starkly against the myriad of gilded panels lining Mother's study. The paneling makes this one of the most admired rooms at Blois. Most visitors see only beauty. I, however, see not the craftsman's art but the treachery that lies beneath. With a touch only she knows how to bestow, Mother can make panels swing open, revealing secret cabinets holding God knows what. Moving to the table, I wonder if my executed marriage contract will be hidden away in such a manner.

The document is long but I need not read it, only sign. The quill lies next to the last page. Just in case I do not see it, Mother picks it up and holds it out. For one wild moment I think of refusing to take it, refusing to seal this dreadful bargain with my name. But what life would be left to me then? Assuming for a moment that I am not forced to sign—by threats and violence—or that my mother is above forging my signature out of the sight of the Queen of Navarre, I cannot imagine anything will await me but imprisonment. To live confined, deprived of the sight of my Henri and the companionship of my friends, perhaps without light, air, music, books. What is such a life but the death of the soul? A real death might be warmer and more welcome. I take the quill. The feather is black. Shall I be a black bird, then? Run to the window, fling myself out? Shall I fly to my death with arms outstretched against a bright spring sky?

No. To defy my mother is madness, but to defy God—to transgress His holy laws—would be worse. It would bring damnation, a never-ending torment of fire and pain. Being the Queen of Navarre is unpalatable, but it is the most palatable choice left me. The thought is so surprising that I laugh. Mother gives me a menacing look. A wasted look, for I am already dipping the quill; I am already signing.

As I lay the pen down Mother puts her hands on my shoulders and kisses me on one cheek and then the other. The Queen of Navarre kisses me as well. "Daughter," she says awkwardly. Like me, she is unsmiling. She holds out a box. A ring lies inside. Elaborate gold scrollwork frames a single diamond set in a bezel. The stone is lovely: a dome of facets catches the spring light. Were it not a betrothal ring, I would surely delight in such an ornament. But under the circumstances I am no more eager to pick it up than I was the quill.

Does Charles see my hesitation or does he respond to a look from my mother or a nudge from the admiral? He lifts the ring, proclaims it *magnifique,* and then says, "My dear sister, you must allow me the pleasure of helping you put this on."

🌼 🌼 🌼

"I cannot wander off to the Tuileries," I tell Henri sternly. Dinner has finished and courtiers are scattering. Normally, this might be an excellent moment to disappear with Henri, and those gardens have become our favorite spot to become "lost." But not today. "Our cousin the Queen of Navarre has been taken ill, and we must visit."

"Why could she not have been taken ill while she was in Vendôme? Far enough away to keep from being an inconvenience," my impatient lover asks.

After my marriage contract was signed, the Court returned to Paris. Mother was eager to begin arranging things for the celebration. I was scarcely less impatient to be in the capital despite the unpleasant smells and blistering heat that ordinarily make it undesirable in summer. After all, Henri was in the city, and my days with him become increasingly uncertain. The Queen of Navarre, however, eschewed Paris, retreating to Vendôme for her health. She was not missed. Yet last week she came dutifully to stay at the Hôtel de Condé. I have heard she is busy ordering wedding clothing for the Prince of Navarre from the best tailors. It is hard for me to imagine any amount of finery making a difference to the gentleman's appearance.

"She was doubtless ill at Vendôme as well. She was certainly often ill while we were at Chenonceau and Blois," I reply. He tries to take my hand but I am too quick for him. "I must go. Her Majesty wishes to make a show. If we are seen to be neglectful, there will be talk."

"Make your show, then. As long as you plan to show me something later." Henri accompanies this last remark with a wicked look.

Leaning toward him, I whisper, "At the fountain nearest the grotto—in the moonlight." Then I go in search of Mother.

When we arrive in the Rue de Grenelle-Saint-Honoré, it is immediately clear Jeanne d'Albret is more seriously ill than she was during the months we passed together. Members of her household are grim-faced even before spotting us. The Queen of Navarre's bedchamber is deep with physicians.

As we draw close to the bed, I realize Jeanne is speaking, very softly, to a gentleman beside her who takes notes. She looks terribly pale and her mouth is stained with blood.

"I forbid my son to use severity toward his sister. I wish him to treat her with gentleness and kindness . . ." Aware of our presence, Jeanne's voice trails off. She no sooner stops speaking than a great paroxysm of coughing takes her, splattering more blood onto the cloth that she raises to her mouth.

"Dear cousin"—Mother stops and puts out an arm to keep me from going closer—"we had no idea you were so poorly. Had we known, His Majesty's personal physician would have come immediately. As it is, he will be here without delay." She snaps her fingers and points to the nearest of her attendants.

"I thank you." Jeanne gives Mother a wry smile. "Meaning no disrespect to the skills of the King's doctor, I do not believe he will be able to do more for me than my own, which is to say nothing at all."

"Surely it is not so serious!"

"When you come to see me next, Madame, I believe it will be to pay your respects. May I ask two favors?"

"Of course."

"I would be buried in the sepulcher of my ancestors in the Cathedral of Lescar, and I would have a moment alone with the Duchesse de Valois."

I have no desire to be alone with Jeanne. But it is not in my power to refuse a woman who thinks herself dying.

Jeanne's eyes remain on me while the rest of the room's occupants exit. I am not particularly uncomfortable under her stare, but I would just as soon she looked elsewhere. When the others are gone, I take a step forward, but she stops me with a gesture. "For my son's sake as well as yours, we cannot be too careful," she says. "This fever might be catching." She begins to cough again. I feel a twinge of pity watching her body wracked by the effort.

Recovering, she says, "I meant to keep an eye on you in the Navarre."

With that single sentence my pity fades.

"You will not be sorry, I think, to escape my watchfulness. But I wish you would believe that I also meant to be a good mother to you. You need a good mother."

"Her Majesty the Queen did not leave me alone with you so that you could insult her."

"I do not have so many breaths left that I wish to waste any on nonsense, or on niceties. I say plainly I wish you had a different mother for your sake, though you would be no use as a bride for my son had that been the case."

Happy thought.

"You have made clear to me that you have no lingering childhood affection for my son," Jeanne continues. "You are a papist and rumored to be a wanton—"

"Madame! You cannot expect me—whether you be dying or not—to remain in the face of such insults."

"I do not ask you to stay much longer, but perhaps you will do me the charity of allowing me to finish my sentence?"

I grit my teeth but remain where I stand.

"I was about to say that, for all that, I persist in believing you to be a good woman."

This may be her most shocking statement yet.

"I appeal to the goodness in you. Be a kind and obedient wife to my son. I will not be here to see you receive the jewels I have purchased these last days for Henri to give you. Know this: their value is nothing compared to the worth of my son. He may not shine as they do, but as I see past appearances in your case, I ask you to attempt to do the same in his."

Extraordinary speech. Some reply is warranted, but I do not know what to say. That Jeanne loves her son and thinks highly of him makes me think more of her. But does not every mother love her sons? It is possible, in fact probable, that a mother will think more of a son than he deserves. Look at Mother and Anjou. The Queen of Navarre's opinion of my cousin cannot supplant mine. But on reflection she does not ask for that. She does not ask me to agree that the Prince of Navarre is wonderful, she only asks me to be kind to him. I can promise this, I think, without perjuring myself.

"Madame, I do not take duty lightly. If I did, I would not be marrying your son in the first instance. I do my duty as a daughter and a sister by undertaking this marriage. I say this not to boast but to reassure you. If I take my marriage vows as the Prince of Navarre's wife, I will owe him the duty of a wife, and I will not shirk in it. I promise you that I will endeavor to show him respect and kindness."

"If."

She misses nothing.

"I should have said 'when,' Madame."

She nods. "Thank you, daughter."

It is only the second time she has styled me such. Unlike the first, there is nothing awkward in the appellation this time.

"I give my blessing to your union, as I fear I will not be present at the wedding to give it. I cannot offer such blessing with an untroubled heart—like you, I have reservations about the match which can only be erased by time, something I no longer have—but I do give it with a mind eased by your promise. Now you may go."

I curtsy but Jeanne does not see. She has closed her eyes. In the anteroom I tell Mother the Queen of Navarre would rest. We are in the courtyard, mounting our horses, when the wailing begins. A window opens and our cousin's chancellor looks down.

"Your Majesty," he says, "the Queen of Navarre is dead."

"I will carry this grievous news to His Majesty, and we will return to mourn her together."

The gentleman nods and shuts the window.

"So, daughter," Mother says, drawing close, "you will not wait for a crown." She does not bother to conceal her satisfaction. "We must go directly to your brother. Charles must claim for himself the sad duty of informing your cousin of his loss. For if the Prince—or should I say King—of Navarre's friends tell him, they may ride too quickly. It would be good if Henri de Bourbon were well on his way to Paris before hearing the news, for we would not wish his grief to delay his wedding."

CHAPTER 16

July 1572—Paris, France

They arrive like the black birds from my childhood nightmares—eight hundred gentlemen, their mourning mantles fluttering slightly as they ride. We receive reports of their entry into the city long before sight or sound of them can be apprehended at the Louvre. But at last the inevitable can be delayed no longer. I must go out and greet the man I will marry.

Despite the considerable effort made to dress me in rich colors, I know my face is as grave and colorless as my cousin's attire. The inhabitants of Paris are somber as well. How else to explain the fact that even as the sound of so many horses' feet becomes audible where we stand, we hear no cheering. The people of Paris feel no joy over my impending marriage, and I love them for it.

The first riders draw into the court of honor. My cousin's party was joined in the Faubourg Saint-Antoine by an escort of four hundred of the King's gentlemen, so the horses and riders seem numberless. At their fore, my groom is flanked by Alençon and Anjou. My Henri rides nearby, his face tight with fury and hurt. My beloved's pain heightens my own. I clench a hand at my side until my nails bite into flesh to keep from crying.

Standing beside me on the steps, Mother instructs me to smile as my brothers and my cousin pull their horses to a halt. When I do not, she puts an arm about my waist and I feel her nails digging into my side through the heavy fabric that encases me, making me all the more miserable in the summer heat.

The man who will be my husband in a month bows over the neck of his horse. "Your Majesties, Your Highness." Nothing else. No speech, no prepared compliments. I have not seen my cousin in over five years. He was not particularly impressive when we parted, and he does not appear improved. His manners show no grace and his ruff is not even straight.

Charles, cutting a fine figure in an immaculate doublet of pale rose embroidered in violet, steps forward. "Henri, Roi de Navarre, we welcome you to our court. You are family and shortly will be doubly so when we bestow our sister's hand upon you. Be at home here and let *l'amitié* and goodwill between us reinforce the peace between Catholics and Protestants throughout France."

Admiral Coligny, sitting on his horse, looks abundantly pleased. He and Mother are the chief beneficiaries of my marriage, but I doubt either of them has a thought to spare for me as they contemplate their good fortune.

The principal gentlemen dismount. Only those of the highest offices and most exalted families will attend the banquet honoring my groom's arrival. Anjou argued strongly that Catholics ought to outnumber Protestants, "to let them know their place from the first." But Mother insisted the numbers be even.

My cousin bounds up the steps two at a time, like a man eager for his dinner. There is absolutely nothing regal about him. He holds out an arm. I place two fingers upon it. I may know my duty and the choreography for this event, but I see no reason to do either exuberantly. I realize, now that we are side by side, my cousin is very little if at all taller than I. I cannot say why, but I take a perverse pleasure in this. I wonder: Am I to pass a lifetime taking pleasure in his failings?

Casting a sidelong glance at my companion as we move toward the great hall, I read sadness and fatigue in his features. I remember my last interview with Jeanne d'Albret—my promise of kindness. The man has lost his mother. And, unlike me, he was not given the opportunity to pay his respects to her as she lay in state. Nor did he attend her burial, as his reaction to her death was so violent, it delayed his travel, and by the time he reached Vendôme she had been interred.

"I am sorry, Your Majesty, that your honored mother is not here to greet you; that after all her work toward this end, she did not live to see us wed."

"Are you?" He searches my face. "I suspect you are the only *dame de la cour* to feel so."

"Sir, I assure you, such is not the case. When the Court went to pay those respects to the Queen of Navarre which her rank and our nearness of blood demanded, I saw tears in the eyes of more than one lady."

"How can I trust such tears, Madame, when I hear your mother wept?" The words are fierce.

My cousin, it seems, is both shrewd and well informed. Still, he ought to have repaid my effort to be civil with civility, not bitter accusations.

As if recollecting as much, the King of Navarre squares his shoulders and, laying a hand with obvious effort upon my own where it rests at the crook of his arm, says, "You are as pretty as you were as a girl."

I nearly laugh out loud. "Faint compliment, Sir, allowing that a woman has become no less attractive! If this is how wooing proceeds in the Navarre, I am surprised anyone is ever wed. Then again, you do not need to woo me—I am already won, or perhaps better say bargained for."

My cousin hands me into my seat, then takes the chair next to mine. "Madame, it was not my intention to insult you, nor shall I be cunningly drawn into agreeing with any statement which makes you sound like chattel. That would reflect well on neither of us."

I long to snap that it is the truth, no matter how badly it reflects. But if my cousin is prepared to play his part in this pageant, I will not be outplayed by this awkward man.

"Perhaps, Sir, it is politic for us to agree that both of us have improved immensely since last we were in company, and that each of us is delighted by that discovery."

"If you like." He shrugs. How could I have forgotten that shrug? My cousin looks past me. Then, without warning, he takes my hand from the table and brings it to his lips. When he lays my hand down once more, he leaves his own atop it. "I am quite delighted to find one thing has altered since we were children," he says rather more loudly than before.

"What is that?" I try to slide my hand from beneath his but he merely closes his fingers around it, holding it fast.

"Do you remember how, when we were young, you insisted I would never be allowed to kiss you?" He lifts my hand again and draws it upward toward his lips. I tense every muscle in my arm, but my efforts are no match for his strength. All I can do is grit my teeth and watch as he very deliberately turns my hand over and kisses my wrist. He offers me a wide, oddly polished smile—the sort any gallant might offer in paying an elaborate compliment. "Well, it seems that I am to have the pleasure of kissing you after all. What man with eyes would not envy me in this?"

Somewhere to my left there is the sound of breaking glass.

My cousin's eyes light up and he releases my hand. Nearby, the Duc de Guise's wine glass lies fallen and shattered against his plate. The hand beside it is clenched into a fist.

So this was my cousin's business! His first swipe at Henri.

Servants move to clear up the mess. My mother's voice draws my attention away from the Duc. "Better glasses than heads broken," she quips to Charles. "Is not peace a wonderful thing?"

Her comments draw a smile from Charles and appreciative laughter from some of those surrounding. I want to slap my cousin despite my promise to his dead mother, but with the eyes of so many upon me I can hardly offer such a naked show of displeasure. Instead I fix the smile of a coquette on my face and, placing my hand on his arm, lean in until my lips nearly brush his ear. I feel him twitch slightly at my proximity. But I am caught off guard as well. There is an unperfumed odor about my cousin—a combination of perspiration and horse—that makes me eager to be at a greater distance. Steeling myself against it, I whisper, "I *promise* you that a hand is the only thing of mine you will ever kiss." Then, as if I have whispered something very charming, I sit back and give a gay little laugh.

My mother nods in approval. What a fool she is. What fools they all are. And my cousin the greatest fool among them.

For the rest of the meal I do not say another word to the King of Navarre, merely nodding in response to whatever he says. To his credit he is quick to perceive this pattern and turns his attention and conversation in the direction of my sister-in-law: complimenting the Queen Consort on her healthy looks, congratulating her on her upcoming confinement, and expressing earnest wishes that the King should have a healthy son.

The person nearest me on the left is the admiral. Since the peace he has risen so much in status and favor that he never sits far from the King he once fought. Charles adores him. Coligny blathers on about all the good my impending marriage will do for France, and all the excellent attributes of my husband-to-be of which I may be unaware. Truly I am in hell.

Mother, of course, has dancing planned. No performance—there will be time enough for those by the score in the weeks that lie between this day and my wedding—but the first of a string of increasingly elaborate balls culminating in the nuptial celebrations themselves. The King of Navarre and I are to open the dancing. But I have had enough of my mother's script. The next part I act will be to my own liking.

As we descend from the dais, I make a little stumble and then, with a small cry, let myself collapse off the bottom step, the corner of which catches me in the lower back, causing me to cry out again—this time in genuine painful surprise. *There will be a bruise there later.* My cousin looks down at me. His eyes are not unkind but nor do they seem concerned. He has either guessed my ruse or truly does not care whether I have injured myself. Her Majesty bustles forward.

"Daughter, what is the matter?" Her tone is all concern but her eyes are sharp.

"Nothing serious, Madame," I declare. Then, trying to sound regretful, "But I fear I have twisted my ankle."

"You cannot dance." It is a statement, not a question. She gestures to a knot of ladies nearby to assist me and, before Charlotte and Henriette can even separate themselves from the throng, turns her back, leaving me to sit where I fell. "Your Majesty," she says to the King of Navarre, "I will be sorry not to see you dance with my daughter on this occasion, but you will have a lifetime to partner the Duchesse de Valois. For this evening I hope you will allow me the pleasure of choosing you a pretty partner to stand in her stead."

"With your permission." I do not realize he is addressing me until I feel all eyes upon me where I stand, balanced on one foot, with an arm around each Henriette and Charlotte. My cousin inclines his head deferentially. "If you wish it, I will be quite content to forgo dancing and bear you company."

Why, I wonder, am I always left feeling vaguely guilty by this man?

"Sir, you must not abridge your evening's entertainments on my account. I will be very happy to watch you dance with another." There is no lie in this.

"Duchesse de Nevers," Mother says, "can you manage the Duchesse de Valois? Good." Mother takes Charlotte's hand. "Your Majesty, may I present the Baronne de Sauve. She will stand well in my daughter's place."

Charlotte offers her famed shy, intriguing smile. She looks slightly in awe of my cousin—like a deer who might be lured in to eat from one's hand or, by a single wrong move, sent bounding into the forest. The look is a lovely lie, of course. My friend is not timid. She is not waiting to be beguiled. She is as much the King of Navarre's as I am—both of us condemned to his use by Mother.

I am nearly forgotten once the music begins. Nearly. Mother glances my way periodically, weighing perhaps both my actions and what may be expected next from me. Henri sees this as he circles the room, unsmiling, and is careful to stay at a distance as he passes me. During one such pass I raise my skirt a bit and wiggle my ankle to make certain he understands my ruse. Even this fails to draw a smile.

Unlike my beloved, the King of Navarre comes more than once to where I sit. On the first occasion he inquires after my ankle. On subsequent ones he introduces me to various gentlemen, each of whom looks vaguely the same in a dark doublet. Each also wears the same polite but distrustful expression, and offers a bow that is correct but betrays no real sense of honor in meeting me.

At last the tedious evening winds to a close. The King of Navarre goes off with his companions and I, on the arm of Henriette and limping noticeably until I am sure we are alone, retreat to my apartment. As we enter my bedchamber, my friend begins at once. "Well, the welcome is over," she says, motioning for me to turn so that she and Gillone can begin to undress me. "You were very clever, contriving not to dance with the King of Navarre. I was not so fortunate."

"And what did you think of my groom?"

"His accent is bad and his odor, *Mon Dieu,* it is worse. My poor dear!" Henriette hugs me impulsively. "You are to be married to a mountain goat, but I dare say you will survive and give him a proper goat's horns. Apropos of which, Guise was pale tonight. And that broken glass! I told him that you will give him every sort of tender reassurance when he comes *ce soir.* But even that seemed insufficient to lighten his mood."

"I will give him more than you think."

"Really? You astonish me! I can think of nothing you have not already given him and nothing he has not given you. I am quite envious, in fact, of all the ways you have enjoyed him. Now that Monsieur has been re-called to Portugal, I have nothing better to take between my legs than my husband. Heaven help me."

"I will give him a promise," I reply, stepping out of the underskirt and farthingale that ring my feet and waiting patiently until Gillone disap-pears into my wardrobe to finish my thought. "A promise of fidelity. Do you know what I told my cousin this evening?"

"I cannot imagine."

"That he will never kiss more than the hand of mine he takes unwill-ingly."

Henriette stops gathering up the balance of my garments and stares at me wide-eyed.

"Margot, you cannot mean it. If you despoil this marriage and break the peace, your mother will have you beaten or worse."

"My mother will know nothing of the matter."

"You think the King of Navarre will be too embarrassed to admit you have refused him? That he will not demand his rights from the King? I would not for a moment count upon that. And only imagine the embar-rassment if Charles or your mother vouchsafe to witness the consumma-tion of your marriage."

I shudder at the image of my mother, her face a twisted, gloating mask, standing beside my bed while my cousin mounts me. This would be a thing so horrible, I doubt I could survive it. But at the moment the idea of being wife to my cousin even *en privé* feels like to kill me.

If I crumble now, I will be lost.

"I cannot count upon the King of Navarre," I say, raising my chin high. "But I am a Valois and a Médicis. Surely I can intimidate my provincial cousin: he will never dare lay a finger on me."

In the morning I find that the King of Navarre is to take me walking at the Tuileries. "But it is so hot!" I say as Mother watches Gillone finish my hair.

"Nonsense! The gardens will be refreshing compared to the rooms of the Louvre. We will be a small party." She reaches out absently and adjusts a jeweled pin on the right side of my head. "And I will keep the others well back so that you and your cousin may converse privately."

"Good heavens, Madame, why? I have nothing to say to the King of Navarre."

"Fine, walk in silence. But do so without incident or, mark me, I will beat you myself." She smiles as if there is no threat between us. "You look lovely. Come, your cousin is waiting."

He is indeed, at the gates of the garden, sweating noticeably—though I can hardly criticize him for that, given the oppressive heat.

"Marguerite," he says, bowing and offering an arm.

I wait until we are a few yards in advance of the others before replying. "I prefer 'Your Highness.'"

"That is silly. I will call you Marguerite and you must call me Henri until you can call me 'husband.'"

I do not know why I failed to foresee this moment, but I realize, with horror, that it is impossible for me to call my cousin by his Christian name. The name Henri is common, but even with a brother called by it, when I say Henri aloud I think always of my beloved Duc.

The King of Navarre stops walking. "Come, I must insist."

"Sir, you are not in a position to insist on anything. My mother may insist I walk with you, but you have not the same power over me."

"A fair point." He shrugs. *Mon Dieu,* I hate that gesture. He begins to move once more, drawing me along. "I am in France and must play the part of guest. It is not a bad role, particularly since, as First Prince of the Blood, none who are not Valois take precedence over me. So I will let you call me as you please—for now. But remember"—he casts a half glance over his shoulder, but the King, with Mother on one arm and the Queen Consort on the other, has turned onto another path, taking his courtiers with him—"once we are married, it will be I and not your mother to whom you owe obedience."

It is a reprimand but my cousin does not seem entirely comfortable with it: he avoids my eyes, looking instead at the cloudless sky. "We have such hot weather in the Navarre but it is different, perhaps because of mountains. I believe you will find it more tolerable."

I do not believe I will find anything in the Navarre tolerable.

We walk on in silence. What a dreadful exercise. I can feel the sweat running down the center of my back. I can hear the lilting tones of the others conversing at a distance while I am stuck with my cousin. To our right lies the grotto. I cannot help glancing in that direction and remembering more pleasant times and more desirable companionship.

"Just what we need," my cousin says, "some shade." His eyes apparently followed mine. How I wish I could have my glance back again. Turning down the side path, he draws me across the threshold and drops my arm. I close my eyes for a moment and think of the last time I was here with Henri, of disrobing before him in the moonlight.

My cousin's voice shatters my revelry. "Marvelous!" I open my eyes to find him running his hand over one of the ceramic lizards. Next he squats down to examine a frog. He is quite as enthusiastic as a child. I am glad no one is near enough to see him.

"You always did like frogs," I say, meaning to mock him.

"I do still," he replies, equally oblivious to my tone and to his utter lack of courtly *sang-froid*. "This little fellow is *tout à fait* perfect. I can nearly hear him sing." And then, unbelievably, he makes a frog call. The low, throaty noise echoes off the walls. What, I wonder, might some stray courtier think we are doing?

"Your Majesty, we should rejoin the others. It is not appropriate for us to be in such a secluded spot alone."

Standing up he says, "You cannot honestly fear I will take liberties, particularly after your little speech yesterday. Or perhaps you think your hand irresistible?"

"I do not. And in fact I do not believe you felt any pressing urge to kiss it at dinner, save as a message."

He smiles. Then, offering his arm, draws me back into the sunlight. Raising a hand to shield my eyes, I look about; I have had enough of being alone with the King of Navarre. Seeing Charles beside a fountain, I say, "Let us join His Majesty. After all, you accepted my hand to be brought closer to the King, did you not?"

Mother eyes us as we approach. "My son," she says, holding out a hand to the King of Navarre. "I hope you will not begrudge me the early use of that pleasant appellation. Bring Marguerite and come and sit beside me that we may be a cozy family."

As if my family has ever been anything of the kind.

"I know you are missing your mother," Her Majesty continues. "Perhaps I may in some part ameliorate her loss by my affections to you."

I remember my cousin's words shortly after he entered the Louvre: he knows what Her Majesty is, and the fact that she does not know him so well—that she thinks she can fool him—gives him an advantage. This is not displeasing. I do believe, though it is a close matter and I could well do without either, I may prefer the rule of my cousin to the rule of my mother.

"Madame," my cousin replies, "my mother's letters did not do you justice."

I must disguise a laugh as a cough.

Charles leans forward to look at our cousin. "When we go to war with Spain, you must have a command." I am surprised Charles is willing to raise intervention in the Low Countries on such an outing. It is a sign of which way his loyalties are leaning in the struggle between Her Majesty and the admiral—at least at the moment.

Mother's face darkens. "We are not going to war with Spain."

"Are we not? Why, the admiral and I were just speaking of it last evening."

As if summoned by the words, Coligny emerges from a side path and strides toward us.

Charles rises and embraces him. *"Mon père."*

I can hear Mother's teeth grind.

"Your Majesty"—the older man's face is grave—"Don Frederic of Toledo has routed the Seigneur de Genlis and his troops at Quiévrain. Not two hundred Frenchmen survived."

"Ha!" Her Majesty's exclamation draws both men's eyes. "Yet you insist, Admiral, that French troops of Protestants and Catholics combined are ready to face the Spanish."

Coligny ignores her. "Genlis ought to have waited for the Prince of Orange and his men. But now he has acted, what will Your Majesty do?"

Mother snaps her fingers. The ladies, including the Queen Consort, rise and scatter. I do not move, content for the first time to remain beside my cousin. Mother narrows her eyes and asks, "Why should His Majesty do anything?"

"Genlis had our blessing," Charles replies.

"He did not." Mother is emphatic. "You would never be foolish enough to condone an attack by any of your subjects on Spanish troops within their own territory."

Charles looks exasperated. "Was Louis of Nassau foolish? His invasion succeeded and everyone upon my council, yourself included, took delight in that."

"Being pleased by someone else's victory and being involved in a military campaign are two different things." Mother is so angry that she visibly shakes. "I say again: you did not condone the actions of Genlis. And you will state so, publicly."

"If the Seigneur has been taken, there may be a letter in his possession which will give the lie to such an assertion."

Mother glares at the admiral. If I were he, I would be prodigiously glad to be armed. Looking back at Charles, she says, "Then lie. Your subjects disobeyed your orders by marching into Flanders. You wish for peace between France and her Catholic ally Spain."

Charles' shoulders droop. Coligny knows this signals capitulation. Bowing to the King he says, "I will return to the Louvre and see what can be done to secure the release of prisoners."

"Fine," Mother says, "so long as you do not expect to ransom them with royal moneys. You Protestants are not without resources: Let *them* be expended."

Charles stands as the admiral departs, but Mother puts a restraining hand on his arm. She is not finished with him—not while there is still a question as to who has the most influence with the King. It is a question I see in the eyes of those surrounding us. "My son," Mother says, "you wring my heart with your foolishness."

"It was only five thousand men, and I did not finance them."

"Not that imprudence—the greater one. You rely too much on one not worthy of your trust."

She does not say the name. She does not need to.

"It is an impossible thing for a mother to see her child in danger and not act. I have devoted my life to preserving and promoting my sons. I have sacrificed much to that exercise, expending my own funds in the crown's defense, going without sleep, traveling in all weathers to be with

Your Majesty or your armies. Yet you prefer to lean upon one who formerly opposed you." She shakes her head slowly. "It is too much. I must beg leave to withdraw from Court."

"You would leave me?" Charles is all agitation. "Where would you go?"

"To Italy. Am I not always called 'that Italian' by those who demonize me?" She draws a kerchief from her sleeve for effect. And His Majesty is affected.

"Whosoever calls you that within my hearing shall have his tongue cut out. There is no question of you being displaced, in my heart or at my council table. And there can be no question of you quitting France."

Mother is not pacified—or at least pretends otherwise.

"As I am Your Majesty's humble subject, I will obey and remain within the kingdom's borders, but I leave for Montceaux today." She sweeps off.

Charles tries to display a look of indifference. "Women!" He laughs but the sound is high-pitched and nervous. "Let us go and admire the roses."

The King of Navarre offers me an arm. Before we join those trailing His Majesty, my cousin looks in the direction of Mother's retreat. "I do not believe any letters could do Her Majesty justice," he says. "She must be seen to be fully understood."

"A woman is not safe in the streets." Henriette breezes into my antechamber where Charlotte and I are ensconced *tête-à-tête* for the morning. When Mother traveled to Montceaux we were left behind. I use my freedom to avoid my cousin, whose awkward attempts at playacted wooing are as tiresome as they are useless, and to do as I like with my friends.

"Surely it is too early for the pickpockets and cutpurses to have arrived for my wedding," I say.

"Those I would know how to deal with," Henriette replies. "Alas, the avenues are thick with Protestants swaggering about, armed and unwilling to suffer the slightest inconvenience or insult." She puts her hand on the hilt of an imaginary sword and struts across the room before collapsing into a chair and accepting the glass from Gillone. "It is a horrible spectacle."

"Too bad Charles did not take some of them with him when he ran after Her Majesty." My brother rode out this morning, able to maintain his feigned nonchalance over Mother's absence for only a single day. The admiral must be bereft. He thought, I suppose, he had liberated the King. What a fool.

"That would have been *very* good of His Majesty, particularly if he had taken the King of Navarre, *n'est-ce pas?*"

"You read my mind."

"I will read it further." Henriette winks. "You may be sorry that gentleman was left behind, but you are delighted that Guise remains in Paris."

"He does?" I did not know this, and "delighted" is an understatement.

"I do." Henri saunters in. He has never been in my apartments in daylight before, never entered them openly by the main door. There is something thrilling about the bold nature of it—thrilling and arousing.

Charlotte makes room beside me.

"Her Grace is quite right"—Henri scowls where I expect him to smile—"the heretics are unbearable. The people of Paris will not tolerate it. If the Protestants continue in such a manner, some of them will be run out of town before the month is out."

"Do not think of the month being out," I chastise him. *Do not think of my wedding being past.* "Do not think of the Protestants with their odd ways and odd smells. Think only of me." I pat my knee. Henri smiles and stretches out on the settle, laying his head in my lap.

Looking into my face, he says, "Yes, let us be happy."

"How is little Henri?" I ask, twirling his hair about my fingers. Oddly, while I hate Henri's wife, I cannot help taking an interest in his children. Perhaps because he delights in them so. His second son is just over a month old and has a rash, thanks to the insufferable heat.

"Improving."

"He would be better still if you would send him out of this sweltering city," Henriette remarks. "And *you* would be better if you sent his mother with him."

I take pride in the fact that although the Duchesse de Guise is Henriette's own sister, my friend's first loyalty is to me.

"Perhaps after the wedding," Henri replies.

For an instant I think he means *my* wedding and I am stung by his casual tone.

"My wife can hardly absent herself from her youngest sister's nuptials," he continues, making it clear that he speaks of the upcoming marriage of Marie de Clèves.

"I too will be traipsing out to Blandy to witness that heretical marriage rite," Henriette replies. "Poor Marie, only days away from becoming the Princesse de Condé. But perhaps I ought not to pity her: marrying Protestants is the fashion this season."

"It is a fashion I do not care for." Henri's voice is thick with disgust.

"Yet another matter, Duc, on which we disagree." The familiar and unwelcome voice startles me. My cousin stands in my doorway. How I wish, despite the stifling heat, it had not been left open!

Snatching my fingers from the Duc's hair, I feel acutely embarrassed. Apparently Henri does not, for he leaves his head in my lap, merely turning it so he can see my cousin better.

"Do we agree on anything?" he asks quietly.

"I believe we agree that my soon-to-be wife is the loveliest of women." The King of Navarre smiles; then meeting my eyes, he says as if nothing were amiss, "I am going to play tennis and wondered if you wished to watch, but it is clear you are occupied."

My face burns. I find I do not know where to put the hand that played in the Duc's curls. "I can come if you like." *Why did I say that?*

"No, no," my cousin replies, with a magnanimous wave of his hand. "You will have ample occasions to watch me beat my gentlemen at sport while your present form of entertainment is coming to an end." Then he is gone.

I sit stunned, but Henriette throws back her head and laughs. "My goodness, that was exciting. I would not have thought the King of Navarre capable of such self-possession, such detachment! Whatever else we think of him, we must applaud that."

Henri sits up, looking at Henriette with disbelief. "He is a coward. He ought to have challenged me."

"Yes, that would have been politic." Henriette looks nearly as disbelieving as Henri.

"Defense of one's honor is not a matter for prudence."

"That is a definite and unequivocal philosophy, but not one likely to lead to a long life or increased offices."

"What about you?" Henri turns to me. "Do you find something to admire in the King of Navarre's display?"

"Indeed not. I have yet to find anything admirable in the gentleman." I say this because I would not side with Henriette against my Duc, but it is not entirely true. If I were honest, I would have to admit to being impressed by my cousin's ability to make us all look foolish in a situation where he might have been expected to do so. He showed an admirable control of his temper. *Unless the sight of the Duc and myself in such an intimate position simply did not raise his ire . . .* The thought both unsettles and nettles me. I want to banish it. Want things to return to the easy way they were before my cousin entered. But the mood is spoiled. This, I realize, is my fate. The King of Navarre will be every day more and more present in my life, in my apartments, in my thoughts. He, or the specter of him, will intrude unexpectedly, making conversations awkward and matters between Henri and me uneasy.

"What shall we do now?" Charlotte asks, trying to break the tension.

"Pray the papal dispensation fails to arrive," Henri says grimly. "Because if it comes, I will be pledged to kill two heretics instead of one."

Charles and Mother return reconciled, helped in their rapprochement by the fact His Majesty's council met at Montceaux without the admiral. The king's commanders—Montpensier, Nevers, Cossé, and Anjou—spoke with one voice for peace, reinforcing Mother's position, and Charles, unaccustomed to standing up to so many, declared he has no intention of going to war with Spain. So, for the moment, mother beams at him and leans upon his arm as she ordinarily leans upon Anjou's.

But while the two appear at peace, all the world else becomes increasingly less so. The heat is partly to blame. Who can be civil in the oven Paris has become? But it is more—it is as Henriette said: there is something about the sight of so many Protestants strolling about both the halls of the Louvre and the avenues of the city as if they were in every manner equal to the Catholics that roils those of the true faith. Priests speak from their pulpits against the "invaders" even though doing so brings the wrath of Her Majesty down upon them.

Within the Court, Anjou and his gentlemen pick fights with my cous-in's men. Every sport becomes serious. Tennis draws blood. Wrestling re-sembles combat. As in the city, Mother does what she can to quiet mounting tensions. And when she has limited success, she acts to assure they will be of the shortest possible duration, having Charles declare all official business suspended during the events of my wedding, and that two days after those celebrations his entire household will quit the city for Fontainebleau, seeking better air for the Queen Consort.

I weep daily. Last evening I began to cry while in bed with Henri, ren-dering him so agitated that I feared he would take his dagger and charge through the rooms of the Louvre in nothing but his shirt, seeking my cousin. His lack of control frightened me. Even as I would avoid marry-ing the King of Navarre if I could, I cannot quite wish him dead. Be-yond my moral compunctions, the death of my cousin at Henri's hands would mean a death sentence for my love in turn. I soothed my Duc and made him swear to me he will not be rash or violent. I cannot, however, keep him from hating, nor from brooding. When we are in company, Henri's eyes are constantly on the King of Navarre.

"Did I not know the odious duty fell to me, I might think the Duc charged with the King of Navarre's seduction," Charlotte jokes from behind her hand.

We are in the King's apartment, four dozen ladies and gentlemen—the choicest members of my brother's household and my cousin's—allegedly enjoying an evening together. My cousin plays dice with the King. Guise walks the perimeter of the room staring at him.

"Were that the case, softer looks might serve Guise better. In fact, they might serve him better now, if you could persuade him to them, Mar-got," Henriette says. "It has taken His Grace full long to be restored to royal favor; it would be foolish for him to harm himself there by offend-ing a prince your mother and brother wish embraced."

I shrug, then curse myself for doing so, as the gesture reminds me of my cousin. "I cannot make Henri other than he is. As he loves me, he cannot bear the King of Navarre."

"Well, he will have to bear him, just as you have had to bear my sister," Henriette replies.

The King of Navarre cries out triumphantly and receives a slap on the shoulder from one of his friends, a man I see him with constantly. Is it the Seigneur de Pilles? I can never remember the names of his gentlemen, perhaps because I do not care to know them. My cousin rises. Charlotte sighs and does likewise.

"Wish me luck," she says before gliding off to fuss over him.

"She is a fool to ask me to wish her luck. I have none myself," I say.

"You do not need luck, for you have beauty and talent." Leaning over between Henriette and me, my brother François holds out a lute and smiles. "Will you play for me?"

Taking the instrument, I smile back at him. "Of course."

François takes a seat on the floor before me. I begin to play and sing softly. Like a siren's call my voice draws Henri. He stops just behind me and rests a hand on my shoulder possessively. The Prince de Condé says, "Cousin, you miss the performance."

My cousin turns from Charlotte, with whom he has been whispering. Not understanding Condé's meaning and seeing me with the lute, he says, "Apologies, Mademoiselle, do you play for us?"

"I play for whoever will listen."

"What an agreeable woman." Condé smiles, but there is no warmth in it. "The Duchesse de Valois is not particular. She will entertain all comers."

Henriette draws an audible breath and puts a hand on my leg. Henri's hand tightens on my shoulder, but it is François who comes to my defense. Springing to his feet he says, "What do you insinuate, Sir?"

The King of Navarre touches Condé's arm.

The Prince ignores him. "Come outside and I will be explicit."

"Gladly, Sir, only let us first send for our swords so that once you have done I may make quick work of you."

The Protestant gentleman I have come to recognize as Seigneur de Pilles laughs, doubtless because François is untried in combat and the Prince a veteran of the wars. That laugh is a mistake. Enraged, François spins, looking for the source. When he cannot identify it, his eyes come to rest on Charles. "Brother, were these Huguenots not your guests I would slay them all and leave none to make light of Valois honor or ability."

"And I would gladly help you." Henri's voice over my shoulder is soft, but not so soft that the King or the Prince de Condé fail to hear it.

"I do not like your chances," Condé replies. "We are as many as you, and none of us have surrendered." This last, an open jab at Anjou and the tale that he killed the Prince's father only after that gentleman was his prisoner, draws gasps.

Anjou, who until now leaned in a corner with Saint-Mégrin enjoying the unfolding spectacle, moves to join François, clapping his arm around my younger brother's shoulder in a rare show of unity. "When we send for the swords, brother," he says, "perhaps we should see if there is an ass in the stables."

Condé takes a step toward Anjou but only one before Charles jumps to his feet. "What is wrong with all of you?" he shouts. "Are you so fond of dying? Fine, but mark this: I am king. You die when and where I command, not here and not now." He looks back and forth between the would-be combatants. The King of Navarre again touches Condé's sleeve, this time to effect. The gentleman steps back. Charles nods in approbation, then looks piercingly at Anjou and Alençon. François moves to join Guise behind me. Anjou gives Condé one last sneer and saunters back toward Saint-Mégrin.

"I am tired of Frenchmen killing Frenchmen," the King proclaims. "The admiral is right: I must send you all to fight the Spanish, if only so that I may have peace." Throwing himself back into his seat, he picks up his glass, drains it, and then holds it out for Marie to refill.

In the corner Anjou gives a little smile. I know what he is thinking: here is something to tell Mother that will remove Charles from her favor again.

Condé stalks to where several Protestant gentlemen were, until the disruption, playing cards. He taps one on the shoulder and that gentleman quickly makes way for him. "Deal," the Prince says. The sound of cards being shuffled breaks the silence.

"That is right," Charles says, "let us return to more pleasurable pastimes."

Crossing to where I sit, my cousin gives me a smile. "It seems I have been negligent in my attentions this evening and look where that brought us. If you will play again, my attention is entirely yours."

I have no desire for my cousin's attention but nor do I wish the evening to devolve further into unpleasantness or violence. So I smile and take the lute up from my lap. As I begin to play, Henriette vacates her seat. "This place is yours, Sir," she says to the King of Navarre. Then, moving to Guise's side: "Brother, you must take me for a turn. We are both, I think, overheated." I feel the Duc's hand leave my shoulder.

As he and my friend stroll away, my cousin says, "With so many Henries it is easy to become confused, so I will be plain. I am not my cousin Condé who would defame you. Nor am I your brother who plays everyone to his own end. But just as I would not have you mistake me for them, do not mistake the Duc de Guise for me—I am the man who will, in less than a week's time, be your husband."

"Sir, I am under no illusion to the contrary. It is that thought which keeps me awake nights."

There is a rumor that, with my ceremony of betrothal and wedding mere days away, the papal dispensation has not arrived. My heart is light. My feet have wings as they carry me in search of Charles. I must know the truth. I am nearly running when I round a corner and come upon my cousin, *sans* doublet, shirt open at the neck.

"You look very happy," he remarks, stopping to bow and forcing me to stop by doing so.

I am stuck for a response. I am happy, but the source of my happiness is hardly something I can disclose without seeming cruel.

I notice he is smiling and take my inspiration there. "You also."

"I've just left your brother Anjou blaming the heat for his loss to me at tennis."

I smile at the thought of this.

"Can it be we are sharing a moment of enjoyment?" My cousin's voice is playful. "I believe we are. Well, then, I will seize the chance to say I hope it will be the first of many."

I do not share his hope, but again, I do not wish to be contrary to no purpose. "I would be glad to see you happy." It is true. My cousin is far from my favorite person, but he becomes more likable as he becomes more familiar. And unlike many I might name, he has never deliberately sought to harm me. "And I am very glad you beat Anjou."

"Soundly," he assures me, his voice both confident and teasing.

I applaud lightly. "The more soundly the better."

He regards me earnestly, as if trying to puzzle something out. "You know, despite the years I passed with this court as a boy, and despite the reports sent by my mother, I find many things not as I expected. Among these nearly every member of your family."

"I can well believe it." I laugh, thinking of what Jeanne de Navarre likely said about me. Doubtless it was no more flattering than what my mother says of the King of Navarre when he is not about. She calls him "the peasant." I wonder how long it will be before she calls him "my friend." When she does, all around will know she thinks him a fool—for that is her traditional use of the phrase, to express a patronizing derision—but he will not. The thought of my mother playing such games with my cousin, and he all unaware, is not pleasing.

"Your Majesty"—I reach out and touch his sleeve, the first time I have ever touched him of my own volition without the pressures of etiquette—"I do not know your gentlemen or how things are in your court. If you are representative, however, I must conclude that your courtiers are unaffected and plainspoken."

"I will take that as a compliment."

"Take it as you like. But understand: we Valois are a changeable lot. To trust in appearance here is to be made a fool, or worse."

"I do not mind being thought an idiot so long as I know I am not one."

I look straight into my cousin's calm, deep-gray eyes. He is no idiot. I nod. "There is safety in being underestimated."

"And your family underestimates many, yourself included." The moment the words are spoken, he seems uncomfortable, as if he has betrayed something he did not intend to.

I am uncomfortable as well, nettled by his perceptiveness, by the truth of his statement, and perhaps most of all by the familiarity of our discussion. Ours are words such as might pass between those with a shared interest. We have none. Or such as might pass between husband and wife and, therefore, decidedly out of place at a moment when I rejoice in a report that His Holiness may render such a union impossible.

Quickly I turn the subject and my mind back to finding Charles. "Was His Majesty among those watching the sport?"

"He left just as I did. Madame Catherine came looking for him."

"I am off to find him, and you are off—"

"To wash."

I am relieved my cousin does not offer to escort me. I stand and watch his retreating back until he is out of sight.

Mother and Charles might be closeted in any number of places, but it is always Her Majesty's preference to be in her own rooms. I will try the secret place.

I wonder, as I ease open the concealed door, if Anjou remembers showing me the vantage point. He ought not to have done that. Once behind the door the short passage must be navigated in silence. I inch forward. I can hear before I can see.

"—delay seems like weakness. I will not have that. I will command the Cardinal de Bourbon to proceed." I put my eyes to the first of the deliberately widened seams. Charles sits, arms crossed over his chest and sullen-faced. Mother paces before him.

"We cannot be certain he will comply," she says. "He answers to the Holy Father. If he knows we lack the dispensation, he will not risk Gregory's ire even to satisfy his king."

"Then I will make him a guest at Vincennes and find someone else to officiate."

"Imprisoning the groom's uncle is unlikely to bring us closer to a wedding. And who would you find to officiate? The Cardinal de Lorraine? I think not."

So the rumor is true!

"What do we do, then? Gregory is no better than Pius. He proclaims himself ready to oblige me but follows this pretense with a list of conditions he knows cannot be met. Can you imagine my cousin kneeling before me and professing the Catholic faith? He is not so keen to marry Margot as that. I doubt even the admiral could achieve it. Must I let the Pope rule France?"

"No. You will show His Holiness that you alone govern here—not by locking up his cardinals, or by asserting your rights in another letter, but by dispensing with the dispensation."

"But you just said the Cardinal de Bourbon will not proceed without it."

"Ah, but if he thought it was coming . . ."

"Your spies say it is not."

"I have better spies than His Eminence. All the Court knows this. So, if you tell the Cardinal the document is on the road between Rome and Paris, none will gainsay you. The Cardinal will be placated and this ugly rumor squelched."

Charles raises a hand to his chin, clearly thinking. What monstrosities he considers: lying to officials of the Holy Church; marrying me off in a ceremony that—without the necessary dispensation—creates an alliance prohibited by canon law . . .

"Yes!" Charles jumps to his feet. "I will do it. Did I not promise Jeanne d'Albret as much? Did I not tell her that if *Monsieur le Pape* conducted himself too absurdly I would take Margot by the hand and marry her to our cousin Henri myself?"

"You did." Mother nods, her face flushed with pleasure. "And I promise you I will not allow you to be embarrassed by His Holiness. I will instruct the governor of Lyons to detain all couriers from Rome until your sister's marriage is sanctified."

Charles laughs. "Do! It would be scandalous if a formal refusal arrived while my sister stood at the altar, or while she and my cousin were consummating the marriage."

"Let us each make haste to do what we must to spread the word the dispensation is on its way, before Guise, Philip of Spain, or, God forbid, your sister hears and believes otherwise."

Too late, Mother. I have heard the truth. Much good may that do me. I let myself slide to the floor of my hiding place. The narrowness of the space pushes my knees to my chest. I rest my cheek upon them. I do not cry. I am too horrified for tears.

What course is open to me? Challenge Charles openly? To what end? A liar does not confess his transgression merely because he is accused of it. And to confront Charles is to risk something. Charles feels a genuine fondness for me. I will not squander his devotion by appealing to it fruitlessly. Having seen my brother's face and heard the vehemence in his voice as he decried the Pope's obstinacy, I know the matter of my marriage is beyond changing. Verily, I believe at this moment he would support a

Protestant rite should it come to that. I shudder. If I am to be married against my will, I would at least have a Catholic ceremony. Anything else forces me into heresy. So I must let Charles' lie stand and proceed with my wedding, pretending to believe in a dispensation I know does not exist.

I close my eyes, feeling empty, without ideas. Then Henri's voice is in my head. He is telling me a battle tale. I am teasing him, because it took him two tries to win a city and he is insisting there is no shame in that, explaining how the lessons of a first defeat may help a commander to victory in the second assault. A very faint thought begins to take shape. There is another reason to make certain my dreaded wedding is a Catholic one. A marriage performed and later found unlawful due to an unexcused degree of consanguinity may be undone. This, insufficient as it may seem, is the hope I will cling to.

I must capitulate now in hopes of a victory later. But I will not surrender completely. I think back to the day that the King of Navarre arrived, to the promise I made him that he should never kiss more than my hand. To the promise I made Henri that I will not sleep with my husband. This is my next battle. I must find a way to keep my word and avoid being taken to wife. Today my cousin and I spoke as friends—that is what I will trade upon. The King of Navarre is smart enough to have realized by now that he has ridden into a nest of vipers. Perhaps he will see the sense in having at least one viper who can be counted upon not to bite him.

It is our last night before I am a married woman. Henri arrives full in equal parts of love and anger. He takes me as a man takes a city—fiercely and without mercy. There is a feeling of desperation in all that we do, in all that we say. And there are things I have promised myself not to reveal that weigh heavily upon me.

"Nothing will be different," I say, rubbing his shoulders where he sits, naked and hunched on the side of my bed.

"Marguerite, do not treat me like a child or a fool. I am neither."

"I do not." I slip from behind him to sit beside him. "Ask yourself: What difference has the Princesse de Porcien made between us? None."

"She is a woman. What rights does she have over me that she dare insist upon?"

"I have given you my word that there are some rights I will never grant the King of Navarre, husband or no."

"So you have." He puts his head momentarily in his hands, running his fingers through the sandy hair I love. When he looks up, his eyes are still despairing. "I believe you were in earnest in your oath. But what you intend and what Henri de Bourbon will allow . . ." His voice trails off.

I struggle to look unconcerned. But I have thought of this. My cousin does not seem a man full of temper, but he has more than once made clear he believes he will be my master once we are wed.

"I cannot understand His Holiness. He promised—" He stops short.

I have no doubt that the House of Lorraine worked behind the scenes to thwart my marriage. But if the Cardinal of Lorraine communicated with the Pope, why did my love not tell me? Perhaps he feared to raise my hopes.

"Never mind what anyone else promised." I squeeze his hand. "We have each of us been betrayed by those who ought to have kept faith with us. So long as we do not betray each other, anything else can be borne."

"Can it? Can I bear to attend your ceremony of betrothal and then see you paraded to the Archbishop's palace tomorrow evening? How? How shall I stand outside as darkness falls, wondering which window is yours, knowing that no ladder will be lowered from it to guide me to you? And the following day . . . I cannot even speak of what comes next."

I understand what he means. Did I not feel the same crushing grief on his wedding day? Yet, perhaps because I did and survived, he ought to take heart. He ought to be stronger. I find myself vexed by his complaints even as they move me. As I am the one currently facing unwelcomed vows, should not *he* be comforting *me*? I swallow the question just as I have been swallowing the words that would tell him the papal dispensation is a fiction.

"What would you have me do?" I ask. "If I refuse the marriage, I am dead to you. If I am not sick within a week and dying, I will be locked away until I am old." I shudder at the thought of being bound to God against my will—of being turned into a black bird by a nun's habit and then caged.

"Better a convent than the King of Navarre."

I am stunned. I never asked this man to give up his future for me. In fact, I begged him to abandon me so that he might keep his prospects. Surely, I reassure myself, this is merely his anger and his exhaustion speaking. "Really, Henri?"

He looks away. For a moment we sit in silence and my discomfort grows. "No," he says at last, returning his eyes to me and bringing one of my hands to his lips.

I exhale, although I did not realize I was holding my breath.

"They say your cousin will abandon his mourning for the wedding. Well, I will don the clothing of grief. It will be easy for you to see me as you look into the crowd of courtiers at Notre Dame. I will be the one clad in somber black."

"Careful, Sir—" even at such a moment I cannot resist teasing him— "you may be mistaken for one of Navarre's Protestants."

He does not smile. "You cannot make me laugh this night, Marguerite. Are you like to laugh yourself?"

"No. But I will settle for not crying. We have hours left until you must leave. Let us not spend them sullen, singing dirges. Let us instead forget a future we cannot alter in an all-consuming passion that is as unchangeable." I climb onto his lap and, leaning in, kiss him. It takes a moment, but first his lips and then his loins respond.

CHAPTER 17

August 18, 1572—Paris, France

I wake with a start. The sun streams into my room. No, not my room: a room belonging to His Grace the Archbishop. Dear God, I remember what day it is and wish I had been beyond waking—that my ladies had arrived to find me dead.

I begin to cry.

Gillone approaches with some trepidation, holding out a *surcote* for me to slip into. Behind her, framed by the window, the sun seems high. After struggling to sleep at all, have I slept away the last morning of my freedom?

"What is the hour?" I ask, wiping my eyes with my fists as if I were an *enfant*.

"Past eleven, Your Highness."

Panic rises like bile in my throat.

"I've brought your breakfast." The thought of eating—well, it seems impossible.

"How long?" I ask.

"Not two hours."

In less than two hours the woman taxed with preparing me for my nuptial Mass will arrive. The thought of a dozen ladies buzzing around me, laughing and making merry, is unbearable.

My crushing longing of the night before returns. Having been paraded here by the whole of my family, I was left alone, and alone I lay awake. How I wanted Henri. If only I could see him now and be reminded that I still have something to live for. But I dare not ask for him. I will see him next in company he despises, for my love, owing to his offices, must accompany the King of Navarre's cortege.

"I wish I could wear black," I say to Gillone, remembering what Henri said of his day's costume. I pull the *surcote* around me tightly as if it were the depth of winter and not a sweltering day in August. "Where is the wig?"

Gillone is stunned. Little wonder. I do not commonly wear wigs, not since Henri told me that he disliked them on me so long ago. Yet one arrived for my wedding. It, like everything else, was selected by Mother to create an image that serves her purposes.

Gillone opens a large leather case and lifts the *coiffure* out. Its pale-colored curls, extravagantly arranged, will do perfectly. They will help me assert and remember that it is Marguerite, Duchesse de Valois and Princess of France, and not Margot the woman, who weds the King of Navarre.

Sooner than it seems possible, servants arrive carrying my fine garments. Gillone helps me don the chemise with its elaborate lace-trimmed collar designed to frame my head. She is holding out my cloth-of-gold slippers when Henriette arrives.

Taking one look at my face, she says, "Your groom abandons mourning for his wedding day, but I see that here a pall remains."

I begin to cry. I have lost count of my bouts of tears since waking.

Shaking her head, my friend says, "Well, it is better to weep now. Once you are dressed, your gown could be spoiled."

"Good!" I reply viciously.

"Being unhappy is no reason to be unattractive. Remember, the Duc's eyes will be upon you, doubtless far more often than your husband's."

Claude arrives with the Baronne de Retz. "Tell the others that they are not needed," I command the Baronne. I desire as few witnesses as possible to my misery.

As she helps me into my bodice, so crusted with jewels that its weight might overwhelm a more fragile woman, my sister makes a feeble attempt to cheer me. "How marvelous this violet velvet looks against your skin."

I cannot resist turning my eyes in the direction of my glass. I am a tribute to my brother's kingdom—my gown so thickly embroidered with gold fleurs-de-lis that one might be forgiven for mistaking me for the Queen of France rather than the soon-to-be Queen of Navarre.

Led to the dressing table, I allow my mind to wander while the ladies apply my makeup and Gillone pins up my hair in preparation for covering it.

"Surely this will rouse her." Henriette's slightly mocking voice draws my attention. The Duchesse holds out a tray where a magnificent necklace rests. Enormous rubies and diamonds alternate along its length, and, intermittently, pearls as large as grapes hang like teardrops. "There is a tiara to match." Henriette motions for the Baronne de Retz to open another box.

"Gifts from our brother," Claude says quickly, as if she is worried I might think the objects come from my cousin. She need have no fear. I have seen my soon-to-be-husband's taste in clothing and jewels. He has none. Such a heedless man could never have selected these things.

As she stoops to clasp the necklace around my neck, Henriette whispers, "It looks well with your gown, but just imagine how divine you would look wearing it *tout seul*. You must model it for Henri." I know which Henri she means, but still I shudder at the idea that my cousin should ever see me naked.

Wigged and crowned I stand again while Gillone winds an ermine *couët* around me. The others wait, each holding a portion of my mantle with its enormous train. As they secure it at my shoulders, Mother enters.

"Daughter." Her nod of acknowledgment is curt. Turning to Henriette, she demands, "Is she ready?"

I begin to cry. I cannot help it. I am doing what Her Majesty desires—marrying my loathsome cousin—still Mother has no word of love or comfort for me.

"Have you nothing to say, Madame, to your daughter on her wedding day?" I sniff.

"Stop crying," she commands. "Half a million écus were spent to make you look the queen. Will you spoil the effect with a red nose?"

In the great gallery my train awaits. Charles looks oddly out of place standing at the head of a column of more than one hundred noblewomen. Many eyes are upon me, but most seem intent on taking in the details of my costume. Only those of the Queen Consort meet my own. She offers an encouraging smile. Mother leads me to the King, then takes her place. All around us there is a murmur of excited voices, yet my brother and I remain silent. Clarions are heard.

"It is the signal!" My sister Claude is not the only one to say it, but I hear her most clearly. Those ladies charged with carrying the train of my mantle rush to unroll it. Now my mother and sister are four ells behind me. Even if they were to offer me last-minute words of advice or encouragement, I could not hear them.

The doors of the hall swing open and ahead the outer doors of the palace stand open as well—a yawning chasm of pure, white light. As we begin to move forward, I can see nothing beyond this threshold. Can this be what a prisoner feels on the day of his execution? Dragged from a dark cell, seeing light, usually the symbol of all that is pure and good, and knowing it marks his doom?

Out I plunge, determined to make a good end. Determined that the tears I shed in my apartment will be my last until I am again in private.

I stand, blinking, on a wooden gallery built to allow me to travel from the Episcopal Palace to a platform before the doors of Notre Dame. Below, a cortege larger than my own approaches. Heralds-at-arms, their tabards emblazoned with the arms of France, and royal guards with clarions and cymbals lead the way for a sea of gentlemen from the King's household, carrying halberds. The glint of the sun off the weapons again brings the image of a hooded executioner to my mind. And there he is, between Anjou and Alençon: my personal executioner. He is clad in yellow satin heavily embroidered in silver and studded with pearls. The coats of my brothers could be doubles. *Does my cousin not see the error in dressing so very like them?* My brothers are tall, with striking dark features. They wear yellow well. It makes the King of Navarre sallow.

My groom's eyes meet mine. Do I see hope? Apprehension? I do not care. Quickly I look away, searching for Henri. The religious conviction of each gentleman in the assembly is abundantly plain, for, unlike my soon-to-be husband, it appears the remainder of his coreligionists have not abandoned their mourning. I nearly laugh out loud: it is as I teased him—my Henri will blend in with the Protestants. But it seems his intention to dress in mourning did not hold. For when my eyes find him beside a scowling Prince de Condé, Henri is as pale as death but wearing silver and rose. The eyes that meet mine are fierce, and they do not leave me until they are forced to as the party passes by.

We stand for what seems an eternity. At last it is our turn. As we process, a sea of faces turns upward to watch. Additional spectators lean from windows and roofs. Yet there is little cheering. I hope my mother remarks this. I am sure my cousin's men do. I can see several in the stands, their eyes wary, their smiles forced. They know that while King Charles professes to love his Catholic and Protestant subjects equally, the people of Paris are not so ecumenical.

Before the Cathedral doors, the King delivers me to my cousin, who holds out his hand. I ignore the gesture, letting my own hand drop to my side. While the ladies who carried it arrange my train, the others of my family take their places. The Cardinal de Bourbon steps to his. He looks remarkably shabby wearing only such vestments as he would for an ordinary occasion. But this is how the King of Navarre's mother wished it to be. The Cardinal begins and I am lost—drifting in the heat, mesmerized by his voice to such a degree that I can make no sense of his words. I hear my cousin speak, then the Cardinal again, then silence. Charles takes a step forward and, rather forcefully, pushes my shoulder. Jarred, I realize I have missed my cue.

"*J'accepte,*" I mumble. It is miserably given, but it is my consent and it is sufficient. My eyes stray to the carvings above the Cardinal—the last judgment—where the archangel Michael weighs the souls of the dead according to the lives they led on earth. At this moment I do not like my chances of entering the kingdom of heaven, married to a heretic in a union that violates canon law. The entire ceremony is impossibly brief for something that changes me from who I was to who I will be, but I am glad of it. My cousin's proximity is unbearable. I wonder if the reason lies in the complete falsehood of our situation. As of this moment, he should be something to me—should be greater and more important than any other person living save my brother the King. Yet he is not. I am glad I will soon be away from him. And I bless Jeanne d'Albret and her myriad of conditions, conditions that will keep my cousin from hearing our nuptial Mass.

Before I am given a respite, however, I must take his hand. There is a fanfare of trumpets as he leads me into the dark, cool church. At the tribune separating the nave from the choir I am handed off to Anjou, who will stand in my cousin's place for the Mass. Ordinarily Anjou's arm is one I studiously avoid. Today I take it gladly. The lesser of two evils— no, not that, for I do believe my brother the more malevolent of the two. Merely an expedient, the first in a new life I fear will be full of them.

"*. . . factum est, et habitavit in nobis et vidimus gloriam ejus, gloriam quasi unigeniti a Patre, plenum gratiae et veritatis. Deo gratias.*"

Mass is over. Before the Cardinal and the Bishop of Digne have descended from the altar someone scurries to retrieve my cousin—my *husband*. I wonder if he knows how loud he and his fellows were as they stood in the cloisters—knows their talking and laughing could be heard, raising eyebrows and hostilities? There is no sign of embarrassment on his face as he approaches. I am ready for his arm. Instead, without warning, he pulls me into an embrace. When I stiffen, he pulls me closer, whispering, "We must give the King of France what he paid for, a symbol of the new *amour* between his Protestants and Catholics, *n'est-ce pas?*"

As we make our way down the nave, covered by the sound of the organ, I reply: "We are symbolic, Sir, but not of Charles' ideal, rather of deceitful appearances. Two mismatched partners smiling for the crowds are very like a *paix* that exists on paper but not in the hearts of men."

"Hearts are difficult to change but they are not so important as actions. We need not love each other to keep from killing one another."

I wonder if he means the Protestants and Catholics of France, or we two.

In our absence, the hall of the Episcopal Palace has been lavishly decorated. We sit in places of honor, beside the King. One would think Charles himself had just married. He beams and I am barely seated before he takes my hand and fervently kisses it.

"My sister, this is a great day. I have ordered every window opened so that my people may hear the sounds of us celebrating."

Looking over my wedding guests, I perceive few signs of joy or mirth, but it is not to my advantage to give voice to that thought. Royal favor is more important than truth.

"Brother," I reply, pausing to lift his hand to my lips in turn, "I hope that though I am now the King of Navarre's wife, you know that I remain your sister first. I pray you will continue to hold me as close to your heart as you are to mine."

"Of course! The King of Navarre may clasp you to his breast but it does not follow I shall root you out of mine." Charles eagerly leans forward to catch my groom's eye. "Cousin, I have given you the most precious gift that was mine to dispose of—not in her dowry but in herself. You must promise to treasure her as I and my brothers have, or I will not be content."

"Your Majesty, you have my word, I shall accord the lady all the respect and caring she has become accustomed to."

I look closely at his face to see if he mocks me on purpose, but my cousin's eyes are mild.

The first course comes. I say nothing to my cousin and he nothing to me. Charles pauses in his effusive praise of everything and everybody only when chewing. As the plates are cleared the King says, "Now we shall have a marvelous surprise." He signals a pair of officers. A dozen heralds-at-arms enter carrying trays heaped with some sort of gold medallions which they begin to toss to the assembly. Charles motions and one of the young men approaches, lifting his tray.

"Take one," Charles commands.

I pick up a medal. A lamb lies curled at its center, resting against a cross. Circling the image are the words, "I announce peace to you."

"Turn it over," my brother urges.

On the back I find my initials entwined with my cousin's, explicit proof that I am the lamb sacrificed in hope of maintaining a two-year-old peace.

Charles smiles, looking for my reaction.

"It is beautiful," I say, nearly choking on the words.

"Cousin, we must share your joy and my bounty. Come, we will toss these to those in the street."

I watch as the two, with Charles carrying the tray he has taken from the herald, make their way to a window and cast out handfuls of gold. Others, I notice, watch as well—not only my beloved Duc but a goodly portion of the Catholic nobles. As my brother and husband turn from the casement smiling and Charles slips an arm around our cousin's shoulders, some number of these guests glower openly. I understand how they feel, then remind myself that the sight of the King and my cousin amicably talking ought to please me. My marriage may make me miserable but it still can elevate me. If it gives me no power or prestige, it gives me nothing.

The two return to the table arm in arm. My cousin smiles at me, then drains his glass of wine in a single gulp. A few weeks ago I would have concluded he is oblivious to the disdain and dislike of some of our guests. But having received proofs that he is shrewder than others suspect, I am inclined to believe he senses the ill will of many attending but chooses to bluster through it.

"Ah, Cousin," Charles says, as the King of Navarre calls for his glass to be refilled, "you have a healthy appetite."

"For life, Your Majesty."

"That is good. I do not trust a man who skulks about." Charles gazes at Anjou. "I think you will turn out to be one of my favorite brothers."

Mother compresses her lips, and both Anjou and Alençon look daggers.

As we rise at the end of the meal, Charlotte and Henriette come to me.

"Your Majesty, stop a moment and we will remove your mantle," Her Grace says.

I pause, eager for a moment with my friends.

The King of Navarre halts as well, as if he would wait, but Henriette waves him on. "Have no fear, Sir, we will bring your bride to you forthwith and much improved, for there will hardly be room for the two of you in one litter while the Queen of Navarre is dressed as she is."

My cousin smiles at the Duchesse, winks at Charlotte, and then says, "And there will hardly be opportunity for gossip if I stand about stupidly." With a bow he goes.

"He knows women," Henriette says, looking after him.

"He knows horses better," I scoff.

"If only you liked him a little more, and the King liked him a little less," Henriette sighs. "As it is, the two of you seem intent on riling the better part of the Court. And how precisely does that help you?"

"I will behave."

"No, you will not. Or have you changed your plans for the evening?"

I make no reply.

"I thought not. Not even to spare Charlotte."

Turning to my other friend, I say, "I am sorry that you must cater to the demands I will rebuff."

"That is all right. I am sure he will not be the worst I have had. At least he is in his prime. A man who wrestles, hunts, and plays tennis as well as the King of Navarre is surely not lacking in physical prowess."

My cousin waits beside our conveyance to hand me in. As he climbs in beside me he asks, "Dust or heat?"

"Sir?"

"If we leave the sides open, we will be choking in dust. If we close them, we will have no breeze."

"Whichever you prefer." *See, Henriette, I can be accommodating.*

"Closed," he says to a lackey. "I think we have been gawked at enough."

"I fear, Your Majesty, the worst is yet to come. Do we not stand for a portrait this afternoon? Is there not a ball this evening?"

"Ah, but painters do not gawk, and all those attending the ball have seen us together before." He pauses. "Those who have never approved of the sight must now accustom themselves to it. And speaking of things that must be gotten used to, the time has come, Madame, when you must find something to call me other than 'Cousin.'"

"How about 'Sir'?"

"It will serve. But as we would not occasion gossip so early in our marriage, and I, at least, have no interest in incurring your mother's displeasure, might I suggest you throw in a 'husband' here and there?" He smiles.

I do not like the idea of calling him "husband." I do, however, wish to encourage such a practical and open approach to our marriage, for such discussions as this treat it as what it is—a political alliance. "Agreed . . . husband."

He smiles again, then looks at me questioningly. "Whatever possessed you to wear that awful wig?"

"The same demon, Sir, that goaded you to wear yellow."

"Your mother, then."

I cannot help myself: I laugh.

"I knew I would either make you laugh or cry this day," he says.

Both actually. As the litter stops and my new husband offers a hand to help me alight, I realize I could never have imagined this brief moment of merriment when I wept this morning.

❖ ❖ ❖

My wedding guests have danced. They have drunk. The sea-themed decorations in the *salle voûtée* were much admired. Étienne Leroy sang with beauty and delicacy during the ballet, but was upstaged by Charles, who arrived dressed as Neptune riding upon the tail of an absolutely enormous gilded hippopotamus. *Enfin,* I am done with the public part of the day's celebrations—though, judging by the state of those left behind, there will be revelers still when the sun rises. A dozen companions accompany me to prepare for the most private part, my wedding night. A dozen *dames de la cour,* but not Mother.

Though I do not desire her company, Mother's absence rankles me. My position as her daughter and my rank surely warrant a royal escort. She herself was brought to her marriage bed by Queen Eleanor. Then I remember: I have the Queen of France with me, at least in name—my sister-in-law, Elisabeth. She walks on one side of me and Henriette on the other, each woman with her arm linked through mine. Henriette knows my mind and by her arm supports my resolve. Elisabeth on the other hand seeks, by her arm and by her gentle hands as I am undressed, to quiet my virginal nerves. I am grateful to her, for I *am* nervous, even if she is mistaken as to the cause.

I still have every intention of saying no to my cousin, but whether he will respect my refusal has never been certain. As I am tucked into bed, I remember how boisterous he was at this evening's celebrations. My husband may not be tall, but he is, as Charlotte pointed out only this afternoon, an avid sportsman and therefore strong. If my words do not stop him from pursuing consummation of our marriage, I have little hope of fighting him off.

"You are pale." Elisabeth leans in kindly and tries to hand me a glass of wine, which I wave away. I believe I have drunk less than anyone else during the course of the day. If my wits are to be my only defense, then they must be sharp.

"I am only tired."

"Too bad you will likely get little sleep tonight," Fleurie de Saussauy quips.

The ladies around my bed laugh, and that laughter is joined by some from beyond my door. My cousin and a handful of his gentlemen have arrived, talking and laughing as they jostle each other. The sight of my lighted room full of lovely women momentarily silences them. Then a gentleman behind my cousin gives the King a shove across the threshold, saying, "Go on, she may be Catholic but she is pretty."

Drunk, I think. The speaker's face is flushed and the top buttons of his doublet are undone. *Definitely drunk.* I look more closely at my cousin, blushing as my ladies stream past him. His ruff is missing and sweat beads his face. Are these merely signs of the day's heat, or is he as inebriated as his friend?

I jump from my bed as if it were on fire, forgetting how sheer my night dress is.

The King of Navarre stares at me openly as his companions lurch away.

Henriette gives me a look for courage then she too is gone. The King of Navarre turns at the sound of the closing door, giving me time to snatch up my *surcote*.

"Madame." My husband tilts his head slightly to acknowledge me. The surprising grace of the movement and the clarity of his speech suggest that however drunk his friends, he is in control of all his faculties. *Thank God*.

Sitting on the nearest chair, he removes his boots. I seem unable to find my voice and am reminded of how tongue-tied I used to feel when called before my mother as a girl. Rising, my cousin begins unbuttoning his doublet. The sight of his flesh at the open neck of his shirt jolts me to action.

"Stop."

His fingers pause.

"Madame?"

"We have something to discuss."

"You have spoken very little to me today, and *now* you would talk? I am tired; talk can wait."

"It cannot."

"All right, then." He crosses his arms.

"I do not want you here," I declare, raising my chin.

"Is that all? You did not want me for a husband either, a fact you made clear on many occasions, but we are wed."

I sense my open defiance is only making him equally defiant. I must try another tack. Remembering our shared moment of laughter in the litter, I realize I must behave as an ally even before an alliance is struck. Stepping forward, I gently place a hand on his arm.

"We are wed, so let us make the best of our union by starting it as friends." It is hard to imagine myself my cousin's friend but not as difficult as it was on the day he rode into Paris. "You are tired. I am tired. If we speak this evening, we will only bait each other. Leave me now and we will talk tomorrow."

"Leave without taking you to bed?"

"Yes. And resolve to not even to think of such an act. My brother the King may have made you my husband in church, but I have no intention of letting you make me your wife in the carnal sense."

I remove my hand from him and take a step back, girding myself for an outburst of anger.

But there is no fury. Instead my cousin looks puzzled. "But it is my right."

"It is your right," I concede. A painful admission, but concessions are key to bargaining. "But if you exercise it you will make an enemy of me. Do you not have enough enemies in Paris?"

He considers me for a few moments, then shrugs and begins to re-button his doublet. "Yours are not the only arms in which I may find pleasure. There is that pretty little Baronne friend of yours who makes eyes at me."

"Pursue Charlotte, by all means," I say, taking care to adopt the most indifferent tone possible. "Bed her. I shall never remark upon it. Bed every woman of the Court and cuckold every husband. I will not be provoked."

"What is the price for all this forbearance?"

My husband is not stupid.

"I wish to be free as well."

"In your affections, you mean."

"Yes, and I shall expect you to be as blind as I."

"Even if you embrace my sworn enemy?"

The taunt *Which one?* rises to my lips but dies, because we both know he means Guise.

"Yes."

"Then you ask me not only to be blind but foolish." My cousin shakes his head.

"No. You may well have been foolish not to turn round and ride back to the Navarre when you heard of your mother's death. But having come to Paris and bound yourself to the House of Valois, it is time to be practical, a quality I believe comes naturally to you. Do you not wish to have one certain friend among the Valois? One dependable ally at the French court?"

"The King embraces me and calls me 'brother.'"

"The King is as changeable as the wind."

This time he nods in the affirmative. Yet I sense he is not entirely convinced. He stands, thinking. "If I lose the King's love," he says at last, "I shall not be without influence. Coligny has His Majesty's ear and is my fixed friend. His friendship, being the result of years, is, if you will pardon me for saying so, more worthy of trust than the one you offer. As for allies, I brought them with me—eight hundred of them."

"Protestant allies at a Catholic court." I shrug, trying to sound as unconcerned as he. "They see only what my mother permits. There is not one among *vos amis* who knows the rooms and halls of this palace or the people who pass through them as I do. Not even the admiral."

"And you would guide me?" He shifts his weight and looks at me intensely.

An easy, meaningless "Yes" dies on my lips. It is my turn to pause and think—to consider how far I am willing to commit myself, knowing that if I say I will be my cousin's guide, I will not find it easy to renege.

I expect neither love nor happiness from my marriage but I do hope to improve my position by it—to be free from the domineering will of my mother, to have my own household. If anything good is to come from being Queen of Navarre, the King of Navarre must thrive. I regard my cousin, his lavish pale yellow doublet askew where he has misbuttoned it, the shadow of a moustache over his unsmiling mouth, his eyes examining my face with earnest concentration. He is out of place here. He is savvier than the others understand, but he will need guidance. I have little influence with Charles. With Anjou and my mother I have none at all. Perhaps I may have some with my husband by making myself useful from the beginning.

"I promise you my honest opinions and advice, so long as you do not impose yourself upon me."

"Agreed." His shoulders relax. It is the first indication I have had that he was nervous. Then, looking down and noticing the poor job he has done fastening his doublet, he begins to unbutton it once more to make it right.

"Leave it. Some disarray in your dress will support the desired illusion."

My husband laughs lightly. "So your first advice to me concerns how to look as if I have done the very thing that our bargain forbids?"

I laugh in response—not as hard as I did in the litter, but as sincerely. There is no attraction between us, but it seems we can be easy together.

And that may be something far more valuable. The apprehension I felt before the King of Navarre's arrival is whisked away. There is nothing menacing in my husband. How silly it seems that only a short while ago I feared he might take me by force.

CHAPTER 18

August 19, 1572—Paris, France

This time there are no tears when I wake. I feel more rested than I have in weeks. How amazing: the thing I dreaded most has come to pass and, far from being destroyed by it, I feel liberated. I am a queen and a married woman, with all the rights and status those things entail. And I am free, utterly free, to pursue my passion . . . until and unless my husband removes me to the Navarre or until both my beloved and my husband march off to a war with Spain.

I push these last thoughts from my mind and rise from bed. I will write to Henri bidding him to come to dinner at the Hôtel d'Anjou with a light heart and a good appetite. His hunger for food and for me shall each be fully satiated in the course of the evening.

As I pad across the floor I remark that the room is stiflingly hot, so either I have slept long or this day will be even more oppressive than the last. I throw open the shutters at the nearest window. The sun is at its apex. The day half gone? Good heavens!

Gillone bustles in.

"Why did you not wake me when the Duchesse de Nevers called?" I ask.

"She has not called, Your Majesty."

"Not called?"

"No one has. The palace was deserted all morning. Everyone rests after your wedding. I heard in the kitchens that even the Queen Mother slept late."

Taking a seat at my escritoire, I uncover my ink.

"Your husband was up with the dawn, however, and is playing at tennis."

Having neither asked nor thought about the whereabouts of the King of Navarre, her comment startles me. "In this heat? I cannot imagine who among his companions would be fit to play; they were all drunk last night."

"As were we," Gillone replies, clearly meaning the Catholic portion of the Court. "Perhaps it is a peculiarity of the Huguenots, rising early. They have many." She retreats, doubtless to get my breakfast, and I busy myself with my note.

When the door opens next it is Henriette, not Gillone, who enters carrying my tray.

"Ah, the bride," she says wryly. "Survived her wedding night, I see. Without incident?"

"Utterly."

"Well, that would confirm the rumor I heard as soon as I passed the wicket."

"Rumor?"

"That the King of Navarre was seen leaving the Baronne de Sauve's chamber this morning, carrying his boots."

"Poor Charlotte," I quip. But, rather oddly, I feel less pity than I expected to.

"Indeed"—Henriette gives a vicious smile as she sets down my tray— "she will taste garlic for a week." She gives an exaggerated shudder and laughs.

"I have a note for the Duc," I say, holding it out.

"You mean you are sending me back into the hot dusty streets?" She tucks the note away deftly in her décolletage. Taking a berry from my tray she pops it into her mouth. "At least it will be a pleasant errand. I should fear to show myself at the Hôtel de Guise had the King of Navarre been seen leaving *your* rooms boots in hand."

I make short work of my breakfast. It is too early to dress for the day's festivities, but, despite the heat, I have no desire to sit idly about in my chemise. I have Gillone dress me in something simple.

"Let us go and watch the King of Navarre at tennis." I speak lightly but Gillone's eyes widen nonetheless. "People will expect it." It is a weak explanation. I hope that Gillone does not question it. I certainly don't intend to.

My cousin is playing with the Marquis de Renel against the Comte de La Rochefoucauld and the Seigneur de Pardaillan. He runs full out, handling his racket with vigor. There is no one watching, so he plays for sport, not show. *It is an illumination of his character,* I think, tucking the fact away. In the shadows of the gallery I enjoy the game. My cousin has an easy, natural athleticism. Scoring the final point, he clasps Renel's arm and congratulates his opponents on their efforts. Then his eyes stray and find me.

Racket in hand, he makes a bow. "Gentlemen," he declares, "Her Majesty the Queen of Navarre honors us with her presence." There is nothing mocking about the statement, but when the unfriendly eyes of his companions fix upon me, I feel awkward.

The remaining gentlemen salute me, then turn back to each other. "Have you had enough?" the King's partner asks the men across the net. "Or must you be beaten again?"

I rise, hoping to escape my embarrassment. My cousin, who has remained looking through the curtain of net that separates us, moves forward and laces his fingers in it. "You are going, Madame? I would be happy to have you cheer me in the next." His eyes are entirely earnest, as if he senses that his companions made me feel ill at ease and regrets it.

"I fear I must, Your Majesty." I give a slight curtsy. "Ladies need far longer for their toilette than gentlemen, and all eyes will be on us when we dine *cette après-midi.*"

"True. But as you, a renowned beauty, need fear no man's eyes, I must suppose you urge me to greater exertions in my own toilette." He smiles slightly. "So much wardrobe advice since we were wed." He is clearly referring to our encounter last night. Why? To remind me of our bargain? Or maybe he merely wishes to re-create the ease we felt.

"I wear silver. You must suit yourself." It strikes me forcibly that, though we may look like a pair at our nuptial festivities, it will take some time for us to be a pair—even a pair of allies. Giving another curtsy, I turn.

As I make my way down the gallery I hear one of the gentlemen on the court mutter, "Spy."

My cheeks burn. It is an old charge, so it stings powerfully. My mother condemned me as a spy for the Duc. Perhaps that is whom my husband's cohorts think I act for now. Or they think me a spy for that same mother who herself labeled me untrustworthy. I am tired of being every person's pawn, trusted by no one. I resolve to prove myself my cousin's ally, the more quickly the better.

I do not see my husband again until he climbs into a litter beside me for the short trip to the Hôtel d'Anjou. Anjou is the host of this dinner and the ball at the Louvre that will follow. I find it both laughable and pleasing that etiquette should force my brother to celebrate my marriage. Laughable because he detests my husband. Pleasing because, given his pride and his elaborate tastes, the events likely cost him a fortune.

Having determined to be on good terms with my cousin, I offer him a smile. "How was the rest of your tennis?"

"*Formidable.* I won every game."

"Truly?"

"No"—he smiles broadly—"but I hoped to get away with claiming as much, given you were not watching."

"No one would ever guess you were a Gascon," I tease.

"Oh, come. They would know it for certain—if not by my boasting, then certainly by my love of garlic. I hear there is much talk of that in Court, especially among the ladies."

I blush, thinking of the myriad comments that have in fact been made suggesting an odor of garlic clings to the King of Navarre.

"What a pity we will all be off to Flanders. It will delay my taking you to the Navarre and introducing you to our cuisine."

"Pray, Sir, do not speak of war with the Spanish tonight, at least not within the hearing of the Queen Mother." My tone is serious but I keep a smile upon my lips for the spectators who line our way.

"I know Her Majesty is not in favor of the enterprise," my cousin responds, adding one of his characteristic shrugs. "But it seems to me His Majesty and the admiral have made up their minds to go forward."

"If they have, that will only make my mother more determined and more dangerous." My voice is so low that the King of Navarre must lean toward me. "If you all go to Flanders and the errand is to your liking, there will be time enough to talk of it. You may even do some of your Gascon boasting, provided you acquit yourself well. But until then, take my advice and stay out of the debate."

I can see he considers the point. "My gentlemen say the opposite. They urge me to support the King pointedly so that he will know we are his allies."

"Are these the same gentlemen who called me 'spy'?"

"They do not know you."

"Neither do you, Sir." I place a hand on his arm to show him that I do not say this in anger. "But I hope to illuminate my character by being true to our agreement and offering the best advice it is in my power to give. I tell you that being Her Majesty's enemy—or even being imagined to be so—is far more dangerous than being thought by Charles to be lukewarm to his war.

"There are better ways to endear yourself to the King. As the weather cools, the gentlemen will ride to the chase. Like you, the King has a great passion for sport. Show yourself as mad for the hunt as he. Bring down a boar with him, and you will be brothers in a way you are not now. I assure you, such tactics will be far more efficacious than speaking of Spain, and far less hazardous."

"Are you suggesting your mother is more dangerous than a cornered boar?"

"She is, though it is you and not I who articulates the thought."

"As you are not a spy, I need have no fear of doing so." His smile never falters but his eyes are not so sure as his lips.

As we alight at our destination, the King of Navarre hesitates, looking about. We both see Charlotte at the same moment.

"Go on."

My husband looks me in the eye.

"I meant what I said last evening—everything I said. Can you, Sir, say the same?" I glance in the direction of Guise. The Duc meets my gaze, his eyes hungry.

"Madame, I am a man who keeps his bargains. May I suggest, however, it is in neither of our interests to openly embarrass the other. I pledge to be discreet."

"As do I." Watching my husband move to Charlotte's side and whisper in her ear, his face glowing, I wonder if I should have warned him Charlotte is Mother's creature. Should I have hinted that Her Majesty may use the Baronne as a weapon? Perhaps, but I am not ready for such a denouncement.

Mother glides to my side. "Do not stare. People will think you are jealous."

It is the first time we have spoken today, and *this* is what she chooses to say?

"I am not."

She draws my arm through hers and we move up the steps. "If you are, you have only yourself to blame. The King of Navarre gave you every opportunity to win his heart and you would not be bothered."

"Madame, a single night in my husband's company has not changed me. I continue to be indifferent."

"That is good. Indifference is power."

"That smacks of bitterness."

"Perhaps." She pauses. "But it certainly reflects experience. I loved your father and it was folly. In the more than twenty-five years we were married, he never cared for me in that way. If I could have been indifferent to him, it would have been to my advantage."

I suppose I ought to show sympathy, for surely this is a painful admission. But I am not inclined to be kind to Mother at the moment. "Then I am more fortunate than you."

"Not yet. I have sons, and you have none. I must exhort you, daughter, not to use your friend Charlotte as an excuse for stinting your duty in that regard."

"I should think, Madame, you would be the last one to cry if the King of Navarre lacked heirs. Another generation of Protestant Bourbons in the south can hardly be to your liking."

"Perhaps they will be Catholic *comme leur mère*. Your cousin's issue will be as much Valois as Bourbon, and that ought to cool religious strife."

"Yes, because we are such a loving family—never jealous, never scheming to best each other." I look pointedly at Anjou where he greets his guests. "After seeing how your sons behave, Madame, I would be afraid to have more than one."

Mother releases me. The look in her eyes is very near to hate. Yet I find I am not afraid. For the first time I feel I may wound the one who has injured me most frequently with relative impunity.

My husband returns to my side and leads me to the table. During the banquet I have only smiles for him, until I notice that my pleasant looks fire the eyes of my Duc with anger. Tricky. I would convince my cousin our alliance is in earnest, but not at the expense of my beloved's peace of mind.

Wait, love, when the dining is done I will be your partner, not his.

By the time the Court makes its way out for the return to the Louvre, a goodly number of its members are staggering. Charles, with one arm around the Comte de La Rochefoucauld and the other around my darling Henri, lectures the two boisterously that they should be friends. Rochefoucauld tries to look gracious. Henri does not. My husband, surrounded by his gentlemen, waves to me before taking a horse, I have no idea whose. A moment later he and two dozen gentlemen, my brothers among them, charge out of the courtyard. This leaves me in sole possession of our litter, an opportunity. Coming up behind Charlotte, I put a hand on her shoulder. "Ride with me."

The moment the curtains are lowered, I ask, "My darling, how are you?"

"Fine. How else should I be?" Her eyes dart from mine and her cheeks color.

"Come, we agreed that we would not let the King of Navarre come between us. You must feel free to gossip and jest as you have about past conquests."

"There is nothing to joke about. I find your cousin refreshing. He does not talk too much, and when he does he says what he means."

I do not know how to respond. A week ago I would surely have made a quip about garlic—the same sort of jibe my cousin brushed off good-naturedly on our ride. Now I cannot. "I am glad you find him less displeasing than you anticipated. Glad that we both do. I will feel less guilty enjoying myself with Guise this evening knowing that I do not leave you in an intolerable situation."

We hold hands and gossip for the rest of our journey about the strangely ardent glances my brother Anjou gave the Princesse de Condé this afternoon.

At the Louvre, dancing commences at once. I dutifully let Charles lead me to the floor. The King of Navarre partners the Queen Consort. Henri is collected by Henriette. When the dance ends, she smiles at me as if to say *Do you dare?*

I do. Without hesitation I move in their direction. "Sir, will you be my next partner?"

"Your next and, were it up to me, your only."

So much has happened since we last stood this close. For more than a day only our eyes have touched, so I feel the first contact between his fingertips and mine with every nerve and sinew. I can tell Henri is equally overwhelmed, for his hand trembles.

When we come together for the third time he finds his voice. "What will Navarre think to see us dancing?"

"Nothing, I assure you. My husband and I have a happy understanding. We plan to live as so many other successful couples do . . . blind to each other's faults."

"So I am a fault?" He smiles to let me know he is not serious.

"You are certainly a vice, from the perspective of more than my husband." I tilt my head in the direction of Mother. She is in conversation with the admiral, but her eyes are on us.

"That only heightens your enjoyment of me, does it not?"

"Of course. A wise man once advised me stolen kisses were the sweetest." I run my tongue across my top lip.

"Then I will steal one now." Henri draws me from the pattern into one of the room's great window alcoves. Bussy d'Amboise stands in the shadows with his hands upon one of the Court's lesser ladies. At the sight of us he makes a hasty retreat, pulling his conquest behind him. While we are screened by the departing couple, Henri pulls me behind one of the draperies standing as substantial as a pillar beside the glittering window.

"You cannot imagine my agony last night," he murmurs. "I paced until dawn and slept only once I had your note."

Putting my hands on either side of his face I pull his head down so that his lips meet mine. Wrapped in a world of soft velvet and music, I move my mouth to his ear and whisper fiercely, "I promised you. Why did you not believe me?"

"I will never doubt again."

His hand rises to my neck and then runs downward to the part of my breast exposed above my gown. His mouth follows the same path. I sigh, wishing the day over, wishing away not only my cousin but the whole of the Court who laugh, drink, and dance so close that their footfall is distinctly audible from where I stand. "Henri, we cannot!"

"No," he concedes, pulling me against him. "We cannot, but dear heaven how I want to."

"You are coming tonight?"

"Tonight, and the next night, and the next—every night for the rest of my life."

Of course I know he speaks hyperbole—he will leave Paris, as he often does; I will doubtless go to the Navarre—but it is what I want to hear, and I have no doubt he wishes it were the truth. I give him a last lingering kiss. "Until later," I whisper. Then I slip back into the light, wandering with a forced nonchalance toward the Duchesse de Nevers. When I am halfway to my friend, my husband steps out of a clutch of his gentlemen.

"Madame, shall we dance?"

"Can you dance?" I know my smile is mocking, but I cannot help myself.

"I gather that my efforts in that vein last night did not impress you, but you granted me only one chance. You must give me an opportunity to better prove my abilities. Besides," he says, taking my hand, "it is expected. We do not want people to talk, or at least we wish to control what they say."

This time my smile is genuine. Casting an eye over him as he leads me to the floor, I am surprised to find nothing out of place. He will never be fashionable, but this evening he is entirely presentable. For the first time I realize that his pearl-gray suit trimmed in silver complements my gown.

My husband's eyes must read mine, for as he pulls me into position he says, "You have promised me sound advice, Madame. A guide is useless if not heeded. And I must say my *valet de chambre* was delighted by my new interest in fashion. I believe Armagnac is destined to become devoted to you."

Gazing into my husband's laughing face, I find myself wishing him well, or at least not wishing him ill, as I did for many months. *We might be happy. Not in the traditional way that husband and wife sometimes are, but parallel to each other.* We are harnessed together like horses, and like horses we may move the fates to our benefit if we pull together. It is a pleasant speculation.

Another day, another celebration, another ride in a litter with my cousin. "Who are you portraying?" I ask as we sit in a long line in the Rue d'Autriche, waiting for our turn to climb out at the Hôtel du Petit Bourbon.

"A knight."

"It is a very odd costume. May I assume from it you are not on the winning side?"

"Your brother Anjou planned the allegory. What chance do you think I had of being on the winning side?"

"*Bien faible.* It seems unfair, as you are the bridegroom and all this show ought to honor you." We move forward slightly. Leaning out, I can see His Majesty and the Queen Consort making their way into the *hôtel*. The sight of Charles reminds me of something. "Sir, have you heard the Duc de Montmorency left Paris this morning? He came to take leave of the King. Charles was not at all pleased and kept asking Montmorency why he could not wait a few days longer and go with the Court to Fontainebleau." I do not know if this information is important, but as I try to build credibility with my new ally, I have resolved to report whatever comes my way.

"I had heard as much from Coligny." He stops for a moment, tilts his head, and considers me. I put a hand to my hair, wondering if my tiara is askew. "*Ventre-saint-Gris!*" My cousin's curse takes me by surprise. "My men insist I should tell you nothing. But how can you counsel me if you do not know what I know? Montmorency urged the admiral to also abandon the city."

"Odd." The hair at the nape of my neck prickles. "Did Coligny say why?"

"Montmorency does not like the look of the crowds in the streets. Or the glances some of those closest to His Majesty throw in his cousin's direction. But the admiral thinks Montmorency an old woman." The King of Navarre punctuates this sentence with one of his characteristic shrugs. "He will not quit Paris without your brother, at least not until they have addressed certain matters."

"The war with Spain?"

"You cautioned me not to speak on that subject, Madame." My cousin brushes off my question. So he wishes to think I am not a spy, but he is not entirely sure.

Our litter draws to a stop for a final time. My cousin holds out a hand. "Oh, I should warn you," he says as we move up the steps, "I end up in hell during today's entertainment and there is a very long ballet while I am there, which makes things even worse."

My cousin is wrong: the ballet is not the worst part of the spectacle. I sit in my place seething. The scenery is splendid, as are the effects, but the whole of the extravagant tale was clearly deliberately designed to demean my new husband and the gentlemen closest to him.

"Madame," I say to Mother, "I wonder you permit such a performance. Surely humiliating the King of Navarre and his friends is contrary to your wish that the Court be exhibited as one and united."

"I did not plan the entertainment."

That may be, but I do not believe for a moment Anjou would stage such a thing without Mother's imprimatur. I give her a sour look.

"Margot, it is all in good fun. In just a moment your husband will be freed and will be back at your side. I did not realize you would be so eager to have him there."

When the dreadful allegory is over, the King of Navarre does not return. Charles throws one arm around my cousin and the other around Coligny, smiling and talking with great vigor. Glancing at Mother, I see her give a little scowl. "Well," I say, "Anjou may wish my husband in hell, but His Majesty clearly loves him. As he loves the admiral. I will wager that you wish that gentleman had left town today with his cousin."

"No, indeed, daughter, I assure you."

❈ ❈ ❈

"Dear God, this weather!" Henri removes his sword and leans it against a chair. "I will be glad to quit Paris."

"You go to Fontainebleau, then?"

"If you do."

"And if I do not?" I have already made up my mind that I will travel with the Court, whether my cousin does or not. But I have no intention of telling Henri that until I hear his reply.

"Then I suppose I must stay here, though it be hot as Hades. Speaking of which, I am enjoying the celebrations of your marriage more than I would have believed possible."

"I am glad someone is," I reply stiffly. I cannot decide which vexes me more: how quickly Henri has accustomed himself to my being another man's wife or the fact that his enjoyment of the festivities is obviously based in great part on the fact they seek to make a fool of that other man.

"Come, Margot! You did not enjoy the evening's allegory?"

"Not at all."

"I am amazed. The only thing that might have made that bit of play-acting more satisfying would have been if Coligny had been consigned to the flames with that wretched gentleman who has been made your husband." Henri closes his eyes and takes a deep breath as if relishing that image. "But the admiral would only have been granted clemency in the end with the others," he continues. "When Coligny is dispatched, I want him more permanently in hell.

"Come"—he puts a possessive arm around me—"let us think and talk no more of the Protestant rabble."

I begin to unbutton his doublet.

"The King showed great affection for your husband this evening. I assume that is because Navarre supports this foolishness in Flanders."

I stop. "I thought we were not speaking of Protestants."

"We are not. We are speaking of courtiers, of influence, of politics. Topics that are not new to us."

Henri is right. I have always speculated on the issues of the day with him, and always sought to help him advance in a court where knowledge, favor, and influence are closely linked. Over the years I have told tales of my brothers and mother—though, I would like to believe, never anything that would allow him to damage my kin. It feels different, however, to make him privy to what I have heard from my cousin.

"I hardly saw the King of Navarre this evening. In fact, I believe I am less in company with him than I was before we wed. Not that I am complaining."

He nods. "Nor I. The less time you pass with that gentleman, the better. Yet you will be called upon to ride, sit, and dance with him, to be in proximity with his gentlemen, and so long as you are I would have you keep your ears and eyes open."

I stare up at him. "You're asking me to spy on the King of Navarre—an action I am already accused of by his followers."

"Why not? He is nothing to you. And the opinion of his gentlemen means still less." He puts a crooked first finger under my chin, tilting my face upward and lowering his mouth to kiss me. I turn so that his lips merely brush my cheek.

Releasing me, he looks puzzled. "Marguerite?"

"He is not *nothing*." My voice is firm. This surprises me, because before this moment I would not have suspected myself equal to a show of loyalty to the King of Navarre under such circumstances. "He is, however, unwilling I was to have him, my husband."

"What is that but a word?"

A good question. Oddly I do not have to struggle for an answer; it just comes. "Marriage is an honorable estate and I wish to behave honorably by it."

Henri gives a short laugh. The sound is unpleasant, more like a bark of a dog than the warm laughter we have shared. "Your sudden embrace of decorum astounds me. We decide what is honorable and what is not. Were it otherwise, what we call love would be merely adultery. Yet I do not recall you objecting to my embraces."

I know Henri's pride speaks, not his heart, but his words prick me.

Why can he not try to see things from my perspective? "I do not ask you to betray your wife's confidences—"

"What would be the point?" he interrupts derisively. "She has nothing interesting to say, and certainly nothing useful." Henri takes a few strides away, then turns back, offering a look of complete exasperation. "Marguerite, I must worry constantly about my influence with the King and must work always to maintain the position of my family. Do you forget that two years ago His Majesty threatened to have me killed and on account of the very love which I now find unreliable? Then you would have done anything for me." Henri's voice catches for a moment. Has he perceived the widening of my eyes, my shock at the implied manipulation in his words?

"You would have done anything to save me," he rephrases carefully.

"And were your life in danger, I would still do whatever was necessary to safeguard it." I approach him slowly, fearful he will turn from me again, but also fearful that his next words—like his last—will disappoint me. "How can you say my love is unreliable?"

When he makes no reply I reach out and touch his sleeve. "The King of Navarre has no claim upon my love, and I deny him the exercise of his rights upon my body. You have both those things. But surely, surely, he is entitled to this much loyalty, entitled to trust that I do not support his rivals in political matters." I close my hand more tightly, feel the heat of the arm that has held me so many times in a lover's embrace. I will him to understand me.

"If you do not aid me against Navarre, how can I be sure that you will not betray me to him?" The question feels like a slap.

"I give you my word."

This must be enough. Yesterday he told me he would never doubt my pledges. I can see the love in Henri's eyes but it is mingled with anger. I expect the love to triumph. Then he deliberately removes my hand from his arm. "A woman's word is as fickle as her affections. You *swore* I would always be everything to you, and yet now you refuse to aid me against a man who, if he could, would oust me from your brother's favor and my offices. More than this, you ally yourself with a heretic who seeks not only to undermine His Majesty's good Catholic servants but to destroy the Holy Church upon which all order in France rests."

My eyes sting. "Love—"

"Do not call me that."

"Henri, please. I love you and I will be everything to you save a teller of tales on the King of Navarre."

Henri retrieves his sword and buckles it on, then pauses. "I am going." He looks at me expectantly.

I am aghast and panicked. Part of me wants to beg for forgiveness and repent of my decision. But the larger portion is tired of being pushed, of being offered love only on the condition that I behave as someone else wants me to. My mother has always loved me thus, and my brother Anjou. Now this man who has proclaimed countless times that he loves me for myself alone wrings my heart for his ambitious purposes. I might forgive him that, but in doing so he vindicates my mother, whose cruel taunts that the Duc loved me only for my connection to the King have never been entirely forgotten.

"If you leave me tonight, Henri—if you abandon me alone with your bitter words and unjust accusations—do not look for a welcome tomorrow." The words come out less forcefully than I would like, but the fact that they come out at all is miraculous.

Turning, he stalks toward the window. For a moment, just before he reaches the sill, I see him hesitate. I hope he will turn back, but he does not. Opening the shutters, he drops the ladder and is gone as quickly and as silently as a specter.

Indeed, in the first moments after his departure, I wonder if our encounter really took place. Perhaps it was all a frightful dream and Henri has yet to arrive for our tryst. I will it to be so, my eyes fixed on the night sky beyond the shutters he left thrown wide. The damp of a tear rolling down my cheek disabuses me of that happy notion. Sinking to the floor in a pool of my own silken gown, I cover my face with my hands and weep.

The Duc has come. The Duc has gone. I have turned away the man I loved but could not marry for the man I have married but will never love.

CHAPTER 19

August 21, 1572—Paris, France

The sun glinting off the armor of the gentlemen waiting to enter the lists hurts my eyes. Banquets, balls, tournaments, I am sick of them all. Nearly as sick of them as of the heat.

Sitting between Mother and the Queen Consort on a balcony erected to give us an excellent view, I find myself desperate to avert my eyes as my brothers advance to be recognized by the crowd. They have Henri with them—one of the favored few. All the King's men are "disguised" as Amazons, and while I might ordinarily find this humorous, my present situation makes mirth impossible. The heart of my bargain with the King of Navarre became meaningless last night. Seeing Henri accepting the approbation of the crowd is a painful reminder of how alone I felt when I awoke this morning—how I could not smell him on my person—and of the fear I experienced that this condition might not be temporary. So I turn my eyes upon my husband, dressed as a Turk. As this is more spectacle than tournament, he is destined by choreography to lose, yet he smiles at me and gestures to my colors, which he wears on his arm. I try to smile back and, failing, move my gaze to the balcony opposite where it is drawn to Henri's mother, the Duchesse de Nemours, who is fanning herself. As I look at her, thinking how Henri has her mouth, blood begins to drip from the hand with which she holds her fan.

I gasp.

Mother looks at me strangely.

I put my hands on the railing before me, breathing deeply in an attempt to collect myself. With breath comes the smell—blood. I know the odor from the chase. Surely I cannot smell the Duchesse's blood from this distance! I stare down to the area below. The mock combat has not yet begun, yet to my eye the ground is crimson. Where does the blood come from? I look at those around me to gauge their reaction, but all smile, clap, or hoot as called for by the theatrical prologue of the gentlemen. None seem shocked or frightened. I look down into the lists once more. The blood is gone. I sway in my seat, clinging yet more tightly to the rail. As soon as I am steady again, I force myself to look across at the Duchesse de Nemours. It is as I suspected, there is no blood upon that lady either.

I try to tell myself it was a trick of the light or an effect of the heat. I slept precious little last night after Henri left, so of course I am subject to being overcome by the unrelenting weather. But a terrible presentiment has hold of me, driving out these rational explanations. I harken back to the tale Mother told me as a girl, of foreseeing my father's mortal wounding. Could I be doing the same? Will the mock combat below end in death? Whose? I watch the King of Navarre attentively as his men press forward and are driven back. Then, in panic, I think that I play sentinel for the wrong soldier. After all, it was Henri's mother whose hand bled. I turn my attention to my Duc. If something should happen to him—if he should be injured or worse while we are at odds! I am all apprehension, and absolutely nothing untoward happens. Nothing. The Amazons are victorious. Combat ends. Those surrounding me applaud. I try to join them and find I have clutched the railing so fiercely, my fingers are numb.

Rising with the other royal ladies, I toss flowers to the victors. I ought to feel relieved. I do not. I scramble from the balcony. I must see Henri. At the bottom of the stairs I spot Charles and his Amazons, but Henri is not with them. The decorative fabric that cascades from the balcony moves slightly, close to where His Majesty stands. There is no breeze. Pushing the drapery aside, I peek inside. In the shade, Henri accepts a bow from a man I have never seen—a man with a narrow face and a dark beard.

"You ought not to have come here." I hear Henri's words clearly as I slip fully into the space beneath the balcony. Seeing me, Henri pushes the man through the curtains behind him. "Madame," he says, "you gave your word last night you would never betray me to Navarre. If that word is good in the light of day, say nothing of what you have observed." Before I can reply, he disappears through the parting of the curtains that the sharp-faced man used.

Bursting into the daylight, intent on going after him, I find myself only a few feet from the King of Navarre. He raises his eyebrows but does not ask why I was concealed. Perhaps he saw Henri exit and thinks we met to exchange whispered words. I do not care what he thinks. I need to warn him, though I do not know of what.

"Sir, I am most earnestly glad to see you and would be grateful for your arm."

He offers it at once.

"Madame, your hand is cold as ice despite the heat. And"—he looks at me more closely—"you shake. What has happened?"

"I feared . . . I feared someone would be injured in the tournament."

My cousin looks confused. "My pride, perhaps. This is the second 'battle' I have been called upon to lose in two days."

"I speak not of reputations but of wounds that bleed," I whisper urgently.

"Madame, I am not bleeding and you are not well. Let me take you to your apartment."

"No." I wrench away from him—equally aggravated with him for not understanding and with myself for not precisely knowing what I wish to convey. "I saw blood. Saw it when there was none."

I brace myself for him to laugh, or to insist once again that I am ill, but he is quiet. Reclaiming my arm, he leads me up to the now deserted balcony. Sitting on the back bench, where he cannot be seen from below, he motions for me to join him. "Where?"

"On the field." I do not think it necessary to mention the Duchesse de Nemours; I sound mad enough as it is.

He waits a moment. I grow hopeful. "Did you see it too?"

"No. But . . ." The pause is long. His expression, usually so cavalier, changes as if a mask has been lifted, revealing a man in doubt. "Yesterday night I played at dice late with the Duc d'Anjou, the Seigneur de Bussy d'Amboise, the Marquis de Renel, and the Seigneur de Pilles. It was not a friendly game. After all Pilles and Anjou stared at each other from the opposite sides of the city walls during the siege of Saint-Jean-d'Angely, and Bussy and Renel, while cousins, are involved in a lawsuit. The taunts between players were more insult than jest. Then the Duc de Guise joined us. I was surprised to see him—"

We both know he means that, given the hour, he assumed Guise would be with me.

"—and had no desire to play with him. I rose to leave but your brother said, 'Come, Cousin, you have taken what the Duc prized most; you must at least give him the opportunity to empty your purse.' So I sat back down, not wishing to precipitate an argument. Anjou took up the dice and as he shook them I saw, or rather thought I saw, blood trickle from between his fingers."

I reach out and grasp my cousin's knee.

"I thought at first he clutched the dice so hard that his nails bit into his flesh, but when he released them, his hand bore no injury and the blood was gone."

I nod comprehendingly.

"The same thing happened when Guise took his turn. I am not superstitious, but when all had rolled and the winnings—mine—were collected, I broke up the game, taking my gentlemen with me. No jeers by Anjou were sufficient to bring me back to the table."

He shrugs, and with the gesture the mask slips back on. "Of course, in my rooms I laughed at myself. To be spooked by my own imagination . . . it is ridiculous."

"Not ridiculous—wise. My mother once told me that only fools dismiss premonitions."

"I am not sure I believe in such omens."

I can see why he wishes to remain a skeptic. Blood cannot be good. But stubbornness in the face of such warnings seems beyond cavalier, it seems reckless. I cannot say this. Lecturing my cousin has never in my memory had the desired effect, and at present I am trying to draw him to me, not drive him away. Indeed, for the moment at least, he is all that is left to me.

"Believe or not, but be on your guard. If for no other reason than because, as you have observed yourself, the fraternity between your gentlemen and my brothers ebbs. The celebrations pertaining to our marriage end tonight. In two days His Majesty is off to Fontainebleau. Where do you go then?"

"*I*?" He looks at me strangely. "*We* follow the King until I am given a commission to march into Flanders."

I am relieved, for I cannot help feeling there is danger here. Perhaps when the Court travels it will be left behind.

In the evening I begin a list of those I would wish to see appointed to my household. The time for my mother's *coucher* comes and goes but I do not stir myself, thinking I will not be missed. I am wrong. Henriette and Charlotte arrive in my apartment when they are done with their duties, complaining of my negligence.

Looking up from my work, I smile. "How I wish I could have you as ladies of my household and never be parted from you."

"What is this nonsense?" Henriette crosses the room and mixes herself some water and wine. "We will not be parted! Does your husband talk of the Navarre?"

"Not to me." I look at Charlotte.

"Constantly," she laughs. "He misses it, particularly the mountains."

"Scenery is all very well, but gazing at mountains cannot compare to observing the machinations of the Court." Henriette glances over my shoulder at my list. "If the Princesse de Condé is persuaded to be your *dame de honneur,* you will pay a heavy price. Would you have Anjou always hanging about?"

"I know he shows an interest in her, but I assume that is only to vex the Prince."

"Then you assume wrongly. Your brother is violently in love."

"Love is contrary to his character."

"Hm." The Duchesse narrows her eyes. "It is the season of unexpected things when it comes to *amours,* is that not so, Charlotte?"

My second friend turns crimson.

"Charlotte?"

"She is infatuated with your husband. Let her deny it if she will—I know the signs."

"I find him pleasant. Is there anything wrong in that?"

"Nothing wrong, but much that is surprising. I will have to stop making jokes at the King of Navarre's expense." Henriette gives an exaggerated sigh, as if this will be the greatest of hardships.

"You might have done that for my sake." I put down my quill and go to pour myself some wine.

"Oh, I am not your mother, Margot. I limit my jests to present company. But now Charlotte will not enjoy them. Perhaps you will not either."

"Meaning?" I lower myself into a chair and put my glass upon a table. I suspect what is coming—I only wonder that Henriette did not find an earlier opportunity to raise the topic.

"You and Guise barely looked at each other today, and those looks that did pass were sad or strained. You did not dance with the Duc, but three times partnered your husband while the Duc glowered. Can it be the King of Navarre comes between you?"

"Of course not!" I have no intention of sharing the source of the quarrel betwixt Henri and me. "Is that the gossip?"

"The gossip is very wild, and began this morning with a report that Guise was seen playing dice last night when he ought to have been with you."

"Lovers argue." I try to sound blasé.

"They do. They even tire of one another. But, Margot, if you are tired of Guise, that will be the most unexpected of all the amorous developments since your wedding day."

It would be. For that reason, whatever I said last night, I am not ready to be done with Henri. I wonder: Is he ready to be done with me?

The sadness such a thought inspires must show, for Henriette takes a seat beside me. "Come, it will all be forgotten. Whatever the cause of your quarrel, I will warrant its true roots lie in this heat. Who can be civil when they are roasting alive?"

"Perhaps I ought to send him a note."

"No, indeed! The fault is not yours."

"How do you know?"

"Because you are my friend and the better of the sexes." Henriette laughs. "So do not trouble me with the truth of the matter. I find, without evidence, that you are the aggrieved party . . ."

"As a matter of fact, I am."

"There, you see. So the Duc must make amends, or at least he must become so desperate to see you that he forgets you are partly at fault in the quarrel. You will not see him tonight."

"No." *But not because I will turn him away.*

"Good. And tomorrow we will begin a campaign to bring him to his knees."

I cannot help but think of the first time I rose early hoping to catch Henri's eye as he played tennis. That day he played Anjou. Today he partners Charles against my husband and the admiral's son-in-law. In the opposite gallery Anjou watches with his head in Mother's lap. The way she plays with his hair reminds me of doing the same with Henri's. Before the gentlemen began, my husband saluted me—or perhaps he saluted Charlotte, who sits beside me. In either case, I noted a certain stiffening in Henri's form which suggests he is not inured to the King of Navarre's attentions to me. Yet, when I catch his eye during a pause, he quickly looks elsewhere.

"If only there were some gentleman handy for you to flirt with," Henriette says, noticing the avoided glance. She cranes her neck. "Ah, the Seigneur de La Mole arrives. He is a heretic, but a handsome one." She slides down to make room then hails him. I give her a look. "Why not?" she whispers. "He may only be one of Alençon's gentlemen, but he is the best dancer at the Court."

La Mole takes the seat between us, looking overwhelmed by his luck. I smile at him, doubting whether Henri will notice or care.

The Seigneur gazes at me like a child at a pastry tray.

What has Henriette started?

Charles scores. We all applaud appreciatively, applause that is interrupted by a cry. "My King, my King, they have shot the admiral!"

The Seigneur de Pilles runs out onto the court, stopping when he reaches Charles.

"What! What is this you say?" the King demands.

"I come from the Rue de Béthisy. They shot the admiral as he made his way from the Louvre."

It is the blood! Oh, I knew it meant something!

Courtiers gasp. Protestant spectators jump to their feet. There are mutterings of every sort, including more than a few, plainly audible "Praise

Gods." On the court Charles physically staggers, then throws his racket to the ground. *"Mort de Dieu!"* he screams, looking first at one gallery and then the other. "When shall I have a moment's peace? When will it stop? Why can you not be contented with peace when I struggle so to give it to you?"

Across from the King, my husband of four days stands, his face pale. His tennis partner, Téligny, looks entirely stricken.

"Is the admiral dead?" Mother's voice is calm. *Strange.*

"No, praise God! By divine intervention he paused to check his shoe, bending just as the ball came. Otherwise I am certain I would bring worse news. But he is badly injured."

"My poor father!" Charles cries. "Amboise Paré must go at once."

"You!" The Seigneur de Pilles looks past the King and points an accusatory finger at Guise. "I see your hand is in this."

The Duc makes no reply, merely staring back with contempt.

"Whoever is to blame, I will find him." Charles looks at the Duc, then Pilles, and finally at my husband. "I will see justice done."

I glance in Mother's direction to assess her reaction. She is gone! So are Anjou and the Baron de Retz, who sat at Her Majesty's other side. Charles storms from the court calling for his counselors. The moment he is gone a hundred bodies are in motion. Joining the throng seems futile. Instead, I move down and press against the mesh separating me from the court. By force of habit my eyes look first for the Duc. Like Mother, Henri has disappeared. My cousin has not. He stands in conversation with Pilles.

"Husband!" The term is calculated to get his attention, for despite our discussion I have never yet accorded him this appellation publicly. It works. The King of Navarre's gaze finds me and he moves toward me, his followers trailing.

"Madame."

"Sad news."

"Yes, though the root of that sadness lies, I suspect, in different things for different people. There are some, I think, distressed not by the violence against the admiral but by his survival."

"Is his survival certain?" The question elicits hostile looks from several of my cousin's men.

"Pilles cannot say: he ran here while Coligny was still being carried to his house."

"You will go." It is not a question.

"Directly."

"Take care in the streets." Behind my cousin, Pardaillan, who called me spy, sneers. My temper flares. "Smirk if you like, Monsieur!" I glare at him. "But whoever wounded the admiral would doubtless like a shot at my husband as well."

"She would know," someone murmurs.

"Come, Margot." Henriette takes my sleeve. "These idiots have not the wits to tell the difference between enemy and friend, and they have the manners of peasants." She spits the last word.

She is right: Why waste my time or concern on men who mock me? I turn from the railing.

"Wait." It is my cousin's voice. Turning back, I find him close to the mesh curtain, his fingers laced in it as they were the morning after our wedding. "I apologize for my gentlemen; they are overwrought." He looks for some acknowledgment, but I offer none. I know very well his followers consider my status as a Catholic and a Valois to be insuperable barriers to trust. I will not pretend otherwise. "When we spoke yesterday," he continues, "you showed great prescience—a prescience that gives your words today increased weight. I will go armed. I will be cautious."

I nod, uncertain why I care—if I care—about my cousin's safety. There are worse things than being a widow.

The streets roil with people. I am glad to be on horseback, for a carriage could not pass. In the Rue de Béthisy there is a makeshift wicket guarded by Protestants. An hour ago Charles ordered those Catholics living near the admiral to give up their houses temporarily so Coligny could be better protected. He also forbade citizens to take up arms, but I notice the glint of swords and glimpse a pistol on a bystander as we dismount. Charles is eager to see Coligny, despite reassurance from Amboise Paré that the gentleman will certainly live. Mother pushes to be beside the King. I press forward as well, using my elbows where necessary. Monsieur Paré waits inside. He looks dismayed by the size of our party—as do the dozen

Protestant gentlemen guarding the door and the stairway leading to the admiral's bedchamber.

"Your Majesty." Paré bows. "I have removed the ball from the admiral's elbow and also the remains of the little finger shattered by the shot."

Charles cringes at this reported amputation.

"The gentleman rests but is eager to see his king. May I ask, however, that not everyone go *en haute*?"

"I do not like it," someone mumbles, "His Majesty alone in a nest of angry hornets."

"Surely, Monsieur, room can be made for a dozen—the admiral has so many who are concerned for him and who cannot be made easy on report alone," Mother says.

The royal physician is not so foolish as to speak in contravention of Her Majesty, so he nods. Charles, Anjou, Mother, and the King's chief councilors head up the stairs. I attach myself to the rear of the party.

The room is stifling. The admiral, lying on his bed, lifts his head. "Your Majesty, I regret I am in no condition to greet you properly."

"And I regret, my dear father, that you have been so brutally attacked." Charles moves to the bedside, displacing my cousin, who goes silently and without looking at me to where Pilles and Téligny stand near an open window.

"I have ordered an inquiry into this cowardly assault," the King says, laying his hand gingerly upon the admiral's bandaged one. "Whoever struck at you struck also at me, for you are my right arm and good counsel."

"I hope, Your Majesty, to shortly be sound enough to sit beside you in council once more. In my absence, I urge you to listen to your conscience, not to those who would steer you in a manner beneficial to themselves but not France."

"Admiral," Mother says, "you need have no fear. I remain steadfastly at His Majesty's side."

I seriously doubt this comforts the gentleman.

Téligny steps forward. "Your Majesty, my father and I have every faith in your justice. To that end, may we hope to hear before this dreadful day ends that the Duc de Guise has been arrested?"

The admiral casts his son-in-law a warning look.

"If you have evidence implicating the Duc," Charles says, "I charge you by the duty you owe me to present it to me."

"Everyone knows Guise vowed as a mere boy to kill my father."

"And everyone also knows," Mother says, "that His Majesty forbade action on that pledge. And yet"—she sighs—"too often men of heated blood disregard their sovereign's will."

I cannot believe it! Mother has just suggested, in a room full of Protestants, that my beloved may be responsible for the admiral's wounding. She has thrown him to the dogs!

"Still," she adds, "inquiries demand evidence, Sir, not conjecture."

"Your Majesties, perhaps you have not yet heard, but an arquebus, still warm from firing, was found on the first floor of a house in the cloisters of Saint-Germain-l'Auxerrois—a house belonging to the Duchesse de Nemours."

I grow cold at the mention of Henri's mother.

"This will be looked into," Charles says.

"There, you have the King's word!" Mother crows triumphantly. "Now let us have no more talk of such things. They are not soothing. The admiral needs rest, is that not so, Monsieur Paré?"

I can see that the admiral's coreligionists are far from satisfied. And those Catholic gentlemen who came with His Majesty are also displeased. I wonder if the admiral, who has lately worked so tirelessly to see Charles' Protestant and Catholic subjects drawn closer, sees that they are being rent asunder over this attempt on his life, or if he is in too much pain to be aware. I am aware—excruciatingly aware. I have the horrible thought that my hand was likely wasted—that I may soon be the wife of a king who is at war with my brother. I look at my cousin where he stands silently taking everything in. Is he enough of a man to bind Bourbon and Valois together in a way his father could not? Can he take the admiral's place at my brother's side if needs be?

"Sir"—Mother stoops over Coligny—"I take my leave. Know that, whatever our disagreements have been, I wish desperately you were not wounded." Mother straightens and beckons to the courtiers we brought. "Come, we leave the admiral among friends. They will, I am sure, lay down their lives before they allow further harm to come to him."

Charles lingers as people file from the room, speaking low to Coligny.

I move to my cousin's side, resolutely ignoring how his companion bristles at my approach. "Sir, do you return to the Louvre with us?"

"No, Madame. I will rest here awhile."

I go to Charles and take his arm. He looks down on the admiral with such sadness that it wrings my heart. "Have faith in me, *mon père,*" he says softly. "I will give you justice, whomever I must punish to do so."

Mother, who waits at the foot of the bed, shifts uneasily.

"In the meantime I will send guards to ensure you rest undisturbed." The King puts his hand over mine where it rests in the crook of his arm. We move through the throngs of somberly clad Protestants and out to our horses. When we are all mounted, Charles turns to Mother. "This wicked deed rose from the enmity between the houses of Châtillon and Guise and the House of Guise shall pay for it," he exclaims. "I will send for the Duc the moment we reach the Louvre."

"Apologies, Your Majesty," Mother says. "His Grace sought permission to leave Paris, fearing some angry Huguenot would take a shot at him before the truth could be known, and I gave it him."

At last, something to be glad of on this wretched day.

By the time I am put to bed, I am exhausted, not because I have done anything very much but from the tension in the Court. Every sort of theory is whispered, from the straightforward and insistent Protestant claim that Henri had the admiral shot, to conspiracies too absurd to be given a second thought—among them that the Huguenots themselves maimed their chief, hoping a wounded admiral would have even more sway with the King. Some of those accusing Guise mention me.

"When asked why the Duc acts at a moment likely to bring the wrath of the King upon him, those who posit Guise's guilt reply that the admiral's support of your marriage was the final provocation," Gillone says as she tucks me beneath the covers.

"Utterly ridiculous!"

"Will the Duc come tonight?"

"He has left the city." I try to say it lightly, as if I am equally unconcerned by the accusations against him and his lengthening absence from my bed.

A strong knock sounds on my outer door. *Who can it be?* "Wait," I call as Gillone turns to go. "Help me into a *surcote*. Whoever it is, I have no intention of receiving them in bed." We go through to my antechamber. She opens the door to reveal my cousin, his page at his side and his men at least four deep behind him.

"I am sorry it is so late, wife," he says, smiling pleasantly. "But I stayed long at the admiral's."

I could not be more confused, nor could Gillone. She stands looking helpless as the King of Navarre and his men sweep in without waiting for my leave. My cousin takes my hand, lifts it to his lips, and kisses it audibly. The whole display has the feel of bad farce.

"Gentlemen," he says, smiling at those around us—not a one of whom smiles back—"I must have a private word with the Queen." He slips an arm around my waist and, utterly bewildered, I let him walk me to the bedchamber. As he releases me to shut the door, I find my tongue.

"Are you mad? This morning you told me my advice was of value to you, and yet tonight you come to my rooms in full state like a true husband, thereby assuring you will receive no more of it."

"Restez tranquille," he says, raising his hands in a gesture of pacification. "I am not here to violate our agreement, but to make the most of it."

"Oh, really? I will admit I do not see how!"

"It seems to me that on a day such as this—when Catholics in the streets cursed me and rattled their swords, and when my own gentlemen have said things about your family too unkind to repeat—all at Court need a reminder that I am bound to the King in a special manner: that we are man and wife. Hence my very public procession to your apartment."

"You were seen coming?"

"By as many as I could manage."

I am so angry that I can do nothing but sputter.

My cousin moves closer. "Madame, truly, I believe this ruse is in both our interests. Do you wish the peace broken?"

His words echo my thoughts of the afternoon: my fears that our marriage will be rendered irrelevant by events. It may be a bad union, but it exists and the only thing I can think of that would make it worse is for it to be made immaterial to the King and to my mother.

"No," I concede. "But I did not anticipate you would need to break my peace in such a manner to preserve the larger one."

"I apologize for doing so."

"Having come in such great state, you have doubtless given the desired reminder. Take your gentlemen and leave me to my sleep."

He does not move other than to shift his weight from one foot to the other. "I wonder if you would honor your pledge of friendship by letting me bide the night."

"Here?"

"In the next room with my gentlemen would suffice. We are used to sleeping rough in the mountains of Navarre and can easily stretch out on the floor. When I leave in the morning, none will be able to say that the wounding of the admiral at the behest of a man rumored to be your lover has driven a wedge between us."

He has me, damn him. "I *have* overheard whisperings that the Duc was driven to act by our marriage."

He nods. "Perhaps he was."

I ignore the remark, because I do not think my cousin means to offend— merely to consider the point.

"So you must stay," I answer matter-of-factly. "But I would have the action stem the gossip not only of Catholic courtiers but of your Protestant gentlemen as well. They have no love for me and no trust either. If you lie with them in the next room, they will know our marriage is a fiction and believe you yourself share their distrust."

His eyes widen.

"So you must sleep here, within the curtains of my bed."

"It can hardly be necessary to subject you to the intrusion."

"It is very necessary. I saw the way your gentlemen looked at me this morning when word came of Coligny's wounding. They think me capable of harming you—"

"No, Madame!"

"Yes!" When he does not reply, I consider the matter settled. "Turn your back," I command. He does so with admirable swiftness. Removing my *surcote,* I cast it onto a chair and get quickly beneath the bedcovers. "Now take off your things and climb in beside me."

He laughs.

"What is so funny?"

"You ordering me into your bed, when not a week ago you made it painfully clear I am not wanted there." I avert my eyes, imagining what Gillone will think; what Henriette will think when she hears tomorrow; what Henri will think. This last gives me pause. For while I do not care if Gillone thinks me intimate with my husband, and while I will be in a position to tell Henriette the truth, I shall have no opportunity to explain to the Duc. Perhaps, given his shameful treatment of me, he does not deserve an explanation.

The curtains on the opposite side of my bed open and my cousin jumps upon the mattress as if he were a boy of ten. Lying down without a word, the man is asleep so quickly I cannot believe it. Considering the events of the day, I would have expected him to lie awake. I do. Staring into the darkness, I try to see his profile and cannot. Many bells toll, yet I continue to stare in his direction—sleepless, sweltering, and wishing he were someone's husband other than mine.

CHAPTER 20

August 23, 1572—Paris, France

Charlotte eyes me oddly as I enter Mother's apartment. She is not the only one. If it were not for the wounding of the admiral, I am certain I would be the center of all gossip today. Then again, were it not for the wounding of the admiral, the King of Navarre should never have passed the night with me.

"What ails everyone?" I ask, taking a seat with my friends. "There is an air of hysteria among Her Majesty's ladies."

"It is not limited to them, I assure you," Henriette says. Then, perhaps seeing some trace of incredulity in my expression, she continues. "You doubt it? Well—"

"There are rumors," Fleurie interrupts, "rumors that the Protestants will take violent revenge upon the King for the wounding of their chief. That they will rise up and begin the next war in the streets of Paris."

Henriette gives me an I-told-you-so look.

"Nonsense," I say. "No one can possibly blame Charles. All know of his devotion to Admiral Coligny."

Fleurie shakes her head in disbelief.

"You think no one can blame your brother?" Henriette asks. "Well, while you were sleeping late, a handful of your husband's gentlemen had a tussle with the royal guards."

"It is said they were trying to force their way into His Majesty's presence," Charlotte adds.

I nearly curse under my breath. "And where is my husband?" When I woke he was gone and I did not bother to look for him.

"The King of Navarre, the Prince de Condé, and a legion of their friends went to the admiral's at dawn. Or so I *heard*." Charlotte gives me an accusatory look.

Henriette shifts closer. "The talk that Protestants will rise in the streets is not confined to the Louvre. And rumors of a plot to kill not only the King but all your family—"

"And to put your husband on the throne," Charlotte interjects.

"—travel through the city like a contagious fever," Henriette finishes.

I am gripped by fear. Not that my cousin and his coreligionists are coming to murder my family—I simply cannot credit that—but that things have so swiftly run out of control.

"Charles ought to take the Court to Fontainebleau at once," I say. "It is too hot here for people to be sensible. If we go and stay away a month, the people of Paris will see there is nothing in these hysterical reports and calm down."

"You are too much the optimist, Margot," Henriette admonishes. "The King has ordered an inquiry into the wounding of the admiral, and Parisians will follow those proceedings—"

"Like dogs track a wounded animal," I say, finishing my friend's thought.

"They will be whipped into a frenzy by them." Henriette nods.

God's blood! "And yet, what could Charles do but seek justice for Coligny, lest he appear a weak king?"

"I would not like to be His Majesty at this moment," my friend replies softly. "Trapped between the Protestants and Catholics he has pulled together. To placate the former, he must punish the guilty. But"—she lowers her voice further still—"this same action will enrage the latter: the people of Paris do not want Guise punished."

I do not want him punished either.

"The Duc is barricaded in his *hôtel*." Fleurie clasps and unclasps her hands as she speaks. "And he is a man who ordinarily fears nothing. Is that not a sign?"

Henri is still en ville!

Renée de Rieux bursts into the room. "They come in force! A huge number of Protestants are in the courtyard!"

Her pronouncement leads to cacophony. Being near the door, I am one of the first to fly from the room. Arriving at a window offering a view down onto the courtyard, I am nearly crushed by other ladies as I work to open it. Very quickly the windows on either side of the one I have claimed fill with *dames de la cour* leaning out and looking down at a sea of gentlemen clothed in black. I recognize the Seigneur de Pilles at their head. I do not see the King of Navarre.

"Idiots! What can they be thinking, coming in such numbers?" Henriette asks over my shoulder. "They will raise the fears of all Paris even higher."

Below, Charles emerges onto the broad steps with Anjou, Mother, and the whole of his council.

Pilles springs from his horse, advances, and bows. "Your Majesty." His voice rings off the walls. "We come, four hundred of your loyal subjects—"

Four hundred.

"—begging, nay demanding, justice for the admiral. We cannot wait. It must be swift. Those who planned Coligny's death must die upon the Gibbet of Montfaucon if you would have us believe you truly love us as you do your Catholic subjects."

I feel dizzy at the audacity of this statement. Mother is plainly incensed. Her eyes burn, her nostrils flare. She looks a full decade younger.

"Seigneur, gentlemen, we *shall* act swiftly," Charles says. His voice lacks the power and confidence of Pilles'. "Two servants working in the house from which the shots were fired have been arrested. They are being questioned. The man who provided a horse that the assassin might flee has been taken."

"From whose stable came the horse?" someone in the crowd calls.

Charles holds up his hand. "We cannot say at this moment."

"*Will* not say," Henriette murmurs. I half turn and she gives me a look.

"Be satisfied that when we can say, we will," Charles continues. "In the meantime, return to the admiral's side and watch him as I would myself were I not engaged in seeking those who tried to fell him." Behind the King, Guast whispers something in Anjou's ear and I see my brother give his favorite an unusually dark look.

"We will, Your Majesty." Pilles bows. As he turns to remount, Henriette taps my shoulder. Grabbing Charlotte's hand, I squeeze between the surrounding ladies.

"The horse is Guise's," Henriette says when we are clear of the crowd.

Oh, God.

"Lovers' quarrel or no, you must urge him to quit the city."

"Surely Charles would not have him executed to satisfy a mob!"

"Who is to say the mob will wait upon the King? In any event, is that a chance you would take?"

Of course not. The three of us run to my apartment, bursting in to find the King of Navarre. Charlotte, apparently quite forgetting my presence, goes directly to him and, slipping her arms around his waist, rests her head upon his breast. "I am so glad you were not with that crowd."

"Not physically—I do not deem it appropriate to call out my newly minted brother in such a setting—but I am with them in spirit. Both Condé and I gave Pilles our blessing."

This time I do curse—audibly.

Looking over Charlotte's head, my cousin says, "Madame, will you grant me a moment?"

"Of course." I hold the door to my bedchamber open. My cousin kisses Charlotte quickly before joining me. Will he tell me about the horse as Henriette did? If so, it will be an act of magnanimity.

For a moment he just stands looking awkward, much as he did as a boy.

"Sir," I say, "I suspect we both have pressing business."

"I can imagine yours," he says wryly.

So much for magnanimity.

"I do not wish to imagine yours," I rejoinder. "Having failed to stop Pilles from marching a virtual army here, it is doubtless to sign your name to some incendiary document that will prove a danger to yourself and others."

He flushes. It is satisfying to know I can provoke him, because as a child I could not. He takes two steps toward the door. Then he stops. "I will not let pettiness prevent me from being a true ally. We need not be friends to be confederates."

Good thing.

"An alarming report circulates in the Rue de Béthisy. It is said the Duchesse de Nemours called upon Queen Catherine three times in as many weeks—under cover of darkness."

"Meaning?"

"The horse may belong to de Guise, and the man who rode it may prove to be in the Duc's employ, but the culpability will be traced higher— much higher."

"So Protestant rumors are as *incroyable* as Catholic ones." I lift my chin indignantly. "Charles adores the admiral. He would never hurt him."

"I did not say His Majesty. You have other brothers, as well as a mother with every reason to be jealous of Coligny's influence."

"I assure you, Sir, jealousy has never made Her Majesty a fool. She is wise enough to know, should she suborn such an act, it would mean the loss of far more than the influence she currently misses." I pause and find myself breathing fast. The idea that Mother had a role in the wounding of the admiral is not entirely dismissible despite what I insist to my cousin. And that terrifies me.

The King of Navarre steps close. "I take solace in the idea that Madame Catherine, while capable of much that is unpleasant, is generally careful to keep herself above suspicion." His voice is soft, as if he is sorry he was compelled to tell me what he did. This bewilders me but also lessens my anger.

"Do you dismiss the tale, Sir? Or do you merely presume that if Her Majesty was involved, there will be no evidence of it?"

"Either will do for the present."

I am stunned. "You would not care if my mother supported the assassination of the admiral?"

"I *would* care—deeply. But the consequences should such a fact become known . . . I cannot imagine them, and that uncertainty fills me with apprehension." He pushes a hand through his hair in a manner not unlike my Henri. "What are your thoughts? You know many of the players in this drama better than I. What do you think His Majesty will do when he hears the rumor—as he surely will before the day is out? What will he do if it is proved?"

What would Charles do if Mother were implicated? I have no ready answer. If Anjou was involved, I certainly believe that Charles would act savagely. But Mother . . .

"I cannot say, Sir, and the question frightens me as it does you."

He nods vigorously. "We are both wise enough to be afraid—far wiser than the rumormongers on either side. They speak without thinking."

It is my turn to nod, for his words express what I felt sitting among Her Majesty's ladies.

"Madame"—he puts a hand on my shoulder—"neither of us can predict what the King will do. You cannot predict what the Catholics will do, and I cannot foretell the actions of my fellows should the trail of blood lead from the admiral's house to the Louvre. I wish you to know one thing, however: I will see no harm comes to you."

It is a strangely gallant thing for him to say, given the situation. It ignites in me both a desire to reassure him and a compulsion to take equal care of his person. These are proprietary feelings—feelings with which I am not comfortable. "Sir, I can take care of myself." I step out from under his hand. "I am not the one who risks the open streets. Keep your wits about you as you return to the admiral's bedside."

"*Bien sûr.*"

"And before you do"—I force a smile so that I will seem less worried than I am—"you had best take care of the Baronne de Sauve's misperceptions. I will not be deprived of a best friend by misplaced jealousy."

He smiles slightly. "You are a most accommodating wife."

"I promised I would be."

I do not follow him to the next room but sit down to pen my note to Henri. Not an easy task. The man to whom, less than a week ago, I confided everything without censoring thought or feeling is suddenly separated from me—in part by my simmering anger, but also by a growing recognition that his interests and mine are no longer one. I settle for the short, plain, and unembellished. Will such a terse message wound? Or will Henri recognize that my sending a note is, alone, proof of my caring? Such questions hardly matter. They are overpowered by a more momentous one: Will my words result in action on his part? I cannot know. All I can be certain of is that if Henri is arrested and, God forbid, banished or worse, the thought that I have tried to save him may salve my conscience but it will not prevent my heart from shattering. And to think I believed it broken already.

"You will not find the Queen in her bedchamber." The Baronne de Retz is alone in Mother's vast antechamber.

"Where, then?" I have spent all afternoon wandering, looking for something more substantial in the way of information than the whisperings that continue to circulate.

"She has gone to the Tuileries."

At such a time? Then it comes to me: no place is more private. "With whom?"

My former *gouvernante* hesitates.

I shrug. "I will go and see for myself."

"Anjou, my husband, the Duc de Nevers, and Cardinal Birague."

Serious company—all Mother's Italian favorites and her favorite son, but not the King. An icy shiver runs up my spine. Such a group raises every sort of alarm. I force myself to smile. Then I go directly toward Charles' apartment. If he does not know where Mother is and with whom, he ought to. As I approach the lesser entrance, the one which only those closest to him use, I am startled to see a hooded figure moving away from that door. The figure raises his head.

"Marguerite!" Henri's eyes meet mine. I see surprise, pain, love, and anger.

"Why are you still in Paris?"

"Why did you—who know me better than anyone—think I would flee it like a coward?"

"Do brave men skulk around hooded?"

He pulls himself up to his full height and pushes back his hood. His eyes soften and I find it in me to soften as well.

"Henri," I say, reaching out a hand to touch his arm, "brave men may die as well as cowards."

"Brave men may die, yes. But they always die better than cowards."

"I would prefer you live to be a very old man." I drop my eyes to the floor.

"Would you?" His voice is imbued with a desire to know. I look back up into his face.

"Of course."

"Do you wish me alive so that you may torture me?" His voice is rough and I know he has heard. "You promised." The accusation is nearly child-like in its raw anger.

I want to tell him that my cousin has not touched me. But the words will not come. He does not deserve to hear them. And saying them would undo a ruse that my cousin and I agreed to. So instead I say, "We each promised many things. Can you say, Henri, you have been entirely faithful to your word? You who deserted me after saying you would love me forever?" If his conscience twinges, I cannot detect as much in his face.

"I must go."

"Go, then. But before you do, I must call upon our long friendship. You know I am told nothing. I have passed all day fearing I know not what. You have been with the King: Can you not at least tell me what passes in fact? For the rumors are too wild to be credited." I do not honestly expect an answer, but, having nothing to lose, a bold play seems the thing.

He hesitates, then says, "I cannot say what your brother will do, and I will not breach the confidence of the others who counseled him. But I advised him to strike the Huguenots before they stop demanding justice and rise up. You see, I too care—I would have you live to old age and your family along with you."

"Strike how? Arrests?"

He ignores my questions, pulling up his hood once more. When he tries to pass, I reach for him again.

"Pilles was a fool to bring four hundred men to the Louvre, but there was no violence. And not every Protestant gentleman was with him."

He tries to shake me off, but I cling tighter. If he will dislodge me, he will have to use force.

"Please"—I am begging, and I take no joy in doing so—"if Charles moves against the Huguenot chiefs, will he be indiscriminate? Will he arrest them all?"

Henri breaks my grip. In the next moment he has hold of my arms— both of them—and he is shaking me. I have never been frightened of him before, but I am now.

"You spy for him, but you would not spy for me! You really are the Queen of Navarre! God weeps for you, Madame. I do not intend to." I expect him to release me, but instead he pulls me closer and kisses me roughly. I wriggle in his grasp, trying to break free. And at last he thrusts me away, doing so with such violence that I stumble, striking the wall and barely managing to remain standing. He stalks off without a backwards glance, leaving me cradling my arm.

"I do not want your tears!" I shout after him. "And you will not have mine!" It is a lie. I begin to cry as soon as he is out of sight, pounding on Charles' door as I do. When it cracks open and my brother looks out, his eyes are wild. He does not admit me. Nor does he say a word. He merely shuts the door in my face.

There is only one place left for me to go. And, damn them all, they have driven me there. Wiping my eyes, I turn in the direction of the King of Navarre's rooms, praying he is returned.

He is back, and not alone. When Armagnac opens the door, my husband's antechamber is full.

"Look who is here." The Prince de Condé accompanies his words with an undisguised sneer. Far across the room my husband looks up.

"Madame." The greeting is polite but not warm.

"We are busy," someone murmurs. "Go away." The looks I am given are filled with hatred.

"Sir"—I have to raise my voice, as many of my cousin's fellows are talking—"a moment."

"I am sorry for your reception," he says when we are alone in his bed-chamber. "Tempers run high. It is rumored the King will let Guise escape. And there is continued talk your family was involved. It is even said Anjou's purse paid the shooter."

I have no time to discuss theories. "Guise may well escape," I say, "but you would do better to plan your own than worry about him. That is why I have come. I too hear rumors; the latest is that if your coreligionists do not temper their calls for justice, and if they continue to show themselves armed in the streets, inciting the ordinary people, there will be arrests."

"His Majesty would not dare! Arrest the guests at his sister's wedding—men he invited to the city—when they have done nothing more than deplore a cowardly attempt to assassinate one of His Majesty's true servants? 'Twould be an ignoble act, and an unwise one."

"Is that a threat?"

My cousin looks startled. "No."

"Well, it sounds like one. Can you not perceive that? So much of what you and your fellows do is being seen as threatening, whatever your intentions. You need to urge restraint upon your gentlemen. No more demands upon the King. Keep off the streets, or at least do not go about so obviously armed."

"Cower?" He looks at me with disgust. "You urge us to cower? No, Madame, we will not. In fact, we will send a delegation to His Majesty tomorrow morning, a delegation I will be a member of, to accuse Guise formally."

"Cousin, you must not. Is Guise's head more valuable to you than your own freedom and safety?"

"Is that what the Duc bid you say? He would like it very well if we did not pursue this."

"Argh!" I throw both my hands into the air. "I cannot help you. Why do I try? Listen to me: If you go to Charles tomorrow, be prepared to fly afterwards. And if you do not do so successfully, do not expect me to visit you in the dungeons of Vincennes."

I assume he will bristle. Instead he gives me the most cavalier of smiles—almost a smirk. This is far more maddening, for it tells me that he thinks he knows better. Fine! I am finished trying to help him, just as I am finished trying to help Henri. These men are fools and must survive—or not—by their own wits. Mine are wasted on them.

I arrive at Her Majesty's apartment to offer a dutiful evening of attendance, and find Mother relaxed as I have not seen her since word came that the admiral had been shot. She embroiders quietly, her hand steady, her smile beatific. *Unnerving.*

Claude, seated *tout près* to Her Majesty, pats the cushion beside her. I seat myself.

"How is the King this evening, Madame?" I ask.

"He was well when I left him."

Well? Under such circumstances? The implausibility of her answer raises my suspicions even further.

"I am glad to hear it." Two can dissemble.

Henriette moves to join Claude and me. When she sits down, she angles herself so that her back is to Mother, partially blocking that lady's view of me. "The *prévôt des marchands* have been here," she says quietly.

There is nothing inherently odd about Charles meeting with the authorities charged with securing Paris, but under the circumstances the news seems significant, as do the looks given me by my sister and my friend.

"Duchesse, would you go to my wool stores and get me another ball of this blue?" The request is pretext. A servant might be sent for the wool. It is clear Mother does not want Henriette speaking to me.

"With pleasure, Your Majesty."

While Mother hands Henriette a sample of the blue, Claude leans in and whispers, "They reminded Charles of Montceaux today."

Of the long-ago kidnapping attempt?

"Who?" I whisper back.

"Birague, Tavannes, Montpensier," she says. "Retz has been with Charles for hours by Mother's express command."

Henriette moves out of Her Majesty's line of vision and Claude sits bolt upright.

What is she trying to tell me? The men she names are influential with the King and all heavily under the influence of Mother. Tavannes is a military man and much inclined, therefore, to military solutions.

"May I have something from your basket to work on?" I ask Claude, careful to speak unconcernedly, as if nothing more than embroidery were on my mind.

She bends down to take up the basket and I with her.

"Mother has bent Charles to her will," Claude whispers frantically. "It is no longer justice he seeks."

Straightening, I am not surprised to find Mother's eyes upon us.

I take up a needle and attempt to thread it, but my hands shake. Is Claude trying to reassure me Henri is safe? If so, why is there terror in her voice? What exactly is there to fear if Charles has given up his investigation into the attempt upon the admiral's life?

"Margot, you look tired," Mother observes. "You must go to bed early. In fact, you may go now." I stare at her, wide-eyed. I do not wish to be dismissed. Not until I have divined what goes on.

"Your Majesty, I thank you for your concern, but I assure you I am fine. Will you not permit me the honor of helping you prepare for bed, as is my right and duty?"

"It is pleasing to have a dutiful child," she replies. "But as your mother I must look to your health before my own pleasure in your company. You can be spared and it is my wish that you return to your rooms."

There is nothing for it. I must go. I hand Claude the basket, stand, and curtsy. As I rise a hand clutches my sleeve. Half turning, I find tears coursing down my sister's face.

"Margot," she says, choking back a sob, "do not go! This is not a night for bed."

"Enough! Claude, you are overwrought and will upset your sister to no purpose."

"Your Majesty, I beg you—"

"Not another word."

Claude hangs her head.

"Good night, then." I move toward the door, keenly aware all eyes are upon me.

When I reach my apartment, Gillone sticks her head out of the next chamber. Within moments she is ghosting away with a note for the King of Navarre. Something dire goes on, and no mistaking.

I am on my knees at my *prie-dieu* when they come *en masse* in response to my summons—my cousin and three dozen of his gentlemen. "Let only the King come through," I instruct, staying where I am. Having humbled myself before Guise earlier, I now mean to do the same before my husband. Well, I tell myself as he crosses the threshold, humility is a virtue before God.

"Wife, you may cease your prayers, for I am come." The joke, the smile—awkward and out of place—put me in mind of all the times he vexed me as a youth.

"I did not pray for your arrival, Sir, but for both our safety."

"You have news."

"The Duchesse de Lorraine tells me the King no longer seeks justice."

"*Ventre-saint-Gris!* Well, we seek it still. If that is all, I will leave you to your devotions."

"Do not be so hasty. I have been with my mother and something has changed. She smiles the sort of smile that generally presages ill for those she considers her enemies."

"Surely I do not fall into that category. If she considered me such, I doubt sincerely she would have given you, her own daughter, to me as a bride, embraced me as a son, and encouraged the King to call me 'brother.'"

"The use of the word 'surely' in conjunction with Her Majesty is a grievous error, Sir. But never mind. I do not need to convince you to be as fearful as I am. I have brought you here to ask a favor."

He tilts his head slightly, clearly both curious and wary.

I swallow and plunge onward. "Stay with me tonight."

"You cannot be eager for my company, so you must truly feel to your bones that something is coming."

"I am as certain as the day I saw blood."

"All right. If you will rest more easily knowing I am here, it will be so. But the hour is early; my gentlemen and I have much to discuss. I will go and return."

I wait for a feeling of relief. It does not come. So I shake my head. "No. Do not return to your rooms. You and your gentlemen may have the use of my antechamber. Gillone and I will stay tucked away here and leave you to your business."

"You wish my gentlemen to remain too?"

"I have seen how they guard you. If the King's men are sent to arrest you, then your own men will buy you time to flee."

"In such an instance I will do my best to escape, for I know I shall have no visitors at Vincennes."

"That is right," I reply, trying to match his bravado. It is yet another of the day's lies, for, without understanding why, I know I would descend to the dungeons to see him were he taken.

Gillone returns. "You grow accustomed to your husband, I think," she says as she helps me change.

"Go to sleep if you like," I tell my shadow. "God and I are not finished." I return to my *prie-dieu*. The rise and fall of voices—sometimes angry— punctuates my devotions. The tapers burn down and the room, dim to begin with, becomes dark. I pray on. So lost am I in my thoughts and mumbled words that I do not hear the door open.

"You do not sleep."

My cousin stands on the threshold, a light in his hand and his *valet de chambre* beside him.

I feel suddenly embarrassed—worried that Armagnac will think I wait up for my husband, and half expecting that same husband to mock my devotion. Instead he says, "Shall we withdraw awhile longer?"

"No, no." I stand. "You must be exhausted, and I am content to rest."

"My man . . ." he says awkwardly.

"Perhaps he would be comfortable at the foot of the bed?"

Armagnac bows, fully and without reservation. I find myself smiling at him. Why not? He is the first of my husband's companions not to temper his show of respect for me with thinly veiled disgust.

Climbing into bed, I wait. Unlike last evening, my cousin does not bounce. As he slides beneath the covers he says, "God grant you rest, Madame."

God does not. I seem to have lost the capacity for rest. Did it leave me when Henri did, climbing down the ladder in his wake and creeping away in darkness? I have not slumbered decently since the night we parted. To-night I am not entirely sure I desire sleep. My sister's admonition that this is not a night for bed weighs upon me, leaving me with the sense I ought to listen for sounds of trouble. For quite a while all I can hear are the voices of my husband's gentlemen. But at last even they fall silent. I make up my mind that some rest is necessary, but when I close my eyes I see Pilles' four hundred in the courtyard, Henri's face as he shook me,

Mother's unnatural smile, Charles' wild eyes through the crack in the door, and I am wide awake once more, my heart racing. I am determined to see dawn break. More than once I claw my way back from the brink of sleep before, at last, losing consciousness.

I awake with a start. My cousin sits upright beside me. "What was that?" he asks.

"What was what?"

He shakes his head in the moonlight that filters through my shutters. "Something woke me, I am sure of it. All the more sure because it woke you too."

Rising, he goes to the nearest window and opens the shutters. The room is flooded with light from the nearly full moon. My cousin peers out.

I struggle to a sitting position. Both of us are silent, ears straining. Nothing. Not a sound. Very quietly I feel, gingerly, for my small clock made by the *Horloger du Roy* at Blois. Unable to see its face, I slide to the other side of the bed and hold it out to my cousin. "What time is it?"

He takes the timepiece and angles it to take advantage of the moon. "Just gone four."

"A strange hour for a noise sufficient to wake a man who sleeps as soundly as you. Perhaps you had a dream."

He shrugs, sets the timepiece on the nearest table, and strikes a light. I watch in surprise as he begins to dress.

"Where are you going?" After all the rumors and my sister's hysterics, I do not like the idea of my cousin wandering about the Louvre in the dark.

"I am awake and not likely to slumber again." He peers at me. "You have circles beneath your eyes and I think will sleep better alone. So I will gather my men and play tennis."

"You are mad. This is not the hour for sport, nor the occasion for it. The Court is agitated and God knows what will happen next."

He shrugs. "As far as I can see, nothing is happening. And nothing will happen unless we press His Majesty. So I will play until the King is awake. Then those of us so deputized will present our petition."

So nothing has changed. Perhaps I ought to argue with him further, but I have not the energy. My cousin is right, I am tired. Bone-tired. Not just from lack of sleep. I am tired of being worried when he is not.

While the King of Navarre finishes dressing Gillone wakes. "For God's sake," I tell her after my cousin and his valet take their leave, "bolt the door and go back to your rest. We will not stir until I am sought by some person of importance. Her Majesty eschewed my services last evening; she can do without them *ce matin*." Sliding down between the covers, I close my eyes. My cousin is right: my bed does suit me better without him in it.

"Navarre! Navarre!" The cry jolts me from my slumber—loud, urgent, and accompanied by such a pounding upon the bedchamber door that I am surprised not to hear wood splinter. Gillone, on her feet, clutches the blanket from her pallet before her. If it is dawn, it is just so.

"The door! Hurry! It may be my husband!"

The cry "Navarre!" comes again as she races forward. It is not my cousin's voice but he may be accompanied. If he must fly, I wonder that he stops here first.

As soon as the bolt is drawn a man, sans doublet, his white shirt covered in blood, staggers in and runs at me. It is the Seigneur de La Mole, with whom I so recently sat at tennis. His eyes are glazed with terror. He cradles one of his arms in the other. When he releases it—to grab the front of my shift with a single bloody hand—he cries out in pain. Before I can say a thing, I know the reason for his terror. Four members of the King's guard dash into my bedchamber. The last actually knocks Gillone to the floor as he passes.

I scramble from my bed with the unfortunate wounded gentleman still clinging to me. The guards stop for a moment at the foot of the bed, then the man in the lead presses toward me.

"Stop!" I cry. "What has this gentleman done that you pursue him into the private chamber of the King's own sister."

"He is a heretic," the soldier replies.

"So is my husband, but what has this man done?"

The man reaches for the back of La Mole's shirt and pulls. I, irritated at not being answered, put my arms about the Seigneur's waist and hold firm, eliciting a groan of pain.

"Sir! Leave my rooms at once or I shall have you beaten within an inch of your life."

The guard does not move, nor does he cease to pull at La Mole. A guard at the foot of the bed actually sniggers.

"Your Majesty," the guard doing the tugging says, "this man is an enemy of the King and we pursue him in accordance with the King's will."

"Well, Sir, I will not be satisfied until I hear that from the King's lips. Meantime, leave my chamber, and leave it without your quarry." As I speak, Monsieur Nançay appears in my doorway. "Captain, your men ignore my commands. Let us see if you can do better. Call them off!"

Nançay's eyes meet mine with a look that contains equal parts puzzlement and respect. "Leave him!" he says to the soldiers. "You waste time. If the Queen of Navarre wants this gentleman, we can spare him. His Majesty may dispose of him later."

The guards file out as I lower the now insensate La Mole to my bed. Nançay bows.

"Monsieur, what goes on?" The question keeps him from departing but is not immediately answered. While I wait for him to speak, I am aware that I do not do so in silence. There is a great deal of noise beyond my apartment—noise of a most disturbing sort, including the sound of feet running and anguished cries.

"Your Majesty"—the captain bows again—"I regret I have neither the time nor the authority to answer you. But, as you are the King's sister and dear to him, do not quit your apartment."

I step forward. "Sir, as we have been always friends, tell me: Where is the King of Navarre?"

"I cannot say."

"Cannot or will not?"

He leaves without replying. I snatch up a *surcote* and pull it over my blood-streaked shift. "As soon as I leave, bolt the door and open to none but myself or the King of Navarre," I instruct Gillone. "Do you understand? No one else. Not the King himself." Opening a casket on my writing desk, I pull out a dagger. "Do your best for the Seigneur in my absence."

My antechamber is in disarray. Is the mess a result of the guards, or were things moved about by my husband's gentlemen who slept here?

Where are those gentlemen now? I crack the outer door and my eye lands immediately on a figure facedown on the stone floor beyond. His head is turned toward me but I cannot know who he was because his face has been kicked beyond recognition. His wide-open eyes convey fear even in death. I recoil. So the guards hunt more than La Mole for some sinister purpose I cannot understand. Drawing a deep breath, I step out of my apartment, glad of the dagger I clutch.

At first I see no one and the noises I hear, while dreadful, are distant. Then the shrieking comes. Ahead of me a man emerges from a chamber. He runs, full speed, in my direction, screaming. Behind him three archers come into view. They pause, take aim, and down the gentleman goes, not ten steps from me, arrows in his back. Yet the shrieking does not stop.

Holy Mary mother of God, am I screaming? I must be. But this fact has no effect on the archers; they merely lower their bows and run past, barely pausing to see that the fallen gentleman is dead. I close my eyes. Surely this is a nightmare. But even before I open them again, I know that the body of the gentleman will remain; the odor of blood fills my nostrils.

I begin to move again, faster and faster. The windows to my right give a view of the courtyard where, when last I looked, four hundred Protestants stood. I hear a barked command echo up the stone walls. Running to the nearest casement, I look down upon a scene from Dante. His Majesty's soldiers run pikes through men who, by their garb, are as Protestant as those who stood demanding justice yesterday. In fact, to my horror, I recognize the Seigneur de Pilles, his breast pierced, lying face upward on the stones. I have no desire to gaze on the terrible scene, but cannot turn away. I find myself frantically searching for my cousin. *Is that him pursued by three guards? No, too tall. Is that him fighting furiously with a sword, then crying out as he is felled?* I hold my breath and am strangely relieved when the victim's head falls back: the face is that of the Seigneur de Pont, not the King of Navarre. Then it dawns on me: I know very few of the King's gentlemen by sight. The fact that I have already identified two below suggests the men being slaughtered are of the highest sort— my cousin's inner circle. I am frozen to the spot by the thought. A window on the other side of the courtyard opens. A gentleman runs directly out of it, his legs pumping in the air as he falls. He lands on the paving stones below with a sickening crack, limbs akimbo. Two of the King's gentlemen wearing strange white crosses upon their sleeves lean out of the casement, laughing. Somehow this spectacle frees my feet. Crossing myself, I set out again at a dead run, hoping I am not too late.

I pass more bodies, bodies of both men and women. I see Marquis de Renel struggling with his cousin Bussy d'Amboise, who stabs Renel again and again. I am not insensible to these sights but they are not my focus. I feel certain my cousin is in mortal danger and worry that I myself may be wounded if I stay in the open. I must reach my sister's apartments. I am nearly at her door when I hear a shout from behind. Spinning, I find myself face-to-face with Monsieur Bourse, so close that I might touch him, just as he is pierced by a halberd. The point emerges from his belly, bringing with it such matter that I nearly swoon. He gasps for breath, then tries to speak but only rattles. Only a sharp pull on the weapon by the guard wielding it keeps the dying gentleman from falling upon me. The guard lets the body drop facedown at my feet, pulls his halberd from it, opens a nearby window and, lifting the still-writhing Bourse, casts him out. Then, his halberd gleaming red, the guard says, "Apologies, Your Majesty."

I bang on Claude's door as I have never knocked anywhere, crying out again and again who I am. When it opens, I drop my dagger and fall into my sister's arms, sobbing.

"Margot! Are you all right?"

"She bleeds!" The second voice causes me to look around. Charles' Queen stands behind my sister.

"Let me see!" Claude wrenches my mantle from me.

"It is not my blood," I say, looking down and realizing just how much there is.

"Thank God, thank God!" Claude hugs me to her.

"What is happening?" I ask.

"Sin and madness," the Queen Consort says. Her face is streaked with tears.

"And the King? Has someone told Charles?"

"He knows," she replies softly.

Dear God, can this be laid at my brother's door, then? "What can we do?"

"I intend to pray," the Queen Consort replies firmly. "I came hither to see that the Duchesse de Lorraine was safe and to ask her to pray with me. I have brought my Book of Hours." She holds it up as if it signifies something in all the chaos.

I believe my sister-in-law to be a truly pious woman, but prayer seems unlikely to save anyone at the present moment. "Who do you pray for? Charles?"

She blushes.

"You waste your breath! If he has a hand in this, he is destined for the flames of hell. Gentlemen of the highest ranks are being hunted and slaughtered without mercy in the chambers, halls, and courtyards of his palace."

"Margot"—Claude puts a hand upon my arm—"Elisabeth takes no part in that, nor do I, but what are we unarmed women to do? Run out among the carnage and die ourselves?"

"You are safe here and may remain so without fear of failing in any duty." I stoop to pick up my dagger, then square my shoulders. "But I cannot. Those I saw dead and wounded were Protestants to a man. I must find the King of Navarre."

Claude places herself between me and the door. "You cannot go out again."

"I can and will, but I need not wander aimlessly. Last evening you knew something of this."

Claude turns her face away.

"You warned me not to retire. The time for warnings is past. I do not ask you to tell me everything you knew or when. I beg you to divulge only one thing: What plans were made for my husband and where should I search for him?"

My sister starts to cry. I have a mind to shake her, but there is no need. The Queen Consort says, "I do not know what was or is planned for the King of Navarre, but he is in Charles' apartment."

I do not even pause to thank her. Pushing past Claude, I slide the bolt, drag the door open, and plunge back into danger.

I pray under my breath every step of the way to Charles' apartment. Pray as I watch men fall under the swords of others. Pray as I see a serving-woman dragged off screaming by men whose eager eyes recall the look I faced when Guast attacked me. Pray as I trip over something that turns out to be a severed arm. Once I leave the more public areas of the palace, I pray for two things: admittance to Charles' rooms, and that I will find my cousin there alive. I cannot say why the last seems with every step more important, but it does.

Restraining both my fear and my urgency, I rap softly at the private door. It cracks and I see the Baron de Retz.

"Your Majesty?" He seems both confused and concerned.

"Let me in."

The confusion grows.

"I was told to let no one pass."

"I am no danger to the King, as you well know. But left out here, I myself am in peril. Will you tell my brother you denied me if I am found injured or worse?"

I have him. He lets me pass into Charles' wardrobe. I have the distinct sense that I will have trouble going further.

"Sir, the Queen Consort and my sister the Duchesse de Lorraine are in that lady's apartment. They are unguarded. I fear for them." I do not need to feign terror, for after the sights I have seen, I remain terrified. "If I swear on my honor to fasten the door and let none enter, will you go and find some members of the King's guard to assign to their protection?"

He eyes me for a moment. What he sees is hardly threatening: a woman barely dressed, streaked with blood, armed with nothing but a dagger. I offer him this last item deliberately. He shakes his head no, unwilling to insult me by that level of distrust. "I will go."

As soon as the door is secure, I move to Charles' bedchamber. It is deserted save for his old nurse, who stands close to a crack in the door to the outer chamber. At the sound of my footfalls, she turns, her face white as death. Well, it might be, for like my cousin she is of the so-called reformed religion.

"Is the King of Navarre within?" I ask in a hushed voice.

"He is. Do you come for him?"

I nod.

"God be praised."

I touch her arm to reassure her as I move past.

"Go cautiously," she whispers. "The Queen Mother is with them."

Heaven help my husband. I swing open the door and there he stands, leaning heavily on the back of a chair. He appears uninjured, but his clothing suggests a struggle. The eyes, which find mine, are quite wild—or so I think, until I gaze into Charles'. My brother, pacing before my cousin, turns to look at me as if he is not quite certain who I am. His face shows that familiar but disturbing mix of lividity and petulance that marks his rages. Is his current mania spent? As I contemplate the question, a throat is cleared. Mother, seated with appearance of tranquillity, seeks my notice. Her eyes are eerily calm.

I walk directly up to the King of Navarre and do something I never expected to do in my life: kiss him on the mouth. "Husband, thank God you are safe."

My cousin looks at me as if to say, *Am I?*

I see the same question in Charles' eyes. This is not heartening.

"Your Majesty"—I leave my cousin and embrace my brother—"I am also profoundly grateful to find you unharmed. Though it be the Lord's day, the halls are filled with evil; there is violence and death everywhere."

"Good Catholics need have no fear," Mother says, "though I suppose a few may fall doing the Lord's work, and the King's."

Taking the hands that Charles worries before him, I ask gently, "*Is* this your work, brother? I do not believe it. I thought you were the king who struck medals for my wedding to celebrate the peace."

"I wanted peace, Margot"—he squeezes my hands—"but they would not let me have it!"

He does not say who "they" are. Perhaps the Protestants' boldness these last days made them seem dangerous to Charles, as I warned my cousin it might. Or perhaps my brother means someone else entirely. *Or perhaps he has gone mad.* The last thought makes me cold.

As I watch, his expression moves from sad to seething. "If I am not to have my dear *père,* then I want none of them. If I am not to have peace between my Catholics and Protestants, then only Catholics shall remain!"

Holy Mary.

"What has become of the admiral?"

Charles pulls away but does not answer.

"His Majesty and I have just seen his head," Mother says.

My stomach lurches, and I see my cousin wince at the casual way in which Her Majesty references the dismemberment of the great man.

"It seems Guise has, at last, avenged his father. Are you not happy for His Grace?"

She says this, of course, for the benefit of my cousin. He trembles slightly. I will not let her use Guise as a wedge between the King of Navarre and myself. Not at this moment. Whatever the justice of the Duc's actions, I have no similarly defensible reason to abandon a husband bound to me before God, however little he suits me.

"If His Majesty gave the Duc his blessing to settle that long grudge, it can be nothing to me."

"No! His Majesty would never do such a thing." The outrage in my mother's voice is wasted: I am not convinced. "Guise would not be governed," she continues. "He is still in the streets—killing. Who knows what may become of him there?"

So she wants Henri too. A court without the admiral and with a weakened House of Lorraine would give her absolute power with the King. My stomach quivers. I do not want Henri dead. Then I remind myself that he is savvy enough not to trust Mother—whatever bargain was struck—and that wherever he is, he is armed and a marvelous fighter.

"Devil take Guise, I want to know what has become of my men," my husband says. "I ask again: Where are the companions you separated from me after my arrest?"

Arrest! What appeared to me so serious a fate yesterday seems nearly laughable now. Never could I have imagined that.

Mother looks at him without pity. "They are dead."

He staggers. Who would not? I reach out and take his arm but he shakes me off. "Pilles? Renel? Quellenec? . . ."

"Lavardin, Rochefoucauld, Pont . . ." Mother takes over the naming, cruelly raising a finger for each. "All. Or if they are not dead yet, they soon will be."

"I do not believe you! They would have fought." My cousin juts out his chin.

"They would have fought, yes, had they been given the chance. I will not discount the advantage given by surprise."

I understand more clearly than ever the brutality of which Mother is capable. Not the killing, no—I knew her capable of that already, and which among the great houses do not keep assassins on their payroll? Her true viciousness lies in the ability to calculate men as if they were numbers and to report calumny as dispassionately as if it were the weather.

"You will never be free of this day," I say.

"Why should I wish to be? These deaths will be celebrated and those who survive will fear the King too much to fight him."

My cousin tenses. I know, or at least suspect, what he will say. Taking his arm once more, I squeeze it—tight. I hear his breath catch and see his jaw clench. *Thank God.*

"His Majesty the King of Navarre has no intention of fighting. He is Charles' own brother and my husband, so I am thankful His Majesty thought to bring him here and kept him safe."

"Ah, but the King of Navarre cannot remain here forever. And you have heard what your brother says. After this there will be no Protestants at Court and few in Paris. Even had His Majesty not set his mind thusly, the people of the city will not tolerate continued heresy."

This time my squeeze has no effect.

"I will not convert," my cousin says.

Mother sighs as if greatly disappointed.

"You cannot execute a sovereign king and First Prince of the Blood for showing obedience to his conscience," I say. "Particularly where he also shows obedience to his king."

"But he does not!" Mother stands. "His Majesty orders him to recant his heresies!"

"Charles, this man is your brother."

"I have brothers to spare."

I hope Mother realizes Charles thinks not only of my husband but doubtless of Anjou.

"You cannot have peace, Charles. I agree it is too late for that. But you can still have honor. Do you wish to be remembered as the king who lured his royal cousin to Paris by false promises, embraced him before all the world, gave him my hand, and then killed him before the leftovers from the wedding feasts had been cleared from the larders?"

Charles stops so close before us that I can feel his rapid breath. I cannot breathe myself. My cousin's life hangs in this moment. "All right," Charles says, "I will spare his life. But if he will not abjure, he will pass his remaining years imprisoned at Vincennes."

"Can there be no other choice? Let our cousin go to the Navarre."

"To raise an army and return?" Mother laughs. "No, indeed. If it is liberty the King of Navarre wants, then perhaps the King should turn him out into the streets. The citizens of Paris may persuade him to abjure where we have failed. We hear reports that many of his sect find it in their hearts to say the rosary when there is a blade at their throats."

"Give me my sword and I will take my chances," the King of Navarre replies.

I lower my voice, though I have no hope of saying anything privately. "You will not get so far as the streets, Sir. You will die a dozen yards beyond the King's door, most likely on the end of a halberd like the others I have seen spitted today as if they were game to be roasted."

The pain in my cousin's eyes burns me. But I am not sorry I am explicit. He has not seen what I have. I must make him understand the true nature of his situation before he gives my family the excuse to leave his fate to the armed men running wild throughout the palace.

Looking at Charles once more, I say, "Decisions of faith are not to be made lightly. If you ask my husband to decide between renouncing his religious beliefs and a dungeon, you must give him time."

"I *must* give him nothing—I am king."

"Well, then I beg time for him."

"Three days, and not an hour more. He will either be my Catholic brother and embraced as such, or he will be my prisoner."

I nod. Mother smiles as if my capitulation were part of her scheme. Rising, she shakes out her skirts. "Let your sister manage her husband. You and I have more important matters to attend to."

Charles' wild eyes flit to the door. "Yes, I am missing everything."

I shiver at what he misses, and at the thought that he desires to see what I devoutly wish I could purge from my memory and know I never shall.

"Margot, you may take your husband away," Mother says. "I will send a company of guard to escort you."

When they are gone, my cousin sinks to the floor, knees pulled to his chest as if he were a young boy, head resting upon those knees, hands grasping his short hair. It takes me some moments to realize he is crying, for he makes no sound. Only the shaking of his shoulders gives him away.

I do not know what to say, because no words will make his situation less grim or his losses less staggering. I feel as if I intrude, but as I move to withdraw, he raises his head.

"Do not leave me."

"I will not. But we must, together, find a way to get to my apartments. I do not know that we will be safe there, but we are not safe here, and we certainly cannot trust whatever guard Her Majesty sends."

"According to your mother, all whom I could trust are dead."

"Then we will call upon those *I* trust. If you trust *me*."

For a moment he stares at me blankly. Then he says, "Call who you like; lead me where you will—even to my doom. I have not the faculties to think clearly, nor the will to act in my own self-preservation. The man who left your rooms this morning is gone as surely as if he died with his many friends."

"Courage, Sir. I will not allow them to kill you so long as I breathe." *It is a fearful promise, and may be hard to keep.*

CHAPTER 21

August 25, 1572—Paris, France

It is a new day, yet the killing continues. Not in the palace but in the streets. I can hear the dreadful cries through my windows. My closed shutters do little to diminish them, merely leaving my rooms dark as if it were perpetually night. It is night—the night of the soul. I feel sick. I cannot eat. I cannot sit still. I cannot even pray. I've tried. My husband fares even worse. The only peace afforded his tortured soul came before dawn when I sang to him as one might a babe, and slumber spared him a few short hours of consciousness.

News filters into my chambers by many sources.

Henriette, accompanied by six armed men to keep her safe on her journey to the Louvre, brought a report of what passed in the Rue de Béthisy when the admiral was slain. The conduct of Guise in that matter disheartened me, and reports that he joined with Anjou to continue killing others of the admiral's sect sickened me. I pray they are not entirely true.

Gillone collects whispers and boasts every time she ventures beyond my apartment. Word in the palace is that Charles has grown sick of the slaughter and insists to any who will listen that he ordered it to stop yesterday at noon. If that be so, it speaks poorly of his power as king.

No, I am not being fair, I think as I complete another circuit of my antechamber with Gillone's anxious eyes upon me. It may well be that the noblemen have heeded his command and are no longer in the streets. They are not needed. Ordinary people do extraordinary things. "Drapers and wine merchants toss the children of their Protestant neighbors into the Seine," Charlotte tells me as she slips in. Her eyes are red-rimmed, her face stricken. "Is he still here?"

I nod.

"You will keep him safe?"

I nod again, unwilling to give voice to a promise I may not be able to keep. "Do you wish to see him?"

"Does he sleep?"

"Yes." I lie to spare my friend. My cousin does not sleep. He mourns. One minute lying curled tight in a ball like a small child, sobbing and pulling at his hair, and the next pacing like a caged beast, casting about wildly for some action he can take to assist those still hunted throughout the city. I do not love him, yet his agony is painful to witness. Charlotte, I begin to suspect, does love him, so his despair would be her own. It would crush her.

"Tell him . . ." Her voice dissolves and silent tears track down her cheeks.

"I will," I promise. "I will."

She slips away, and I square my shoulders for a return to my bedchamber. I have put off this moment since smuggling my cousin from the King's apartment more than four and twenty hours ago, but it can wait no longer. Whatever my husband's grief, whatever his state, we must speak sensibly of his future or he may have none.

The King of Navarre sits on the floor, his back against one post of my bed. The sound of the door causes him to draw his dagger. When he sees it is I, he sheathes it again.

"Apologies, Madame." He tries to give one of his wry smiles, as if he would make a joke out of his alarm.

"Do not apologize for a sensible precaution. I've given Gillone a dagger and I have one as well. If I had a pistol I would bring it to you, but alas, I do not."

"How many could I shoot anyway should Charles change his mind and send the guard?" His shoulders rise to a shrug out of habit. Then more quietly: "But I suppose I could deprive them of the pleasure of assassinating me as they did Coligny. If I am to die I would prefer not to do it with Guise's boot in my face."

"Do not speak so."

"Of the Duc?"

"Of your own death." I move forward and crouch at his side. I would take his hand but the gesture seems presumptuous. "You have escaped the worst; why should you die now?"

"Why should you assume the worst is over?"

"Because," I reply, giving voice to my raw thoughts, "to imagine otherwise would be unbearable. If we would not run mad, we must believe this nightmare draws to a close."

"So many are dead already, I suppose it must." He puts his face in his hands. Unwilling to disturb him, I remain silent. In a few moments he lifts his head. His face is so close to mine. Closer than it has ever been. His eyes burn. "The Duchesse de Nevers told you all the gentlemen who surrounded the admiral in his most desperate hour have perished. I had forty gentlemen with me when I was dragged before His Majesty. They are all dead. What Protestant noblemen can be left to slaughter? Only I and my cousin Condé. I suppose there is little sport in killing two more when you have slain hundreds."

"Not sport but politics will determine whether those few of you who yet remain are safe."

"True."

"Yesterday Charles granted you your life, but his mind . . ." I hesitate, thinking of my brother's mercurial mood swings. Is he mad? If so, is it but the madness of these hours or is it permanent? In either case I cannot bring myself to say he is out of his wits, so I say, "His mind is as changeable as my mother's mood. You must secure a more official reprieve."

"The council." My husband nods.

"Yes, you must go before them and ask them to grant you your life. And"—swallowing hard I lay a hand on his arm—"you must be prepared to pay."

"Abjuration? My honor for my life? I will be ridiculed in every corner of France. Despised by my fellows for weakness. Laughed at by Catholics as your family parades me around like the latest acquisition for the royal menagerie."

"But you will laugh last. What better blow can you strike against your enemies at this moment than to survive?"

My cousin's hand shoots out; his fingers encircle my wrist. "And you would go with me to the council?"

"If you wish." I use my free hand to push my hair back from my face so that he can see my eyes better and know that I do not lie.

His fingers close more tightly. "Why? Why should you care if I live or die? My enemies are those closest to you—by blood and by affection."

I shake my head. "I do not know why." It is the truth. I have no love for this man, and if we are becoming friends, we certainly picked an inopportune time. "Perhaps because I gave you my word—promised to be your ally." I am not satisfied by this answer and neither is my cousin, for his grasp does not loosen.

"His Majesty told the admiral he loved him, and gave his word as Coligny lay injured that he should have royal protection. Poor La Rochefoucauld played at cards with your brother only hours before his throat was slit, and was embraced as a friend when they parted. This is not a season for trusted allies or promises kept."

"It is not, Sir. Yet I swear again, my word to you is good."

We remain, eyes locked, very still. Like animals hiding, driven into the same hole.

"I will play the Catholic," he says at last. "You may have them bring me a priest. Or better still, as you swear you are my friend, undertake my instruction yourself. I will not have to lie to you. I will only have to memorize. Lying before everyone at once—including God—is lying enough, I think."

I do not know what to say. To hear him speak so brazenly about falsely recanting his heresies is not a pleasant thing. Yet, did not Christ admonish us to beware condemning others when we are sinners also? I made false oaths before man and God when I married him.

"God forgives much, Sir. And there are many this morning whose sins are so grave that they make yours in falsely professing the Catholic faith seem but a feather in the scales."

There is a sharp knock on the outer door. My cousin releases my wrist. I know Gillone will not open without me. Those are her orders. Rising, I take two steps. *The ladder.* Returning to the bedside, I kneel, reach beneath the bed, and draw it out. Another knock sounds.

"Here." I shove the bundle at him. "This will take you down to the fosse. I like your chances better in the Louvre than in the streets, but if they have come for you and they are many, I will say, 'The King of Navarre is not here.' Let that be a signal for you to make your escape, and good luck to you."

"Merci." His thanks tighten my chest and bring tears to my eyes. I wipe them furiously on my sleeve as I open the door to the next room. "Lock it," I command without turning.

As soon as he complies I signal Gillone to open the outer door. Mother glides in.

"Get dressed to go out."

Whatever I expected her to say, it was certainly not this.

"Out, Madame? The streets run with blood and ring with the cries of the dying! Who but a lunatic would wish to venture into them?"

"They will be safe enough for us."

The truth of her words disgusts rather than reassures me.

"What would Your Majesty propose? Will you take us all to church? Prayers for your soul and for the souls of my brothers can as easily be said in the chapel here, and to as little effect."

"Such histrionics. We have no reason to fear the wrath of God or godly men—quite the contrary. A Franciscan brings word that a hawthorn in the *Cimetière des Innocents* has burst into bloom. It is a sign from God that he commends the work of his Catholic children."

"What work? You cannot mean the slaughter of their Protestant brothers." *Dear God, all around me is madness, and it is celebrated as miracle.*

Mother offers me a dismissive smile. My outrage is clearly not worthy of response. "We will make a pilgrimage to see the bush, and you will come with us."

"I will not."

I glimpse Gillone's face over Mother's shoulder: her fear is palpable. But after the horrific sights of yesterday, and the tales I've heard since, my mother lacks the power to frighten me.

"The King commands your attendance. You refuse to obey him?"

"I do."

The smile fades, the eyes narrow. "You will be made to go."

"How? By force? I warn you, Madame, should you order the strongest of His Majesty's guards to transport me, they will have an awful time of it. And how will it serve either your purpose or the King's to have me carried kicking and screaming through the streets? Or do you mean to have me bound and gagged. That would be a spectacle for the populace to enjoy."

"Marriage to a heretic has made you obstinate."

"I believe it has." As I speak I understand in a blinding flash why I have decided to protect my husband and why I must be stubborn now. If I am not, I will be damned. Never did I imagine that the guests at my wedding would be slaughtered before they could return home. But who will believe it? And more particularly who will believe it if I am seen celebrating those events at the *cimetière*? I *know* I am innocent. I am even willing to believe that the King and my mother had no inkling such events would transpire as I took my vows. But nothing can save *them* from being linked with the massacre now.

I will not have my name spoken in the same breath as theirs when this horror is recounted.

Mother shakes her head slowly. I am transfixed by the motion. Simple as it is, it seems threatening. "Let us see if you have lost all ability to reason. I have Jean d'Armagnac."

"The King of Navarre's *valet de chambre*? My husband thinks him dead."

"Not yet. Do you want him?"

The room jerks, or perhaps I stagger. My eyes lock with Her Majesty's. Can she possibly be so cruel? Can I be so foolish as to doubt it? I just told my cousin he must sacrifice honor for survival; how, then, can I flinch?

"I want him here."

"After."

"Before. When I have seen him I give you my word I will dress."

"Why should I accept your word when you decline to accept mine?"

"Because the only blood my hands are stained with is that of those I saved on Saint Bartholomew's morn, while yours are red from the slaughter."

"I'll be back."

"White," I say as the door shuts behind Mother. "I want to wear white. The color of mourning."

I do not return to my husband, because I do not know what to say to him. To claim credit for saving Armagnac—just the thought sends me into dry heaves. To admit I will ride out with my family to celebrate the decimation of his friends and followers—that thought is even worse. And the fear of what I will surely see in the streets of Paris nearly paralyzes me.

I wait, my mind wandering nowhere, numb.

When the door opens next, Mother is not alone. A member of the Swiss Guard, his uniform streaked with grime and blood, pushes Armagnac before him.

"Sir, are you unharmed?" The question sounds absurd. It *is* absurd.

"Your Majesty, yes."

Mother nods sharply. The guard shoves Armagnac forward so that he stumbles into my arms. "We leave within the hour."

I close my arm protectively about my husband's valet, pulling his head onto my shoulder. "Get out."

The guard obeys at once, but Mother lingers.

"Is Navarre here?"

"Yes."

"I wonder how long he will be content to live as a prisoner."

"He has not yet decided for Vincennes."

She laughs. "There are all kinds of prisons, daughter. Even should he return to the Church, he will not be at liberty. Nor, thanks to your show of disobedience, will you. Today's outing will be your last for some time."

"Madame, do you expect confinement in the Louvre to be a hardship to me? How so when I have never been free? My whole life has been directed by your will, my brother's whims, and even by chance pieces of gossip—everything but my wishes. I have no wings for you to clip."

As she departs I feel Armagnac's shoulders shake as he begins to weep on my shoulder.

Just reaching my horse is horror enough. The halls of the Louvre have been cleared of the dead, but random garments and weapons left behind, along with the quiet that pervades spaces usually overflowing with people, are reminders of what has passed. As I emerge into the courtyard I am confronted by a figure sprawled where he fell, doubtless one of those unfortunate souls who threw himself from a window yesterday in a desperate bid for escape. I cannot see his face and that is just as well, because all the sadness I feel must be swallowed. Mother is watching. May I be damned if she sees me break.

A large party has assembled. Among them, just next to my mount, is Henriette. Looking past her, I see Henri. He gazes at me with a mixture of triumph and concern. Behind him a pile of bodies, some with pikes still in them, stands in the blistering sunlight as if it was composed of something more benign, like hay for the horses. Meeting the Duc's eyes, I spit, then climb into my saddle.

"What was that?" Henriette asks under her breath, but I merely shake my head.

As we form up to pass through the gates, I spot Charles at our head with a pair of priests. We move into the road in a tight pack. We could not pass otherwise. The Rue Saint-Honoré is a broad thoroughfare, but it is greatly constricted by bodies, many of them, after so many hours, stripped naked. Yet pickpockets and scavengers have not given up hope of finding something of value. They look up at the sound of our horses' hooves, and scurry off like rats at the sight of the Swiss Guard.

A small child in his nightshift lies at the side of the road just ahead. His hand is within a hair's breadth of a woman's, doubtless his mother, who was equally unable to save him or to retain his hand in death. I cannot take my eyes off those hands. As we pass, my head turns over my shoulder to see the pair of them. The effort of holding back my tears is physically painful. My chest burns. My stomach is hollow. I glance at Henriette but she looks straight ahead.

What monsters we are.

I try to keep my eyes from returning to the road, looking at the back of the King's head, at the cloudless sky, at anything but the fallen— anything but the fallen or the large ceremonial cross carried by one of the priests. God has no place in this moment. Of this I am certain.

Guise pulls his horse alongside Henriette's. "I suppose we ought to have thought of the stench and thrown more of them in the river. By tomorrow the odor will be unbearable."

Anjou, riding just in front of me, laughs and turns back over his shoulder. "I have it on good authority that near the Pont aux Meuniers the river could hold no more bodies. One could traverse from bank to bank upon them without wetting one's feet. But never fear, Guise, we shall send soldiers to clear what the thieves and the grieving relatives do not. And only think how much better Paris will smell this fall with cooler weather and fewer heretics to pollute it."

The Duc smiles. I never thought to see Henri reduced to my brother's level. Their conduct always distinguished them one from the other—with all of the good on Henri's side—as did their antagonism. Yet here they are, joking together, and over what? The deaths of innocents.

"And how will you remove the stench from your persons?" My voice is low; I have not enough breath to speak more loudly and not enough self-control to stop shouting if I start. "No amount of the perfumes you favor, brother, will banish the scent of death from you. It will cling to you until you are a corpse yourself."

"Spoken like a woman whose husband smells of dogs and garlic," Anjou replies.

Henri snorts.

I turn to him across the figure of my friend. "What is garlic compared to the odor of the grave?" I will myself to look into his eyes, daring him to break the stare. "If moral decay had a stench like the decay of the flesh does, you, Sir, would be given a wide berth by all. As it is, I am profoundly thankful for the odor of my horse at this moment."

His eyes drop, but not before I have the satisfaction of seeing a flare of pain in them. Before this I could not have imagined causing Henri pain without feeling it myself.

I am relieved to reach the *cimetière*. Here at least the dead are below-ground. I experience a strange urge to spring from my horse and run to hide among the bones stacked in the charnel house, but what behavior toward me might be excused if it appears I have run mad? I will not offer myself as sacrifice to my mother and brothers, nor will I offer the King of Navarre.

The bush is old and frames a grave so ancient, the name has been worn from the marker by the drops of a thousand rains. A single branch blooms. I must admit, the white of the blossoms is startling against so much gnarled wood. Against so much death. We dismount and the priests move forward, praying as they go. The King and Mother follow. I am allowed, momentarily at least, to hang back, clinging to the reins of my horse. Henriette comes to my side.

"Margot, calling out the Duc d'Anjou and the Duc de Guise! What possessed you?" Her voice is a whisper but chastisement nonetheless.

"Grief and guilt—maladies which seem to affect far too few in our party."

Taking my arm, Henriette leads me to the far side of my horse. "Who have you lost that you should grieve? You had little liking for your husband's companions, and your acquaintance with them was so fleeting that you had yet to learn many of their names."

"But they were my guests nevertheless. If I cannot mourn them as men, may I not despise the fact that my wedding put them in the way of dying?"

"You *may* do whatever you like. But whether you should . . . that is a different matter." The dismay in my friend's face leads me to feel dismayed in turn. "How do such thoughts and actions help you?" she asks. "It is a foolish thing in war to side with the losers, most particularly where the losers are already dead. *La mort n'a point d'ami.*"

"We were at peace."

"And we will be so again. Who precisely is left to raise arms against His Majesty? Whatever you think of the actions of yesterday, a generation of Huguenot leaders is dead. They drag the admiral's body through the streets."

I pry her hand from me. "You speak of that as if it were nothing. You who dined with Coligny, and hunted with him! Just a week ago he was everywhere we went, a royal advisor, one of the most powerful men in Charles' court."

"Too powerful."

"Too powerful for the House of Lorraine."

"And"—Henriette's voice drops so low that it comes out as a hiss—"for the House of Valois. Did you consider *that* when you savaged Guise? He is not the only one who wanted Coligny dead, or who had a hand in the first attempt."

"There is plenty of blame to go around," I whisper back furiously.

"Thus laying blame is both futile and dangerous. We are here to celebrate. Put on a smile, if only as an act of political expedience. If it is less than honorable to kill women and children in their beds, be glad common men, not courtiers, did that dirty work. Henri finished the admiral, yes, and in doing so avenged his father. Is that not the act of an honorable man? I thought you loved him."

And, without waiting for my reply, she is gone. When I slide from behind my horse, she is with the others, in a ring about the bush, head bowed. Henri is not far from her. Looking at the profile I know so well, at the sandy hair I have tousled in play and in lust, I know that I did love him. I love him still. Perhaps that is why I find myself unable to embrace Henriette's justifications of his actions.

Mother casts a look in my direction. I glare back but move to join the others, bowing my head as if in prayer, though my thoughts are more temporal.

Guise is not the only man who committed murder last evening. Without question, such a massacre, however it began, could not have proceeded without the acquiescence of my family. Doubtless Anjou wet his hands in blood driven by petty grievances and ambition more than by any desire to rid France of heresy or safeguard Charles' reign. And Charles owned that what was done inside the Louvre was done in his name when I confronted him. But Henri is not supposed to be as my brothers are—governed solely by self-interests and whims as given rein or checked by Mother. He is charged, as I love him, with being a man of honor possessed of a conscience, guided by God. Glancing at the Duc, his eyes shut in prayer, my heart aches. I am bitterly disappointed in him for being less than he appeared through my loving eyes.

I realize those around me are moving, filing forward toward the bush. At the front, Charles receives a blessing and stoops to kiss the white blossoms. Courtier after courtier follows suit. My feet will not move. I stand rooted like a bush myself as others pass. Then my hand is drawn through an arm. I know even before I see his profile that my escort is Guise. He does not turn to meet my gaze but very softly says, "If you will not have a care for yourself, I must do it."

He draws me onward and then, as the bush is reached, steps back so I am in front of him. Just before me, Amboise d'Bussy accepts the blessing, murmurs "Thanks be to God" and kisses the blinding-white flowers. Advancing upon me, the priest makes the sign of the cross, then lifts the branch so I may offer thanks and kiss it in my turn. I have no intention of doing any such thing. Then I think of poor Armagnac sobbing on my shoulder. I have things, even at this horrible moment, I should be grateful for. If they are not the same things commemorated in the others' prayers, so much the better.

"*Deo gratias!*" Unlike the others I do not mumble, but say it clearly so all can hear. *Deo gratias,* I think, *for giving me the strength to save La Mole from the archers and Armagnac from my mother. Deo gratias for the life of the King of Navarre.* As I kiss the blossoms, I ask for God's help in keeping my husband alive awhile longer. Then I move back to my horse as quickly as possible. I am done with this place. I wish it were as easy to break with some of the people in it.

* * *

When I return to my apartment, the King of Navarre is sitting at my table, writing with Armagnac beside him. Both gentlemen have changed into fresh clothing. I give Gillone a questioning look.

"I went to His Majesty's rooms and collected some of his things."

"For which I am profoundly grateful." My cousin looks up. He is a man entirely different than the one I left sitting on the floor of my bedchamber. He has marshaled his composure, and the strength such an act reveals impresses me deeply. "As I am for greater acts of compassion." His eyes move in Armagnac's direction.

I look away, still unwilling to take credit for the *valet de chambre*'s life, as the price I paid for it is so loathsome to me.

"What are you writing?"

"An accounting of those I know to be dead. Perhaps you can assist me."
I wince.

"Or not." His voice is gentle. "It is a grim task, but I think it important, for perhaps those not yet dead can be preserved."

Hope, it seems, is in Navarre's nature.

"If you think it to be valuable, Sir, I will help. When we have a list, I shall ask the Duchesse de Nevers to examine it. Her knowledge will be greater than either of ours."

"You could ask the Duc de Guise for his list. He must know how many and who he killed. Or perhaps he killed so many he lost track." The words are as quiet as his last, but they are angry—the first angry words he has spoken that seem, at least in part, directed at me.

"I could not. I believe it will be a long time before I speak with the Duc again."

There is a knock. Gillone cracks the door. Her eyes widen. The hand she slips through the crack returns, clasping a note. I know the moment I see the handwriting it is from the same man whose company I have just forsworn. Only three words: "Talk to me."

"I must go out." I know my face betrays surprise and perhaps even dread, but certainly there might be many causes for such a reaction. The King of Navarre cannot suspect the Duc waits on the other side of the oak. And this is well, for if he did there might be violence. There has been enough of that.

Slipping into the corridor, I find Henri waiting, his eyes traversing the space from end to end. When they find me I cannot distinguish if they contain surprise or hope. Perhaps both.

"You do not invite me in." Awareness comes upon him, slowly changing his expression. "He is with you."

"If you mean my husband, then yes. He has been with me since the King saved him yesterday."

"The King saved him?"

"Of course! You could not honestly have believed His Majesty would permit the murder of a man linked to him by both blood and marriage." There is absolutely no reason for me to reveal how uncertain I was upon that very point yesterday.

"I hoped he would. Just as your brother Anjou doubtless prayed Condé would lie among the dead."

A horrible admission but hardly surprising. Henri hates my cousin not just as a heretic but as the man who holds the place he wanted himself. I have felt the same about the Princesse de Porcien, and, if I am honest, I would, I think, have been glad of my cousin's death before I wedded him. Would I have cared who killed him or how?

"Is this what you have come to tell me?" I ask.

He looks about again.

"Is there not somewhere we can go?"

How many times have I heard those words? This time I am struck by the fact that, thanks to the slaughter, it has never been easier to be alone without subterfuge. Countless rooms stand empty, with no chance their tenants will return. The closest belong to my husband.

When we arrive, I am shocked by how normal everything looks. Perhaps the guards seeking to arrest the King of Navarre found them empty and simply had no reason to cause destruction. I have never asked my cousin how or where he was taken, assuming the recitation of the event would increase his pain.

I stand facing Henri, waiting for him to begin.

"Marguerite, as I love you and you once said you loved me, I want to know why you treated me as you did this morning."

I am being called to account? Me?

"Sir, I find it discouraging that you cannot arrive at such a conclusion on your own. Are you not the man who slew the admiral? The man who joked this morning about the dead lying naked in the avenues?"

"I do not understand," he says. I can see that—in Henri's eyes, in his defensive posture. "You have always known what I was. And you have always known I was sworn to kill Coligny. When I marched to the last war, you wept and told me to kill as many heretics as I liked, and certainly as many as I needed to come back safely. You wished me luck in avenging my father's death. Now I have had that luck and done a son's duty, yet you seem to think I should be ashamed."

How can I explain? I do not believe I have changed so much—or perhaps I do not wish to believe it. I would like to think that Henri's manner of killing the admiral would have mattered to me even long ago.

"I knew you would kill Coligny, yes," I reply. "But I thought it would be in battle, or sword to sword in the combat that befits gentlemen. I could never have imagined you would have an injured gentleman pulled from his bed and thrown from the window of his own *hôtel*."

He flinches slightly at my account, and this moves me more than anything he has said or any look he has yet given me. Then his eyes harden.

"One might kill a dog in such a manner," he says. "Coligny was a dog."

"No. A heretic, yes, but a gentleman. And even were he not, you are one. It ought to have been beneath you to kill him as you did."

I wonder what will happen if he hangs his head in shame and admits his fault. If he pleads a sudden madness. Surely many who roamed the Louvre and the streets that night were mad. I think that if he is contrite, I will take him in my arms and soothe him.

"I cannot be sorry the admiral is dead," he says. "And rethinking the manner of his death is entirely futile." Lowering his voice, he steps forward, closing the gap between us. "Marguerite, there *are* things about the long night which make me sorry."

"Yes?" I keep my voice cold, but my heart leaps.

"Children ought not to have been slaughtered. They were but innocents who might have been brought to see the error of their parents' ways and reclaimed for the Holy Church. Even some of the adults abjured."

"God cannot reclaim a heart by force." I think of my husband facing the pain of his own abjuration, of his guilt and of the loathing he so obviously feels for himself at the prospect of becoming Catholic in name again.

Henri throws up a hand. "And it seems that I cannot reclaim your heart no matter what I say! What would you have me do? Shed tears because we have rid His Majesty's kingdom of his worst enemies and God's?"

He paces away, and I think our conversation is over. But, rounding, he returns, this time stopping much closer, intimately close. "Is this truly about dead Protestants, or is this really about my asking you to spy on the King of Navarre, and turning from you when you would not? That spat ought never to have been allowed to continue for so long. I have lain awake more than one night reliving my long climb down the ladder from your room and the moment when, at the bottom, I thought to scramble back again and take you in my arms. I have wished countless times I had acted on that impulse. And I tell you now that though my body may have left you standing alone in darkness, my soul in good part did not leave you and has never left you since."

So I have not been *tout seul* in my loneliness. There is comfort in that—comfort and something more. I feel the understanding between us rekindling. The spark is weak but it is there. I do not wish to speak for fear I will speak wrongly and extinguish it. Henri weighs my silence, examines my eyes, and presses onward.

"Do not spy on the King of Navarre if you do not like it. Such a little matter must not be allowed to separate two hearts meant to be conjoined."

This concession—which would have made me happy as late as the day before yesterday—fails to satisfy. How surprising. How infuriating.

"I will grant you this: it is a 'little matter' now," I say. "You no longer need anyone to spy on the King of Navarre. You, my brothers, and Her Majesty have made certain he is a lonely, friendless prisoner. Who can he conspire with now when all his gentlemen lie dead—some in pieces? You think to be magnanimous, but you have missed the mark. You offer nothing of value."

"I offer you my love," he says quietly. "Something I did believe you held dear, as I treasured yours."

He is right, of course. I valued his love. I lived for it. Even at this moment, when I am confused, angry, hurt, and terrified for my future and the future of France, I find it difficult to imagine a life without our mutual affection. Our love, having gone on so long and survived such hardships, seems part of the warp and weft of me. I close my eyes for a moment to see my own thoughts more clearly.

Henri's voice again cuts through my silence.

"Are we really finished, then? Separated by a victory for the Church you hold as dear as I do and by a man whom you do not love?"

Opening my eyes again, seeing Henri before me, I find that, despite his great sins of late—and they are mortal, to be sure—I am not ready to foreclose the possibility that he will be my own again, and I his. He may repent. God may forgive him. So why not I? But I do not feel that forgiveness in my breast at this moment.

"Peace, Henri," I say.

His eyes soften at my use of his Christian name.

I lay a hand on his arm. It feels strange to do so, strange but not unpleasant. "Mayhap things between us will be restored, but at present too much happens that is larger than both of us. We are in the grip of history. You and my brothers think to mold it. I have no such pretentions. But I believe all of us, myself included, will be molded by it. I charge you, as I have loved you, to reflect upon that. Who you will be when these dark days come to a close—who I will be—I cannot foresee. I hope I will be a woman you can love. I hope you will be a man I can embrace once more without reservation."

"And in the meantime?" he asks.

"In the meantime, take your leave and do as you feel you must. God go with you."

"God and a kiss?"

I hesitate. A great part of me wants to lean forward and taste his familiar lips. I wonder if doing so would make all that has been ugly between us disappear. Then I remember where we are. These rooms are filled with my cousin's things. The King of Navarre trusts me. Not as wife, perhaps, but as friend. I do not think his trust would long survive should he see me kiss his mortal enemy. He is not here, of course, and would never hear of any such kiss, but knowing how it would make him feel makes the kiss wrong.

"God and my good wishes," I reply. Then I move past him quickly. I do not want to see Henri's disappointment or acknowledge my own.

CHAPTER 22

August 31, 1572—Paris, France

On the one-week anniversary of what is being called the Saint Bartholomew's Day Massacre, the royal council grants my cousin his life. I stand beside him to hear them pronounce it. I am with him everywhere now. The massacre bound us in a way that our childhood and our marriage utterly failed to. As we leave the council chamber, the King of Navarre turns to me.

"Madame, I owe you my life twice over."

"That is not the case, Sir. You overestimate my influence with the council. I have none. I promised I would go with you and I did. But it is you who spoke eloquently on your own behalf."

"All my words would have availed me nothing were I not your husband. That title alone saved me—not 'King of Navarre' or 'First Prince of the Blood.'"

"Nonsense. The Prince de Condé was also granted his life. I tell you, the mania for killing has exhausted itself, at least in Paris." I am not so certain as I try to sound, and both of us are keenly aware that the carnage so lately halted here has spread to Meaux, Troyes, La Charité—so many cities.

"Perhaps," my cousin says. "There were several present whose eyes looked murderous. Did you notice the expression on Anjou's face? And he was not the only duc unhappy with the council's decision."

He refers to Guise, of course. Henri lacked his usual self-control. When he saw me enter with my cousin, he looked personally wounded. When the grant of clemency was made, his disappointment was palpable.

We walk in the direction of my apartment—our sanctuary and prison, waking or sleeping. I am afraid to let my cousin live in his apartment alone, and neither of us desire to participate in Court events. We have been ordered to some, and those the most horrible of all. Two days ago we were compelled to take part in a procession to Mountfaucon, where the remains of Coligny were displayed. My cousin was forced to look at the poor tortured body, and so was the admiral's seventeen-year-old son. The young man cried. My husband did not. But in his sleep that night he called out for Coligny, and I, retreating to the next room after soothing him, cried for both men, and for myself too.

As we come in sight of my door, my cousin sighs. Glancing at him from the corner of my eye, I see a man being eaten alive by captivity, as Mother predicted. This frightens me. If my cousin can be lured into doing something stupid, even the council's pardon may not be enough to keep him from being consigned to a grave like his fellows.

"Thank God, the Cardinal de Bourbon does not come today. I do not believe I could sit through his catechism though my life depends on it." My cousin paces to the window. "Two weeks, Madame," he says with his back to me. "Two weeks from today I must embarrass myself with a false conversion. And before that I must find a way to choke down my pride and write a letter beseeching the forgiveness of the Holy Father." He turns to me, his face animated. "Why should I apologize to him when it is said he organizes a great *Te Deum* at Rome to celebrate the deaths of those I held most dear?"

"It is not a matter of should."

"You are right." His shoulders fall and he appears older than his years.

"Sir, you must find a weapon—a shield to protect yourself—or you will be broken by the aftermath of a horror which failed to kill you."

"I have never felt more impotent."

"I have felt impotent all my life." The admission surprises him, but me more.

"How have you survived?"

I am not sure that I have. My life at the moment is no life at all. I have no consequence; I am alienated from the man whose love I thought would sustain me always; I have not even the facile distractions of Court entertainments.

"By subterfuge. You would do well to clothe yourself in that bravado which used to mark your speech and actions. The more my family can determine what hurts you, the more accurate their blows become."

He nods. "All the roles I played in the pageants surrounding our wedding were given me. You urge me to create my next role myself. I would be the King of Navarre, free and far from here. I must find a way to escape south and raise an army."

"Yes, but such a flight will take time. Do it precipitously and you will be displayed at Mountfaucon for the crows to desecrate. Until your chances of escape improve, while you may live for revenge, you must find some other occupation."

Looking at my cousin, I ask myself what I miss most in my own life. The answer is immediate: love. That is something I cannot give him. But I know who can. Charlotte has made several attempts to see my cousin these last days, but he has been unwilling to receive her. It is time for him to start.

"Sir, why not pass an afternoon with the Baronne de Sauve? Surely that would be better than sitting here with me, contemplating my family's sins."

He colors. "It seems wrong, Madame, to repay your kindnesses with infidelity."

"Political allies do not demand that sort of faithfulness," I reply. "If they did, then no man would ever have one." He ought to laugh but he does not. "Come, Sir, you know the nature of our agreement and by its terms your dalliance has my blessing."

He looks at me incredulously. "I feel as though our bargain has been overtaken by events."

"*Everything* has been overtaken by events. If we are to have control of our lives once more, we must wrest it back."

"All right," he says. "I will take comfort in another, if only so you may have your rooms to yourself again for a few hours." He smiles and even manages a touch of insouciance.

"I will find Charlotte."

I am moving through the halls with a lighter step than in many days when I hear it—a wild, croaking cry, then another. They ring in such a way as to suggest they come from the courtyard. My blood runs cold. Rushing to the nearest window, I peer out. An enormous crow sits on the cobblestones below. Raising his head, he meets my eyes, then sounds again. Birds begin to fall from the sky—no, not fall, plunge—down into the courtyard with a great flapping of wings. I stand transfixed. Soon there are too many to count, yet more arrive. Unlike the first bird who drew me to the window, these are silent, eerily so. When there is no more room on the ground, birds perch on outcroppings in the architecture. One lands on the ledge outside the window where I stand. It tilts its head and considers me with its beady black eyes. I open my mouth to say I know not what, and he opens his black beak, issuing something very like a scream. His cry is but a beginning. The moment he makes it, his fellows join him in a concert of shrieking, groaning, and howling.

I have the wild thought that these are the souls of my husband's men come back to the scene of their murders. I want to run but I cannot move—cannot turn away or even raise my hands to cover my ears. I am aware of movement around me. People stream to the windows as they did on the day Pilles brought his four hundred. Within moments the cries of the crows are joined by the wailing of ladies. I feel a hand on my shoulder. Someone leans forward until his lips nearly touch my ear. " 'And shall not God avenge His elect, which cry to Him day and night?'" The voice is my husband's.

I begin to tremble, for I believe I hear the cries of the dead, and I am certain God must. My cousin, moving beside me, puts his arm about me and pulls me close against his side. There is a great commotion. The King arrives with Mother at his elbow.

"You see," she says as Charles looks down upon the cloud of screeching birds. "They are only crows. There was no need to send your guard into the streets."

So Charles too mistook the cries for human.

The King looks at my husband. "Make them stop!" His shrieking sounds very much like the birds'.

"Your Majesty, if I could, I would, for they frighten my wife. But the birds of the sky are no more my subjects than yours."

"It is an omen." Anjou sidles up to the King. "I told you it was a mistake to leave any alive."

The Duc de Guise, standing just behind my brother, nods.

"Henri," I say, "I have heard and seen enough."

It takes my cousin a moment to realize I speak to him—takes him far longer to react than it takes Guise. At the sound of his shared Christian name applied to his hated rival, the Duc blanches and his hand twitches across the pommel of his sword. He casts my husband a look of pure hatred.

As my cousin turns me from the scene, his arm still about me, I realize I have made a misstep. Much as I wanted to pain Guise, I ought not to have left him so long with the false impression that I have been intimate with my husband. The thought clearly feeds Guise's hatred, making him more dangerous. As we move through the crowd, I spot Charlotte, whom I sought in the first instance. I mouth the words "Henriette" and "Come."

Despite the distance, I can still hear the birds in my apartment. The others must be able to as well, but, like me, they studiously avoid remarking on the fact. We three ladies draw together and put our arms around one another—a unit as we have not been since the violence began. Then Henriette notices that Charlotte and I are crying.

"Come, my beloveds, there have been enough tears already. Where we three are together there ought to be smiles, or at very least schemes."

"The latter is what I had in mind," I reply. "Charlotte, you and the King of Navarre have been too long apart."

My friend, who had been drying her tears, begins to weep again. "I fear we will be parted more permanently. Her Majesty declares I am no longer to see him."

She has forgotten that my cousin never knew of the Queen's sanction. I cannot see his face from where I stand, but Charlotte can. Whatever she sees brings horror to her eyes. She covers her face with her hands and sobs. The King of Navarre turns his back on my friend.

"The time has come for truth," I say, putting a hand on his shoulder. "At least between the four of us. If we can be honest with each other, then we shall have a great advantage over those others who go about the Court." I take a deep breath. "The Baronne was set upon you by my mother, just as I married you by her will. But what does that signify?"

My cousin spins to face me, his expression full of disbelief and fury. I put up a hand before he can speak. "Hear me out. I had no desire to marry you, yet we have since pledged ourselves of our own accord and on our own terms. Charlotte seduced you for my mother's purposes, but I suspect she cries now at the loss of you for herself."

"It is so," Charlotte says.

"You see, Sir. What does the beginning matter if the end is love?"

His eyes soften slightly. I push harder. "Are there so many who love you in France that you will let pride keep you from embracing a true heart?"

"No." He opens his arms and Charlotte runs to him.

"Charlotte," I say, "as a wife I have no objections to your *amour,* but as an ally of the King of Navarre I must ask for your word that you will no longer carry tales to Her Majesty. She has forbidden you from continuing with my cousin. Let her think that you obey."

Charlotte looks into my husband's face. "You have my word. I will cut out my tongue before I will say aught that will damage you, Sir."

"Now off with you. While all the Court wails over a flock of crows, you two have better things to do."

"Ally of Protestants, matchmaker, your marriage has made you many surprising things," Henriette says when we are left behind by the departing pair. "But I would venture to say it has not made you happy."

"No. Yet I can hardly complain, because this does not seem an auspicious time for happiness in the court of France. If you can tell me one person who is happy presently, I will be astonished. My mother, perhaps?"

"Not even she, not completely. She is celebrated by the common people as savior of the kingdom and she is taking credit for the events of last week where that will help her, but did you not see her face this morning as His Majesty ranted?"

"She fears losing control of the King and the situation," I say.

She nods. "Neither His Majesty nor France is known for fidelity of opinion. And the latter has always had a healthy skepticism where Madame Catherine is concerned. So Her Majesty still reaches. My husband worried that all the begging I urged him to would be insufficient to save Condé."

"So you are an ally of Protestants too."

"Not at all." Henriette manages a wry smile. "But I would not let a sister's husband die if I could prevent it. Neither of my sisters' husbands."

"Surely Guise is in no danger."

"Not from Her Majesty. At least, not at this moment. But I believe he is in very great danger from you. He is being torn apart and changed in unbecoming ways by your rupture. He wanted Condé's blood, though he is also related to that gentleman by marriage."

"I will not accept blame for Henri's bloodlust. It is the very reason we have no rapprochement, and I told him so. What concerns me now is that he clearly longs for my cousin's blood, and that is in part my fault. I have allowed the Duc to believe, as the rest of the Court does, that my cousin is my true husband."

Henriette's eyes open wide. "No wonder he wants Navarre dead."

"Go put that particular fear to rest. Tell Henri I was true to my pledge and that—as he claims still to love me—I rely upon him to guard this knowledge, which I have good reason to wish kept secret."

As I watch Henriette go I find myself hoping that somehow my confession will both protect my cousin and provide the next step back into the Duc's arms. For with my cousin restored to Charlotte, I have the presentiment that my own loneliness will be harder to bear.

My husband sends word as night falls that he will remain in his apartment. I hope this is not foolish even as I smile at the thought that two among my friends are happy this night. Climbing beneath the covers, I think how good it will be to be spared my cousin's snoring. An hour later, when I am still awake, I wonder if that same snoring might not soothe me.

Rising, I pad to the next chamber, where Gillone sits at the table in a small ring of light, replacing some pearls on one of my partlets. I send her to the kitchens to fetch me a sleep pillow of lavender and chamomile. The relative dark of the chamber bothers me as it never has before. *Am I become a child again?* I think, angrily. *No: even as a child the dark was not among my fears.* I close my eyes, but a sudden vision of Gillone lying dead with a halberd through her forces them open. I shake my head to clear it. I must put aside such morbid imaginings. Why should anyone harm Gillone?

Yet my stern thoughts are not sufficient to set me right. I take the lamp from the table and begin to rekindle every light in the room, lifting shades with shaking hands. Perhaps action will restore my self-possession where sheer will has failed.

I have my back to the door when it opens.

I turn, expecting my little shadow, and nearly scream. My mother stands just inside. Here is a thing more justly feared than the dark.

"Daughter," she says, "I've come to have a little talk." Her smooth, unctuous tone turns the blood in my veins to ice, but I will not give her the pleasure of seeing me shiver in the summer heat and work hard to keep the hand holding the lamp from shaking as I place it back upon the table.

"What demons do you hope to banish with all this light?" Her question is oddly knowing, as if she could see into my soul. *But,* I try to assure myself, *she cannot.* Foresight she may have, but the power to see into hearts surely lies beyond her.

"I banish nothing," I reply. "I would read and do not wish to do so in the next room where I might disturb my husband." I pray she takes me at my word.

"Husband. Hm." Without being invited to do so, she takes a seat at the table. Unwilling to stand before her like a naughty child, I too take a chair.

"Would it surprise you to know that I am sorry?"

The list of things my mother ought rightfully to be remorseful for is enormous. But I feel certain the greatest of her sins do not trouble her.

"Sorry?" I reply. "Madame, I can think of no apology you need make to me—at least, none which would be timely."

"Ah, you still cleave to old grievances . . . to old loves . . ." She lets her voice trail off and turns her eyes to her own fingers, which trace the pearl pattern on the partlet that lies between us.

"You are mistaken. I do not dwell on the wrongs you have done me in the past. But nor can I forget them. Only a fool allows herself to be burned by the same candle twice. Surely you did not raise a fool."

She smiles. Not one of her false or mocking expressions, but a genuine smile. "No, Margot, you are *not* a fool. Bravo. In this you achieve a great deal more than many. It is because you know how to weigh your own interests that we have something to speak of. I said I am sorry, and I am. Sorry that I forced you into a marriage with Navarre."

She pauses to allow me to respond, but I cannot divine what is best to say, and even were I sure, my tongue cleaves to my mouth. Reaching out, she places her hand on top of mine where it rests. I cannot bear her touch. Drawing my hand away, I stand, walk to my fireplace, and turn to face her again.

"The King and I believed your marriage would bolster the *Paix de Saint-Germain-en-Laye,* so we urged you to overlook your qualms of conscience and your inclination. As you have ever been *une fille de France* and a dutiful daughter, you did so."

I would laugh at this description of myself if the memories of how I implored Charles on my knees to give me a different husband did not pain me so.

"And now it seems your sacrifice was wasted."

"Do you not mean my *hand* was wasted?" I snap. "The King and Your Majesty meant to benefit from my marriage. You needed to keep the King of Navarre close and to make it less likely he would lead troops against the crown. My marriage was intended to do that and might well have succeeded had you given the matter time. My hand could have soothed your enemies. But you were impatient and found other hands willing to slaughter them." I stop, expecting Mother to lash out. Instead she shrugs. How very different her shrug is from the one I have become accustomed to seeing my cousin give—a shrug I used to hate but now understand. It seems to me that her gesture is uncaring and dismissive, while my cousin's seeks to avoid disagreement or to show a brave indifference where he is anything but.

"Phrase it as you like. Yes, your hand was wasted. The question is: Will you allow it to remain so? This last week you have perceived your fortunes to be coupled to your cousin's and acted accordingly." She nods understandingly. Most alarming. "But look again. Now that your cousin is under the King's thumb, held here as securely as if he were a boy once more, might you not prefer the freedom to make better, more beneficial allies?"

"You would have my marriage annulled." Strangely, the image of my husband as a boy comes to me as I speak: he is in the Great Gallery at Fontainebleau, his hose are twisted, and he is speaking fiercely of his return to Béarn. I did not like him then. I like him now, but I do not love him.

"Yes. You can be free of Henri de Bourbon. But you must assist in your own case for the annulment."

"Meaning?" My mother cannot need me to tell the Pope that I was married without dispensation. The Holy Father certainly knows this, even if a vast majority of the Court remains unaware of it. Therein, I suspect, lies the problem. Charles and Mother cannot be eager to trumpet the fact that they flouted papal authority just as they are being embraced as champions of the faith.

Raising her eyebrows, Mother leans forward, breaking her pose of studied nonchalance. "I spoke with Guise today. He tells me that perhaps you are not really the King of Navarre's wife after all."

So that is the game. The words I sent to Henri to soothe him—words I asked him to hold in confidence—were betrayed to Mother within hours, giving her grounds for an annulment without needing to admit there was no dispensation. Oh, Henri, where is the faith in this? Where is the honor? While I am lost in a swirl of thoughts and emotions, Mother speaks again.

"I have explained to His Majesty that such an admission might be mortifying to you and persuaded him that, if you were willing to attest that your marriage is a matter of paper and no more, he ought, as recompense, to grant you the right to choose your next husband without limits." She smiles magnanimously.

"The man I would have chosen is no longer free."

"For the right price, anyone can be made free."

My eyes sting. The union that Henri and I planned so many years ago and were denied might still be within our grasp. I might yet be happy. I might be loved. And if my life has taught me any lesson, it is that to be truly loved by no one is to be lonely beyond measure. I swallow the lump that rises in my throat.

I may be loved, but at what price?

"What of the King of Navarre? Would you allow him to go south?" It is a trick question, for I know that Mother will never willingly permit my cousin to go where he might effectively lead what remains of the Protestants.

"That could be discussed." She says this without a flicker of guilt for the lie. "His Majesty will consult with his friends and advisors, your new husband among them."

A fearful price.

In that one sentence it is clear to me: once I am freed from the King of Navarre, he will perish. Mother wishes it so. Henri does as well. My cousin will not, like his friends who lost their lives in the massacre, be killed openly in the halls of the Louvre. He will be assassinated cleverly: by poison, in a street brawl, or as he travels home, if he is ostensibly permitted to go. My mother and my brothers may be willing—nay, delighted—to be credited with the deaths of thousands, but my family is too chary to take my cousin's blood upon their hands.

It will be on mine.

No, no, no! I fight the thought. Surely the choice here is not so stark!

Mother comes to stand beside me and slips her arm around me. "My dear Margot, tell me: Is your husband a man?"

"What else should he be, Madame?" I sidestep the intent of her question, postponing the moment that must decide my cousin's fate. "You have seen him enough times at table and at the chase to know that he has the appetites of one. And you have doubtless had more intimate reports from the Baronne de Sauve, whom you set upon him."

"The King of Navarre's foolish preference for a woman not your equal in wit or beauty is another reason to be done with him," Mother says. "He has a peasant's tastes which his crown cannot mask." Mother releases me. "I have come here to be satisfied, daughter. Tell me plainly: Has your marriage been consummated?"

Thoughts swirl about me like the swarms of small insects that descend on Paris in the summer, pricking me from every side. All I need do is tell the truth and I will be unmarried. Free, if my mother is to be believed, to follow my heart. *But when has my mother ever been true to her word, at least where that word was given to me?* More than this, can I purchase my freedom with another's life? The murder of an honorable man—and my cousin is honorable—by dishonorable means—this is sin. Not even the *Te Deums* that have resounded through Paris this last week, celebrating the slaughter of my husband's coreligionists, can convince me otherwise. I am *not* my mother, willing to do anything to achieve my personal ends.

"Madame, it has."

Mother starts. Putting her hand on my shoulder, she stares commandingly into my eyes. Her dark eyes remind me of the crow on the windowsill. She is waiting for me to twitch, to look away, to concede defeat and say what she wants to hear. "Will you swear to it? Remembering that a false oath is a serious thing?"

I have a nearly overwhelming desire to laugh, a reaction which would be most unwise. An oath is a serious thing? Is murder not more serious? Is betraying your children in favor of your own power and political aims not more loathsome? I am about to swear falsely but my heart is light.

"I give you my word as a devout *femme catholique* and a daughter of France that I consider myself truly joined to my husband."

For one unguarded moment, Mother's face falls. Then she is herself again, utterly composed. But that moment was a triumph for me and it is enough. I am free! Not of my husband, nor of the walls of this palace. It seems to me Henri and I will be held prisoner here some while longer. Rather, my mother's hold over me is broken. My years of struggling to please, of seeking to garner her attention and gain her love through obedience—of being disappointed when her affection proved to be nothing but affectation—are at an end. I am a woman grown, a queen and worthy of that title in this moment for the first time. I do not know if the crows have left the Louvre's courtyard, but the black birds in my soul have flown and I do not fear their return.

AUTHOR'S NOTE

If only Marguerite de Valois had been born in England.

That is what I found myself thinking as I researched and wrote about this much-maligned princess. Setting aside the myths about her (and I will get to those in a minute), and looking at the historical record, it is clear that Marguerite was highly intelligent, politically astute, and, in her later years, a serious force in the literary life of France. Arguably her political acumen exceeded that of her brothers, making her more similar to her strong-willed, politically expert mother, Catherine de Médicis. Yet, as the Valois princes died one by one and left Marguerite the last legitimate royal of her line, Salic Law kept her from ruling in France as her contemporary, Elizabeth I, was doing so ably in England. She might have made another great sovereign queen, but fate was not kind to Marguerite de Valois.

Nor was history.

As long as a royal line endures, those who go before will be memorialized by people with a vested interest in maintaining their reputations. When a dynasty expires, its last years are recounted by people who often have agendas that make it tempting to denigrate their predecessors. Such was the fate of Valois in the late sixteenth century. No member of the royal family was exempt from the attacks of anonymous political pamphlets during their lifetimes or after. Anti-Valois propagandists seeking to degrade

Marguerite—like the pamphleteers who, in a later era, skewered Marie Antoinette—chose that easiest and most ancient path for destroying a woman: allegations of rabid sexual desire and wanton conduct. Marguerite owes most of the defamation of her character to a single such work, *Le divorce Satyrique.* This pernicious tract mocked and insulted her as it stated, purportedly in the first-person voice of her husband, grounds for the annulment of her marriage—an annulment essential to the production of a Bourbon heir for the man who was no longer merely King of the Navarre but King of France. That such propaganda should have been taken for fact seems astounding today. But early chroniclers of history were often not particularly concerned with objectivity. As Robert J. Sealy argues in *The Myth of the Reine Margot: Toward the Elimination of a Legend,* "The documentary sources for our knowledge . . . were written during the wars of religion and, all too frequently, are colored by political expediency . . ." Even some later histories written in the nineteenth and early twentieth centuries make no pretense at objectivity. The authors unabashedly announce in their prefaces which side they are on. I hope in *Médicis Daughter* that I have done Marguerite justice. Better justice than she received from Valois disparagers, and from those later historians who saw no reason to look more closely at a figure considered insignificant.

What about Catherine de Médicis, then? If I am discarding what can be clearly identified as propaganda and rehabilitating Marguerite, can't Catherine be more the sainted "mother of a nation" and less *La Serpente?* Catherine is a trickier figure. While the Queen Mother was by no means the cartoon villainess or "black queen" as she was dubbed by her most ardent contemporary detractors, historians disagree strongly on both the content and efficacy of her policies with respect to the Wars of Religion— and just about everything else. Unquestionably, Catherine was a woman of influence who preserved her sons and wielded power for and through them. As such, she can be given credit for that which went well in the post–Henri II Valois era. But she must also take her share of the blame for what went disastrously. To insist that she was effective as a political operative when the resulting events are viewed as laudable, yet argue she was utterly unable to influence events that turned out to be less than savory (and the most blatant Catherine apologists do this), is too logically inconsistent for my taste. Also, such assertions strip Catherine of her agency, doing her no justice as one of the sixteenth century's impressively powerful women. As historian R. J. Knecht asserted, "Whitewashing Catherine can be taken too far. She may have been given more than her fair share of blame, but she was no saint and had dabbled in assassination . . ."

Happily, unlike academic historians, I was not obliged to parse out Catherine's motivations or moral culpability. My story is told from the point of view of her daughter, and even the best mother is seldom seen objectively through a daughter's eyes. Marguerite de Valois had valid personal reasons to feel hurt and angered by Catherine. Those feelings act as a filter for how Catherine is portrayed in *Médicis Daughter*.

No author's note would be complete without a disclaimer of sorts. In bringing you a Valois Court in the throes of the Wars of Religion, I strove to be true to history. But I also had another mission: to tell a compelling story. Driven by considerations of plot and theme, I occasionally engaged in the gentle tweaking of history. Sometimes this meant moving events slightly in either time or space to avoid confusion or streamline the narrative. On other occasions it involved giving Marguerite eyewitness status to events that actually took place outside her presence. Certain aspects of the book required not so much an adjustment of history as an informed decision between conflicting historical opinions. For example, one of the critical events in Marguerite's life is her appointment by her brother Anjou as his partisan, and her corresponding promotion to a position as confidante to their mother. Historical accounts cite competing dates for the start of this new intimacy. I've accepted the assertion, made by Leonie Frieda among others, that Margot's elevation in fortune dates to a Court visit paid by the Duc d'Anjou to report his victory at Jarnac.

And what about the cause of the rupture between Anjou and Margot? After years of being everything to each other, I sought a convincing reason that Anjou would turn so viciously on his sister. A dislike of the Duc de Guise driven purely by military and political rivalry did not seem sufficient. There have long been rumors about Marguerite's alleged incestuous relationship with one or more of her brothers. While I reject the idea that she slept with any of them, I chose to accept the premise that Anjou came to feel a romantic attraction to her. After all, hell hath no fury like a man spurned, and if Anjou saw Guise as a rival for his sister's love, his violent reaction to Marguerite's attachment to Guise becomes understandable, as does the antagonism between brother and sister that replaced their former *amitié*.

Finally, there is an event in the book created out of whole cloth. On June 4, 1572, Jeanne d'Albret was seized by a fever that was to be her final illness. On her deathbed she went unvisited by any member of the royal family, though they made a great show of paying their respects when she lay in state. This behavior probably contributed to rumors that Jeanne had been poisoned, even though an autopsy by the royal physicians suggested she died of tuberculosis. I added a fictional visit to Jeanne as she lay dying because it seemed a dramatic moment for the discussion in which the Queen of Navarre asked Margot to promise to be kind to her son, a pledge that led to unexpected places.

The Valois dynasty's last years were plagued by bloodshed, betrayal, scandal, and fanaticism, and marred most shamefully by the Saint Bartholomew's Day Massacre. But the best of the Valois came into her own during that massacre when she saved the life of Henri of Navarre, who would become Henri IV of France. *Henri le Grand* granted religious toleration to the Huguenots, brought discipline and regularity to the finances of France, increased the prosperity of his subjects, and became one of the most beloved kings in French history. Marguerite de Valois may have been ill treated by her family and slandered by history, but her forgotten strength, faith, and resourcefulness paved the way for France's salvation—a legacy worthy of any sovereign queen.

ACKNOWLEDGMENTS

An author may put the first words of a manuscript on the page, but it takes a team to produce a novel. My faithful critique partners, Frances and Kate, see things in my manuscripts that I am often too close to recognize, and their honesty and humor in commenting on my work not only helps me to make my books better but keeps me sane. I am immensely grateful for the support, guidance, and hard work of my agent, Jacques de Spoelberch—a gentleman in an era when they are increasingly rare. I am thankful also for my editors, Toni Kirkpatrick and Jennifer Letwack, whose enthusiasm for *Médicis Daughter* equaled my own.

Finally, my husband, Michael, and my parents, Barbara and Henry, believe I can do anything and everything, and all have been exceedingly patient while I tried.